Downturn Abbey

ROSS O'CARROLL-KELLY
(as told to Paul Howard)

Illustrated by
ALAN CLARKE

PENGUIN BOOKS

PENGUIN BOOKS

Published by the Penguin Group
Penguin Books Ltd, 80 Strand, London WC2R ORL, England
Penguin Group (USA) Inc., 375 Hudson Street, New York, New York 10014, USA
Penguin Group (Canada), 90 Eglinton Avenue East, Suite 700, Toronto, Ontario, Canada M4P 2Y3
(a division of Pearson Penguin Canada Inc.)
Penguin Ireland, 25 St Stephen's Green, Dublin 2, Ireland (a division of Penguin Books Ltd)
Penguin Group (Australia), 707 Collins Street, Melbourne, Victoria 3008, Australia
(a division of Pearson Australia Group Pty Ltd)
Penguin Books India Pvt Ltd, 11 Community Centre, Panchsheel Park, New Delhi – 110 017, India
Penguin Group (NZ), 67 Apollo Drive, Rosedale, Auckland 0632, New Zealand
(a division of Pearson New Zealand Ltd)
Penguin Books (South Africa) (Pty) Ltd, Block D, Rosebank Office Park,
181 Jan Smuts Avenue, Parktown North, Gauteng 2193, South Africa

Penguin Books Ltd, Registered Offices: 80 Strand, London WC2R ORL, England

www.penguin.com

First published by Penguin Ireland 2013
Published in Penguin Books 2014
003

Copyright © Paul Howard, 2013
Illustrations copyright © Alan Clarke, 2013
All rights reserved

Penguin Ireland thanks O'Brien Press for its agreement to Penguin Ireland
using the same design approach and typography, and the same artist,
as O'Brien Press used in the first four Ross O'Carroll-Kelly titles

The moral right of the author and of the illustrator has been asserted

Typeset by Jouve (UK), Milton Keynes
Printed in Great Britain by Clays Ltd, St Ives plc

ISBN: 978-0-241-96279-4

www.greenpenguin.co.uk

Penguin Books is committed to a sustainable
future for our business, our readers and our planet.
This book is made from Forest Stewardship
Council™ certified paper.

For my friend, Eoin Hennigan. Dearly missed.

Contents

Prologue: *How Nice!*

I'm watching her in the orangery, with the autumn sun on her face, running her hand along the exposed red brickwork wall, half smiling, but half confused, like someone from the Midlands having the digital switchover explained to them – kind of getting it, but at the same time thinking, 'Is that even English I'm listening to?'

She says we might actually put the piano in here. Her voice echoes off the walls of the big, empty room. She says she's always, like, *wanted* a music room? She can play a load of shit on the piano and she reached grade four on either the piccolo or the bassoon – I can never remember which.

'Oh my God,' she goes. 'I would love it if Honor discovered what an amazing, amazing thing music can, like, *be*?'

We're suddenly watching our six-year-old daughter through the window, stomping around the gorden while pointing her iPhone to the heavens, to try to find more than a single bor of coverage. 'For fock's sake,' she's going, 'it's supposed to be actual *Killiney*?' First World problems. That's a phrase my old man sometimes uses.

In the space of, like, three days our lives have changed and there's a lot for us all to suddenly take in. Sorcha, especially, is still struggling to get her head around the fact that her childhood home, the famous Honalee on the Vico Road – described by the *Irish Times* property supplement as 'well-appointed' and 'contemporary, yet at once classic' and by An Taisce as 'a permanent blight on what is otherwise one of the most beautiful bays in Europe' – now belongs to her slash us.

'Where are we going to put everything?' she goes, even though the real problem is how are we going to fill this pretty much mansion with, like, *our* few possessions?

I end up just shrugging. I'm there, 'Hey, we've got the rest of our lives to fill it, don't we?'

Except she doesn't answer. Like I said, it's a lot to – I'm going to use the word – *process*?

It's some focking pile of bricks, all the same. I've always said it. We're talking fourteen bedrooms, a humungous kitchen, an actual walk-in pantry, three living rooms, two dining rooms, a library, and then fockloads of rooms that aren't actually *anything*? You stick your head around a door and genuinely go, 'I don't think anyone's even *been* in this room since the focking millennium.' You can see why Sorcha's old pair were broken-horted to have to actually sell it.

That's on her mind, too. I know my wife well enough to see that she's feeling for some reason guilty that the gaff is now hers slash mine.

She walks out of the room without saying anything, then I hear her footsteps on the refinished hordwood stairs. I stay where I am, leaning against an, I suppose, windowpane, suddenly thinking about mainly Ronan. To be honest, I barely closed my eyes in the last few nights thinking about him. Fourteen and soon to be a father. You read about these things in the likes of the *Herald* and you presume they're exaggerating, just to sell papers. Then it's suddenly *your* son? I drove straight to Finglas when I heard the news, not a thought for my own welfare. And there was Ro, sitting in front of the horseracing, smoking one of his world-famous rollies, taking it all in his stride – or at least *pretending* to?

'It's a fact,' he went. 'All you can do is deal with it.'

I was like, 'What about school?' which was weak, I know, especially coming from me. What I possibly meant was, what about your childhood? What about your life?

I was there, 'Jesus, Ronan, could you not have been, I don't know, careful?' which, again, was a bit rich. I mean, if *I'd* been careful, there wouldn't even *be* a Ronan. And I can't imagine what the world would be like if that was the case.

Still, the real shock possibly only hit me a couple of hours later, as we were watching Real Gone Kid romp home in the 2.50 at Huntington. For fock's sake, I remember thinking, I'm going to be a grandfather at thirty-one. Jeremy Kyle would kill for an hour of airtime with me.

Ronan just went back to his *Racing Post*, studying the form. 'Like I said,' he went, 'it's a fact now.'

I make the trek upstairs and find Sorcha in her old bedroom. She's, like, staring at the walls, probably trying to decide whether they need a new coat of paint or not. She's become a massive fan lately of adobe as an actual shade.

A memory suddenly comes back to me of us having sex in this room. It might have been the first time we did it in an actual bed – while her old pair were at the National Concert Hall for a performance of Lehár, Tchaikovsky and the Masters of Waltz by the Icelandic Symphony Orchestra. It's funny the things you remember, isn't it? I made my exit by way of the window after the two of them arrived home unexpectedly early. Edmund – the dick – had, like, a nosebleed during the interval that basically wouldn't stop. I had to drop, like, twenty feet to the gravel below, then make a run for it. *He* happened to look out the window in time to catch me disappearing down the driveway, still pulling up my chinos. Ever since that night, he's hated me in a way that goes way beyond the normal father-in-law, son-in-law, hey-I'm-rattling-your-daughter vibe.

'Do you think you can do this?' Sorcha suddenly goes.

I'm like, 'As in?'

'As in, do you think you're capable this time? Of being married? Are you prepared to make a proper go of being an actual husband to me?'

'I really do. Yeah, definitely.'

'Because in a month's time, six months' time, a year, I don't want to hear, "She pretty much threw herself at me, Sorcha!" or "Hate the game, Baby, not the player!" or any of your other stupid lines.'

'I've done a lot of growing up, Babes.'

'I expect you to honour the vows that we both took on our wedding day.'

'Okay,' I go, pausing slightly. 'I'll read them.'

She's like, '*Read* them?' Not a happy rabbit.

'What I meant to say was that I'll read them every day.'

'You shouldn't have to read them every day. You took a vow to be faithful to me. Do you think you can remember that?'

'Er, yeah.'

'This time?'

'I'm saying definitely.'

She stares at me for a long time to try to, like, gauge how *serious* I am? I maintain full eye contact with her using a visualization technique I learned kicking points for Castlerock College back in the day. Even though I'm not lying to the girl. I genuinely think I'm possibly ready for this.

She pulls me in for a hug. She smells of vanilla and juniper and maybe one or two other things. After a few seconds, we separate ourselves and I go, 'Have you thought about what *he's* going to say?'

She's like, 'Who?' pretending not to know.

I'm there, 'You *know* who, Sorcha. Your old man. We all have to accept that he's never been a fan of mine. He's always ignored a lot of my genuinely amazing qualities and chosen to focus on the negative stuff. I can't help but wonder what his reaction is going to be when he finds out that I'm back with the apple of his eye – *and* I'm suddenly the master of *his* old house.'

'Why are you smiling, Ross?'

'I wasn't smiling.'

'You smiled. I hope you're not taking some perverse pleasure from this.'

'I'm not.'

'Or, if you are, I hope you'll resist the temptation to show it in front of him.'

'I'll definitely do my best. When are we going to tell him? Tell *them*? We could do it now.'

'We can't,' she goes. 'They're away this week.'

Shit, I forgot. They're in, like, London. Her old man is thinking of going on one of these bankruptcy holidays. Twelve months in purgatory – well, he has a brother in South Kensington, who me and Sorcha have stayed with once or twice – then he can come back to Ireland and stort all over. Jesus. Stort all over. The man is, like, fifty-eight. There's a lot of that about, I suppose.

'It gives me a few days,' she goes, 'to try to get my own head around it. It's going to be a huge adjustment.'

I'm like, 'Not just for us,' suddenly thinking about Honor again. 'God knows what it's going to do to our daughter's life if she can't get mobile phone coverage.'

It's a good line. The girl has been pretty much permanently on Twitter since Nicki Minaj – *actual* Nicki Minaj – favourited a Tweet of hers about something or other. Sorcha smiles – like I said, it's a good line – but then she's suddenly sad.

'What are we going to do about her?' she goes. 'Her behaviour has just become, like, oh my God.'

'I know. A consolation for us should be that we don't have any questions to ask ourselves in terms of how we, like, brought her up and shit?'

Sorcha suddenly doesn't look so sure. She goes, 'We should never have let her be in that film.'

She's talking about the movie that the Hallmork Channel made of my old dear's misery lit book, *Mom, They Said They'd Never Heard of Sundried Tomatoes*. Honor played the lead – little Zara Mesbur – and Sorcha thinks the whole experience went to her head.

'Come on,' I go, 'she was a little wagon before she ever did that movie, let's be honest about that fact.'

I mean, this is a girl who rang Childline and said she was a poverty risk because her mother was managing a Euro discount store in the Powerscourt Townhouse Centre. Sorcha forgets.

'Well, whether she was or not,' she goes, 'I wish we'd never agreed to let her be in that movie. If there was some way of stopping it ever being shown, I would.'

The next thing either of us hears is Honor go, 'Talking about me?'

I end up nearly shitting my pants. She's standing immediately behind us. I'm like, 'Whatever you think you heard, Honor, we didn't mean it.'

It's, like, an *automatic* thing?

Sorcha goes, '*I* meant it,' because she's better at standing up to her than I am. 'I don't like using negative language to you, Honor, but your behaviour recently has fallen way below the standard that we consider acceptable.'

Honor goes, 'In your opinion,' looking her dead in the eye.

'Yes, in my opinion. And your father's.'

I nod, just to let her know that me and her old dear are pretty much a team again.

She's there, 'There's no mobile signal,' like it's something she expects us to instantly fix.

'Look at this beautiful home that you're going to be living in,' Sorcha tries to go. 'There are more important things than your phone, Honor.'

Honor turns her back on us and that's when I hear it. Under her breath, she goes, 'Fock you.'

I've honestly never seen Sorcha look so shocked. I mean, usually you'd have to wait until they're in, like, second or third year in Mount Anville before they say that to you.

I decide it's time to say my piece. 'Honor,' I go, 'possibly don't speak to your mother like that.'

She turns around, her hand on her hip, and goes, 'Er, it's a line in a song?'

'What song?'

'Er, Cee Lo Green?'

I turn around to Sorcha. 'She has us there,' I go. 'It is from a song.'

'Anyhooo,' Honor goes, sounding totally bored with us now, 'I'll be waiting in the car whenever you two are finished whatever it is you're doing. Hashtag – it's been emosh.' And off she trots.

Neither of us says anything for a good, like, thirty seconds. Eventually, roysh – mainly for the want of something to say – I go, 'Ronan's got it all ahead of him. I wouldn't focking envy him.'

Sorcha – totally out of the blue – goes, 'Where are they going to live, Ross?'

I'm like, 'Who?'

'Ronan and Shadden. When the baby arrives.'

'I don't know. I just presumed . . . I don't know what I presumed. I'm driving out to Pram Springs to see *her* old pair tomorrow. There's obviously shit we need to talk about.'

'Because they could live here.'

'Here? With us?'

'Look around you, Ross. Look at all this space we have.'

6

'I suppose.'

'The baby could have an – oh my God – magical childhood growing up here, full of wonder. Like I did.'

'It'd be great to have Ro here. Jesus, can you imagine the crack?'

'It's, like, so an amazing idea. I mean, I'm not being a snob or anything, but there are, like, so many more advantages for children growing up on this side of the city.'

'There's not as much lead in the air – I know that for a fact.'

'And the other beauty of it is that I could look after the baby all day if Ronan and Shadden wanted to finish school. They'd be living in an amazing, amazing house *and* have, like, a full-time, live-in nanny.'

'Like I said, I'd love if they were here.'

'It'd be the solution to – oh my God – so many problems. When are you going to see Shadden's parents again?'

'Tomorrow. Tina's going to be there as well, just to say. It's, like, a summit to discuss the crisis.'

'Well, maybe I'll come as well.'

'You? I wouldn't have thought Finglas would be your kind of place.'

'Someone needs to make the case, Ross, that, okay, this thing has happened – and it's maybe not what everyone envisaged, for Ronan *or* for Shadden – but it could still work out happily for everyone involved.'

'Finglas, though. I mean, what would you even wear?'

'Ross, it doesn't matter what I'm going to wear. What matters is that we let them know that this little baby could have an amazing childhood here in Killiney, growing up in this incredible house, with its mother and father, its grandfather . . .'

The sound of someone leaning on a cor horn snaps us suddenly back to reality.

'And of course Honor,' I go.

Sorcha's like, 'Of course,' looking suddenly sad again. 'Who could forget Honor?'

From outside, we hear the sound of our daughter leaning on the cor horn again. 'Okay, getting bored here,' she shouts. 'Getting very, very bored.'

How Marvellous!

There's a washing machine in the gorden. I could have nearly predicted there'd be a washing machine in the focking gorden. These people love clichés like they love chunky jewellery and MDF furniture.

Sorcha's sitting beside me in the front passenger seat with a determined look on her face – the same expression she wears whenever a newsreader announces that viewers may find the following scenes disturbing. Which is pretty much the exact same thing I tell her as we're, like, sitting there outside the gaff.

'You can watch all the episodes of *Love/Hate* in the world,' I go, 'but there's still no preparing yourself for the reality of a family like the Tuites.'

She shoots me a look – *withering* is the word you often hear used?

I'm like, 'Hey, you haven't met them yet. You're in for a serious focking treat. And by the way, I don't know why you bothered your orse making *that*,' because she's brought one of her salted caramel custard pies, with Chantilly crust and organic, fumigant-free strawberries.

She's there, 'Ross, you are *so* a snob.'

'Yeah, no, I *am* a snob?' I go. 'But I'm also, like, a realist. And don't expect to get that cake plate back, I'm warning you now. It's the last you're going to see of it.'

We get out of the cor, then up the focking path we go. Sorcha's eyes are, like, caught in the tractor beam of the washing machine, rusting away on its side for God knows how long now, with leaves and papers spilling out of the round hole where the door used to be. I can tell she's shocked. She has to eventually tear her eyes away from it. While she looks for the non-existent doorbell, I give the old letterbox a rattle.

The door opens and suddenly Kennet Tuite is standing in front of us in all his finery. Which in his case is the usual plain white Dunnes Stores dress shirt, tucked tightly into a pair of ice-blue 501s that have been washed to the point of having no shape – *and*, of course, black slip-on shoes.

He's there, 'Th . . . Th . . . Th . . . Th . . . There thee are!'

Shadden's old man has a horrendous MC Hammer, I don't know if I mentioned.

He goes, 'H . . . H . . . Howiya, Ross!' and he says it with a big focking smile on his face, like he always does, like I'm the butt of some focking joke that I'm not even aware of. 'You f . . . f . . . fowunt us alreet, wha'?'

I'm there, 'Yeah, whatever.'

'And you must be S . . . S . . . S . . . Surrogate.'

Sorcha goes, 'Yes, but it's actually pronounced *Sorcha*?' smiling, determined to keep the porty polite. 'As in, like, *Sorcha*?'

'Surrogate,' he goes.

'No, no. Can you say *sore*?'

Jesus Christ, it's like talking to focking aliens. 'So-urr.'

'*A*?'

'A.'

'*Ka*?'

'Ka.'

'Now put them all together. Sore-a-ka!'

'Surrogate.'

'Sore. A. Ka.'

'Surrogate.'

I decide to break it up then, because I can feel myself wanting to throw a punch at him. I'm there, 'Sorry, Kennet, we can't stand around here all day trying to teach you the basics of the English language. I think we'd all agree that we've got, like, shit to talk about.'

'Sh . . . Sh . . . Shewer,' he goes, opening the door fully. ''Mon in.'

In we go.

'Says I,' he goes, 'to D . . . D . . . Dordeen, "Hee-er, Dordeen, the p . . . p . . . poshies are coming over today. Berror get the hoover out, wha'? Give the place the once-over!"'

I look at the floor. She obviously didn't bother in the end.

Kennet leads us down to the kitchen, where Dordeen is sitting at the table smoking a cigarette and watching the repeat of last night's *X Factor* on a black-and-white portable. I didn't know they even still existed.

Someone – it might be Johnny Robinson – is bawling his eyes out and saying how much winning the *X Factor* would mean to him – 'just the world' – and how devastated he would be – 'it would be the end of everything – it'd be, like, the end of my life' – if he *didn't* win it?

Focking ridiculous nonsense.

Kennet clears his throat to let her know that they have company, then Dordeen turns her head and goes, 'There yiz eer – yiz fowunt us!' again like it's some private joke. It's like they find the very fact of my *existence* funny? She crushes what's left of a Johnny Blue into the ashtray and, at the same time, stands up to greet us.

'Howiya, Ross,' she goes. 'And who's tis wit ye?'

I'm like, 'This is my wife – as in, Sorcha?'

She doesn't even attempt to say it, just goes, 'That Indian, is it?'

Sorcha's there, 'No, it's actually Irish? It means Sarah.'

'It's easier if you just say Surrogate,' Kennet goes. 'I've just been s . . . s . . . sayin Surrogate.'

I'm just glad we left Honor with Claire from Bray. Not that there was ever any chance she'd cross the Liffey with us.

Sorcha hands over the pie and explains what's in it. Of course, she might as well be reading a donkey his focking horoscope for all the response she gets. At the very mention of salted caramel custard and organic strawberries, Dordeen pulls a face that seems to say, *Oh, well – excuuuse me!* and puts the cake onto the top of this, like, *press*, with the speed and skill of me offloading a rugby ball back in the day.

'So anyhow,' she goes to *me* then, 'congratulayshiddens.'

I can't actually believe my ears. I'm like, 'On?'

'Ronan,' she goes, grinning like a wanking Chinaman, like what she's about to say is the most natural thing in the world. 'He's gonna be a fadder.'

'I'm not sure congratulations is the actual word,' I go. 'He's four-teen years of age.'

She's there, 'He's nearly fifteen, but. And I wadn't much older when me and Kennet had hour foorst.'

I'm actually trying to think of something really insulting to say – but at the same time *clever*? – when Kennet goes, 'Look, it's a fact now. Alls *we* can do is gerron wirrit.'

That's when I end up totally losing it with them. I'm there, 'Whoa, what *is* all this *it's a fact* horseshit? Maybe *your* family is ready to just accept it. I'm pretty interested in finding out how it actually *happened*?'

I'm obviously a lot angrier than I even realized.

Sorcha goes, 'Ross!' trying to calm me down.

Kennet's there, 'I'm shewer you don't need me to tell you the ways of the w . . . w . . . wurdled, Ross. Thee were having the sex . . .'

'Well,' I go, 'they shouldn't have been having *the sex*, as you call it. I would have thought Shadden was old enough to know better.'

That goes down like Josef Fritzl at a family reunion.

'Who ta fook do you think you eer?' it's Dordeen who goes, 'coming into *eer* house and meeking accusashiddens?'

'I'm just pointing out that your daughter's, like, sixteen – as in, two years *older* than him? I'm making the point that *she* should have had more basic sense.'

I hate saying that because Shadden's a great girl.

'Well,' Kennet goes, 'Ine m . . . m . . . makin ta point tat tis is s . . . s . . . sometin tat was goin on in *yooer* apeertment.'

'Excuse me?'

'Tat's where thee were doin it.'

'Er, *I* wasn't *living* there at the time? Ronan stole the actual key from me. I don't think *I* can be blamed.'

'Well, Dordeen and I woorunt have lerrit happen unter *hour* roof.'

'And I didn't let it happen under my roof!'

All of a sudden, Sorcha goes, 'Okay, time out!' and she actually makes the T shape with her two hands. 'Time out!'

She did that two-week Certificate in Mediation course the summer after she finished her degree. She's good in these situations.

'Okay,' she goes, 'may *I* humbly point out that this mode of debate isn't actually *helpful*? I think everyone needs to move on from the hows and the whys and talk about what *is* important? In other words, how all the relevant stakeholders – i.e. Ronan, Shadden and their respective families – can accommodate this change of circumstances into their lives in a way that's good for everyone, especially the baby.'

Jesus. Even I'm left open-mouthed. See, that's the Smurfit Business School, isn't it?

'Hee-er,' Kennet goes. 'She's reet. Alls tat's important is tat t . . . t . . . tis babby is b . . . b . . . borden into a luvin family and wants for n . . . n . . . nuttin.'

I'm there, 'Er, agreed.'

Kennet then goes, 'I'll give Shadden and Roatnan a shout – they're up in the g . . . g . . . good room,' and then he stands at the door of the kitchen and storts going, 'Shadden! Shadden!' into the hall, and then, 'M . . . M . . . Mon down here. And bring Roatnan. Ross is hee-er – he's f . . . f . . . fadder. And Surrogate.'

I turn around to Dordeen and I'm there, 'By the way, is there any chance you could switch that TV off?'

Kitty Brucknell singing 'Don't Stop Me Now'. For fock's sake.

Dordeen stares at me for a few seconds – like she wants to actually *slap* me? – then does as she's told.

Ronan suddenly appears in the kitchen, followed by Shadden. It's a shock to the system, I have to admit, to see how much she's showing. She's thirty-something weeks gone, I suppose, but they managed to hide it from me for all that time. It was Tina who ended up having to tell me in the end.

Shadden goes, 'Howiya, Ross? Howiya, Sorcha?'

Shadden, I think I mentioned it before, is a lovely kid. By some fluke of, I don't know, genetics, she's actually clever and has basic *manners*? It's honestly like she was raised in a different home and only met these people she calls her parents in the last hour.

She looks at Sorcha a bit, I don't know, sheepishly, like it's *her* opinion she cares about more than anyone else's. Women can be total bitches to each other, don't forget. But Sorcha throws open her orms and grabs her in a hug, which is a lovely thing to see, even if it *is* a bit OTT? She ends up nearly breaking the kid's glasses, she grabs her that hord, and you can see Kennet and Dordeen wondering, literally, what the fock? But then Sorcha's a people person – very much like me.

'How *are* you?' she goes.

Shadden's like, 'I'm fine, thanks.'

Like I said, unbelievably nice – there must have been a focking switch at the hospital. It's the only explanation.

'And how's it all going – the pregnancy?'

'Ine really toyered.'

'You *will* be. You're going to think this final trimester will never end! With Honor, I was – oh my God – *praying* that I'd go early?'

They stort talking baby shite, so I turn around to Ro and I go, 'Hey, Ro – how the hell are you?'

He's like, 'Alreet, Rosser?' playing it über-cool as ever. 'Ine grant, so I am.'

I'm there, 'Hey, that's good – that's real good like Gielgud!' which is a thing I picked up from Brian O'Driscoll.

Suddenly, there's a knock on the door – well, again, the focking letterbox.

Ronan goes, 'That'll be me ma.'

Tina. Shit.

Kennet goes out to answer the door. I'm wondering has she actually calmed down in the time since she told me the news, or is she still blaming basically *me* for the entire thing? I get my answer pretty quickly from the filthy she shoots me when she walks into the kitchen.

I go, 'Hey, Tina,' just to be civil, and she gives me a look – like I said, a total filthy – shoots Ronan and Shadden a look of disappointment, then turns to Dordeen and goes, 'Soddy, whorr am I even doin hee-er?'

It's, like, Kennet who answers her. 'Ross and Surrogate t . . . t . . . taught irrit make s . . . s . . . s . . . sense to get all ta p . . . p . . . p . . . peerdents togedder – to talk about ta arrangements – knowmean?'

Tina's like, 'What *arrangements*?' now giving Kennet the cold, hord stare.

'Well, we're all gonna have to pull thegedder,' Dordeen goes, 'when the babby arrives.'

It's like watching a focking stand-off between two T-Rexes.

Tina's like, 'Pull togettor?'

'Thegedder, yeah.'

Sorcha makes the mistake of trying to come between them then. I would have honestly told her to stay the fock out of it if she'd bothered her hole to ask me.

She goes, 'I think what Dordeen is saying is that we have to decide in practical terms how we now respond to events? Where, for instance, are Ronan and Shadden going to live after the baby is born? Will it be somewhere that maximizes the opportunities that are available to the child and provides it with an upbringing that's full of wonder? How are Ronan and Shadden going to support their baby? Who'll be looking after it if they choose to return to their academic careers?'

Tina turns dog on Sorcha all of a sudden. She goes, 'You're not a peerdent,' without even looking at her.

Sorcha's there, 'I am so a parent,' just defending herself.

Tina goes, 'Not of addyone dat's involved in dis.'

I think it's always pissed Tina off that I ended up with an actual genuine looker, while she herself has a face like a kicked-in rubbish bin.

'She's *my* wife,' I instantly go, 'which means she's Ronan's stepmother. Which means she's entitled to an opinion. End of.'

Tina decides to ignore my point. She turns back to Dordeen and goes, 'So come on den – what *are* de arrangements? I'm shewer yizzuv it all woorked out awretty.'

She hates the Tuites. In fairness, she said they were scum from day one – she told Ronan to have nothing to do with them.

Kennet goes, 'I doatunt think ters any question of where thee'll live. Thee'll live hee-er w . . . w . . . wirrus – until the babby's borden . . .'

'The boat of dem?' Tina goes. 'Livin wonther *yoo-er* roof?'

'Wh . . . Wh . . . What's wrong wit tat?'

'He's fowerteen years owult – dat's what's wrong wirrit. He belongs at home – wit he's mutter.'

That's when Ronan suddenly pipes up. 'Ma,' he goes, 'I wanna be with Shadden. I wanna be wit Shadden and the baby.'

You'd nearly feel sorry for Tina because her hort is obviously *breaking*? I suppose mine is as well, even though I'm trying to be more, I don't know, *pragmatical* about shit.

'We went to see ta Council on Friday,' Dordeen goes. 'We put their nayums down on ta housing list. Next door's arthur becoming empty.'

'Mrs Sheerlock,' Kennet goes, 'Lorta m . . . m . . . meercy on her.'

'Thee said, cos of eer ceercumstaddences, thee might look favourdably on us gettin next door and mebbe knockin troo ta wall.'

Tina looks at Ronan. She's like, 'What about skewell?' although what she probably means is, 'Is this it? Is this the future?' All that promise he showed – an IQ of fock knows what – and *this* is what it's come to? Fourteen years of age with a baby on the way and lodging with one of Ireland's most notorious scumbag families.

'Ine gonna take a year or two out,' Ronan goes.

He's, like, properly gifted. Six months ago, he was talking about college, the lot.

Tina's like, 'You'll nevor go back.'

'I will,' he goes. 'Mebbe when the baby's owulter.'

Tina looks like she's about to burst into tears.

I'm like, 'So what are you going to do to, like, support the three of you?' thinking I probably should weigh in here, as his actual father.

Kennet goes, 'He's gonna w . . . w . . . woork – have you ever heard of it befower?' which is a dig at me – a *definite* dig.

'He's fourteen,' I go. 'Where's he *gonna w . . . w . . . w . . . woork*?'

'I'll gerrim woork – don't you w . . . w . . . woody about tat.'

'Yeah,' I go, 'we all know what you lot consider *woork.*'

It's a well-known fact that the entire Tuite family income comes from benefit fraud and bogus personal injury claims.

Sorcha, who's been silent since Tina slapped her down, obviously decides she's not leaving here without them hearing her pitch.

'Okay,' she goes, 'can *I* just suggest something here?' and no one immediately objects, so off she goes. 'Ross and I have just inherited an amazing, amazing house on the Vico Road in Killiney. It's, like, the house I grew up in? It's got – oh my God – *so* much space. Including, like, fourteen bedrooms and a beautiful gorden with a view of Killiney Bay . . .'

I'm thinking, okay, okay, don't rub their focking noses in it, Sorcha.

'. . . so . . . they could move in with us. Ross and I are home all day, so we could, like, help Shadden out with the baby when he or she arrives. And it'd mean Ronan could continue going to school. And I could be, like, a live-in nanny if Shadden wanted to go back next September. Holy Child Killiney is only up the road. It's a really, really good school. We debated against them – oh my God – loads of times over the years.'

I know that Ronan loves the idea because I notice him suddenly perk up. I'm not imagining it – the corners of his mouth actually turn upwards into, like, a smile? He rips the piss out of me on a regular basis, but we're a great double act.

'N . . . N . . . No,' Kennet goes, straight away shooting the idea down. 'I doatunt want tum livin on tat s . . . s . . . side of ta cirry.'

I'm like, 'What's wrong with that side of the city?' I'm very defensive about it, of course.

'It's so f . . . f . . . feer away from everyting.'

'What do you mean, *f . . . f . . . far away from everyting*? It's not far away from Dalkey. It's not far away from Sandycove. It's not far away from Dundrum Town Centre.'

'It's feer away from Shadden's howum,' he goes. 'M . . . M . . . Mirras well be Australia for all w . . . w . . . we'd see of her. They're stayin hee-er wirrus and tat's all there is t . . . t . . . to it.'

Dordeen's contribution on the subject is, 'Six munts over tat side of the cirry and we wouldn't be able to wontherstand eer own thaughter,' and then she says to Sorcha, 'And tat's no offence to *you*, love.'

I'm tempted to go, 'Everything about you is a focking offence to us,' except I don't.

'Well,' Tina goes, 'it sowunts like yizzuv it all woorked out,' and she turns around to just leave. She hasn't even sat down, bear in mind.

Ronan's like, 'Ma!' but Tina's too upset. She morches out to the front door and shouts back into the house. 'I rue de day you gor involved wit dis family, Ronan,' which has got to be a hord thing for poor Shadden to hear. 'I rue it now, so I do. And I know dat one day I'll rue it even mower.' She slams the door on her way out. Poor Ronan looks on the point of basic tears.

Sorcha looks at me. 'We, er, probably should get going ourselves, Ross,' obviously realizing that there's no reasoning with these people.

I'm like, 'Er, yeah, cool,' still staring at Ro, making sure he's okay. 'We probably should be getting back to civilization alright.'

Ronan looks totally crushed.

Kennet shows us to the door. As he opens it, two – what Ronan would call – *shams* walk into the house. Kennet introduces them as Eddie and Dadden, the two eldest of God knows how many kids they have. They're, like, both in their mid-twenties – a pair of basically identikit skobies. Dadden, I notice, has a tattoo on his neck of a dove, then underneath it a hand, which I recognize straight away as – I shit you not – the logo of the Deportment of Social Welfare.

They both stort checking Sorcha out, although *she's* too innocent to cop them basically leering at her – especially at her torps.

Kennet suddenly storts giving out yords to them. He's like, 'Where are yizzer collars?'

'What?' it's Dadden who goes.

'Why ardent yiz weerdin yisser bleaten c . . . c . . . collars?'

I realize that what he's talking about is their *surgical* collars? There's, like, seven or eight of them hanging up on hooks in the hallway – that's not a focking lie – all to be worn presumably in support of bogus whiplash claims.

He's like, 'I told yiz not to go out wirrout your c . . . c . . . collars. They're w . . . w . . . watching us. I've me f . . . f . . . fooken case, don't forget.'

I just go, 'Okay, we're going to leave you to enjoy some family time,' and we head out to the cor.

I turn the key in the ignition and as I'm turning the Lambo around, I notice Ronan in the window of one of the upstairs bedrooms. He sad-smiles me, then gives me a little wave. I go to wave back to him, except by the time I've done it, he's already gone.

I can't tell you how suddenly depressed I am. And I get the instant feeling that Sorcha feels the same way. Neither of us says a word until we drive over the East Link Bridge and even then all I can think to go is, 'Didn't I tell you that you wouldn't get your cake plate back?'

Sorcha's there, 'I don't care about the cake plate, Ross.'

And I go, 'I'm just making the point that I said you wouldn't get it back.'

I laugh. I can't help it. I can't even begin to tell you what a complete and utter tit Christian looks in the uniform – and I'm saying that as his best friend.

It's, like, a green polo shirt with the word 'Footlong' on the left breast. Except it's not, like, a *nice* green? It's the kind of green you'd expect to see coming out of the orse of a Labradoodle that's shivering sick.

And then there's the trousers, which are, like, grey. And even though they *look* like chinos and *feel* like chinos, they're cut like actual slacks – as in, they're bet onto his thighs and into his crotch so tightly that you can nearly read the raised lettering on the Visa cord in his pocket.

And then, to top it all off, there's a visor. A literally visor. Like I said, I laugh. He looks like a total clown.

'Ross,' he goes, 'if you're here just to take the piss . . .'

I'm like, 'Dude, I'm here to support you on your first day in your new job. We all are.'

Here, by the way, is Chatham Street, which is, like, random, I realize. I turn to Oisinn and JP and they both nod, except they're at least *trying* to hold in the laughter? It's possible to support your friend *and* rip the pistachio out of him. Christian's become so serious since he moved back from the States. I think Lauren has his balls in a vice on a pretty much permanent basis.

'In fact,' I go, studying the menu board, 'I think I'm going to eat something,' because I'm focking storving. Possibly the best way to describe Footlong is that it's *like* Subway, but it's *not* Subway? 'I think I'll have the old Macho Melt,' because I'm a huge, huge fan of subs generally.

He goes, 'You can't have a Macho Melt,' and he says it straight out. 'That's on the breakfast menu.'

I'm like, 'So?'

'The breakfast menu finishes at eleven o'clock,' he goes and – get this – he makes a big show of turning around and looking at the clock over his shoulder. 'It's now twenty past.'

You'd want to focking hear the way he says it as well, like we've never even *met*?

I'm like, 'Dude, you're supposedly the manager here,' at the same time looking at JP and Oisinn for back-up.

'There are rules that come with the franchise, Ross.'

'And one of them is you can't serve breakfast after eleven o'clock?'

'Yes.'

'Even to former team-mates on the rugby field?'

'Yes, even to you, Ross. And if you've a problem with that, I suggest you take it up with head office in New York.'

'They're in New York? Jesus Christ. How the fock would they even find out?'

Oisinn throws his two yoyos into the mix then. 'Mystery shoppers,' he goes. 'They send people in – *company* people – pretending to be customers, to make sure the rules are being adhered to. Corporate compliance, they call it.'

I'm there, 'Well, I *still* say it's focked up. Okay, I'll have the Midday Melt then. Presuming head office are happy with that, of course – I mean, it's only, like, twenty past eleven.'

Christian's like, 'You can have the Midday Melt.'

I turn around to JP. 'Which is bacon, sausage and cheese, by the way. The only difference between *it* and the Macho Melt is the focking egg. So basically they're saying you can't have an egg after eleven o'clock,' and then I turn around to the three or four customers behind us – all Spanish students, by the looks of them – and I go, 'You can't have an egg after eleven o'clock, everyone, because New York says so!' and it's genuinely hilarious.

Christian could do with growing a pair. That is all.

Oisinn's there, 'Yeah, I'll have the same as Ross.'

'Yeah, no,' JP goes, 'a Midday Melt is good for me as well.'

Christian storts cutting the rolls from end to end. He tells the Spanish people that he'll be with them in a minute. We find a table and sit down.

'So, Dude,' JP goes to me, 'tell me again what you told me on the phone.'

I laugh. I'm there, 'It's all true, J Town.'

'I thought you were hammered.'

'I *was* hammered. But it's also true.'

'Your granny bought Sorcha's old pair's gaff . . .'

'Yeah, no, a couple of weeks before she died.'

'And she, like, *left* it to you?'

'To me and Sorcha. Well, *actually* to Sorcha. But we're back together now. Going to maybe give it a proper go this time.'

JP shakes his head – we're talking pure admiration. 'Talk about falling on your feet!'

Oisinn goes, 'How did Sorcha's old man take the news?' because he knows the dude wouldn't be a big supporter of mine.

I'm like, 'He doesn't know yet. As in, he's been out of the country. I think we're telling him this weekend. The dick. Actually, we'll have to tell him – we're supposedly moving *in* next week.'

'It's some focking house,' Oisinn goes. 'I mean, shit the bed.'

I'm there, 'I know. The goy is going to lay a focking egg when he finds out that not only am I back with his precious daughter, I've also got my Reet Petites under his old table, while he's living in a rented focking dog box in Sandyford Industrial Estate. I can't wait to stort ringing him every focking day to ask him how shit works. The immersion. The sprinklers. Blah, blah, blah.'

Suddenly, we hear a voice – an accusing voice, some would even say angry – go, 'Who used that toilet?'

I turn around and it's, like, Lauren, with little Ross Junior in tow. She's referring to the wheelchair toilet, by the way. She pulls the door shut – really gives it a good bang. I don't know why she's looking at me.

'I asked a question,' she goes. 'Who used that toilet?' and – under serious pressure – I have no choice but to subtly nod my head in the direction of the Spanish people.

Christian decides to give me up, though. 'It was Ross,' he goes. 'And, yes, I told him not to use it.'

She's like, 'Stay out of that toilet.'

I'm there, 'Well, it's just the men's is a bit of a hike upstairs.'

'That's the wheelchair-accessible toilet.'

'I know. But I just can't see myself trudging up the stairs every time I want to drop a lobster in the pot. I dare say other customers are going to feel the same.'

She actually points at me and goes, 'Do *not* go in there again,' then she joins Christian behind the counter and apologizes to the Spanish – I think the phrase for a group of them is Spaniards – for keeping them waiting.

Little Ross Junior, by the way, is away in his own little world, with a doll in either hand – and we're not talking action figures here, we're talking, like, full-on Cindy slash *Borbie*-type dolls? – and he's performing a little play on the table next to ours.

'You have a three o'clock appointment for a full Thwedish math-age?' he goes. 'Yeth, but I'm altho thinking of having a thkin peel.'

Jesus.

Me, JP and Oisinn exchange a look. A four-year-old boy shouldn't be talking like that, I think we all accept, although it's possibly not our place to say it.

Christian brings us over our Midday Melts, which are incredible, by the way – I'm going to admit that – egg or no egg. We horse them down and stort generally just catching up. JP and his old man are back in the housing game. Distressed property auctions – I might have mentioned it already. Oisinn is still dismantling decking for cash-in-hand. The poor focker's not even allowed to own a bank account under the terms of his bankruptcy. He seems cool with it, though. I've honestly never seen the dude as chilled.

I don't mention that I'm about to become a grandfather. I don't *know* why? Maybe I still need time to come to terms with it myself. And, yes, the embarrassment. Honor is going to be an auntie at six years of age. I can't think of anything more working class. Except maybe Argos. And being especially close to your grandmother.

All of a sudden, no pre-warning, Ross Junior storts going, 'Roth, my mawmy hath three pairth of thkinny jeanth.'

I shit you not. Those are his exact words. I decide to just blank him. It's the only way to get the kid to snap out of it. You can see even the Spaniard people looking crooked at him as they sit down two tables over from us with their Ranch House Melts and their whatever else.

'Roth,' the kid keeps going, pulling at the sleeve of my sailing jacket this time, 'my mawmy hath three pairth of thkinny jeanth. Roth, my mawmy hath three pairth of thkinny jeanth . . .'

Again, I keep focused on my sub. It's great cheese, by the way, even if it is just processed. 'By the way,' I turn around to JP and go, 'how's Fionn getting on in Umbongo? Does anyone even read his blog?'

All of a sudden, I can feel the weight of Lauren staring at me. I look at her. She's like, 'Are you not going to answer him?'

I go, 'Answer him?'

'Ross is talking to you.'

'Well, I'm not really sure there *is* an answer to what he's saying, though, Lauren.'

'Well, could you even acknowledge that he is talking to you?'

So I look at the kid and I go, 'Er, that's great, Ross. Skinny jeans. Sounds amazing.'

Then *he* goes, 'She hath three pairth of thkinny jeanth and five pairth of ballet flath.'

There's, like, silence for three or four seconds, then I make the mistake of going, to the general audience, 'Am I the only one who thinks that's a bit, I don't know, *weird*?'

Lauren goes, '*Excuse me?*' and she says it in a did-you-just-say-what-I-think-you-said kind of a way. There's something about me that just rubs the girl up the wrong way.

I'm there, 'I don't know, just, well, a kid of his age – a boy, basically – banging on about women's clothes. And then what's the Jack with the whole playing-with-dolls thing?'

Lauren ends up having a total knicker-fit. 'Who the hell do you think you are, telling people how to raise their kids?'

I'm there, 'I'm not telling you how to raise him, Lauren. I'm just saying it's a bit odd. I think everyone in this restaurant would back me up on that.'

No one does, by the way. They all keep their focking Von Trapps well and truly shut – Oisinn and JP included.

Lauren goes straight for the jugular then. 'I'll tell you what's a bit odd,' she goes. 'A fourteen-year-old boy about to become a father.'

Oisinn, JP and Christian all suddenly look at me with their eyes wide open.

'That's right,' Lauren goes, loving embarrassing me. 'I bumped into Sorcha coming out of L'Occitane.'

Women are like elderly relatives – yeah, you love them, but they can't hold their piss.

'Yeah, no, fair enough,' I go. 'That was my other news that I was going to hit you all with later. I'm about to become a grandfather.'

'A grandfather?' the goys, all at the exact same time, go. '*Fock!*'

Fock is right. If you had to come up with one word to describe the turn that my life has taken in the past week, you couldn't come up with a better one than that.

You'd nearly *have* to feel sorry for Sorcha's old pair – well, her old dear anyway. From a mansion on the Vico Road to a two-bedroom aportment near the Beacon in Sandyford is a serious comedown. From Bel Eire to South Central – and we're talking literally.

'Now, let me do the talking,' Sorcha goes, as she throws the old Mercury Mariner Hybird into the Luas cor pork opposite Rock-brook. 'It's a lot for them to suddenly take in, Ross – especially my dad.'

I'm like, 'Kool and the Gang, Babes,' getting out of the cor quickly.

'I mean it – no gloating.'

'What do you mean, gloating?'

'You know what I'm talking about, Ross.'

See, she can see how John B focking keen I am to get up there to him. I'm walking, like, seven or eight paces ahead of her.

She goes, 'I know you two can never resist going at each other, but today is not the day.'

Sorcha turns around and notices that Honor is walking, like, way behind us – her eyes pretty much glued as usual to that phone of hers. Sorcha goes, 'Come on, Honor, hold my hand crossing the road,' like you would to any normal six-year-old. 'You can go on Twitter later,' and then she goes to grab her by the hand.

Honor shakes her hand loose and goes, 'Er, I think I can cross the road by myself. Hashtag – I'm not retorded.'

I don't say a word, even though I possibly *should*?

Sixty seconds later, we're at the door of the building. Sorcha keys in the aportment number, then hits the bell and suddenly her old dear's voice comes through the little speaker, going, 'Sorcha! What a lovely surprise! Edmund and I have just opened a bottle of Chardonnay!' and she buzzes us in.

Chardonnay at, like, quarter past one on a Saturday afternoon. They might be living in the middle of an industrial estate, but they're keeping the dream alive. You'd nearly be tempted to say, 'Fair focks.'

We take the elevator to the third floor. The old dear obviously thought it was going to be *just* Sorcha? She's a bit surprised to see the Rossmeister General tagging along like a champ.

She in fact goes, 'Oh . . . Ross . . . as well,' and you can hear the definite disappointment in her voice. '*And* Honor!'

Honor doesn't even acknowledge her, by the way. I at least give her a nice big hug and tell her she smells great. I'm in that kind of form. A bit full of myself, I have to admit – all the time thinking, okay, where the fock is *he*?

The next thing, he steps out into the hall with his orms outstretched, going, 'Sorcha! What a lovely –' and then he cops me and stops dead, the wind suddenly knocked out of him, like he's just walked into a focking porking meter or something.

'There's the man!' I go, making sure to give him a big shit-eating grin. I'm a shocker, I know. He looks at Sorcha for an explanation. The expression on her face is enough to tell him that she's come to break bad news – that's how well he knows his daughter – and he instantly thinks worst-case scenario.

'No!' he goes, looking from her to me, then back to her again. 'Oh, no! Please, no!'

It'd nearly give you a complex.

'Dad,' Sorcha just goes, 'I have something to tell you. And I know it's going to be very difficult for you to hear.'

'You don't *need* to tell me,' he goes. 'I can see it in the . . . the . . . lost look in your eyes and the smile on *his* idiot face . . .'

'Edmund!' the old dear goes. 'Let's at least hear what Sorcha has to say before we rush to judgement. Let's have a drink and at least discuss it in a civil manner.'

We go into the living room. It's about the same size as the *en suite* in our new bedroom, and that's not me being a wanker.

Sorcha tries to lighten the atmos by talking general blah. She brings up the whole, I don't know, presidential election thing. 'Oh my God, I *so* hope Michael D. wins,' she goes, because I think it's happening next week. 'He could end up being *our* actual Obama.'

Her old man, by the way, can't take his eyes off me.

'Love the new gaff,' I go, looking around me. 'Is that an Aldi I saw downstairs?'

I actually *know* it's an Aldi because Sorcha's sister – Euphemia or Helvetica Extra Bold or whatever the fock she's called – is supposedly working there as a district manager intern, whatever they even do. Sorcha's old pair are insisting that she pays her way if she's going to live with them. That's how bad things have gone generally.

The old man knows I'm ripping the piss out of him. 'You're like a virus,' he goes. 'A virus that can't be eradicated. It just keeps coming back in a different form.'

'Sit down,' the old dear goes, which we all end up doing – me and Sorcha on the sofa, Honor at a tiny desk in front of the window, where the first thing she does is switch on Sorcha's old man's laptop. 'I'm using this computer,' she goes, 'in case anyone has an issue with that.'

Sorcha's old man has an issue – but it's not with Honor using his Vaio. He is one pissed bear.

The old dear goes, 'Let's listen to what Sorcha has to tell us,' as she pours us each a glass of wine. It's Chardonnay alright, but it's, like, a Tesco one in a screw-top bottle. They used to have a cellar. Like I keep saying, it's some fall from grace.

'I *know* what she has to tell us,' Sorcha's old man goes. 'She's back with *him*. I said it would happen. As soon as she took him in – a period of convalescence, she said! – I knew he'd worm his way back into her bloody affections.'

Sorcha goes, 'Yes, Dad, Ross and I *have* decided to give our marriage another try.'

He suddenly loses it. He ends up actually *shouting*? 'Years I've spent trying to extricate you from that bloody mess that you so blithely call a marriage!'

Sorcha's there, 'I think it's unfair to call it a . . .'

'Don't cut me off, Sorcha!' he goes. 'I'm entitled to my say! I put hundreds of hours into your divorce! Worked day *and* night. And through it all, there was the consolation that at least you could one day walk away from the . . . the . . . the worst mistake you've ever made.'

'Hey,' I go, 'I'm still here, you know.'

He turns to me and he's like, 'Yes! Don't I know it!' which is a good line, I'll give him that.

Sorcha tries the Daddy's Little Princess turn then. 'Dad,' she goes, 'I remember you told me once that you'd always support me, whatever I chose to do in life.'

He's like, 'That was when you were thinking of going back to college to do environmental law.'

'You said *whatever* I chose to do.'

'Environmental law. Something academic. Not this.'

'So what you're *actually* saying is that you don't trust my *judgement*?'

'Not when it comes to him, no. I don't trust your judgement. No.'

'Oh, well, that's nice to hear. Thanks for your honesty, Dad!'

'He'll break your heart, Sorcha, like he's broken it a thousand times in the past. People like him, they don't change.'

That hangs in the air for a good few seconds. I decide not to say anything. I don't need to.

Sorcha goes, 'Well, since we're here, there's something else.'

The poor focker looks at her with his mouth just open in shock, like he's about to be creamed by a 46A, but it's too late to get out of the basic way. 'Something *else*?'

'Okay,' she goes, 'I'm not sure *how* you're going to take this one. The house.'

'What house?'

'*Your* house. The old house.'

'What about it? It's sold.'

'I know. The buyer . . . the buyer was Ross's grandmother.'

The old dear looks instantly confused. 'But she died, didn't she?'

Her husband is a lot quicker on the uptake. He used to be a barrister, of course, and they're *never* dipshits. He just stares me down. 'She left it to you, didn't she?'

I feel my mouth twist into a smile. It can't be helped.

'No,' Sorcha goes. 'She left it to *me*?'

He laughs, nodding at the same time. 'Yes! Of course! So you feel duty-bound to take *him* back, because it's what that . . . *woman* wanted.'

I'm like, 'Careful,' and I actually mean it. 'She was my grandmother.'

He stands up really quickly. He's like, 'Don't you dare threaten me in my own home!'

Sorcha can see that he's at actual boiling point now, so she goes, 'Ross, could you maybe take Honor outside for a minute?' and she nods in the direction of the French doors leading out to the presumably *balcony*? 'Honor, go outside with your father.'

Honor goes, 'Yeah, don't mind me. I've no interest in your bullshit conversation.'

And Sorcha, who I don't think I've ever heard raise her voice to our daughter, suddenly goes, 'Go outside now!' her face all red and her eyes pretty much bulging. 'And don't cheek me back!'

Honor stands up and goes, 'I see a great need in you,' and then, tutting, rolling her eyes and dragging her Uggs across the laminate flooring, she joins me outside on the balcony.

'Okay, your wife is having a nervous focking breakdown,' she goes.

I'm like, 'Maybe don't talk about your mother like that,' for once standing up for the girl, like she's always standing up for me.

'Hashtag,' Honor goes, 'just saying.'

I lean over the balcony rail, staring out at the factories and the cor showrooms and the shell of the unfinished block between us and the clinic, which looks like something out of, I don't know, some place that America bombed the shit out of. Below our feet there's a queue of traffic heading for the M50 and obviously Dundrum.

'What *is* all of this?' Honor goes, her face screwed up in, like, confusion. It's like she spends so much time on Twitter that she doesn't notice what's happening in the actual *world*?

'It's an industrial estate,' I go.

'An industrial estate?'

'As in, factories, showrooms, blah, blah, blah.'

She shakes her head. 'Why would anyone want a balcony overlooking an industrial estate?'

'That was the Celtic Tiger, Honor. A lot of things went on that are difficult to explain now.'

I think about the Rugby World Cup final tomorrow, how much I focking hate France, but I still want them to beat the All Blacks.

Through the glass, I can hear Sorcha's old man working on her, trying to get her to see sense. I pick up the odd phrase – 'mindless buffoon', 'moral eunuch', 'waste of good protoplasm' – presumably all in reference to me. Then I hear him go, 'Your friend Claire!' and 'Your friend Sophie!' and 'Your friend Chloe!' and I realize that he's giving her a recap of some of my previous crimes slash conquests. He goes, 'Your sister, for God's sake! Your own sister!'

Her old dear throws in the odd line as well. It's all, 'We just want to make sure you're going into this with your eyes open,' and 'I'm not sure people like Ross are *capable* of being faithful,' because she's always had a soft spot for me.

The old man adds, 'He's like one of the lower primates.'

Except Sorcha obviously isn't listening – *Amare et sapere vix deo conceditur*, as the nuns out in Goatstown used to tell them – because the next thing I hear is the old man go, 'This is, comfortably, the worst day of my life,' and then I hear the French doors open and he steps out onto the balcony with a face on him like a half-sucked mango.

Honor focks off back inside to use the computer – 'Yeah, about time!' she goes – leaving me alone with him.

He stands a couple of feet away from me, just looking me up and down. I imagine he's wondering how much strength it would take to lift me up and fock me over the rail there.

'Don't worry,' he goes, as if reading my mind, 'if I thought a fall from the third floor would kill you, you'd already be down there, bleeding out.' The next thing he says is, 'How does a six-year-old girl end up speaking to her mother in that way?'

All I can do is go, 'I know. She's a bitch.'

'Do you think it's funny?'

'Dude, I'm agreeing with you. It's probably one of the few things we *do* agree on.'

'She speaks to her mother in that way because she doesn't have any respect for her. And the reason she doesn't have any respect for her is because she's taking her lead from her father.'

'That's horsh.'

'It's also true.'

I thought it was me moving into his old gaff that was going to piss him off more than anything. But he almost doesn't *care* about the house? It's me being back with his daughter – as in *back* back – that's really grinding his gears.

'When Sorcha was Honor's age,' he goes, suddenly changing the angle of attack, 'do you know what she wanted to be when she grew up?'

I'm like, 'I don't know. Something to do with animals would be my guess.'

'Ireland's first female Attorney General.'

'Oh.'

'Ireland's first female Attorney General. That's what she told me. Six years of age. Do you know where it all went wrong?'

'I'm tempted to say it was doing Orts in UCD. It's not a degree you can do a lot with, in fairness to it.'

He ends up totally losing it with me. 'It was nothing to do with her choice of course! It was you!'

'Me?'

'Meeting you. That was the moment when the . . . the . . . the regression began. And look at her now. Thirty-two years old. No career. No job. A failure for a husband and a brat for a daughter.'

'Well,' I go, 'if it's any consolation, I'm going to stay loyal to her this time.'

'That's no consolation! It's no consolation at all! She's attractive. She's intelligent. She's loving. She could have any man in the world she wants . . .'

That's actually pushing it.

'. . . but for some reason that her mother and I have never been able to fathom, she wants you. It's like some kind of fatal compulsion.'

I'm there, 'Hey, *I've* got qualities that *I* could list.'

He ignores this.

'You'll let her down again. You will break her heart. That's why I'm going to do everything in my power to remind her what you really are.'

'And what basically is that?'

'A man of no moral worth.'

I'm there, 'I might end up surprising you.'

He goes, 'I seriously doubt it,' and then he says something that I would imagine very few people have ever heard their father-in-law say. 'You know, I've always had this fear about the way this is going to end, that one day I'll just snap and kill you with my bare hands.'

A dude on the TV is saying that the election of Michael D. Higgins as Ireland's ninth President is an indicator that a people who've been let down by the political, banking and religious elites in which they once placed their faith are finally ready to make the case for a real republic. And I'm stuck behind some stupid bitch in a Škoda Citigo who doesn't know that the right-hand lane is for driving fast and the left-hand lane is for driving slow. Where do they get their licences, these women? I'm about to give her a couple of blasts of my full lights when my mobile all of a sudden rings. I make the mistake of answering it without checking who it is first. It turns out to be the old dear.

I'm like, 'Okay, why are *you* ringing me?' because it never pays to be too friendly to her. 'Focking Face Ache.'

She goes, 'I'm just ringing to say goodbye. I'm going to California tomorrow, to meet with my producers.'

She's talking about the Hallmork Channel. I still can't believe they made an actual movie out of *Mom, They Said They'd Never Heard of Sundried Tomatoes.*

She sounds in good form – California in late October, why wouldn't she be? – which is the reason I decide to hit her with the news.

'You're going to be a great-grandmother,' I go, just blurting it out like that.

For a good ten seconds, she doesn't say a word. I can picture her big bee-stung lips opening and closing. 'Who's having a baby?' she eventually goes.

I'm there, 'Well, it's hordly Honor, seeing as she's six years old.'

'You're talking about Ronan then?'

'Hooray! The penny focking drops!'

'You mean that little girlfriend of his . . .'

'Shadden.'

'She's pregnant?'

'Hey, that's life in the big city, I'm afraid. And what it means for you is that you're going to feel suddenly ancient.'

She's not a happy rabbit. That much is obvious from her silence. Eventually, she goes, 'Can we . . .' except she doesn't finish her sentence.

'You were going to say, "Can we keep this quiet?" weren't you?'

She's un-focking-believable.

'I'm just thinking of my profile. Great-grandmother. It makes me sound so . . .'

'Old,' I go. 'Happy focking travels,' and then I hang up on her.

The bird in the Škoda Citigo is still hogging the fast lane, doing forty or something equally ridiculous. What is it about the Stillorgan dualler? I go to, like, undertake her, but the second I go to switch lanes, she decides to do the exact same thing and I end up having to brake hord to stop myself running into the back of her.

I give her four or five blasts of my horn, then when we hit a red light opposite the old Spirit of Gracious Living, I pull up alongside her and open the window on my front passenger side.

She's not great-looking, if I have to be honest. If I'd a mickey tree in the gorden, I wouldn't let her look over the wall.

She gives me a little wave of apology, like it wasn't a major deal.

'Yeah, typical woman,' I shout at her. She actually seems surprised that I'm even pissed off.

'I beg your pardon!'

'You expect us to spend an hour looking for the G-spot and you won't spend two seconds looking at your blind spot.'

It's an amazing, amazing line – I'm going to have to admit that. Her mouth opens wide to form an H – presumably the stort of 'How dare you!' – but I'm like, 'You must have been wearing a low top the day you passed your driving test,' and then the light turns suddenly green, and I'm out of there in, like, a serious screech of tyres.

'Oh my God!' Sorcha goes.

We're standing in her old man's old lumber room – his *junk* room basically?

'I can't believe my dad left this behind.'

It looks like an old, I don't know, clothes rail or something.

I'm like, 'What even *is* it?'

'It's my old ballet barre from when I was a little girl. I used to use it to practise in front of the mirror in my room.'

She runs her hand along it and she smiles to herself, as if just touching the wood is enough to, like, stir up old memories. 'I wish you could have seen me do *Coppélia*,' she goes. 'With Mrs Bell. In the Taney Parish Centre. It was the first time I ever did a *pas de chaval*,' and she suddenly gets carried away by the moment and makes the mistake of trying to bring our *daughter* in on it?

'Honor!' she goes. 'Honor, come in here and see this!'

But Honor shouts back, 'Nooo,' in a really, like, bored way, 'because it's almost certainly lame,' and Sorcha just smiles sadly, obviously wishing she was different.

We *both* do?

I go, '*I* don't think it's lame.'

She smiles again – still sad, though.

'Thanks,' she goes, then after a moment of, I suppose, thought, she stands on one leg, on the tips of her toes, then swings the other leg out sideways, rests it on the top of the bor, raises her right orm like she's hailing a taxi and stares into the mid-distance, wearing one of those forced smiles you associate with ballet and, well, Mount Anville in general.

I'm there, 'You've stayed in amazing shape, in fairness to you.'

She goes, 'A lot of that has to do with pilates. I've looked after my core.'

'No one's questioning that.'

I suddenly want her. Her face is all flushed from the effort of bringing our boxes into the house from the rental van and her nids look incredible in that tight, baby-pink, Abercrombie airtex.

I make a grab for the merchandise.

She's like, 'What are you doing?' pulling away from me – a little bit appalled, but still smiling.

I'm there, 'Er, it's a little thing called *foreplay*?'

'Ross, we've got – oh my God – *so* much work to do.'

'Come on, we've got the rest of our lives to unpack this shit.'

'But Honor's just along the passageway.'

Which is a hilarious thing to hear. A week ago, we had a landing. Now, we've got a focking passageway. I go, 'Here, let's lock her in the basement until we're done.'

She's there, 'Ross!'

I laugh. 'Come on, Sorcha, *she's* not going to hear us. Jesus, the house could be burning down around her ears and she wouldn't know she was dying of smoke inhalation unless she read it on Twitter.'

I put my orm around her and try to unhook the catch of her bra through her T-shirt – an old trick of the trade – except she pulls away and goes, 'Stop it!' like she actually *means* it?

It turns out it has nothing to do with Honor or even the job of moving all our shit into the new gaff. And it's not one of her famous period dramas either.

'Look,' she goes, 'I've decided we should wait. Before we, you know . . .'

I'm like, 'Wait?' My face must look like I've just been given, I don't know, devastating news. Rosanna getting married. Sexton leaving Leinster.

She goes, 'I was thinking about what my dad said.'

I nod my head. I'm like, 'I might have known *he'd* have something to do with it.'

'Ross, don't dismiss him like that.'

'He got to you.'

'He didn't *get* to me. He just pointed out certain – oh my God – realities . . . Ross, you've never, in fourteen years, been able to stay loyal to me!'

'I told you, this time is going to be definitely different.'

'Well, I want you to prove it. I want you to show me that you're capable of abstaining – as a demonstration of your commitment to me.'

'Abstaining? Jesus Christ, how long are we talking about here, Sorcha?'

'I don't know.'

'A week? Two weeks?'

'I don't *know*, Ross. It'll be . . . when it suddenly feels right. I'll let you know.'

I'm there, 'Can I just check with you, does this abstaining thing cover everything? As in, not only full sex, but all the other bits and pieces as well?'

'All sexual contact, Ross. It shouldn't be too difficult for you.'

I roll my eyes and shake my head.

Now, in normal circs, if a bird said that to me about waiting, the next sound she'd hear would be me shutting the door on my way out. The fact that I'm still here is a sign of maybe my growing maturity.

'I'm going to end up with balls like focking Jupiter,' I go. 'But if that's what you want, it's your loss.'

The next thing either of us hears is, 'Where are they? Love's young dream!'

I wander out to the – I'm just going to go with the word here – *passageway*. I look over the banister and there's my old man, standing in the entrance hall with Helen and what looks very much to me like a rocking chair.

'What the fock is that?' I go.

He's like, 'It's a rocking chair!' which is exactly what I thought it was. 'A house-warming gift from Helen and me.'

Usually, roysh, I'd say something like, 'Leave it there, it'll do for focking firewood,' but this time I don't. I actually go, 'Thanks,' which is yet another sign that I'm maybe growing up at last.

Me and Sorcha tip downstairs. There's the usual air-kissing and the usual blah. The old man asks Sorcha if she thought the right man won the election. He's like, 'I was rather hoping it would be Sean Gallagher.'

'I was a Michael D. supporter from, like, day one,' Sorcha goes. 'What this country needs right now is – oh my God – hope. And that's what he offers. I've said all along he's the closest thing we have to an Obama.'

Me and the old man carry the chair down to the kitchen – the focking parlour, as Sorcha's old pair used to call it – and we stick it in the corner, next to the genuine wood-burning stove.

'So,' it's Helen who goes, 'how's the move coming along? Is it strange?'

She's a really, really cool person. I'm glad my old man ended up with someone like her.

Sorcha's like, 'Oh my God, Helen, I can't actually believe I'm back living in my childhood home. It's like – *hello?* – a dream?'

She puts the kettle on and the old man goes, 'The rocking chair, by the way, isn't a wry commentary on your age, Ross – or, more pointedly, the fact that you're poised to become a grandparent!'

The old dear must have told him. But he says it in such an easy-breezy way, I end up going, 'Are you not, like, sad about it – sad, disappointed, whatever?'

He whips a *Romeo y Julieta* out of his pocket and it's genuinely the size of Isaac Boss. He doesn't actually smoke them since his hort attack. He just likes the feel of them between his teeth. 'Look,' he goes, holding it between two fingers, 'it's obviously not the future any of us would have chosen for the little chap. But what can you say, Ross? It's a human life! And that's a wonderful, wonderful thing.'

I'm there, 'I suppose.'

Helen goes, 'How's Ronan coping with it? I expect he's a bit overawed.'

I'm like, 'Good question, Helen. And good word, as well. I think he's in definite shock. He's talking like he's cool with the whole thing, but I don't think it's actually hit him yet – as in, what's about to *happen*?'

'Well,' the old man goes – and this is a pretty incredible compliment he pays me – 'with you at his side, he has nothing to fear. If it's lessons he's looking for in how to be a good father, well, he's already received a master-class from the very best.'

I turn to Sorcha. I'm like, 'That's an amazing boost for my confidence.'

Sorcha goes, 'Well, Charles is right. You're an amazing, amazing father.'

Like I said, it's great to get that recognition.

The old man makes a big show of looking around him then. 'Speaking of your successes as parents – and I'm including you in that, Sorcha – where's that beautiful granddaughter of mine?'

I sort of, like, snort. It's funny.

'Upstairs,' I go. 'Unpacking her stuff.'

He's like, 'I'll pop up and say hello,' and I'm about to go, 'Yeah, good luck with that!' when I spot the fifty yoyo note already in his hand and I think, yeah, that'll buy you five or ten minutes of pleasantness.

Helen goes upstairs with him.

'It's the fourth door along the passageway,' Sorcha shouts up to them.

I laugh. I don't think I'll ever get used to calling it that.

Sorcha listens closely until she's sure they've gone upstairs, then she goes, 'Charles is right, Ross.'

I'm like, 'About?'

'About you being an amazing father.'

'Yeah, I've accepted that.'

'I just think it'd be great when the baby arrives if Ronan could spend as much time around you as possible.'

'Well, that's not going to happen, is it? With us over here and him, Shadden and the baby out in – I'm not being a snob or anything – but Knackeragua?'

She's just like, 'Hmmm,' and anyone who's in any way familiar with the deadlier of the species will know the noise I'm talking about.

I'm like, 'Okay, what do you mean by that?'

'I've just been thinking about the whole Ronan and Shadden moving in here thing.'

'Come on, Sorcha, we've been through this.'

'It's just – oh my God – they would have *so* an amazing life here, Ross. Especially if the baby was, like, a *girl*? I'm not being a snob either, but can you imagine – ballet, horseriding, recitals? She won't have any of that living in – okay, I'm going to say it – a local authority house in Finglas.'

'Look,' I go, 'I'd do anything to get the three of them away from that family of basically scumbags.'

She closes her eyes in pretend disgust at what I've said.

'A nicer way of putting it, Ross, is that there are fewer social advantages for young people in that port of Dublin. I rang Holy Child Killiney, Ross, and they sent me out their prospectus. Shadden would love it. There's, like, two whole pages on the school's ethos – all about leading fully human lives and striving to meet the wants of the age.''

'But you heard what K . . . K . . . K . . . K . . . Kennet said. He wants Ro and Shadden living with them – in the gaff next door.'

'But it might not be his decision to make.'

'What do you mean?'

She, like, hesitates for a second. 'Okay,' she goes, 'I've also been doing quite a bit of research.' That much is obvious. 'I think you and I should maybe talk to the social worker in the case.'

I'm like, 'What social worker?'

'There'll *be* a social worker, Ross.'

'Will there?'

'When two young people who are under the legal age of consent are having a baby, social services are going to be, oh my God, all over the case.'

'Okay, so what are we going to say to this supposed social worker? That these people are, like, the lowest of the low?'

'Ross, please don't talk about other human beings in that way. All I'm saying is that we should at least let this social worker know that Ronan and Shadden have options open to them.'

'And how do we do that?'

'We invite the social worker here. When the house is, like, properly done up. And then the social worker will hopefully decide – especially when we get the floors polished and all the antique cornices painted – that this is the perfect environment in which to bring up a child.'

'Do you know what it sounds like to me?' Christian goes.

See, this is what I missed when he was in the States. Pints and honesty. I told him about Sorcha pushing the whole Ronan and Shadden living with *us* thing? He knocks back a mouthful of the golden wonder – this is in, like, Neary's, by the way – and he gives me his verdict.

He's like, 'She's clucky.'

I actually laugh. 'Yeah, no, I don't think so.'

'Well,' he goes, 'I'm just telling you what it sounds like. She's suddenly got this huge nest and she wants to fill it.'

'Dude, genuinely. She won't even let me near her at the moment.'

'What do you mean?'

'Yeah, no, she's brought in this rule. No one-plus-one-equals-three until I prove that I can stay, I suppose, faithful to her. I can't tell you how gagging I am for it either.'

'That doesn't mean she's not clucky. In fact, she's probably just testing how secure the foundations are before she decides if she should have another one.'

'Jesus, I don't know about another one. I think Honor's more than enough for us.'

He gives me a sympathetic look. All the goys know what she's like.

He goes, 'She's no better?'

I laugh. 'Look,' I go, 'I don't believe in speaking ill of your kids. But it's like that movie, *We Need to Talk About Kevin*. You'd nearly be wondering was it something *we* did – or is she just naturally a little focker?'

Christian is actually the easiest person in the world to talk to. I love when it's, like, *just* us? No Lauren to come between us and try to get Christian to stort focusing on my negatives.

'We're going again ourselves,' he suddenly goes.

I'm like, 'No way!'

'Well, we're trying.'

It's on the tip of my tongue to go, 'Let's hope to fock it's a boy this time!' just because I'm a slave to a good one-liner. But I somehow manage to resist the temptation. Instead, I just go, 'Things are obviously better – as in, between you and Lauren?'

A few months ago, I could have seen them actually breaking up.

He nods. 'I definitely went through something when I lost my job.'

See, he *was* the project manager on the Star Wars casino in Vegas – until he got the road.

He goes, 'Being back working has made such a difference to my self-esteem. Look, I know it's only a submarine sandwich franchise . . .'

'Er, they're focking *unbelievable* submarine sandwiches.'

'I don't know if they're *unbelievable*.'

'Well, that's the word I'm using. And you're going to be seeing a hell of a lot of me in that place, I can tell you.'

'Well, just stay out of the wheelchair toilet,' he goes, smiling, even though he's *serious*?

'I just can't see myself trekking all the way upstairs every time.'

'Ross, seriously. You have no idea how pissed off Lauren was about it the last day.'

'Dude, I've already explained the situation to her. I just can't see it.'

'Seriously, Ross . . .'

'Dude, let's agree to differ. Let's just agree to differ.'

After a few seconds of silence, he goes, 'I can't believe you're about to be a grandfather. I have to say, young Padwan, I'm struggling with it.'

It's a long time since he called me Padwan. It's nice.

'Yeah, no,' I go, 'it was only when Lauren said it that day in the shop that it finally hit home – as in, *properly* hit home?'

'It's a lot to get your head around.'

'I felt, I don't know, instantly old.'

'I can understand that.'

'I'm trying to think of that thing that Father Fehily used to say. Life is like a toilet roll – the nearer you get to the end, the quicker it seems to disappear.'

'I miss him,' Christian goes. 'Especially, like, his wisdom.'

I'm like, 'Hey, the dude lives on through his quotes.'

That's when my phone suddenly rings. I pick it up off the bor and just look at the screen. It turns out to be Ronan. I answer by going, 'Hey, Ro, we were just talking about you!'

I suddenly remember he's in town with Shadden tonight doing a bit of late-night shopping.

He goes, 'Where are ye?' and that's when I know there's something instantly wrong.

I'm like, 'Ro, what's happened?'

He's there, 'Shadden's bleedin', Rosser.'

'What?'

'There's blood.'

I'm straight off my stool. 'Where are you?'

'Mutter Keer.'

'Okay, which Mothercare are we talking? The one in the Stephen's Green Shopping Centre?'

'Stephen's Gureen, yeah.'

I'm there, 'Have you rung an ambulance?'

And that's when he says the most incredible thing. He goes, 'I'm ringing *you*, Rosser.'

This is, like, Ronan turning to me for help – as in, I'm his first phone call. It doesn't happen often. He knows far more about the world and how it works than I do. I just go, 'Sorry, Christian – emergency,' and I run out of Neary's with the phone still clamped to my ear.

I'm there, 'Try to get to the front door of the shopping centre, Ro. I'm going to grab an Andy McNab for us.'

Which is exactly what ends up happening. I jump into the front passenger seat of the first cor on the rank, the driver does a U-y and Ronan arrives over with his orm around Shadden, then the two of them get into the back.

'We'll go to Holles Street,' I go, turning around to them. 'Down Dawson Street, along Nassau Street, then we're pretty much there. Is that okay with you, Shadden?'

She goes, 'Yeah. Thanks, Ross.'

I'm like, 'Hey, this is what I do. Are you in pain at all?'

'No, there was just blood coming out of me.'

'Okay.'

'It was a lot of blood.'

I'm there, 'Yeah, we've all gathered that,' because I'm a little bit squeamish. 'Just try to relax, okay? Both of you.'

They both just nod. They're putting their total trust in me. And suddenly I'm seeing them for what they are – just a couple of frightened kids.

Big moments have always brought the best out of me. That's a thing that's been said by a lot of people.

I'm suddenly going, 'Don't worry, Shadden. It's probably nothing. I'd nearly guarantee it. We're nearly there,' just reassuring them the entire way to the hospital.

We pull up outside. I throw the driver a Brody Jenner and I tell him to keep the change. I don't give a fock about money at this precise moment in time. Then in we go.

Fair focks to Holles Street. I never thought I'd hear myself say those words. But once we tell them the problem, Shadden is taken in to see a doctor pretty much straight away and I end up just sitting outside the door with Ro, talking to him quietly, just trying to keep him calm, like I used to do to Oisinn back in the day, when we were playing someone like Clongowes or Terenure or any school that really riled him.

I'm there, 'I was actually born in this hospital, if you can believe that.'

'Really?'

'Your grandmother was in the National Gallery when her waters broke. The whole way here she kept screaming, "I beg of you, in the name of humanity, take me to Mount Cormel!" She'd tell you that story herself.'

There's, like, depths to me. Ronan at least *tries* to smile? Then, out of the blue, he goes, 'Ine scared, Rosser.'

I'm there, 'Hey, don't be. It's going to be fine. It's going to be nothing. Trust me.'

'Ine thinkin about . . .'

'Come on, tell me – what are you thinking about?'

'I ditn't want it, Rosser. When I foorst fowunt out.'

'You're talking about the baby?'

He nods his little head.

I'm there, 'You're fourteen years old. Of course you didn't. Jesus, I can't imagine how scared you were . . . You know, you didn't need to keep it from me, Ro.'

'I ditn't know what you'd say.'

I shake my head. 'I'd never judge you, Ro. I mean, look at me. Look at what a total fock-up I'm constantly making of things.'

I look down and I notice that he's holding a black-and-white photograph, which turns out to be a scan of my actual grandchild. I take it from him. It's weird, roysh, I just automatically laugh, except actual tears stort pouring out of my eyes. I wipe them away with my hand before Ro notices.

He goes, 'Alls I can think is, if athin happens . . .'

I hand him back the photograph and put my orm around

him. 'Hey,' I go, 'nothing's gonna happen. I've already guaranteed that.'

'What if she loses it, but?'

'She's not going to lose it. It's going to be nothing. I was talking about Father Fehily earlier. You know what he used to also say? "Worry will keep you awake all night. But faith makes one hell of a pillow." He actually used to say that.'

'I'm blemmin meself, Rosser.'

'Don't be blaming yourself. But just as a matter of interest, why?'

'I should have got Shadden out of that house.'

'What house? The Tuites' house?'

He nods.

I'm there, 'I thought I picked up on something. When Sorcha suggested you come and live with us, you were up for it, weren't you?'

He just nods.

'But what about Shadden?'

'She could be persuaded.'

'Really?'

'She dudn't want to hoort her ma and her da's feelings, but. She loves her ma and da, Rosser.'

'But at the same time, she possibly knows that that house isn't the best place for the baby?'

'The fooken smoke alone, Rosser. Kennet, Dordeen, Dadden – they're all at it.'

'You're saying they're smoking in *front* of Shadden?'

'It's not good for the baby. I said it to them befower. Loads of times.'

'You shouldn't have had to say it, Ro. Shouldn't have had to.'

'And then just the fooken . . . stress.'

'What kind of stress are we talking?'

'It's a fooken madhouse, Rosser. The rows. The social are follying them arowunt. You don't know when the Geerds are gonna boorst in.'

'I can imagine.'

'It's no envirdonment to bring up a baby, knowmsayin?'

Before I get a chance to say anything, the door opens and Shadden

44

walks out, followed by a doctor – a woman in her, I'd say, mid-forties. But still hot. She looks at me, then at Ro, and it's obvious she's having trouble picturing either of us as the father.

In the end, Shadden has to make the introductions. 'Dis is Ronan,' she goes. 'Me fella. And dis is Ross, he's da.'

The doctor forces a smile by way of a hello to me. I'm possibly imagining it, but I get the impression she's wondering what kind of a father I must be.

'The good news,' she goes, and I feel my shoulders instantly loosen up, 'is that it's nothing to be worried about. The baby is fine. Just a small bleed from a polyp in the . . .'

I instantly screw up my face and stort making a loud humming noise to drown out the words. Like I said, I hate hearing that shit. The doctor shoots me a look like she doesn't appreciate it. Then off she goes.

Ronan and Shadden throw their orms around each other. And then – and I'm not expecting this – they break away from each other and they both at the same time throw their orms around *me*?

Shadden goes, 'Thank you so much, Ross,' and Ronan's like, 'Thanks, Rosser,' and it's a real cut-out-and-keep moment.

When I've finally sent them off home in a Jo Maxi – with a twenty for the fare – I ring Sorcha. She answers by going, 'Oh my God, Honor is being such a bitch to me. Everything I say to her, it's, "In case I care!" Are you and Christian enjoying your night out?'

I'm like, 'Er, no, something came up.'

'What?'

She sounds instantly worried.

'Yeah, no, I'll tell you about it later. Look, let's find out the name of that social worker.'

'Oh my God, really?'

She's delighted.

I'm there, 'Really. I've come around to your way of thinking. I want Ronan, Shadden and that beautiful little baby with us.'

2.

How Wonderful!

I'm watching some fashion programme on TV and I'm wondering what it'd be like to have phone sex with a stylist. You'd ring up, in the mood for a serious pedal, and you'd go, 'Hey, what are you wearing?' and the stylist – this is what I'm imagining – would go, 'Today, I'm wearing a Roberto Cavalli mohair and duchess silk satin jacket, an über-covetable glass bead bandeau top by Stella McCartney and Alexander McQueen silk twill trousers – as worn recently by Erin Wasson, our current *crush du jour* – complemented by an amazing gold-plated, brass and hemalyke necklace, which are very much on-trend at the moment.'

It's been too long since I've had my rock and roll. I think that's what I'm saying.

I don't know why, roysh, but that's when Erika suddenly pops into my head. I'm wondering where in the world she is right now, what she's doing, how she's coping with the disgrace of jilting Fionn at the altar and running off with a focking showjumper from Orgentina.

I whip out my phone and – out of mostly curiosity – I type her name into Google. Nothing comes up. Well, loads comes up, but nothing about her, just people with the exact same name. She was never into, like, Facebook and Twitter and all that shite. She thought it was a waste of time.

So I end up having a total brainwave and Googling *him*? Fabrizio Bettega. I type it in. There's, like, pages and pages of shit about him. He's represented Orgentina at the Olympics and blah, blah, blah. Won a medal. Or his horse did. He's even got his own Wikipedia page, the knob.

I type in 'Fabrizio Bettega' and then 'news' and up comes a

story about him winning some World Cup event in a place called – honestly – Montevideo.

I click on the story, although it's more the photographs I'm interested in, because I don't consider showjumping to be a sport like rugby is a sport. There's a picture of him going over the fence on a horse called *Arricifes* – the animal doing all the work, as usual – then a photograph of him collecting a piece of what looks like Waterford Crystal for his troubles. I click on the second photograph and, with my thumb and forefinger, I make it lorger.

There she is, in the background, just over his shoulder, looking incredibly well – and I'm saying that as her half-brother – wearing a really classy-looking navy dress that's cut just low enough to showcase her fantastic tweeters.

I check out her boat-race. It's, like, tanned and line-free. But at the same time I think I see something else in it – a *sadness*? I don't know. Maybe I'm imagining it. Let's be honest, Erika never looks happy, even when she *is*? I try to make the picture even bigger, except her face ends up being just pixels. And from those pixels it's impossible to tell whether the dream worked out the way she thought it would.

We're standing outside Killiney Dort Station when the train pulls in and we watch Ronan help Shadden – eight and a half months pregnant, remember – up the steps and over the pedestrian bridge. Sorcha's on edge, like it's actual royalty we're meeting. She's obviously keen that today should go well.

'Oh! My God!' she shouts, when the two of them aren't even over the bridge yet. 'Look! At you!'

The girl looks like she's about to pop alright – basically any minute.

A few seconds later, the two of them come through the ticket barrier and outside to us. There ends up being air-kisses and all the rest of it, except not between me and Ro, because that would be weird. Instead, he gives me the usual, 'Alreet, Rosser?' and I go, 'Alright, Ro?' and then he calls me a bender – I'd miss it if he didn't – and we all hop in Sorcha's cor, me and Sorcha in the front, Ro and Shadden in the back.

47

'I'm *so* pleased you and your baby are okay,' Sorcha goes, pointing the cor in the direction of the house. 'When Ross told me about the hospital, I was like, Oh! My God! Wasn't I, Ross?'

I'm like, 'She was, yeah. Very much, in fact.'

Shadden goes, 'It's lucky Ross was there, so it was,' pushing her glasses up on her nose. 'We were boat so skeered. But Ross was amazing.'

She's a terrific kid. I honestly couldn't have hoped for someone better for my son.

'Yeah,' Ronan goes, 'nice one, Rosser.'

I'm like, 'Hey, I'm not looking for pats on the back, or to be called very much the man of the hour, or any of it. In a case like that, instinct just takes over. I faced a million situations like it on the rugby field, where something happens and, without even thinking about it, you end up just doing what has to be done. That doesn't necessarily make me a hero.'

Two or three minutes later, we're pulling up outside the gaff. They're both pretty mesmerized by it, I can instantly tell. I catch Shadden looking at Ro with her mouth just open. 'It's like Downton Abbey,' she goes.

Sorcha laughs as she steps out onto the gravel. She goes, 'That's what a lot of people say, including – I don't know if you've ever heard of her – but Felicity Fox, when my mum and dad were originally *selling* the place? And I am *so* a Lady Mary! Ross will even tell you that!'

I have no focking idea what she's talking about. But we all laugh, mainly because we're supposed to. Her voice – it suddenly hits me – has become a postcode or two posher since we moved into the place.

Shadden goes, 'I luff *Downton Abbey*, doatunt I, Ro-Ro?'

Ro-Ro! That's what she calls him. Hilarious. I say nothing, though.

He's like, 'You do alreet. You're always watching it.'

'Oh my God,' Sorcha goes, 'who's your favourite character?'

Shadden's like, 'Probably Mister Bates.'

'Isn't he *such* a sweethort? Okay, I *actually* wish he was my uncle!

Actually, Ross – oh my God, brainwave – we should have a house-warming porty with a *Downton* theme.'

I'm there, 'Er, what?'

Sorcha turns back to Shadden and goes, 'Would you come? The two of you? We could make it fancy dress – everyone has to come as an acutal character from the show! I could get caterers in to serve – oh my God! – authentic *Downton* food. Lobster rissoles! Truffled eggs on toast! We could have it the night of the Season Two finale!'

Shadden's like, 'We'd love to come.'

After a bit more blah, we finally step into the house. Ronan and Shadden get treated to the full guided tour, with Sorcha giving them a trip back through her happy childhood as she leads them from room to room.

It's all, 'This was my bedroom when I was a little girl. My dad painted – oh my God – a beautiful dragon on that wall. Oh my God, I was obsessed. That's how the house ended up being *called* Honalee?'

Or it's, 'This is the room where I studied for my Leaving Cert. The sound of the sea is – oh my God – so, I suppose, *therapeutic*? I got, like, five As and two Bs and that was while even cramming.'

And then it's, 'The acoustics in this room are *so* amazing. When we did *A Chorus Line*, when we were in, like, transition year – oh my God – *all* the girls wanted to come out here to rehearse the musical numbers because of the way the sound bounces off the actual wall. Listen,' and then she storts – I swear to fock – actually singing, '*God, I hope I get it. I hope I get it. How many people does he need?*'

She's seriously over-egging it, if you want my opinion. But that's when I remember what Christian said, about her being possibly clucky. And how this is pretty much all the same shit she tried to interest Honor in, except Honor went, 'Yeah, and you're *how* old now?' or she went, 'Insert enthusiastic exclamation here!' or she went, 'Meanwhile, in the real world . . .'

And though I'm not the shorpest tool in the drawer, I suddenly realize that Sorcha sees Ronan and Shadden's baby as her chance to possibly stort all over again.

We tip down to the kitchen slash parlour. Sorcha lashes the kettle on, then there ends up being this, I don't know, awkward silence, while Sorcha looks for a way to, like, broach the subject of why we're all actually *here*?

'Shadden,' she eventually goes, at the same time taking out the Ladurée macaroons, 'you've got – whatever it is – three weeks to go until the baby arrives. So it's only natural that you're going to be thinking about what kind of environment your baby is going to grow up in . . .'

She's sailing dangerously close to saying Finglas is a shitbox.

'Ross was saying that you and Ronan coming to live here with us after the baby is born is something you might be prepared to consider in, like, a favourable way?'

Shadden looks at Ro, then goes, 'There'd be more room,' obviously not wanting to say straight out the real reason, which is that her family are basically scumbags. 'And I know Ronan would luff to be around he's da.'

I laugh. 'Is that true, Ro?'

He gets all embarrassed, of course. He's like, 'Leave it, Rosser, will ye?'

Sorcha pours the tea and goes, 'Okay, I'm not trying to convince you one way or the other. But what I would say – and this *isn't* me being a snob – is that this is an area of definite social advantage, especially for a baby growing up . . . Here, try one of the pistachio ones, Shadden . . . I mean, I've probably already given you an idea of what it was like for me growing up in this house. I had a childhood full of wonder . . .'

'The thing is,' Ronan goes, cutting across her – he's like a little adult – 'what me and Shadden need more than athin is just peace and quiet to able to gerron wit things. That's not to be running your famidy down, Shadden. But there does be a lot going on.'

He's a little diplomat. Sorcha is another.

'Again,' she goes, 'without pushing one set of options ahead of another – and just to reiterate what I said that day in your mom and dad's house – one of the advantages of you two living here with us is that you'd have me as, like, a live-in nanny if you decided to go back to school next September.'

Shadden's little face lights up. She's another smort cookie, see – her and Ronan met on that Saturday course they did in DCU for kids who are, like, über-gifted.

'I *would* like to go back to school,' she goes.

Sorcha's like, 'Well – again, not pushing you – I mentioned Holy Child Killiney to you the last day. And I asked them to send me out their prospectus – I hope you don't mind . . .'

Sorcha produces it from a drawer and puts it down on the free-standing island. Shadden picks it up and storts flicking through it.

'There's a whole thing in there about Mother Cornelia Connelly,' Sorcha goes, 'the founder of the Society of the Holy Child of Jesus. She was an – oh my God – amazing person with, like, really strong beliefs. She was a big believer in, like, social justice. And on the Leaving Certificate results table, they're . . . I don't know where, but it's something, like, really *high*?'

From the way they're nodding to each other, it's obvious that Ronan and Shadden are already pretty much convinced.

'Plus,' Sorcha goes, 'you probably know this already, Shadden, but in a lot of schools, girls can be – oh my God – total bitches. Except there, they're, like, *not*? Ross, you knew a lot of Holy Child Killiney girls when you were at school, didn't you?'

I certainly did. I went through those girls like a fat kid through a bag of Pick 'n' Mix. Made a real pig of myself. Happy, happy days. Although Sorcha knows pretty much none of that. I was actually going out with her at the time.

'Look,' Ronan goes, 'me and Shadden are all for it. The boat of us. But needer of us wants to hoort Kennet and Dordeen's feelings.'

Sorcha's like, 'No one wants that.'

'Thee were really good when thee fowunt out I was pregnant,' Shadden goes.

They were focking delighted. More child benefit coming in. They're probably already claiming for twins. I manage to resist the temptation to say that, though.

'Can I just suggest something then?' Sorcha goes. 'Look, why don't Ross and I speak to the social worker in the case? I'm presuming there's a social worker.'

Shadden nods. 'Patriona is her name. Patriona Pratshke.'

I laugh – for no other reason than it just sounds funny.

'Patriona Pratshke,' Sorcha goes, putting the name into her phone. 'Well, why don't Ross and I speak to her, just to let her know that you two *do* have options with regard to what happens next? Again, I'm not being a snob, but we can tell her what we've just told you and she can decide what kind of upbringing would be more advantageous to the baby.'

Ronan goes, 'Leave us ourrof it, but.'

Sorcha's like, 'Ronan, you have my word. This conversation we're having today never took place.'

Ronan nods. Then Shadden gives Sorcha this Patriona bird's digits.

We finish our tea, then Shadden looks out the window and goes, 'You have a lovely garden.'

This is the point I'm trying to get across. It's her manners as well as brains. She's, like, a Tuite in name only.

'Go out and explore it,' Sorcha goes. 'Check out the really old sycamore tree. There's a little Princess Castle – like a treehouse – that my dad had built in the branches and it's still there!'

Ronan and Shadden tip outside. I watch them through the window, wandering around the gorden, orm in orm, taking in the view of the sea. They seem actually excited. Not half as excited as Sorcha, though.

'Oh my God,' she goes. 'Ross, they really want this.'

I'm like, 'They certainly seem to. Let's not get ahead of ourselves, though.'

'Oh my God, do you know what we should do? We should turn one of the bedrooms – one with a view of the bay – into a nursery,' and she storts opening and closing drawers. I know what she's looking for is the Ikea catalogue.

I'm like, 'Is *that* not getting ahead of ourselves, Babes?'

But suddenly she's a woman with a mission. She goes, 'What if Patriona asks us if we're ready to take this new baby? We haven't even got, like, a crib. We have to prepare for it, Ross, like it's us who are actually *having* the baby?'

I realize that there's no point in having it out with her. The one thing that keeps going through *my* mind, though, is how Honor will react, if and when it actually happens. Another child in the house? She'll shit her focking molars.

I suddenly look at the clock and realize that it's already after two. 'Look at the focking time,' I go. 'I better go and collect Honor from school.'

I'm not shitting you when I say this, but Sorcha – I swear to God – goes, 'Who?'

One of the nicest things about having a second crack at your marriage is that you suddenly stort remembering all the reasons you fell for the other person in the first place. One of the qualities that Sorcha has always loved about me, just as an example, was my competitiveness in pretty much everything I do. The memory of it suddenly hits her when I'm pushing the trolley towards the checkout in Superquinn in Blackrock and I turn around to her and Honor and go, 'Okay, you two leave the packing to me.'

Honor doesn't look up from her phone, just goes, 'Er, *natch*?' but Sorcha actually laughs. She's like, 'Oh my God, don't tell me you still do that!'

She remembers.

Whenever we did the big grocery shop together back in the day, I always set myself the challenge of having nothing left to bag up by the time the bird on the till scanned the final item through. Even as I'm approaching the checkout area with the trolley, I'm already thinking tactically. The trick, when you're putting everything on the conveyor belt, is to space out the items that have, like, security tags attached to them – shit like bottles of wine, razor blades, DVDs and whatever else – to stop the checkout bird getting a proper momentum going.

In rugby terms, it's called breaking up the play.

Sorcha shakes her head. But she accepts that it's just, like, one of my things.

I deliberately choose a checkout where there's, like, a woman customer ahead of me. Women are famous for being exact change freaks. The time she spends rummaging through the shrapnel in her purse for the thirty-five cents or the ninety-three cents or the seventy-eight cents or the forty-seven cents gives me time to stort getting shit down on the actual conveyor belt.

It's like when you play Wales. A good, early lead is essential.

I take the fruit and veg out of the trolley first. It's also part of the challenge to keep all similar items together, so that all the meat, cleaning products, stuff from the bakery and whatever else are all in their own separate bags.

So I stort throwing it all down on the belt. Apples. Bananas. Helda beans. Sweet potatoes. Kiwis. Pineapples. Broccoli tender stems. Aubergines. Sugar snaps. Blueberries. Raspberries. Blackberries. Conference pears. Courgettes. Wineglass onions. Avocados. Pomellos.

The bird on the till hasn't even *got* to my shit yet.

Then I put down a CD – *Christmas* by Michael Bublé. There's a good, like, seven seconds of work in, like, removing the security packaging from that, which will give me time to get the fruit and veg bagged up, before moving onto the cheese, general dairy and chilled foods.

You get the idea.

'I have some news,' Sorcha goes.

I'm there, 'News?' but not without breaking my focus.

'I spoke to Patriona, Ross. As in, Patriona Pratshke?'

'Keep talking.'

'I rang her this morning. I just explained that I was Ronan's stepmum – and obviously *as* his stepmum, I was interested in his welfare. She is, like, *so* a nice person, Ross.'

I've already emptied the trolley and I'm, like, through the checkout and poised with the bags when the bird storts ringing through my items, which is exactly where I want to be.

I'm like, 'Continue, Babes. I'm listening,' even though the race is now very much on and the checkout bird knows it. I watch a little smile pass across her face, even though she wouldn't be much to look at. But she's got a customer who wants to play.

'The point I'm making,' Sorcha goes, 'is that she seemed really interested in what I had to say.'

'Did she?'

'I just explained our situation. And she did acknowledge that Shadden's family home was a bit on the crowded side. I mean, how many kids do they actually have?'

'I don't think even *they* can put a number on it. Could be five. Could be seven. But you may bet they're claiming children's allowance for twice the actual number.'

'Ross, that's a horrible thing to say.'

Here comes Bublé. A pawn in my game.

'I'm only saying it because it's true, Sorcha. Here, you didn't tell her that Shadden and Ronan are all on for moving in with us, did you?'

'No, I didn't.'

That's when Honor looks up from her phone, suddenly picking up the thread of the conversation.

She's like, '*Excuse* me?' and she says it with a serious amount of 'tude, like she can't actually believe what she thinks she just heard.

Sorcha just blanks her. 'Anyway,' she goes, 'Patriona wants to interview us.'

I'm there, '*Interview* us? It's suddenly all a bit thorough, isn't it?'

'Of course it's thorough, Ross. This is the welfare of a beautiful little baby and two, remember, still teenagers we're talking about.'

The Roquefort, the Low Fat Super Milk, the Petits Filous, the cottage cheese, the unsalted butter and the Actimels come at me in a pretty much blizzard. You can see that the checkout bird is all delighted with herself, thinking she has me already beaten, but then there's suddenly a bottle of Château Montlabert 2008 in front of her, and it takes her, like, six or seven goes to get the actual tag off the neck of the bottle – she keeps having to belt it off whatever that little device is called – allowing me to get all the dairy stuff bagged and in the trolley before she hands it to me.

The woman is up against a tactical master and she suddenly knows it.

'So where are we supposedly meeting this Patriona?' I go. 'That is one seriously focked-up name, by the way.'

Sorcha's like, 'In her office. I made an appointment for next Wednesday.'

Honor goes, 'Hello?' still trying to get our attention.

This isn't how I'd have chosen to break the news to her, I have to admit.

I'm like, 'Yeah, no, I'm free that day, you'll be happy to know. So what do we have to do – put on a show?'

'It's not about putting on a show, Ross. We're just going to talk to her. She's already been to see the Tuites. She's hopefully seen how they live.'

'God focking help her.'

'I'm going to bring along some pictures of our beautiful home and hopefully she'll see the – oh my God – *amazing* life we could offer the baby and decide that the best place for Ronan and Shadden to be is with us.'

Honor goes, 'Okay, *what* the fock are you talking about?'

Like I said, there were possibly better ways of telling her.

Sorcha smiles at her, obviously expecting her to be excited, and goes, 'Ronan and Shadden might be coming to live with us, with their brand-new baby!'

She's possibly jumping the gun a bit, I think.

'Okay,' Honor goes, her body suddenly going all rigid, 'you're *actually* joking.'

'I'm not joking.'

'Do you expect me to be focking pleased or something?'

'It's a little baby, Honor!'

Honor goes, 'A little baby that has nothing to do with me.'

Sorcha looks at her open-mouthed. 'Of course, the baby has something to do with you! Ronan's your half-brother. That means the baby will be your little niece or nephew.'

'Half-niece or half-nephew,' I go, even though I'm not sure if those are actual things.

Sorcha goes, 'I think we can say just niece or nephew, Ross.'

I have to focus here. There's suddenly, like, a build-up of focaccias and Vienna rolls and chocolate Hobnobs and date loaves and charcoal crackers and *pains au chocolat* and Tuc crackers waiting to be bagged. The bird on the checkout obviously senses that I'm in trouble because she picks up the pace as she puts the Battenberg and the four-pack of Lancashire Barm Cakes and the Mr Kipling Angel Slices through with a definite smile on her face, suddenly clogging up the packing area.

'I think we might go to Ikea on Saturday,' Sorcha goes.

Ikea is kind of, like, *my* Afghanistan? I've done one or two tours there and I've no real desire to go back.

I'm there, 'Why are we going to Ikea?'

'To get the bits for the nursery, Ross.'

'Okay, can *I* just remind you,' Honor goes, her face all red, 'that it's not *you* who's having this baby?'

She's as mad as a focking meat hammer.

Sorcha's there, 'Cheer up, Honor, it'll be like having a little brother or sister in the house.'

'Oh, I'm *so* excited,' Honor goes, 'I think some pee came out!' except she's being, like, *sarcastic*?

'Well, you're going to have to get used to the idea.'

'I'm not going to. I'm telling you that now.'

Focking yes! Another bottle – this time of Grey Goose – with a security tag on it. Again, it's a stubborn one. It comes off at, like, the fifth attempt, by which time I've managed to get everything that *was* in the packing area into actual bags. That's when the checkout bird finally realizes she's beaten. I can see it in the way she puts the last items through, like she couldn't be orsed any more – the twenty-four pack of Superquinn sausages, the Ardennes pâté, the North Atlantic smoked salmon, the gourmet minced lamb, mint and pancetta burgers – like she knows she's pissing into the wind now.

Not only do I manage to bag them up, but I have my credit cord and my reward cord out of my wallet and ready to give to her by the time she puts the last piece of shopping through – a five-pack of Gillette Sensor Excel blades. They're in, like, a plastic security box, which she has to go to the enormous trouble of opening and, by the time she gets the actual blades out, I'm holding open the last shopping bag for her to drop them in.

The critics can say what they like about me – thick as a ditch, bad father, too good-looking to ever be loyal to any one woman – but one thing no one can deny is that I'm an unbelievable competitor. I even go, 'How can the IRFU say that I've got nothing left to contribute to the game? The focking nerve of these people.'

Even the checkout bird gives me a little smile of recognition as she's handing me back my cord and receipt.

That's when I catch Honor suddenly staring daggers at *me*. She goes, 'Will you please talk some sense into this woman?'

I'm like, 'Honor, it's like she said, this kid – *if* we manage to get it – could be like an actual brother or sister to you.'

That's when she storts going, 'I don't want a brother or sister! I don't focking *want* a brother or sister! I don't focking *want* a brother or sister!' loud enough for pretty much the entire Blackrock Shopping Centre to hear.

I'd say there's one or two in the Frascati Centre who can nearly hear her as well.

'Ignore her,' Sorcha goes. 'Come on,' and she storts walking towards the travelator, leaving Honor behind in the supermorket, with literally steam coming off her. We stort heading downstairs, in the direction of the cor pork.

I look back. 'Do you not think we should maybe go back and get her?' I go. 'It possibly wasn't the most *sensitive* way we could have broken the news?'

'We're going to have to stort ignoring these little tantrums of hers,' Sorcha goes, her face set hord as a traffic warden's hort. 'She's bullied us for far too long, Ross. And with another child possibly about to enter our home, I've decided that it's not going to continue.'

Honor is suddenly hanging over the gord rail above us, still screaming at the top of her lungs, her eyes popping and her face all red, going, 'I don't want a brother or sister! I don't want a brother or sister! I have focking rights!'

*

The old man squints the length of the fifth fairway – this is in, like, Elm Pork. I don't *know* why. He must have played this hole, like, two hundred times before.

'So Enda Kenny,' he goes, 'your friend and mine, Ross, is to address the nation on television. To tell us all, no doubt, what a good boy he's being and how he's doing everything he's told to do by our betters in Europe.'

'Fucking Germans,' Hennessy goes. And then he actually spits – although he has just bitten the butt end off a Davidoff Millennium Churchill. 'And the French. There's words I could use, Charlie. Ugly ones.'

The old man laughs, then he addresses the ball.

'Didn't mean to get you riled, old scout. You've always had your doubts about the, quote-unquote, European project. Right from the off. I know that. I'm giving you credit for saying it back in nineteen-seventy-whatever-it-was. We're better off out of it – those were your exact words. We were in the Shelbourne Bar.'

The old man hits the ball – sweetly, it has to be said – to within, like, one decent chipped shot of the green. He turns around with a little look of, like, triumph on his face. 'But at the same time, Hennessy, I think we'd all have to agree that independence hasn't really worked out for the Irish. The best thing we could do now is go to Britain, our friends across the water, and say, "Bygones be bygones and so forth. Is there any danger you might take us back?"'

Hennessy's like, 'Take us back?' and he's not a happy rabbit. He looks like he wants to bend one of his Callaways around the old man's head.

'It's only been a hundred years,' the old man goes. 'A little less. No, I'm sure they'd understand. It's like young people today. They move out of home, full of optimism, of course, that they're going to have tremendous fun *and* be in a position to pay the bills. Then they realize, uh-oh, I possibly wasn't ready for this – wonder if Mum and Dad have converted my old room into a home study yet? Ross, how many times did you leave home, only to turn up again like a bad penny, with a cheery "What's cooking? It smells revolting, but I'd eat anything at this stage", then handing me your final notices to pay for you?'

I'm like, 'Who's up next?' except Hennessy doesn't answer, so I go ahead and tee up my ball.

There's a definite tension between us, which is what you'd obviously expect. It's the first time we've laid eyes on each other since he conned me out of the €1.7 mills I extorted from Regina Rathfriland and I got Ronan's mate, Nudger, to burn his yacht in retaliation.

The old man knows none of this, of course.

I take one or two practice swings, but I can feel the dude, like, staring at me, his eyes burrowing into the back of my head. I end up totally shanking it and the ball ends up in the small wood off to the right of the actual fairway.

The old man's like, 'Something up, Ross?'

I'm there, 'Sorry?'

'Unlike you to slice the ball like that. It's all this talk of politics, I expect. I know you have your views.'

I have literally no views. I often think that if you cracked my head open, you'd find two giraffes in there playing badminton.

Hennessy puts the ball down.

'So, Kicker,' the old man goes, 'did you hear your godfather's news?'

I'm like, 'No.'

'He's off to the U. S. of A., don't you know! For a year! To help out one or two chaps – no names, no pack-drill — who are being chased for money by NAMA.'

Hennessy hits a beautiful drive – fully, like, straight – to within ten feet of the old man's ball.

'Good shot,' I go, not sucking up to him, more happy to let the past just be the past.

'I expect today will be the last you two will see of each other for a while,' the old man goes.

I breathe a sigh of – I'm not going to deny it – relief. I wander over towards the, again, wooded area, to try to, like, find my ball. That's when I hear Hennessy go, 'I'm going to help Ross find where it went,' and I know instantly that he wants to get me on my own.

I'm, like, combing the long grass between the trees, when he's suddenly standing right behind me – uncomfortably close, it has to be said – not even helping me. I try to get the subject onto something happy.

I go, 'That sandwich place of Lauren and Christian's seems to be flying. You must be proud of *her*,' because Lauren's his actual daughter. 'If you're going to have anything, have the Midday Melt. I'm going to use the word gorgeous, even though it wouldn't be a typical Ross word.'

I tend to just babble when I'm shitting myself. Hennessy doesn't want to talk about Lauren and he doesn't want to talk about sandwiches, submarine or otherwise.

'You burned my fucking boat,' he goes.

I decide to just, like, balls it out. I'm like, 'Do you have proof of that?'

He goes, 'I'd only require proof if I was going to seek my retribution in a court of law,' and he says it in a definitely threatening way.

'You're saying you're going to try to get revenge?'

'I'm saying it's not over – me and you. I won't always be in the States. I'll be back. One day. And when you see me again, you should get worried.'

The old man suddenly shouts over to us. He's like, 'What are you two talking about? Politics, no doubt! I expect Ross has drawn you into one of his famous debates, with some suitably ribald comment on the shortcomings of the present administration!'

'Your ball's over there,' Hennessy goes, pointing with his nine-iron to an area of, like, undergrowth. Then, still staring daggers at me, he walks off.

I pick up my ball. I'm about to just fock it out of the rough and onto the fairway when my phone all of a sudden rings. I check the screen. It's K . . . K . . . Kennet Tuite. I answer by going, 'Ross O'Carroll-Kelly – since 1980,' which is a funny thing I sometimes say.

He goes, 'You fooking p . . . p . . . p . . .'

I cut across him. I'm like, 'Dude, I'm enjoying a round of golf here with the old man and his solicitor. Just tell me, am I going to have time to play my next shot before you finish that sentence?'

'Prick,' he goes.

Obviously not. How do I *make* so many enemies? That's what I wouldn't mind knowing.

I'm like, 'Okay, *why* am I a prick?'

'Yiz rang ta sociaddle woorker . . . b . . . b . . . behoyunt me b . . . b . . . back?'

'Yeah, if you have a point, you better make it quick.'

'Yiz had no reet.'

'We had every right.'

'Yiz ardent t . . . takin eer thaughter an eer granchoyult off us.'

'We're not *trying* to take your daughter or grandchild off you. Our basic point is that I'm as much this baby's grandfather as you are – which means I'm *as* entitled as you are to a say in what happens to the kid after it comes along.'

'The b . . . b . . . b . . . babby'll live hee-er wirrus. I alretty toalt yiz.'

'Well, that's what remains to be decided.'

He's there, 'It's not a competition,' even though we both know, deep down, that it kind of *is* one? That's why he then goes, 'What are you going to s . . . s . . . s . . . say tooer?'

I'm like, 'What do you mean?'

'I mean t . . . t . . . teddin stordies abourrus – what we're like.'

I'm there, 'Dude, she's met you, I presume?'

He goes, 'She's been hee-er tooer tree toyums, yeah.'

'Then I won't need to tell her anything. Look, we'll tell her about *our* set-up – massive gaff, overlooking the sea, great schools all within driving distance – and then we'll get her verdict. A view of Killiney Bay or a view of – what's that thing opposite your gaff? – an off-licence built inside a cage to keep the focking ram-raiders out. Yeah, no, I don't envy her *that* choice.'

He goes, 'Ye d . . . d . . . d . . . d . . . doorty-looking . . .'

I'm like, 'Dude, I'd love to hang around for the conclusion of that sentence, but like I said, I've got shit on.'

Then I hang up and fock my ball out into an actually playable position.

'A text from Jamie Heaslip,' I go, holding up my phone as proof.

I'm still buzzing on what we did to Munster yesterday in the old Rabble Direct. I'm possibly still a bit mulled as well.

Sorcha goes, 'Hmmm,' not really listening to me. She's driving around and around the cor pork of Ikea in Ballymun, looking for somewhere to stick the old Mariner. There's, like, tonnes of focking spaces, by the way, but she always insists on finding one that's as close as possible to the entrance to the actual store. Five nights a week, you'll find my wife walking the roads of South Dublin, swinging her orms like a focking lunatic, to try to lose weight. But when it comes to, like, shopping centres, she'll spend an hour driving around to save herself a ten-second walk.

'Yeah, no,' I go, 'I texted him last night, just to say fair focks for basically destroying Munster last night. Then he comes back to me a minute ago with this. It's like, "Thanks. Means a lot coming from you, Legend!" which is an amazing thing to say. He didn't have to say it.'

'He's probably just humouring you,' Honor suddenly pipes up from the back. 'He probably looked at your text this morning and went, "Oh my God, who is this randomer suddenly texting me?" He probably doesn't even know who you are.'

She's got a face on her like she's just drunk battery acid out of one of Zak Dingle's wellies. She's still in a fouler over this baby business.

I'm there, 'Oh, Jamie Heaslip knows who I am alright. He actually nodded to me in Bear two months ago – as in Bear, the restaurant he owns? – and when the bill finally came, they only chorged me for the ten-ounce rib. The fries and the horseradish sauce weren't even on it. I wouldn't imagine he'd do that for someone he didn't recognize and definitely respect.'

Honor rolls her eyes, tells me I'm *actually* sad, then goes, 'Why are you always talking about rugby anyway?'

'Because,' I go, 'it's a massive, massive port of my life, Honor. And it probably always will be.'

'I don't know why. You obviously weren't very good at it.'

That hurts. Especially coming from my own flesh and blood. But

I realize she's just pushing my buttons – *she's* hurt, so she's lashing out – and that's the reason I decide to remain calm.

'There's a lot of people who would disagree with that analysis, Honor. George Hook reckoned I had the potential to be as good as Mike Gibson. Derek Foley said I was a definite future Ireland captain.'

'But you weren't. So you were a failure.'

Sorcha comes steaming in to defend me – fair focks. She saw me when I was at my peak, remember – even though the girl knows fock-all about the game. She's like, 'Stop picking on your father, Honor.'

'Er, I'm *not* picking on him? I'm just asking him why he never made it as a rugby player – *if* he was as good as he always says he was.'

'Injuries,' I instantly go. 'Plus bad luck. Plus I said a few things to Warren Gatland one night in the Berkeley Court with a few drinks on me that possibly didn't help my cause. I did the same with Eddie O'Sullivan – except that was in Jury's in Cork.'

She doesn't respond to that. She just stares at the back of Sorcha's head as we finally pull into a space, and goes, 'So he needs you to fight his battles for him now, does he? Er, *lame* much?'

We get out of the cor and we walk the short distance to the shop.

Sorcha goes, 'Even if we get, like, two or three pieces today, Ross. A crib and maybe a little wardrobe – just to be ready, if and when it happens.'

I should tell her that she's maybe counting her chickens. Instead, I go, 'Er, yeah, whatever.'

Honor goes, 'Oh my God, you don't even know that you're *getting* this baby. Hashtag – desperado!'

Sorcha's like, 'We want to be prepared, Honor,' and then to me she goes, 'We should also see if they have any leaflets on baby-proofing a house. We should definitely be thinking in terms of baby-proofing.'

Honor, for no reason, suddenly kicks the back of my heels and I trip and sort of, like, stagger *forward*? 'Oh, soz,' she goes, cracking on that it was an accident. 'I'm *such* a klutz!'

I don't say anything. I decide not to give her the pleasure.

'Okay,' Sorcha goes, as we're walking into the place, 'now, it's up to you, Honor. Do you want to come with us to choose items for the new nursery, or do you want to go to Småland?' which is what Ikea call the crèche.

Or Spa Land, which is what Honor calls it.

Honor sighs, like it's all too much for her, then goes, 'Oh my God, the crèche if those are my only choices,' and then a second or two later, 'You know I'm going to be mixing with northside children and probably bogger kids as well. Yeah, *rul* good parenting, Mom!'

We get her signed in. One of the crèche workers, who I think looks like Rozanna Purcell – note to self: I need to have sex very soon – points out the ball pit and the climbing ropes and the games and the paints and shit. Except Honor gives her, like, a seriously filthy look, takes out her iPhone and goes, 'I have plenty to keep me busy, thank you.'

The woman looks at us, as if to say, 'Okay, what's this kid's deal?' then me and Sorcha turn away quickly, in case she changes her mind about taking her. As we do, some poor unfortunate little girl makes the mistake of trying to be friends with her and we hear Honor go, 'Please don't speak to me. I don't want to pick up an accent.'

Fifteen minutes later, me and Sorcha are in, like, the children's furniture section, traipsing up and down the aisles, neither of us saying a word, roysh, trying to think about the kid we might be getting but *actually* thinking about the one we've already got.

'She's just acting out,' Sorcha goes, as if reading my mind. She's checking out this Sundvik crib, wondering do they have it in any colour other than Norwegian goat willow. 'I'm not saying it's going to be easy on her, coming to terms with the arrival of a new baby. But it's time she realized, Ross, that she's not the actual centre of the universe.'

I go, 'Imagine what she's going to be like when this movie of hers hits the TV screens?'

She's like, 'I don't even want to think about it.'

I'm there, 'That shit she said to me in the cor, though,' and I end up sort of, like, slapping this Leka Cirkus mobile with my hand. 'She definitely knows what buttons to press with me.'

'Don't let her get to you.'

'Calling me a loser. A lot of people would disagree with that assessment.'

I suddenly realize that I'm on the point of actual tears here. Sorcha can obviously hear it in my voice because she touches my shoulder, then turns me around to face her. 'Ross,' she goes, 'you're not a loser. You're *so* not. That thing that George Hook said about you. That will always stand.'

'That's my point.'

'*And* that text from Jamie Heaslip.'

'I didn't think you were listening to me.'

'Of course I was listening to you. Are you going to save it?'

'I was thinking I might.'

'You should.'

'I probably will then.'

That's when we hear it. A man's voice suddenly comes over the P. A. going, 'A customer announcement – would Ross and Sorcha O'Carroll-Kelly please return to Småland to collect your daughter? That's Ross and Sorcha O'Carroll-Kelly – please return to Småland to collect your daughter – immediately!'

I look at Sorcha, except she's got this look of, like, stubbornness on her face that I recognize from all the times in the past when I asked her to take me back. She's like, 'We're *not* going back to Småland, Ross.'

I'm there, 'Yeah, no, but it sounded pretty urgent, Sorcha. They used the word immediately.'

'Well, what we're doing right now is urgent, too. We have to pre-pare a room for a newborn baby.'

'What if Honor's, I don't know, maimed another kid?'

'She won't have maimed another kid.'

'I'd like to think that as well, Babes. But I'd nearly believe any-thing of her at this stage.'

'Ross, it's *all* classic acting-out behaviour. She knows there's pos-sibly another baby on the way and she wants our attention. And the worst thing we can do is feed that craving. Sharing is something she's going to have to get used to – and that includes sharing us. Now come on, concentrate.'

'I don't know.'

'Look, we can just say we didn't hear any message. She'll still be there when we finish our shopping.'

If you'd told me a year ago that my wife would one day say those words, I honestly wouldn't have believed you.

'Once again,' the same voice goes, 'would Ross and Sorcha O'Carroll-Kelly please return to Småland to collect their daughter. Please. Come now. Please.'

Sorcha goes, 'That Sniglar changing table is – oh my God – so cute. I wonder should we make Scandinavian coastal conifer the actual colour theme?'

See, that's Sorcha when her mind is made up about something. There's literally no changing it. So, like her, I try to ignore the announcements, which stort coming every, like, three or four minutes for the next two and a half hours, the dude's voice sounding more and more desperate and – I have to admit – sad.

I can hear other customers tutting and saying shit like, 'The poor little girl – the parents are probably in the pub!' and 'Why doesn't the shop just call the Gardaí?'

But Sorcha manages to shut everything out for those – like I said – two and a bit hours, while she fills a pallet truck and a shopping trolley with shit before she decides we're finally through.

We head for the checkouts. The bird on our till – don't ask, she's a focking dog; what is it with these shops? – gets the scanner gun out and storts totting everything up. Three Trofast wall storage combinations. Two Mammut topple-proof kiddies' wardrobes. A Sudvik crib in – yes – Scandinavian coastal conifer that converts into a toddler bed. A set of Spoka LED nightlights in the shape of lady-birds. A Gulliver baby bath. A Mammut children's table with four Mammut children's chairs. The Sniglar changing table that she loved. An ergonomically designed Lilla potty with an anti-slip base. A Leka Cirkus playmat. An Ekorre toddler walker with building blocks in it. A rocking moose called Rasmus and a cuddly hedgehog called Vandring Igelkott.

And as I'm watching our till receipt grow longer and longer, I'm still listening to the same voice going, 'Ross and Sorcha

O'Carroll-Kelly. Unless you return within the next five minutes, your daughter will be treated as an abandoned child and we will be forced to inform the authorities.'

I genuinely don't think Sorcha can even hear it any more. She turns around to me and goes, 'By the way, don't forget to mention the housewarming porty to the goys.'

I'm like, 'Have we decided we're actually having one then?'

'Ross, we have to have a housewarming porty.'

'Yeah, no, but the whole *Downton Abbey* thing – we're not focking dressing up, are we?'

'Come on, Ross, it'll be – oh my God – so much fun.'

'That's one thousand, eight hundred and seventy-five euros,' the till bird goes, 'and sixty-eight cents.'

Jesus Christ.

I hand over the plastic and pay for the lot. Then I stort pushing the trolley in the direction of Småland.

Sorcha's behind me, still going, 'We could do, like, a draw to decide who's going to dress up as who. I'm presuming no one's going to want to be Daisy or Mrs Patmore. Or actually Lady Edith.'

I think Lady Edith is the ugly sister.

'Yeah, no, fair enough,' I go. 'But we better step it up here, Babes. Instead of two kids, we might actually end up with none.'

Even from, like, fifty yords away, I can see that Småland slash Spa Land – whatever you want to call it – is a scene of focking chaos. There's, like, paint all over the walls. There's paint all over the kids. Plastic balls from the dry pool are scattered all over the floor. Tables and chairs have been upturned. There are, like, fifteen or sixteen children being comforted by Ikea staff, some of them crying, some of them just staring into space, basically traumatized, like they've just been pulled out of a burning bus.

I hear one little boy – who's covered from head to toe in paint – turn around to a member of staff and go, 'She's evil,' obviously referring to our daughter.

And there she is, sitting alone in the corner – people afraid to go near her – her little thumb working away on her phone, texting or Tweeting or fock knows what.

She suddenly looks up and sees us. 'You took your time,' she goes.

And Sorcha's there, 'Yes, we did, Honor. Because we know what this is about. And we're not going to give in to you. You're going to have to get used to the idea of sharing our home with another small person. So you can give up these little attention-seeking displays.'

Honor suddenly looks at the trolley and the pallet truck that are loaded high with all the shit we've bought. She shakes her head, goes, 'You're actually *both* losers,' then morches past us, in the direction we came in.

As we go to follow her back to the cor, one of the crèche workers – the one who's a ringer for Rozanna Purcell – turns to me and goes, 'Don't ever bring her here again.'

Sorcha tells me to let her do the talking. She's wearing her Stella tailored blazer over a white Jill Sander shirt – a sure sign that she means business. I'm pretty insulted, it has to be said.

'What,' I go, 'you expect me to just sit here – like *Weekend at* focking *Bernie's*?'

Actually, that's a great movie. I definitely need to watch it again soon. It was once every three months when I was in college.

'I'm not suggesting you just sit there,' Sorcha goes. 'What I mean is, let me take the lead.'

'But I've possibly got shit to say myself, Sorcha.'

'All I'm saying is that I've done courses, Ross – as in, recognized courses?'

'I know all about your courses.'

'So I'm just saying, yes, by all means, talk. But let me set the agenda.'

We're sitting outside this Patriona whatever-the-fock's office. Our appointment was for, like, twenty minutes ago, but she's supposedly running late. Her secretary – who's not *that* unlike Leigh Lezark, in fairness to her – tells us that she should be off that call soon and we just smile at her, roysh, and tell her it's cool.

'And don't use the F-word,' Sorcha goes, out of the corner of her mouth.

I'm like, 'Why would I use the F-word?'

'Because you use it all the time, Ross. And God forbid this baby should end up with a mouth like Honor's.'

She blames me for a lot of shit that isn't my basic fault.

All of a sudden, Patriona's door opens, she comes out and she wanders over to her secretary's desk.

'Oh, fock,' I instantly go, with my hand over my face.

Sorcha's like, 'What?'

'I think I know her.'

This conversation ends up being whispered, by the way.

'What?' Sorcha goes, straight away worried. 'How do you know her? Oh my God, you didn't sleep with her, did you?'

I'm like, 'Jesus Christ, Sorcha, what do you take me for?'

She's focking horrendous-looking, this woman. Cillit Bang wouldn't shift her.

'So how do you know her?'

'I think I may have insulted her on the N11 a couple of weeks ago. She can't drive for shit – and I'm saying that in my defence.'

Sorcha suddenly has her head in her hands. 'What did you say to her, Ross?'

I'm there, 'Er, I can't actually *remember* the specifics? I'm pretty sure she won't know it's me, though. I don't think she got that good a look.'

I'm wrong, of course. The second she turns and storts walking towards us with her hand outstretched, I cop the instant flicker of recognition in her eyes.

'Ross,' she goes, 'and Sorcha,' except she barely looks at Sorcha. She keeps staring at me, obviously trying to remember where she *knows* me from? 'I'm sorry I kept you waiting. Do you want to come into my office?'

We follow her in. I'm jinxed. I genuinely believe that. We sit on the opposite side of the desk to her and she goes, 'I'm sorry, we've met before, haven't we?'

I'm like, 'I don't remember you. And I'm a sucker for a pretty face,' just trying to keep it light.

She suddenly realizes who I am, though, the second I open my mouth.

'Didn't you shout something at me a few weeks ago? At traffic lights on the Stillorgan Road?'

'Again, I'm going to have to say the face isn't ringing a bell.'

'Was it, "You want us to look for the G spot, but you couldn't be bothered looking at your blind spot"?'

I'm there, 'Doesn't sound like one of my lines.'

But Sorcha has to go and make a liar out of me then. 'Ross, just tell her,' she goes. 'It's important that we have transparency. Yes, Patriona, it *was* him.'

She has a mouth on her like a focking hippopotamus.

'You did change lanes without actually indicating,' I go, just in my defence.

Patriona goes, 'For which I apologized with a wave of my hand. And no, by the way, I wasn't wearing a low-cut top the day I passed my driving test.'

I can sense Sorcha suddenly stiffening. She's heard me use that line before. 'Okay,' she suddenly goes, trying to retake control of the conversation, 'now that we've accepted that, I just want to say thank you for agreeing to see us today, Patriona. Like I said to you on the phone, Ross and I obviously have an interest in the case. Ross is Ronan's father and I'm, I suppose, his stepmother and we get on – oh my God – *so* well.'

'Yes, you explained that to me on the phone.'

She's hord work, this woman. I suppose you have to be in her line.

Sorcha goes, 'I think the point we really want to make today is that, okay, this unfortunate thing has happened. It's not an ideal situation, what with Ronan and Shadden being still so young. But they do have options open to them.'

Patriona's like, 'What options are you referring to?'

She's a serious wagon.

'Okay, I'm glad you asked me that question,' Sorcha goes, in job interview mode. 'We'd be more than happy for them to come and live with us. We'd like to become their legal guardians and help them raise the baby.'

'And what makes you think you'd be suitable guardians?'

'Again, that's a good question and I'm more than happy to answer it. We've just moved into an amazing house in Killiney and – without being a snob – it's an area that would be considered, I suppose, privileged. I grew up in the same house and it was a childhood filled with – I'm always using the word – wonder. There are lots of really good schools in the area, with students from, like, ethnically diverse backgrounds and just a really good ethos, which I think is important . . .'

Patriona shuts her up with just a patronizing smile. 'With all due respect,' she goes, 'it's not necessarily *about* privilege, or – what was that word – *wonder*? It's about who can provide Ronan and Shadden with the most stable home environment.'

'Well, that's definitely us,' I go – I end up just blurting it out.

She's like, 'Is it?' and then she opens a file on the desk in front of her – presumably *ours*? – and storts making a big show of flicking through it. 'It's very worrying when we hear that young people of their age – especially Ronan's – are sexually active.'

I'm like, 'Welcome to the real world, Patriona,' because she's pissed me off here this morning.

'Is it true it happened in your apartment?' she suddenly goes.

I'm like, 'Excuse me?'

'Is it true they were using your apartment for sex?'

I end up pretty much losing it. 'I know who told you that! It was K . . . K . . . K . . . Kennet, the stuttering fock. He knows well it was fock-all to do with me. I wasn't even living there. Ronan robbed the key. I can't believe that focker . . .'

Sorcha and Patriona are just left staring at me and I end up having to apologize.

'I hope you don't mind me saying,' Sorcha goes, 'but I don't think you're giving us a fair hearing, Patriona.'

Patriona's like, 'Well, I don't know what you expected. Did you think you could just walk in here, tell me you lived in a big house in a privileged area and I'd agree to remove a sixteen-year-old girl from a stable home environment and make an order that she lives with you?'

I decide to just say it – even though it makes me technically a grass. 'What if she doesn't want to live there when the baby arrives? What if Ronan and her both want to live with us?'

'Have they indicated that to you?'

'Possibly.'

Patriona suddenly closes the file. 'Like I said, I'm not going to make a decision based on this discussion. I think I *would* like to hear what Shadden and Ronan have to say. And I'd like to arrange a home visit.'

Sorcha's like, 'A home visit? To *our* home?' and she seems delighted, obviously thinking she's going to be won over by the gaff.

'I'd like to see what you're like at home. You have a daughter, don't you?'

I'm like, 'You're saying you'd definitely need to meet her, are you?'

She goes, 'Why wouldn't I want to meet her?'

I look at Sorcha, then back at her. I'm there, 'No reason.'

'When is this likely to happen?' Sorcha goes.

Patriona's like, 'I'll contact you,' and then, with her eyes, she indicates the door.

I actually hate Garret, as in the dude who's married to Claire from Brayrut. I seriously, seriously hate him. It's, like, everything about the focker just grinds my gears. It's the head on him. It's those stupid bits of coloured wool he wears around his wrists, each one apparently a memento of some friend he made while he was off supposedly travelling the world. It's the fact that no matter where you tell him you've been, he pulls a face, says it's 'a bit touristy' and then tells you about a place five miles up the coast that you should have gone to instead.

It'd be fair to say that he and I have never hit it off. There's basically way too much history between me and his wife for us ever to get on. I've seen Claire probably a dozen times with her legs over her head, making her focking zoo noises, and he's not mature enough to handle that fact.

Oh, yeah, and he's also *always* banging on about The Machine. As in, if he sees someone he knows suddenly wearing a suit, he's all, 'Working for The Machine, huh?' like earning a focking living is something to be suddenly ashamed of. A dude, by the way, who's living rent-free in a house in Bray that his granny moved out of when she had to go into a nursing home.

Him and Claire have spent the last twelve months trying to set up an organic bakery on the Quinnsboro Road called Wheat Bray Love, except no bank will give them the money. This, of course, is the fault of The Machine and not the fact that the country is focked and that offering organic food to the people of Bray is as pointless as giving me a long-division problem to solve.

He's just a dick.

He's in Kielys with us, roysh, and he's going, 'I was walking along the Quays the other night. I think it was North Wall Quay. And I was looking at this building. A. N. Other Multinational,' and he laughs to himself. He's delighted with that. 'Anyway, all the lights were on, which meant you could actually see in. You could see people working at their desks. You could see people eating in the canteen. And on the third floor, you could see people in the gym, running on treadmills. And I thought, oh my God, it's a hamster cage. That's what it is! It's a human hamster cage! I texted that to you, didn't I, Claire?'

Claire just nods, like the dope that she is.

'It's only people earning a living,' I go. 'Trying to pay the bills. Make ends meet. We can't *all* live in *your* focking granny's house.'

He doesn't like that. I have a quick look at Christian, Oisinn and JP – they're delighted to see me put him in his box.

'Don't you two stort,' Sorcha suddenly goes. 'Here,' and she hands me a scissors and a piece of paper with loads of names on it – we're talking me, Sorcha, Chloe, Sophie, Amie with an ie, Claire and Fock Features, Christian, Oisinn, JP, Lauren, Ronan and Shadden, Honor, then one or two others. 'Cut those up and put them in there,' meaning this little green velvet bag with drawstrings, which I think came from the Scrabble set she found the other night while poking around in the eaves. 'We're going to do the draw to decide who's dressing up as what character!'

I do as I'm told, cutting up the names, then folding them and dropping them into the bag.

'Oh my God,' Chloe goes, 'I love *Downton Abbey*. The gallantry. The barbed remarks. The stolen kisses.'

Sophie's like, 'The stilted manners. The whispered indiscretions. All those looks into the distance.'

'We are total *Abbey*philes, aren't we, Sophie?'

'Oh my God, *total*!'

Amie with an ie goes, 'I took a lover with no thought of marriage. Think of that!' and then everyone just storts firing out random focking quotes to show that they know more about the show than anyone else.

Sorcha: 'The Kaiser is such a mercurial figure, don't you think? One minute a warmonger, the next a poet!'

Chloe: 'How many times am I to be ordered to marry the man sitting next to me at dinner?'

Sophie: 'What's a weekend?'

Chloe again: 'The telephone? It's like something from an H. G. Wells novel.'

And then focking Claire ends up going, 'I'm going upstairs to rest – wake me at the dressing gong!'

I just roll my eyes. The cheek of *her* trying to get in on the act. 'Yeah, no,' I go, 'I'd say they love that show in Bray, alright. People in wellies playing with shotguns and marrying their own focking cousins.'

There's a few sniggers – especially from the goys – before Sorcha calls everyone to order. 'Okay,' she goes, holding up her little Moleskin notebook, 'I'm going to read out the name of each character in turn and then Ross is going to draw a name from the bag.'

No one voices any objection.

'First of all, Robert Crawley, the Earl of Grantham . . .'

I pull out a name. It ends up being mine.

'Fix!' JP and Oisinn storts going. 'Fix!' really just ripping the piss.

'Okay, settle down,' Sorcha goes. 'Cora Crawley, the Countess of Grantham.'

I feel around in the bag and whip out another. I'm like, 'Sophie.' And that's how it basically continues on.

'Lady Mary Crawley . . . is going to be JP.'

That gets a huge cheer.

'Lady Edith Crawley . . . is going to be Chloe.'

'Lady Sybil Crawley . . . is going to be Honor – if she could be orsed, which I doubt.'

'Violet Crawley, the Dowager Countess of Grantham . . . that's going to be you, Sorcha.'

She seems happy enough with that.

'Matthew Crawley . . . is going to be Lauren.'

'Tom Branson . . . is going to be Amie with an ie.'

'Isobel Crawley . . . is going to be Christian.'

'Okay, now we move onto the staff. Carson the butler . . .'

All the girls go, 'Oh my God, I *love* Carson!'

'. . . is going to be Ronan.'

'John Bates . . . is going to be Shadden – if she's up to it.'

'Mrs Patmore, the cook . . . is going to be – I'm focking delighted! – Garret!'

'Daisy, the kitchen maid – this gets funnier and funnier – it's you, Claire.'

'Mrs O'Brien . . .'

Chloe goes, 'Oh my God, Mrs O'Brien is an *actual* bitch!'

Sophie's like, 'Oh my God, there are times when I want to slap her!'

I'm there, 'Mrs O'Brien is going to be . . . Oisinn!'

Oisinn cracks his hole laughing. Everyone seems happy, in fact, except for Garret and Claire. They're both just sitting there with faces on them, not happy that they've ended up being the kitchen focking skivs.

'You did that on purpose,' Claire goes.

I'm like, 'Excuse me?' all innocence.

'Are you saying it's just a coincidence that me and Garret – who you actually hate – get picked to be the two lowliest staff in the actual house?'

Sorcha goes, 'Claire, it's only a bit of fun.'

I'm like, 'Yeah, no, plus it was random. You saw me draw the names out.'

Claire ends up making a total show of herself, going through all the bits of paper on the table and giving it, 'Look, the pieces of paper with our names on were folded in three. All the others were folded in two. Except his own, which was folded in a triangle, look.'

She hands the pieces of paper to Garret, who looks at them, then shakes his head, like he's disappointed with me. Except no one ends up believing them.

Amie with an ie even goes, 'Claire, it's only a fancy dress party – come on!' and suddenly Claire is being made to feel pathetic for even bringing it up.

Garret just, like, *glowers* at me? I've got a big, shit-eating grin on my face, of course. There's very few things I enjoy more than focking people over. I'm like, 'Yeah, no, it's like Sorcha said, Claire. It's all just fun and games.'

Sorcha says it's too big.

I'm like, 'It's not too big.'

I'm standing there with the thing in my hand.

She goes, 'Ross, it's not going to fit in the hole.'

'We'll see about that.'

'Oh my God, don't force it!'

She's holding the assembly instructions for the Mammut topple-proof kiddies' wardrobe, which by the way has more ports to it than that focking probe they managed to land on actual Mars.

I'm like, 'Does it even matter which screws go where?'

Like most men, if it was down to me, those instructions – with their focking *Achtung!* and their *Waarschuwing!* – would already be in the bin downstairs. But Sorcha's always been a big believer in doing shit by the book.

'Yes, it does matter,' she goes. 'The screws that go into that hole are these ones – the 110519s. The ones that you have there are the 118331s.'

'I don't see much of a difference, Babes.'

'There's a subtle difference.'

There's a reason, by the way, that they give you an Allen key and not a screwdriver with these things. Ikea is the Swedish word for divorce, while flat-pack comes from Flåtpâk, which is their word for domestic homicide.

'Hey,' I go, because I've suddenly got a better idea, 'all this serious brain activity has given me a bit of a . . .'

She cuts me off straight away. 'Forget it, Ross.'

'You don't even know what I was going to say.'

'You were going to suggest we go into our bedroom and have sex.'

'It doesn't even have to be our bedroom.'

'The answer's no. I want to get this nursery built in case this thing actually happens. And anyway I haven't decided yet that I'm ready to commit to you physically.'

'Fock's sake, Sorcha, it's been literally weeks. Come on, I think I've pretty much proved that I'm not going to stray.'

I reach for the old jolly jugs of joy, except she slaps my two hands away.

'Ross!' she goes. 'I'm serious. I told you that *I'd* let *you* know when I'm ready.'

And there the conversation ends because my phone all of a sudden rings and it ends up being my old dear. I answer by going, 'What the fock do you want?' possibly taking my frustration out on her.

She goes, 'I'm in Los Angeles. At the Beverly Hills Hotel.'

'Yeah, no, that wasn't the question I asked.'

'I've just come from a meeting with the Hallmark people – in Studio City. I need to talk to you and Sorcha.'

'What about?'

'I don't want to say over the phone.'

'So why are you focking ringing me?'

'Just to say I'd like to see you both when I get back next week. Come to the house. I'll cook supper.'

'I'd rather eat the fluff from under the fridge,' I go, except she doesn't hear me, because she's already hung up.

'What'll it be?' Ronan goes.

It has to be said, he's really made the effort to get into the character of Carson. He's wearing a tux with a white bowtie and has a side-porting held in place with about a pound and a half of Brylcreem.

He's doing a pretty good job as a borman as well.

We're having, like, pre-dinner drinks in the room just off the dining room, which we're all supposed to suddenly call the Library for the evening.

'Yeah, no, I'll have the usual Hydrogen,' I go.

Except Sorcha happens to breeze by at that exact moment and goes, 'No beer, Ross. We're trying to make it as authentic as possible.'

I'm like, 'So what am I supposed to drink then?'

'There's a cocktail list.'

'Is a Jägerbomb on it?'

She goes, 'A Jägerbomb isn't a cocktail, Ross!' another one who's definitely going with her character, pursing her lips like I've seen Maggie Smith do. 'You can have a Lady Mary . . .'

'Lillet Blanc,' Ronan goes, 'freshly squeezed lemon juice, basil and Billecart-Salmon.'

'A Lady Edith . . .'

'Sloe gin, ruby-red grapefruit juice and Ballatore Spumante Rosso.'

'Or a Lady Sybil . . .'

'Sloe gin, Saint Germain elderflower liqueur and Billecart-Salmon.'

Sorcha goes, 'Served in a flute. Those are your only choices, Ross . . . Heavens, look who's arrived!' and she wanders over to the door to greet Chloe as Edith, Sophie as Cora and Amie with an ie as Branson the chauffeur.

It's going to be a long focking night.

Ro makes me a Lady Mary and I tell him about our meeting with so-called Patriona Pratshke. 'It went okay,' I go. 'I mean, we had to get over the fact I accused her of flashing her focking orbs to get her driving licence. Once that was out of the way, she definitely listened to what we had to say.'

'So can we move in, Rosser?'

'I don't think it's going to be as easy as that, Ro. She said she's definitely going to come out here and check out our set-up. But she also wants to hear what you and Shadden have to say.'

I suddenly realize that Shadden's standing right beside me. I hope she didn't hear what I said about her social worker's orbs.

'Shadden caddent tell her ma and da she dudn't want to live with them,' Ronan goes.

Shadden's like, 'I taught de soshiddle woorker would just decide.'

'Yeah, no,' I go, 'we're just going to have to come up with a way of persuading her that this is the best place for you to live, without you actually saying it. I don't know what that is yet, but Sorcha is very much on the case.'

Shadden suddenly pulls a face and puts her hand on her, like, bump.

Ronan's there, 'Are ye okay?'

'It's just . . . cramps,' she goes.

He's like, 'Are ye shewer?'

She nods.

I excuse myself – I actually go, 'Do excuse me,' kind of getting in on the whole vibe myself – and I tip over to Christian (Isobel), JP (Lady Mary) and, the funniest of all, Oisinn (Miss O'Brien). It's not right seeing one of your mates dressed up in a French maid's outfit.

'I may never have another erection again!' is my opening line. The goys all love it, of course, although Lauren (Cousin focking Matthew) looks at me and shakes her head disapprovingly – whether she's acting or not, I don't even ask.

They're talking about JP's new line.

'So what exactly *is* a distressed property?' Christian goes.

I have to say, it's nice to see JP and his old man back in the beautiful game.

'There's no mystique to it,' JP goes. 'It's just a property that's been repossessed and that's, like, lying vacant. The banks don't want to be left holding thousands of gaffs that they can't offload. They're not in the business of selling property anyway, even if there *was* still a market for it? So they turn to people with expertise in the area – goys like my old man – to dispose of it for them. It's, like, fire-sale stuff – the bargains you can pick up are unbelievable.'

It's hilarious hearing him say all this in a pink chiffon evening dress and pearls.

'Well, fair focks!' I go. And I actually mean it. Seeing a vulture like

JP's dad doing well for himself makes me believe that we can get the old days back again.

'We're having our first auction in January,' he goes. 'You'll all have to come.'

We're all like, 'We definitely will.'

Us all talking about how well things are going for JP makes me feel instantly bad for Oisinn. 'Are you alright?' I go – except quietly, not making a major deal of it. I can't imagine what it'd be like to be, like, bankrupt.

He goes, 'Dude, it's okay. I had my time. And I honestly wouldn't go back to 2006 for all the money in the world.'

He doesn't mean it – he couldn't – but I decide to just let it go, roysh, because all of a sudden in walk Garret and Claire, him as Mrs Patmore, with the focking pinny and big red wig, and her as Daisy, with the pinny as well and the little cook's hat.

It's actually hilarious – the faces on the two of them. They're literally bulling.

A gong suddenly sounds. I shit you not. That's what Sorcha must have been picking up this morning from Sandycove Fine Orts.

'Dinner is being served,' she goes.

I don't know if I mentioned that she's got actual caterers in. Silver focking service, the lot. We all wander into the dining room and there are, like, definite gasps of approval from everyone, including Sophie, Chloe and Amie with an ie, who are usually total bitches. The table looks incredible. I doubt if anyone has ever seen a housewarming like it.

'We're having a medley of storters,' Sorcha goes. 'Salmon toasts with mustard butter, oysters à la Russe, beef and Yorkshire pudding canapés and autumn figs stuffed with Stilton cheese. For the main course it's going to be Calvados-glazed duckling with an asparagus salad and a Champagne saffron vinaigrette. Then for dessert it's Apple Charlotte.'

Apple Charlotte. It's a focking pity Patriona Pratshke isn't here to witness this.

We all sit down and the caterers – in full focking tuxes, by the way – stort dishing out the nosebag. That's when Honor (who was supposed to be Lady Sybil) decides to make an appearance. She hasn't bothered her hole wearing the Alice Temperley evening dress that Sorcha forked out over four hundred snots for. She's actually dressed for bed.

'Do you have any plans to feed your daughter?' she goes to Sorcha in front of everyone. 'Or are you too busy playing dressing up?'

Sorcha – obviously embarrassed – tries to go, 'Come and sit down, Honor. It's fun!'

Honor goes, 'It's sad,' and storts putting together a plate for herself from the various serving dishes, presumably to bring back upstairs to her room.

Shadden, roysh, actually makes the effort with her. She goes, 'Honor, come and sit beside me and Ronan,' and this is, like, despite the cramps and everything. 'There's a seat here.'

But Honor just, like, bitch-smiles her, and goes, 'Yeah, unlike other people in this house, I have no interest in you *or* your baby,' then she takes her food and focks off back upstairs to her room.

Shadden just bursts into tears and Ronan ends up having to try to comfort her.

'She's a bitch,' I go. 'An absolute bitch. Ignore her, Shadden.'

Sorcha's like, 'Ross!' but she knows I'm just telling it like it is.

There ends up being, like, twenty seconds of awkward silence then, before Chloe goes, 'Oh my God, I am *so* looking forward to tonight's final episode. I wonder will Matthew marry Lavinia?'

Claire instantly goes, 'I actually know what happens.'

'Oh my God!' practically everyone shouts. 'Don't tell us! Don't tell us!'

She goes, 'I'm not going to tell you – don't worry!'

I'm fairly throwing the Madeira wine into me at this stage, bear in mind. I'm like, 'Why focking mention it then?'

I love giving her a hord time.

He – as in Garret – comes rushing to her aid. 'We accidentally read a spoiler online, that's all.'

Why mention it, though? That's what I want to know.

'Oh my God,' *she* goes then, 'we should actually set up a Downton Club. Do this once a month. Obviously not as lavish as this,

Sorcha. But we could get together, watch episodes and then, like, discuss them.'

Jesus focking Christ.

'Like a book club?' Sorcha goes. 'That's *so* an amazing idea.'

I need to have sex. I need to have sex with someone soon.

Claire turns to Garret then. '*We* could host the next one?'

I notice the sudden change in Sorcha's expression. She presumed Claire meant it would always happen here. 'You?' Sorcha goes. 'I mean, do you have the room?'

'I think what Sorcha's trying to say,' I go, 'in a polite way, is that no one here wants to *go* to Bray,' and I can't tell you how funny they look dressed up as the *Downton* kitchen dregs. 'And by the way, you two are doing the washing-up.'

Garret ends up totally losing it. He suddenly jumps to his feet and storts pointing at me, going, 'I am sick to death of you running down Bray!'

'Someone ring for an ambulance,' Ronan goes.

I just laugh. 'I don't think that's going to be necessary, Ro. This dude couldn't deck me in a dream.'

But that's when Shadden suddenly goes, 'Me waters are just after breaking.'

And Ronan – as calm as anything – is like, 'The baby's coming, Rosser. It's coming now.'

I hear laughter. It's at, like, my expense, I realize, even though I'm only really waking up.

'The f . . . f . . . fooken dribble on he's face, look.'

It's obviously Kennet. I mean, who else do I know who talks like that?

'What time is it?' I go, somehow managing to open my eyes.

I'm sitting in a corridor – in, it's coming back to me now, the Rotunda.

'Tree o'clock,' Dordeen goes.

I think about this for a few seconds. I'm like, 'Is it morning or afternoon?'

They laugh like this is for some reason funny. 'Arthur noon,' *he* goes.

Shadden was admitted at, like, nine o'clock last night, which means we've been here . . . I don't know – you do the maths.

I'm like, 'What time did I fall asleep?'

Dordeen goes, 'Seven o'clock tus morning. You're arthur missing it all.'

'Missing it all? Missing what?'

'You've a grand thaughter,' Kennet goes. 'B . . . B . . . Borden at twenty-two minutes arthur the hour of n . . . n . . . noyun.'

I'm there, 'Could you not have, like, woken me up?'

He goes, 'If you caddent stay aweek to celebreet ta moment you become a grand fadder, that's yooer problem.'

My neck hurts. It's, like, stiff *and* sore?

I'm there, 'Did you say it was a grand-*daughter*?'

'A little girdle,' *she* goes. 'She's bayooriful, idn't she, Kennet?'

'Bayooriful's ta word alreet.'

I'm like, 'You've seen her then?'

He goes, 'J . . . J . . . Just tru ta glass of the oul incubator, knowmean?'

I check my phone. I've got, like, thirty-seven missed calls from Sorcha, obviously looking for news. I must have stuck it on silent.

'Ta f . . . f . . . fooken state of you, by the way!'

'We had a porty,' I go, 'with, like, a *Downton Abbey* theme. That's the only reason I'm dressed like this. How's Shadden?'

'Knackered,' Kennet goes. 'It was a l . . . l . . . long owult labour for ta pooer girdle.'

'It definitely seems to have been.'

All of a sudden, a door opens at the far end of the corridor and through it steps Ronan.

I stand up. I feel shit. It's possibly the biggest regret of my life that I wasn't there to see him being born. And now I've slept through *his* big moment.

It was all that focking Madeira wine.

'I s . . . s . . . see your f . . . f . . . f . . . fadder's finally aweek!' Kennet goes.

86

I'm like, 'Congratulations, Ro.'

And Ronan's like, 'Thanks, Rosser.'

'Are we able to see her?' Dordeen goes.

Ronan's there, 'Shadden or the baby?'

'Eeder.'

'They're boat asleep at the moment. Mebbe come back the night.'

'Tat's what we'll do,' Kennet goes. 'We'll come back arowunt s . . . s . . . seven or eight the night. We'll go and get a sleep. We didn't all m . . . m . . . maddage to get ta full eight hours – did we, Ross? Not like some feddas.'

The two of them shuffle off in the direction of the elevator. When they've disappeared, I turn around to Ronan and I go, 'Ro, I'm sorry. I must have been more hammered than I actually realized.'

He looks over both shoulders – I'm only fifty-fifty about whether this is even a word – but *conspitatorially*?

He goes, 'Wait hee-er.'

I'm like, 'Where are you going?'

'Just wait hee-er.'

He disappears back through the door he first came through, then he reappears again maybe thirty seconds later, holding a little bundle of something wrapped in a white blanket.

I'm suddenly off.

'Stop crying,' he goes, walking towards me with her.

'I'm not sure I can stop, Ro.'

'Stop crying,' he goes, laughing at me now, 'ya fooken benny.'

'Like I said, I'm not sure it's even possible.'

He puts her into my hands. She's, like, tiny – as in *tiny* tiny? Little ears. Little nose. Little fingers. Ronan's eyes. Ronan's mouth. Hair. Lots of it. She's perfect.

Father Fehily used to talk about those rare moments in life when something happens that makes you feel like the world has slipped on its axis and nothing looks the same and you think nothing ever will again.

'I haven't even asked you her name,' I go, still blubbing like a fockwit.

'Rihanna-Brogan,' he goes.

I'm like, 'Rihanna after . . .'

'The obvious, yeah.'

'And Brogan after . . .'

'Burden It.'

Burden It Brogan. The Dublin footballer. One of his heroes. I feel my mouth twist into a sudden *smile*?

'It suits her.'

I go to hand her back to him, except Ronan just shakes his head. 'Keep holding her, Ross. Fact, Ine gonna leaf you for a few minutes to get to know her – that alreet?'

And I just nod – again, dumbly. Off Ronan goes. And for the next twenty minutes, doctors and nurses, staff and patients, all sorts of people walk past me in both directions. A woman goes by on a trolley, screaming with labour pains. The fire alorm goes off. A man has a row with his Asian wife in a language I don't understand. A Mike Hunt is paged over and over again, even though he probably doesn't exist. Someone refills the vending machine. A cleaner polishes the floor around me.

And not once do I look up. I just continue sitting there, staring at this perfect little baby in my orms, tracing and retracing the shape of her tiny little features, trying to burn them into my mind as, like, a memory, terrified that I'll one day forget even a second of what this moment actually feels like.

3.

How Sad!

The old dear has let someone have a crack at her face again. Her skin is all tight and shiny, like it's been shrink-wrapped in plastic film, and her lips are swollen into a permanent pout.

She looks like a monkey sucking a Locket.

'Oh my God, you never seem to age,' Sorcha goes – she was always a bit of a crawler where my old dear was concerned. 'I'd love to know your secret, Fionnuala.'

I just laugh. I'm there, 'Women like her *don't* age. The ratio between what's real and what's artificial just keeps changing.'

Sorcha goes, 'Ross, don't be so horrible.'

I'm like, 'Hey, I've never been afraid to call it. Right now I'd say the woman is about thirty percent skin and bone and fifty percent collagen. The other twenty percent is Bombay gin and insincerity.'

'Ross!'

'Like I said – calling it!'

We're in, like, the old dear's gaff in Foxrock and we're eating spiced pork belly stuffed with prunes, with cinnamon squash and orange and pistachio sprouts. It's possibly the nicest meal I've ever focking eaten, although the trick with the old dear is obviously never to let on, which means rolling my eyes and shaking my head with every mouthful, just to let her know that I can't believe I'm even eating something that *she* cooked.

She goes, 'Ignore him, Sorcha. I do. Now tell me your news. How are you settling into your new home?'

Sorcha goes, 'Oh my God, Fionnuala, I still have to pinch myself to believe that it's even ours.'

'How lovely!'

'And of course it's, like, *so* full of memories for me. I had an amazing, amazing childhood there. But we still need – oh my God – *so* much new furniture to fill it.'

The old dear smiles. It's a horrible sight. It's like watching a horse have its lips ripped off by a hurricane. 'Choose something from here,' she goes.

Sorcha's like, 'Excuse me?'

'I'm serious. I want to give you and Ross a special housewarming gift,' and she storts making a big show of looking around her. 'Choose something of mine.'

'We couldn't, Fionnuala.'

'That credenza over there. Or the armoire. Or the Medici secretary desk with hutch.'

I go, 'But not the liquor cabinet, though. She'd let us take anything but the liquor cabinet.'

This she chooses to ignore – the serious lush.

'There's also a beautiful chiffonier upstairs in one of the guestrooms.'

'Fionnuala,' Sorcha goes, 'I'd feel so bad.'

'No, you won't! The secretary desk and the chiffonier – that's decided then!'

'That is – oh my God! – *so* a kind gesture, isn't it, Ross?'

'Well,' the old dear goes, flashing that horrific focking smile again, 'it's just so wonderful to see you two back together again,' and then she turns to me and – this is, like, word for word – she goes, 'And don't you go messing it up this time.'

There's, like, no way I'm going to let her get away with that. So I go, 'I can't believe you haven't asked me a single question about Ronan.'

She's like, 'Well, what is there to ask?'

I end up having to just shake my head. 'Yeah, you have an *actual* great-granddaughter. And she's beautiful, by the way.'

'She is!' Sorcha goes. 'Oh my God, Fionnuala, you will just want to gobble her up!'

With that focking mouth, I wouldn't be surprised if she did.

I'm like, 'Are you not even going to ask us her name?'

'Okay,' she goes, 'well, what's her name?'

I'm like, 'Rihanna-Brogan.'

I watch her try to feel something. It involves all sorts of cogs turning and levers shifting inside her face to try to produce something that at least *looks* like a smile.

'Lovely,' she goes.

I'm like, 'Yeah, you could at least sound like you mean it.'

'Well,' she goes – again, this is word for word – 'it's just so awful, isn't it? The whole business. He's still so young. It's just . . . unspeakable.'

'It is,' Sorcha goes, actually agreeing with her. 'But Ross and I have come up with a plan, Fionnuala, that might end up being to, like, *everyone's* advantage?'

The old dear's like, 'Oh?' as she pours us both another glass of Belle Epoque, this limited edition cuvée that costs, like, three hundred snots in Horvey Nichs. The world economic meltdown was only ever a rumour to my so-called mother.

Sorcha goes, 'We're hoping that Ronan, Shadden and little Rihanna-Brogan are going to come to live with us!'

The old dear's like, 'With *you*?'

'We have the room, Fionnuala. And we're trying to make the point that there are – oh my God – *so* many more opportunities for a child growing up on this side of the city as opposed to, well, any other side.'

'Well of course there are!'

'And that's not me being a bitch. I'm thinking about things like Imaginosity. Amazing, amazing Montessori schools. Hockey. There's, like, gaelscoils, if she's interested in her heritage. Equestrian centres . . .'

'Oh, you're absolutely right, Sorcha. Even the air quality. I find it difficult to breathe on the other side of the city. I always think it's like something Dickens dreamt up.'

'Well – again, not being a snob – I just think the southside has *so* much more going for it. We've told the social worker in the case that we're interested in becoming Ronan and Shadden's legal guardians. She's planning a home visit.'

'A home visit! Then you're taking the armoire as well, Sorcha. No arguments.'

Finally – basically tired of her horseshit – I go, 'Sorry, wasn't there something you wanted to talk to us about? I mean, I presume there's a reason we're here – and that it's not just to eat your muck.'

The old dear suddenly goes all – it may or may not be a word – but, *solemn*?

'Yes,' she goes. 'Look, I feel awful for having to tell you this, especially when you have so much going on in your lives as it is. But I'm afraid I'm the bearer of some rather bad news.'

Sorcha looks at me, then back at the old dear, her face full of worry. 'What kind of bad news, Fionnuala?'

'Well, I don't know whether to tell you now, at the risk of spoiling your dessert, or to wait until after you've had it. It's a sweet fig tarte tatin with shaved Manchego.'

Sorcha looks at me again. 'I think we'd prefer to know now – wouldn't we, Ross?'

I go, 'Just focking get on with it, will you? Stop hogging the lime-light. Focking shaved Manchego.'

It sounds incredible, by the way.

'Well,' she goes, 'it's about my movie.'

I laugh. 'Yeah, so-called.'

Sorcha's there, 'They haven't cancelled it, have they, Fionnuala?'

'No, they haven't cancelled it. But, well . . . Honor didn't test well.'

I'm like, 'Test well? What does that even mean?'

'Oh, it's an industry phrase,' she tries to go, focking thrilled with herself. 'Before a movie or television show is put on general release, producers arrange a test screening in front of a representative cross-section of the public, to gauge what the likely audience response will be.'

I'm there, 'And you're saying they hated her?'

'They didn't hate her. They just felt the accent was, well, wrong.'

Sorcha looks instantly confused. 'Wrong? But, Fionnuala, that's how little girls in South Dublin speak.'

'*I* know that, Sorcha. And *you* know that. But, unfortunately, making a successful movie – especially a TV movie – means pandering to the lowest common denominator. Americans have a view of Ireland and sadly it's *The Quiet Man*. I read the completed questionnaires. Where were all the begorrahs and the have-you-a-drop-of-anything-wets and the sure-'tis-a-bold-colleen-you-are-indeeds? That's what they wanted to know.'

'I suppose it *is* the Hallmork channel,' Sorcha goes, trying to put a positive spin on it.

I'm like, 'So what's going to happen?'

'They're going to reshoot the movie,' the old dear goes.

'Without *our* actual daughter?'

'Yes, sadly, without Honor. It's out of my control, I'm afraid. They've found another girl who can do the accent they want. She's from San Bernadino.'

She stands and gathers up our plates. 'I'm so sorry,' she goes. 'I really feel I've let you down.'

Sorcha's like, 'Don't be silly, Fionnuala. You *so* haven't.'

'Don't listen to Sorcha,' I go. 'You have let us down. *And* in a big-time way.'

Sorcha's like, 'Don't listen to him, Fionnuala. There was nothing you could have done.'

The old dear goes, 'I'll just go and get dessert,' playing the mortyr. She focks off to the kitchen.

'Nothing she could have done?' I go. 'She could have walked. She could have told them to shove their movie up their orses.'

Except Sorcha doesn't *seem* that upset? She goes, 'Ross, you know my feelings on the matter. I think this could be a blessing in disguise. You know I regretted letting her ever do that movie.'

'And I made the point that she was a bitch before she did it.'

'Well, whether she was or not, I think what Honor needs now more than anything is a life more ordinary.'

'Okay, what does that even mean?'

'As in, like, more *grounded*?'

The old dear suddenly shouts to us from the kitchen. She's there, 'Would you like crème fraîche with it?'

And I go, 'Yeah – anything that takes the focking taste away.'

I knock back a mouthful of the cuvée. It *is* good shit.

'The only problem,' Sorcha suddenly goes, 'is how are we going to break the news to her?'

I'm there, 'I don't know. Do we not just tell her? You've been dropped. Deal with it. That kind of vibe.'

'Oh my God, Ross, young people of Honor's age have *such* fragile psyches. We don't want to destroy her confidence.'

'Yeah, I wouldn't be a hundred percent sure that's even possible.'

'And of course the other question,' she goes, 'is *when* do we tell her?'

I'm like, 'As in?'

'As in, she's not going to like it, Ross. We're all familiar with her tantrums. We've got a social worker coming to visit us at home sometime between now and hopefully Christmas.'

'Honor's already anti the whole Rihanna-Brogan living with us thing.'

'We don't want her making trouble for us, Ross.'

'And she would. I think she definitely would.'

'So let's not tell her for now. Let's keep it to ourselves.'

It feels a bit sneaky. But I go, 'Yeah, no, it's possibly for the best.'

She's like, 'On pain of death, Ross.'

'Whooda best girl? Huh? *Whooda* best girl? You! Yes, you! Youda best girl! *Yooouda* best girl!'

It's funny, Sorcha was always anti the whole talking shite to babies thing. She read somewhere that it was bad for their early intellectual development and always insisted that I talk to Honor in, like, *actual* words and complete *sentences*?

But then look how *she* turned out.

We're in my old man's house – we're talking me, her, Sorcha, Ronan, Shadden and little R&B, as I've already storted calling the little one – and she hasn't once looked away from *True Hollywood Story* on E!

Shadden's already tried talking to her. She asked her when she was going to be on TV herself. Me and Sorcha couldn't even look at each other. Honor's eyes didn't move from the screen. They're doing a special profile of Selena Gomez. 'I'm sorry,' Honor went, 'I'm too busy to invest right now.'

Shadden just gave up.

'Whooda best girl?' Sorcha keeps going. She's, like, pacing the old man and Helen's living room, with little R&B in her orms. 'Rihanna-Brogan da best girl! Rihanna-Brogan da best girl! Yes, she is! You can understand me, can't you! I think you can! I think you can! I think you can because you're smiling at me! Yes, you are! Yes, you are!'

Honor goes, 'Could someone please bang that woman on the side of the head? Either that or give her a Valium.'

In fairness, it was kind of pissing me off as well, but I still go, 'Yeah, no, Honor, try and be a good girl today.'

Helen asks who's for more tea? She's, like, such a cool person. Everyone's seems to be alright for tea, though. Then the old man goes, 'Perhaps we'd all like something a little stronger! I've a bottle of XO in the sideboard there. What say you we see what damage we can do to it?'

I'm like, 'Yeah, I'll definitely have one,' and Ronan goes, 'Yeah, brandy's good for me, Grandda,' and even though my instinct is to remind him that he's still only fourteen years of age, I eventually think, you know what, fock it, he's an adult now – whatever it says on his birth certificate.

The old man pours three glasses for us. He gives ridiculously good measures, in fairness to the focker.

'So,' he goes, 'are we all looking forward to Enda Kenny's address to the nation?'

I laugh. 'Yeah, no,' I go, 'good luck getting the TV from Honor.'

He goes, 'We can watch it in one of the other rooms,' because *he's* as terrified of her as the rest of us. 'Enda's no Churchill, but I'm still rather keen to hear what he has to say. It'll be tighten our belts, no doubt. Quote-unquote.'

Helen's there, 'Whatever he tries to tell us this evening, it's clear that our children are going to be paying for the greed and the stupidity of our generation. And not only our children, but our children's children.'

There's something about that phrase – our children's children – that strikes an instant chord with me. I look at my little granddaughter gurgling away there in Sorcha's orms and I wonder what kind of world she's going to grow up in. And it's weird, roysh, but for the first time in my life I actually *care*?

'I'm going to watch this so-called speech,' I go. 'Definitely.'

The old man goes, 'Of course you are! You and your politics!'

'I mean, I might end up drifting in and out – as in, mentally – but I'm definitely going to sit through the entire thing. I just think we owe it to, I don't know, future generations.'

'Well, if I know you half as well as I think I know you, you'll be bloody well heckling throughout!'

Sorcha's been holding R&B for, like, half an hour now. I feel like I nearly have to remind her that she's not actually *ours*?

Helen asks Shadden if it's true she's planning to go back to school.

'I'm hoping to,' Shadden goes – her and Sorcha exchanging a smile. 'Maybe next September. I want to sit the Leaving and then hopefully college.'

There's no *hopefully* about it – she'll be one of those kids who ends up on *Six One* for getting maximum points. Or pretty close.

I watch Sorcha's nose suddenly twitch. I instantly know what that means. When Honor was in nappies, it would have been my cue to leave the room.

'I think a litta bitty baby not too far from here needs changing!' Sorcha goes, kissing her on the forehead. 'Does this litta bitty baby need changing? Is it this litta bitty baby? Is it this lidda bitty baby here?'

Shadden puts her orms out and goes, 'I'll take her.'

Except Sorcha's instantly there, 'I don't mind changing her.'

Shadden goes, 'No, no, I'll do it,' and it ends up turning into a bit of a stand-off.

'Shadden, I really don't mind.'

And that's when Honor suddenly goes, 'I've a good idea! Why doesn't *her mother* change her? And by the way, Mummy dearest, that *isn't* you! Hashtag – stop embarrassing yourself!'

It's a real traffic-stopping moment. There's no doubt about

that. No one actually says anything for a good ten seconds, then I watch Sorcha hand the baby over to Shadden and the old man goes, 'So, are we going to see what this chap has to say about how badly off this country really is?' just trying to keep things chivvying along.

We all pile into his study, where he's also got a TV. I turn to Sorcha and I go, 'Are you okay?' and she doesn't answer, just shakes her head, like she couldn't trust herself to open her mouth because she'd probably actually *cry*?

I go, 'I'm beginning to think that Honor might be the universe's revenge on me for being such a dick to my own old pair.'

She doesn't laugh. I suppose it's no laughing matter.

And speaking of which . . .

'Tonight,' the dude on the TV storts suddenly going, 'I'm taking the opportunity to speak to you directly on the challenge we face as a community, as an economy and as a country . . .'

I'm like, 'Is that him?' and I'm being serious. I don't know what the focker even looks like.

The old man laughs, then turns to Helen and goes, 'A wonderfully droll piece of commentary on the Taoiseach's hitherto reluctance to engage directly with the electorate! If Martyn Turner said that in a cartoon, they'd say he was a genius!'

'I know this is an exceptional event,' the dude on TV keeps going, 'but we live in exceptional times, and we face an exceptional challenge. It's important that you know the truth of the scale of that challenge and how we are addressing it . . .'

No, he's already losing me.

'At the end of last year, our economy was in deep crisis, and while steps to recover from the crisis have been taken, we remain in crisis today. I would love to tell you tonight that our economic problems are solved, and that the worst is over, but for far too many of you, that is simply not the truth.'

I'm thinking, a pink tie does not go with that suit.

An old friend of Oisinn's who went to Columba's back in the day is telling us about a three-in-the-bed he once had with a woman he met in Vanilla – she supposedly worked in, like, event management? – the only problem with the story being that the third person in the bed was the woman's husband, who I *think* he said was a software development project manager.

Now, I don't know where this dude learned maths – well, Columba's, I'm presuming, and quite possibly the Institute – but two men plus one woman does *not* a three-in-the-bed make. It's what's known in the old lovemaking business as a Devil's Threesome.

We don't say a word, though.

'The husband was a pretty much spectator,' he keeps going – maybe he can see from our faces that we're all Scooby Dubious. 'He has his own company. He's back and forth to Florida the entire time.'

'That's, er, great,' JP tells him. 'Fair focks,' and eventually the dude heads off.

'Devil's Threesome,' Oisinn goes, out of the corner of his mouth.

JP's there, '*I* wouldn't do it. Not in a focking million.'

I'm like, 'I wouldn't either. And you know me, J-Town, I'm pretty open-minded about what goes on between the duvet and memory foam. But mine must be the only cock in the room. Call me an old-fashioned gentleman, but a threesome, in my book, is two women plus me.'

Christian arrives – late, but just in time to get the round in. Kielys is rammers tonight, which is always good to see. I direct him to the bor with my eyes before he makes his way over to us through the, I suppose, *throng*? He holds up, like, four fingers and I just nod. No need to even ask what everyone's drinking.

Christian arrives over, followed by one of the lounge girls carrying a tray of pints. I make a big show of looking at my wrist, where a watch would have been in the days before they put a clock on everyone's mobile.

'Sorry I'm late,' he goes, at least picking up on it. *We're* already, like, three pints in. 'I was collecting my son from drama.'

I go, 'From what?' and I'm not trying to embarrass the dude. I genuinely think I might have, like, *misheard* him?

'Drama,' he goes, trying to make it sound like the most natural thing in the world for a four-year-old boy to want to do. 'And don't raise your eyebrows like that, Ross.'

I'm there, 'I didn't raise my eyebrows.'

I put my pint to my lips and have a subtle look at the other two goys for their reaction. They're obviously thinking the same thing as me. A boy of that age should be playing an actual sport – and more to the point, that sport should be rugby.

I decide to just leave it, though.

'Hey, congratulations,' JP goes, suddenly remembering why we're all here – in other words, to wet my granddaughter's head. The goys all raise their drinks, in fairness to them.

I'm there, 'Ah, she's beautiful, goys. Just . . . You know me, I'm very seldom short of something to say – forever calling it – but words actually fail me.'

'A grandfather at thirty-one,' JP goes. He's not the only one struggling to get his head around it.

I'm there, 'Thirty-two in January,' as if there's a difference. 'Yeah, no, I genuinely don't *give* a fock? She's healthy, that's all I care about. And beautiful. Did I mention that she's beautiful?'

They all laugh.

'So what's the deal?' JP goes. 'Are they going to be living with you and Sorcha?'

'Yeah, no, we're hoping that plan is still a goer. It just means persuading this social worker bird that we're suitable people to be their, like, legal gordians.'

'Jesus,' Oisinn goes, like I've just told him I'm trying to learn, I don't know, Irish history through Japanese. 'Good luck with that, Ross.'

I'm like, 'Thanks, Dude. I'm worried about Sorcha, though. She's really got her hort set on this thing happening. I just hope she's not setting herself up for a disappointment.'

They all just nod.

'Right,' I go, 'I need to take a quick Wiki,' and there's a general chorus of, 'Yeah, thanks for that information, Ross!'

Anyway, I'm, like, literally ten yords away from the shitter door when I end up bumping into – as in, *literally* bumping into – this bird, who just so happens to also be a total stunner. Just to put it in, like, context for you, she's a ringer for Daniella Moyles.

I'm like, 'Oops, sorry,' and then I nod at the door of the jacks and go, 'Beer in, beer out!'

Like I said, I've been fairly hounding the Britneys tonight.

She actually ends up loving it as a line. 'Beer in, beer out,' she goes, laughing. 'That's really good. Okay, that's *actually* really good.'

I'm there, 'Do you think so?' I don't know why I'm surprised.

She shrugs. 'I mean, it's funny, isn't it?'

I'm there, 'Hey, I've got a load of lines like that. I could do that shit all night long.'

She goes, 'I'm Grainne!' and offers me her hand.

She has a fantastic set of norks on her, it's impossible not to notice. Sense of humour. Nice boat. Great bottle rockets. In normal circs, she'd be ticking a lot of boxes for me.

I'm there, 'Sorry, say that name again,' because I wasn't really listening to her.

'It's Grainne.'

'Hey,' I go, 'it's nice to meet you, Grainne,' laying it on good and thick, full eye contact, everything. 'I'm Ross.'

She smiles. 'I know who you are.'

'Do you?'

'Doesn't everyone? I remember you playing rugby.'

I have to say, after the shit that Honor hit me with in the cor pork of Ikea a few weeks back, it's muesli to my ears. 'You couldn't remember me playing rugby,' I go. 'How even old are you – if that's not too rude a question?'

'I'm thirty-one.'

'Thirty-one? Oh my God, you do *not* look it. You very much don't look it.'

I'm on fire here, suddenly remembering – and this is going to sound bad – how much I loved being *single*?

'Okay,' she goes, 'this is – oh my God – so embarrassing. But when I was in, like, Alexandra College, we used to follow you around.'

'A lot did.'

'We used to practically stalk you, though. You were a really amazing player.'

'All I'd say in response to that analysis is that I enjoyed my rugby.'

'You were amazing. As in, Oh! My God!'

'Well, what I said still stands.'

Her next question comes, like, totally out of left-field. 'So are you, like, with anyone these days? As in, like, *with* with?'

It's weird, roysh. I automatically look over my shoulder for Sorcha, even though she's at home with Honor. This is the first major test of my, I suppose, *commitment* to her? My answer here is going to say a lot about my character.

'You seem suddenly interested in my status?' I go, deciding to keep it vague. It's better than a straight, 'Yeah, no, I'm single,' which I think shows signs of definite emotional growth.

Having said that, this no-sex pact has me backed up like a focking hospital waiting list and I'm curious about how far I could actually push this.

'I'm just asking,' she goes. 'I know you *were* married, to that girl – was she, like, head girl or deputy head girl in Mount Anville?'

I check over my shoulder again. The survival instinct is strong in me. 'Yeah, no, look,' I go, 'I'm going to be honest with you, I am still technically married. We did break up but we've decided to give it another go. Sorcha happens to be the girl's name.'

'Sorcha! That was it. Oh my God, she was a great debater.'

'Yeah, so she never tires of mentioning! Look, I like you, don't get me wrong. Great face. Great sense of humour. All the rest. And I think you like me, certainly from the vibes you're giving off.'

'I do.'

'Well, unfortunately, I don't want to do anything that might, I suppose, jeopardize what me and Sorcha have got – certainly not this early on.'

She's disappointed. I can see it.

'Oh, well,' she goes, smiling like a good loser, which, it has to be said, would have been typical of Alex girls back in the day, whether it was hockey or whatever. 'If your circumstances ever change . . .'

She gives me an incredible smile and I realize that I'm horder than Crumlin here.

'Like I said,' I go, 'I have to piss.'

She's there, 'It was lovely to meet you, Ross,' then off she trots, with her ying-yangs practically bursting out of her top.

I'm like, 'Yeah, no, you too.'

'What the fock is this?'

I pick up the iPad with the intention of Google searching for photographs of Dinara Safina and Nadia Petrova, and Sorcha's got some page open with photographs of a bunch of – this is possibly seriously racist – but *black* kids, sitting under a tree, in front of an, again, blackboard.

Like I told you, I'm like, 'What the fock is this?'

Sorcha goes, 'I was reading Fionn's blog.'

Fionn's gone to Uganda or Ugando – whatever you want to call it – for two years to actually teach.

'*You* should read it,' Sorcha goes. 'It's so an amazing thing that he's doing, Ross. He's in a tiny little village just outside Mbale.'

I'm like, 'Yeah, I'm saying fair focks, Sorcha. It's just I don't know if I'd have the time to read, like, an entire focking blog on what he's up to. Jesus, there's a lot here, isn't there?'

We're talking literally pages and pages. What is it about Irish people that they can't just go away and enjoy themselves without asking every focker they've ever known in their lives to spend an hour of every day reading about how they saw an actual coral reef or fired a focking bazooka at a gnu?

If Kathryn Thomas couldn't interest me in the world beyond South Dublin, I don't fancy Fionn's chances.

I'm like, 'Gimme the highlights, Babes. What's he up to? Is he riding any of the other teachers?' hoping that the answer is yes. It's nearly, like, six months since Erika ditched him at the altar. It'd be nice to think of him getting it regular again.

'He doesn't have time for all that,' she goes. 'He has, like, six hours of classes a day.'

'Six hours a day? Jesus, what the fock are they teaching these kids?'

'Everything. And then he spends another six hours a day doing building work.'

'Building work? We're talking actual manual labour?'

'Yeah, they're building a proper permanent school. Look! The entire building is going to run on solar energy and have a rain-fed water system!'

Her phone all of a sudden rings. She looks at the screen and her mouth just drops. 'It's Patriona,' she goes.

I'm like, 'Answer it.'

This is us just sitting in Idlewilde in Dalkey, by the way.

Sorcha's like, 'Hello?' putting on the posh but still polite voice she reserves for people like her old headmistress and the maître d' in Patrick Guilbaud. 'Yes, Patriona. Yes, that date would suit us, Patriona. Yes, morning or afternoon. That's perfect, Patriona. Thanks, Patriona,' and then she hangs up.

'So was it Patriona?' I go, just ripping the piss.

It goes totally over Sorcha's head, of course. 'Yeah, it was her. The thirteenth of December.'

I'm like, 'That's when she's coming?'

She goes, 'We'll have to make sure the house is looking – oh my God – amazing!' and as she says it, she storts flicking through the December edition of House and Home magazine, which she just so happened to buy earlier. 'Ross, I have to show you this room!'

I'm there, 'Er, didn't Patriona mention the last day in her office that it wasn't so much about the house as about what kind of people we are?'

Except she just thrusts the magazine in front of my face anyway. She's like, 'We so should do that.'

It's a photograph of a room with, like, a massive focking Christmas tree in one corner, surrounded by presents – including a rocking horse with, like, a bow on it – then a humungous log fire, then a table, set for Christmas dinner, like one of the ones you see in the window of House of Ireland.

She goes, 'We should copy it.'

I'm like, 'What would be the point of that?'

She's there, 'It's about creating an impression, Ross. I want her to walk into our home and go, "Oh! My God!"'

'Again,' I go, 'I think it's more about whether she actually likes *us*?' which, by the way, I don't think she does.

'Don't worry,' she goes, 'I'm not going to ask you to do anything, Ross. Except get a tree.'

'A tree?'

'A Christmas tree. Like the one in the magazine.'

'Er, okay.'

'They sell them in Blackrock College – in aid of, I think it's, like, St Vincent de Paul?'.

I'm like, 'Yeah, no, that's no problem, Babes,' and of course you can probably guess what's immediately going through my mind. There's no way in this world I'd give Blackrock College the money – charity or no charity.

Don't get me wrong. I've got a healthy amount of respect for the fockers. Without Blackrock College, there'd be no Brian O'Driscoll. There'd be no Leo Cullen. There'd be no Something de Valera. But I won't give them money. It'd go against everything Father Fehily believed in.

I'm there, 'I'll get you a tree, Babes, don't you worry.'

I actually know where there's one going.

JP says he's pretty sure that what we're doing here is illegal. This coming from the man who once described Newtownmountkennedy as 'combining the quiet gentility of the Irish countryside with the bustling, can-do energy of Europe's most vibrant capital city'.

He was lucky he was never locked up. I say that to him as well.

'But this is criminal damage,' he tries to go.

I'm there, 'We're chopping down a Christmas tree. It's hordly criminal damage. It's, like, nature, isn't it?'

'Well,' he goes, 'at the very least it's trespassing.'

I'm like, 'Firstly, I simply refuse to give Blackrock College the money. And secondly, how could it be trespassing when my old man's a member here?' and then I turn to Oisinn. '*You're* a member as well, aren't you?'

He goes, 'I *was*. And from memory, Ross, membership allows

you to play the course and use the bar and restaurant. I don't think it entitles you to . . . logging rights.'

'Well,' I go, 'it's a good job I'm going to do the actual chopping down then. You're only here to help me carry the thing to the truck.'

JP still has the flatbed he used to drive when he and his old man moved into, like, repossessions temporarily.

He's like, 'Which tree even is it?'

'I don't know,' I go, because it's, like, nine o'clock at night and pitch dork? 'It's definitely somewhere around here, though. I sliced my drive off the fifth tee and this is where it ended up.'

Oisinn shakes his head. See, golf was never really my game. But I definitely saw a Christmas tree when I was looking for my ball.

I suddenly spot it.

I'm like, 'There it is!' even though it's actually bigger than I remembered it. That's what possibly *threw* me? JP and Oisinn stare at it, just nodding. I think we're all in agreement that it's an incredible specimen, insofar as we're any kind of judges of what a nice tree looks like.

I'm like, 'Give me the axe.'

Oisinn hands it to me. I run my thumb along the blade, testing it – I don't know why.

JP goes, 'Have you ever used one of those things before?'

I'm like, 'Jesus, I can't imagine it's that hord, Dude.'

I tell the two goys to step back, which they do, then I swing the thing at the tree, pretty close to the base. The blade goes right into it – it actually gets stuck – and I end up having to move the axe up and down to free it. Then I swing it again. The trick is obviously to keep hitting roughly the same spot, which is what I try to do. Nothing gets said, but I think the goys are pretty impressed with how well I end up handling the equipment.

'By the way,' JP goes, while I'm still hord at it, 'who was that bird you were talking to in Kielys the other night?'

I'm like, 'Nice, huh?'

'I actually thought it was Daniella Moyles.'

'I'm glad *you* said that – because you're my proof.'

Oisinn's there, 'She was nice alright.'

I'm like, 'There's no doubt about that. *And* she knew her rugby. She basically offered herself to me on a plate as well.'

'Fock off!'

'On a plate, Dude.'

I swing the axe at the tree again. It's not going to take much more for it to fall.

'And you weren't tempted?' JP goes.

I'm like, 'Tempted?' wiping the sweat off my forehead, even though it's, like, two degrees or something focking ridiculous. 'Of course I was focking tempted. But like I told her, I'm going to try and give the whole marriage thing a serious go. It's focking typical, though, isn't it? I've been thinking about some of the absolute focking horse-beasts I ended up with when I was actually single.'

'Eye broccoli,' Oisinn goes, like *he* can afford to talk. 'Pure eye broccoli.'

I'm there, 'It was grizzly chickens, 2 a.m. beauty queens and focking crockadillapigs throwing themselves at me. Now, for the first time in my life, I'm trying to do the whole monogamy thing and that's the kind of material that's suddenly on offer.'

'They've got, like, a sixth sense for it,' Oisinn goes, 'as in, women. The best offers you will ever get are when you're already involved in something else. That's a stone cold fact.'

I hit the tree again – one more time – and suddenly it goes down. We all do the whole, 'Timmmbbbeeerrr!!!' bit, as it falls with a bigger thud than any of us expected.

It's, like, heavier than we expected as well and it takes, honestly, all of our strength to lift the thing onto our shoulders and carry it – like three coffin-bearers – across the golf course and out to where the truck is porked on Nutley Lane.

We're traipsing across – I *think* – the first green, when my phone all of a sudden rings. I manage to get it out of my pocket and it ends up being, hilariously, Sorcha.

'Ross,' she goes, 'where are you?'

I'm there, 'I've, er, just picked up a Christmas tree . . .'

Which isn't a lie.

'. . . from Blackrock College.'

Which is.

'Is it definitely environmentally friendly?' she goes.

I laugh. 'It's a focking tree, Sorcha, it doesn't come any more environmentally friendly than that.'

Oisinn and JP – in front of me, carrying the heavy end – have a little chuckle to themselves. They know what she's like, see.

'I mean, did you ask them whether the grower has sustainability built into his business plan?'

'Er, explain sustainability, Babes.'

'As in, does he plant a new tree for every one he cuts down?'

'Actually, yeah, I did ask the goys that now that you mention it.'

'And?'

'Yeah, it's all good, Babes.'

'You're sure?'

'Yeah, no, a hundred percent. In fact, yeah, they actually plant *two* trees for every one tree they hack down.'

I can see the goys both shake their heads, as if to say, this goy will never change – and let's all just celebrate that basic fact.

'Two for one?' Sorcha goes. 'That's actually very generous. And the grower *was* committed to organic forestry, was he?'

I'm like, 'Yeah, they mentioned that as well.'

'His operation is pesticide- and chemical-free?'

'Big time.'

'And do you know how many road miles it travelled.'

Jesus focking Christ.

'As in?'

'As in, was it hauled across five counties in a lorry belching CO_2 into the environment?'

'No, definitely not. I wouldn't have bought it if it was.'

'So you're saying it was definitely sourced locally?'

I laugh. 'Trust me,' I go. 'By the time I get it home to you, it won't have travelled longer than the length of the 46a route. That much I *can* guarantee.'

The next thing any of us hears is, 'Hey! You!' and without even looking around we all know it's time to exit this scene – and fast.

I'm like, 'Er, got to go, Sorcha. I'll see you back at the ranch,' and I hang up – just as the light of a torch suddenly comes on us.

'Okay,' I go, 'let's step up the pace, goys.'

JP and Oisinn don't need to be told twice. Actually, they don't need to be told once. They're already running, insofar as you *can* run while carrying a humungous Christmas tree between three of you. We're all running from the knees down, basically.

'Come back here with that tree!' the voice goes again. And of course then we all end up getting a fit of the old giggles. We all end up thinking the same thing – it's like we're back in college.

He's, like, twenty or thirty yords behind us.

I go, 'Keep running, goys,' somehow managing to get the words out between literally sobs of laughter. 'Don't even look back.'

We reach the flatbed truck. JP jumps in the front and, like, storts the engine, while me and Oisinn throw the tree on the back, then jump on top of it, like we're clearing out a ruck back in the day. There's no time to tie it down, so we end up having to lie on it – still laughing our heads off – as JP puts his foot on the accelerator and we tear down Nutley Lane.

There's, like, a security gord standing on the side of the road, waving his finger at us, telling us that he's calling the Gordaí and I'm suddenly thinking, it's a good job there's no focking licence plate on this beast.

JP floors it down Nutley Lane and through an orange light onto the Merrion Road, with me and Oisinn literally holding on for dear life, but at the same laughing, and remembering what a great thing it is to have true mates.

Oh! My! God!

That's Sorcha reaction when she sees the tree I managed to get and the job I've done actually decorating the thing.

'Oh! My! God!'

She says it, like, four or five times. And then she goes, 'I can't wait to see Patriona's reaction,' and it's then that I should possibly throw in a line.

I should go, 'There's always the possibility – given that it's me involved – that this might not turn out the way we're hoping it's *going* to?'

Except I don't – the reason being that she leans in close to me and gives me the kind of kiss on the lips that would normally be my cue to take the Blouse Brothers out for a quick spin, then suggest we take the porty upstairs.

She straight away senses that I want more, of course. I'm gagging for her. For anyone.

'No sex,' she goes. 'Seriously, Ross, calm down.'

'Jesus, you storted it.'

'Let's just finish the tree.'

It's as I'm getting ready to put the stor on the top that she suddenly says it. 'Oh, by the way,' she goes, 'I did something today that you might not wholly agree with.'

Shit.

'Yeah, no, continue,' I go and I brace myself for the worst.

'I invited Kennet and Dordeen out here. The whole Tuite family, in fact.'

'What? When?'

'The same day as Patriona. I'm going to do a cold Christmas buffet.'

'Jesus Christ, Sorcha . . .'

'Now don't stort saying cruel things, Ross, about them stealing the silverware. You know I hate that kind of talk. I was chair of the Peace and Justice group at school and I don't want to listen to . . .'

'I was just going to ask why – as in, why would you invite them *here*?'

'It's very simple, Ross. Ronan and Shadden want to live here . . .'

'Go on.'

'But they don't want to tell Kennet and Dordeen that they don't want to live with them.'

'Okay.'

'Kennet and Dordeen are reasonable people, Ross.'

'Yeah, no, they're actually not.'

'And they're intelligent.'

'Again, I think you're possibly giving them a bit too much credit.'

'I'm confident that they're going to come here, see our amazing, amazing home and then – like Patriona – actually decide for themselves that this is the best place for Ronan, Shadden and little Rihanna-Brogan to be.'

'I don't know, Babes.'

'You forget, Ross, how persuasive I can actually be.'

Again, I should say something, just to dampen down her optimism. Don't get me wrong, Sorcha is well capable of making her case. But standing up in front of the Model U. N. and arguing that this house regrets the slaughter of some focking crowd by some other focking crowd is nothing compared to the lifetime the Tuites have spent pulling the wool over the eyes of social workers, juries, the Deportment of Social Welfare and blah, blah, blah.

I don't say that, though. I just put the stor on top of the tree and go, 'Let's hope you're right.'

Laura Whitmore's on *Xposé*, looking all lovely like she's hurting no one. Married or not, if I thought I had half a sniff, I'd be all over her like a dog on a dropped waffle.

It goes to an ad break.

I flick through the channels, except there's fock-all on. It's basically all talk about this Budget today.

Shit for those in work. Shit for those out of work. Shit for the young. Shit for the old. Shit for homeowners. Shit for people renting. Shit for smokers. Shit for drinkers. Shit for drivers. That seems to just about cover the main points.

It'd possibly depress you if you let it.

I check out what's stored on the old Sky Box. A lot of Sorcha's old *Revenge*s and *Off the Rails*es and then – er, *paydirt*? – I suddenly remember that I have the Miracle Match stored. Leinster versus Northampton in the Ken Cup final. It's very much a case of, like, winning!

I tip out to the kitchen, grab a can of Hydrogen from the fridge, then settle down in front of the TV again, just nicely happy. Sorcha's in Dundrum, picking up bits for the visit of Patriona and the focking Tuites tomorrow – it's turning into a bit of an event – while Honor's upstairs doing, well, who cares what.

It's, like, the simple pleasures and blah, blah, blah.

Anyway, five minutes into the game, I get the feeling of being suddenly watched. I look around and there's my daughter, standing in the doorway of the living room with a big, sulky look on her boat.

She goes, 'Is this an important match?' a line she learned from her old dear. Roughly translated it means, can you please switch that off so I can watch something else instead?

I'm there, 'It's rugby, Honor. They're *all* important matches!' and I end up having a little chuckle to myself, because it's a really, really good line that I'm definitely going to have to remember.

She doesn't buy it, though. I see her eyes go to the little light on the front of the box, then she goes, 'Er, this is *recorded*?'

I'm like, 'So?'

'Er, *so* you can watch it anytime. I want to write my Santa List.'

I'm like, 'Your Santa List?' at the same time trying to come up with a way to get out of it. I go, 'Okay, look – the thing is Honor . . .' and for five, maybe ten seconds – I'm not proud of this – I actually consider telling her the truth about who *actually* puts the presents under the tree, just so we can drop it as a subject.

That's how much I love my rugby.

In the end, I don't. I go, 'Can you maybe wait until your mother comes home? I actually don't own a pen *or* a piece of paper.'

But she's on it like vomit.

'You do,' she goes, lifting up one of the sofa cushions and pulling out the A4 pad that I use as a kind of tactics book while I'm watching rugby on TV. It's basically all the shit that *I'd* do in certain match situations if I was the Leinster or Ireland coach, with little illustrations and blah, blah, blah. 'We can write it in your Sad Book.'

I'm like, 'Yeah, there's no need to call it that.'

'Well, it *is* sad.'

'It's just my thoughts on rugby.'

'Yeah, whatever.'

She hands me the pad and the pen, then she picks up the remote and mutes the TV.

'Hey, Honor,' I go, still trying to worm my way out of it, 'I'm just thinking back to last year. Do you remember you said that what you wanted more than anything for Christmas was to see your mom and dad get back together again? Well, let's just say your big present arrived a year late! What's that thing you always hear people say? Santa Claus works in mysterious ways!'

She just stares me down.

'Okay,' she goes, 'just so you know, I'm *humouring* you with the whole Santa Claus thing? Mainly because you seem to get a kick out of it,' and then she taps the notepad with her finger and goes, 'Okay, start writing this stuff down as I call it out. And make sure you take down the brands as well.'

I'm like, 'Er, okay.'

How did she become such a cow?

'A Joanne Hynes embellished collar. An iPad mini. A pink Barbour jacket. A coatigan by Cyrillus. A cream gilet by SuperTrash. An I Love Gorgeous pink tulle dress, the one that Alyson Hannigan's daughter, Satyana, is wearing in a magazine I have upstairs. A bottle of *Love, Chloé* perfume. A Mint Jun dress by Roksanda Ilinčić – she's this, like, amazing designer from Belgrade . . .'

I'm there, 'Belgrade?' basically trying to slow her down. 'Where *is* Belgrade?'

'Okay,' she goes, 'what's the point of telling you what country Belgrade is in when you won't have even heard of it?'

'Try me.'

'It's in Serbia.'

'Okay, point proven. Move on.'

'A Michael Kors watch – something chunky to make my wrist look thinner. A Mulberry bag. *Or* a Miu Miu. *Or* both. But definitely a Mulberry. And preferably both. The Alyssa Mary Jane shoes by Ralph Lauren that Suri Cruise wore on her first day at school. The Matilda dress in amethyst by Little Ella Moss that Jennifer Garner's daughter Violet wore recently. A Michael Roberts Anna Wintour

T-shirt. A Magic Cube portable projection keyboard – I'm thinking of storting a blog. Victoria Beckham sunglasses – I like the Metal Charles in Mink, the Round in Honey and the Granny Cat in Fresh White. Two of those three. Or preferably all three. A miniature dog, though I haven't decided what breed yet. The Joce dress by Stella McCartney Kids and the pink coat by Monnalisa that Ben Affleck's daughter Seraphina was wearing in the last issue of *Heat*. Why are you writing Seraphina down?'

'I don't know. I thought it might be relevant.'

'It's not relevant. I'm just telling you where I saw it. Okay, can you, like, focus? A Louis Vuitton Minaudière Petit Trésor. I'm going to spell that for you because I can see you're already struggling with it . . . M . . . I . . . N . . .'

It goes on for, like, five or ten minutes more. When I get the sense that we're slipping into the high five-figure territory, I go, 'Just to warn you, Honor, you might not get *all* of this stuff.'

She's like, 'Excuse me?'

'It's a lot, is all I'm saying. You're talking, like sixty or seventy Ks worth of stuff. Enda Kenny was on TV the other night saying we're basically focked – and that's as a country. I slept through some of it. But that seems to have been the general message.'

Honor throws her eyes up to heaven, then goes, 'Whatevs! Just tell me which ones you and Mom are going to get me, then I'll pay for the rest myself.'

I laugh. I'm like, 'And how are you proposing to do that?'

'Er,' she goes, 'with *my* money?'

I'm like, 'What money?'

'My *movie* money? Hashtag – are you brain-dead?'

'Your movie money?' I go. My brain is telling my mouth to shut the fock up, but my mouth lets it go to the message-minder. 'Yeah, no, there might not be as much of that as we originally thought, Honor.'

I watch her little face drop.

She's like, 'What do you mean?'

I'm there, 'Er, nothing. I'm just saying.'

'You *know* something.'

'I don't. I swear.'

'You do. That's the same look Mom had when I mentioned my movie money last night. What's going on?'

'Nothing.'

'There *is* something.'

'I said the words "I swear", Honor. That should mean something to you.'

She picks up the remote for the Sky Box again and she hits the delete programme button. A message comes up on the screen. It's like, 'Delete Programme?' and then underneath it offers the Yes and No options.

'Tell me,' she goes, 'or I'm going to delete this game.'

I try to grab the remote, except she pulls her hand away and hides it behind her back. She's like, 'I'm going to press Yes.'

I'm like, 'Honor, please!'

'I'm going to press it. Three . . .'

'Honor, I'm begging you.'

'Two . . .'

It's the Miracle Match!'

'One . . .'

'Okay, okay! I'll tell you! Jesus Christ! Look, the unfortunate fact is you're not going to *be* in any movie.'

'*Excuse* me?'

'Yeah, no, the old dear told us – a week ago. You didn't test well apparently. They're getting some other kid to do it. From San Somewhere-or-other.'

I watch her eyes suddenly fill up with tears, which is something I didn't *expect*? She's such a little weapon so much of the time that you can forget that she's still a little girl who's capable of being, I don't know, hurt.

She's like, 'What do you mean, I didn't test well?'

'They tested the movie on an audience. The old dear explained the ins and outs of how it works. I only took a bit of it in. You know me.' I'm babbling, I realize.

She goes, 'They've got *another* girl?'

I'm there, 'That seems to be the general upshot, Honor.'

'*You* did this,' she all of a sudden goes, turning on me. 'You and Mom . . .'

I'm like, 'Honor . . .'

'You did! You pulled me from it. You told them you didn't want me to be in it.'

'That's where your facts are wrong.'

'You never wanted me to be in it.'

'Honor . . .'

'You didn't. I heard you talking. Mom said she wished she'd never let me do it. I heard her say it.'

Shit. I've never regretted opening my mouth so much. Sorcha is going to literally kill me.

That's when, totally out of the blue, she goes, 'I focking hate you!' and she says it with her eyes narrowed and her face full of – I'm going to use the word – *spite*?

'You don't mean it,' I go.

Then she says it again – over and over, in fact. 'I focking hate you! I focking hate you! I focking hate you! I focking *hate* you!'

She shouts it right in my face, then she turns and storms back upstairs to her room, still shouting it over her shoulder – 'I focking hate you! I focking hate you! I focking hate you! I focking hate you!' – and then I hear her bedroom door slam, loud enough to cause a focking landslide, and then her sobs echoing through our big, still mostly empty house.

I put the match back on. I find it very difficult to concentrate on it, though.

Fifteen, possibly twenty minutes later, Sorcha arrives home, carrying bags and bags of shit. She goes, 'I got everything. Including some beautiful table decorations from House of Fraser. I even got an – oh my God – dotey little rocking horse in Mamas & Papas. They are, like, *so* nice in that shop. They even helped me carry it to the cor.'

Her eyes suddenly turn to the TV. She's like, 'Is this an important match?'

'It's rugby,' I go. 'They're all important matches, Babes.'

'Because I was going to ask you to get the rocking horse out of the boot and then help me set the table.'

'You mean now?'

'Ross, they're all coming tomorrow.'

'I know.'

'We don't have a lot of time.'

'I realize that.'

'I just want everything to be perfect, Ross.'

I end up just nodding and she suddenly stops. It's something she just sees in my face. She's like, 'Oh my God, what's happened?'

She can read me like a focking *Bob the Builder* book.

I'm there, 'Honor knows.'

She goes, 'Knows? Knows what?'

'Knows about the movie – about being dropped from it.'

'How?'

'You're asking me how? Okay, look, she basically got it out of me.'

'You told her?'

'Like I said, she put the pressure on me and I folded. I folded like an Italian scrum.'

She sits down, like she realizes this is suddenly serious. 'Oh my God! And how did she react?'

I'm like, 'Er, about as well as you'd expect. She said she hated me – although, I think that was directed at the two of us.'

'Oh, no.'

'She thinks we pulled her from it. Well, mainly you.'

Sorcha has her head suddenly in her hands. 'Ross, we've got a social worker coming to the house tomorrow. What if Honor decides to . . .'

The two of us turn our heads at the exact same time to see Honor standing in the doorway. I don't know if you've ever seen the movie *Carrie*, but that's pretty much the vibe.

She goes, 'Oh, don't worry,' except in a really, like, *bitchy* way? 'I'll be on my *best* behaviour tomorrow. Because I know how much this little baby means to you.'

★

I'm wondering is this not actual *bribery*? Sorcha says she doesn't care what it's called. 'Today is – oh my God – *such* a big day for us, Ross. I don't want Honor ruining it. So if that means us having to buy her good behaviour for one day of the year, then so be it.'

I'm wondering how that fits in with all those good parenting manuals she used to read. Mind you, a fat lot of focking good they were to us.

She's like, 'What did you get her?'

I'm walking back up Grafton Street towards the Stephen's Green Shopping Centre, which is where I'm porked.

I'm like, 'The Michael Kors watch. The Joanne Hynes embellished collar. The Lara Bohinc cashmere and silk scorf with blurred leopard-print detail. That pink tulle dress by I can't remember who. And the other one by Roksanda something – I have it written down.'

'What about the embellished leather clutch by Corto Maltedo?'

'Yeah, no, how could I forget? It was thirteen hundred snots – a focking handbag for a six-year-old. I also got the Betmar red balsa hat.'

'Is that all?'

'No, that T-shirt by Lanvin. And the perfume. *Love, Chloé*. And those shoes that Suri focking Cruise apparently has.'

'Okay. Well done. Let's just hope it's enough.'

I'm like, 'Only time will tell, Babes.'

I'm passing, like, Dubray Books, when all of a sudden someone touches my elbow. I turn around and it ends up being Grainne, the bird from Kielys that night – I suppose I'd have to call her my fan.

She mouths the word *sorry* – she didn't realize I was on the old Sharon Stone. And I go, 'Yeah, no, Sorcha, I'll see you back in the ranch,' and I hang up on her.

I'm like, 'How the hell are you?'

She goes, 'I'm good. Oh my God – *someone's* been shopping!'

I'm like Julia focking Roberts on Rodeo Drive here.

'It's just a few presents for my daughter,' I go. 'People go on about spoiling children. I don't think that's even possible . . . It *was* Grainne, wasn't it?'

'Grainne, yeah. And, oh my God, you must think I'm *actually* stalking you now!'

I laugh. I'm like, 'Hey, stalk away. I'd nearly consider it flattering,' because, like I said, she is a total honey with a seriously tremendous rack.

'Okay,' she goes, 'I need to apologize for my behaviour in Kielys that night. It was so rude of me to be so forward.'

I'm like, 'Hey, you saw something you wanted and you went for it. That wasn't against the law the last time I checked. And like I said, if I was a single goy . . .'

I genuinely never thought I'd hear myself talk this way. She decides to just change the subject – to something less painful for her.

She's like, 'Did you see the match on Sunday?'

Leinster beat Bath 18–13 in the Ken Cup.

I'm there, 'I did. I would have liked to see them score one or two tries in the second half. They had the chances. There's no denying that.'

And that's when she says one of the most unbelievable things a girl has ever said to me. 'Gordon D'Arcy played a pass to, I think, Luke Fitzgerald. I've seen him play that pass a hundred times before. And the more I see it, the more convinced I am that he copied it from you.'

My jaw practically hits the floor. Only two people have ever pointed that out before. I'm one. The other was Fionn.

I go, 'When you were talking about rugby in Kielys that night, I actually thought you were just talking shit like a lot of girls. But you seem to actually know the game.'

She laughs. 'I'm sure there's a compliment in there somewhere.'

I'm there, 'There is. A big-time compliment. Dorce learned a lot from me – more than he's ever acknowledged in interviews.'

I realize that I could actually fall in love with this bird and it'd be dangerous for me to stay standing here.

'Anyway,' I go, 'I better get back to the Batmobile.'

She laughs. A sense of humour is so important, and luckily she loves mine.

We say goodbye. There's no digits exchanged or anything. I stort walking back towards the Stephen's Green Shopping Centre and it's then that I realize that I'm bursting for a piss.

And I happen to know just the place for one.

Christian and Lauren's business is flying. It must be. That's if the queue is anything to go by. It's out the focking door and up Chatham Street as far as Muji. They've got, like, five staff working for them now as well, including a little hottie who I can't help but notice is a ringer for Alexandra Breckenridge, except with blonde hair and even bigger Berthas.

She's the one who points the lunch queue out to me – with a breadknife, as it happens. She's like, 'The line starts outside there.'

But I'm there, 'Hey, it's cool. I'm not here for food. I'm a friend of the boss,' and I give her one of my nice and sleazy winks.

I'm going to do my best to stay faithful to Sorcha, but I can't turn off the famous Ross O'Carroll-Kelly chorm.

Christian is showing another bird – who's obviously just storted working here – how to make a Caprese Melt.

I go, 'Alright, Dude?' and he looks up.

He's like, 'Hey, Ross,' and I have to say he doesn't look half as hassle-hoffed as he did the last time I was in here.

I'm like, 'No Lauren?'

He goes, 'No, she'll be in at two o'clock. Ross, I can't let you skip the queue,' because I can hear one or two grumbles now from the old lunchtime crowd.

I'm like, 'I'm not here to eat, Dude. I'm here to piss,' and I head for the usual ground-floor slash wheelchair toilet. 'Although I might take one of those Caprese things to go. They smell incredible.'

He loses it with me then. He storts going, 'Ross, don't go in there! Do *not* go in there!' but – fock him – I end up totally blanking him. I go in, shut the door and lock it behind me. I stort whipping my lad out as I'm turning away from the door, which is a habit I've always had.

Christian needs to stort manning up, I'm thinking to myself.

I take a step towards the toilet and that's when I get a fright that nearly empties my focking bladder there on the spot.

There's a man sitting on the bowl.

I try to apologize, except no actual *words* come out of my mouth? *He* can't speak either – he seems to be as much in shock as I am. He's an old dude – probably in his early sixties. Jesus Christ. I notice his wheelchair and then – and this is the real shock – his missing leg.

I'm like, 'Look . . . er . . . em . . .' and – oh shit! – I suddenly realize I've still got my dong in my hand.

Something, possibly instinct, tells me that I'm not going to be able to smooth-talk my way out of this one. There's fight and there's flight, and I haven't stayed alive for as many years as I have without knowing when to ditch one and do the other.

In one fast and fluid movement I put Elvis away, turn around again and stort walking, very focking quickly, in the direction of the door.

That's when the *shouting* suddenly storts?

'Help!' the dude storts going. 'Help! Help me! Someone call the Guards!'

At the mention of that crowd, I decide it's time to put some serious distance between us. A lot was said *and* written back in the day about my turn of pace over the first ten yords. Well, the lunchtime crowd on Chatham Street is suddenly being treated to a real trip down memory lane, as I come tearing out of the jacks – still doing up my fly buttons – past the line of goggling faces, past Christian and the rest of the staff, out onto the road and off in the direction of Grafton Street.

I just run and run and run. I'm like Forrest focking Gump. And I don't stop until I get back to the cor.

The buffet table has been laid and I can say that I've honestly never seen anything like it. We're talking duck and pork terrine with cranberries and pistachios. We're talking miniature turkey and cranberry pies. We're talking butternut-squash soup shots – in actual shot *glasses*? – with crispy pancetta soldiers. We're talking prawn and spiced-beef skewers with gremolata.

The sound of Leonard Bernstein and the New York Philhormonic Orchestra doing 'O Tannenbaum' and other Christmas classics drifts through the gaff. There's, like, presents under the tree, a roaring fire in the grate and the entire downstairs of our new home smells of burning wood and of the rum-infused, stor-topped mince pies and the cranberry and white chocolate cookies that are gently warming in the oven.

I feel like Daddy focking Warbucks here.

'What time is it?' Sorcha goes.

I'm like, 'It's five minutes after the last time you asked me. Try and calm down, Babes.'

She's, like, pacing the floor, looking out the window every ten seconds. She goes, 'How did Honor seem?'

I'm there, 'When?'

'When you gave her all the stuff. What did she think of the Lara Bohinc cashmere and silk scorf especially?'

'She didn't open it. She didn't open any of it.'

Which is true. She looked up from her iPhone, saw me standing at the door of her room with my orms laden with presents, and went, 'Oh, so we're trying to *buy* me off, are we? Hashtag – hillare!'

I put the presents on the floor at the foot of her bed and then, as I was leaving the room, she went, 'I know what a big day it is for you and Mom. Don't worry, I'm going to be *so* on my best behaviour.'

I put my orm on Sorcha's shoulder. I'm like, 'Let's just hope she means that literally,' even though I know, deep down, that she possibly doesn't.

The next thing either of us hears is the sound of, like, tyres on the gravel outside. 'It's Patriona!' Sorcha goes. 'Oh my God! Oh my God! Oh my God!'

I'm like, 'Deep breaths, Sorcha,' trying to think positively. 'She's going to love us – how could she not?'

She takes control of her breathing, nods, then this look of – I suppose – *resolve* comes over her? Which I recognize straight away as her game face.

She opens the front door and steps outside, giving it, 'Welcome, Patriona! Welcome to our home! I see you're admiring the garden. You'll have to come back in the summer, when there's hibiscus everywhere – it's *so* a strong memory for me from childhood.'

I would have thought it was a bit OTT, but she obviously knows what she's doing.

They step into the house. Looks-wise, I think I've already mentioned that Patriona is a focking disgrace.

I give her a friendly 'Hey, how the hell are you?' and she gives me a cautious 'Yes, hello, again.'

Sorcha calls up the stairs to Honor. She's like, 'Honor – Patriona is here!' except there's no sound of Honor even stirring.

Sorcha leads the way to the dining room.

Patriona's jaw hits the, literally, floor when she sees the spread. We might be living through a world economic crisis, but we're not *all* using single-ply jacks roll – and it's important that point comes across. She's like, 'I said on the phone that a cup of tea would be fine,' but Sorcha – hilariously – tries to crack on that this is the way we *always* live?

She goes, 'It's just a simple buffet. Sorry, I am *such* a sucker for this time of year. So many of my lovely, lovely memories from my childhood in this house involve Christmas. Would you like the tour, by the way?'

The woman's like, 'The tour?'

She has a face like a rally cor mudflap.

'The original structure was mock Gandon,' Sorcha tries to go, 'but a lot of the actual features, like the turrets and the mock Renaissance strapwork, were added later on . . .'

Patriona cuts her off. She's like, 'Like I said to you when we met in my office, this visit is more about you and your husband . . .'

'But I just thought . . .'

'Rather than the house – *if* that's okay.'

It's a serious slap-down and Sorcha reacts in what I would call a typically South Dublin female way. 'Of course,' she goes, bitch-smiling her. 'Ask us any questions you like, Patriona.'

All of a sudden we hear the sound of the letterbox rattle. It's obviously the Tuites. I mean, they don't have a doorbell themselves, so why would they bother their holes using ours?

Sorcha goes out to answer it, then, twenty seconds later, in they focking troop. Kennet, then Dordeen, then the kids – I count five in all – which includes Shadden, who walks in last, pushing R&B in her little stroller, with Ronan just in front of her, carrying the various bags of this, that and the other that you need for a baby.

I give Ro a wink, roysh, just to let him know that it's going to be okay. He goes, 'Alreet, Rosser.'

I'm like, 'It's all good, Ro. It's all good.'

Kennet's one of those fockers, though, who always has to be the centre of the room. He's like, 'Howiyiz?' big chirpy focking head on him and not even making the effort to tone down his accent for the occasion. 'Howiya, Patriona?'

Patriona's like, 'Hello, Kennet,' in a really friendly way.

He goes, 'You m . . . m . . . member the kids – Eddie, Dadden, Kadden, Shadden and Enrique.'

I shit you not. The youngest – who was obviously an afterthought because he's, like, eight, while the others are well into their teens – was named after, I'm *presuming*, Enrique Iglesias.

I mean, *there's* a reason for Patriona to take him into care, right there.

I've never seen a tougher-looking kid than Enrique. He's just, like, shaven-headed – he's a definite ginge – and unsmiling and he stares at you like he's just waiting for you to give him shit about his name so he can tear out your Adam's apple.

Eddie and Dadden, I already told you about. They're pure focking ID parade fodder. You look at them in their twenty-yoyo jeans and their three-hundred-yoyo runners and you instantly remember that you meant to increase the value of your contents insurance.

They're both wearing their neck collars, by the way – as is Kennet.

Kadden is a sight. In my mind, I've already christened her The Girl With The Slutty Lower Back Tattoo, because she's got this, like, tat of a tribal design with a butterfly in the centre and it's visible over the top of her low-rise, ice-blue Levis when she bends over to inspect the buffet. She's got one of those, like, severe faces as well, her lips slightly pushed out, her eyes slightly narrowed, like the entire world is a focking offence to her.

I can actually see her and Honor really hitting it off.

'What ta fook is all tis?' is her reaction to the meal that Sorcha was up since six o'clock this morning preparing.

Dadden's like, 'It's fooken lubbley,' while going at the bacon, chipolata and prune rolls with both hands.

'Er, it was intended as, like, a *sit-down* buffet?' Sorcha goes, still trying to be nice. See, that's why people take the piss. 'I was going to suggest we fill our plates, then all sit around the table, so we can, like, talk. Shadden, I'll put together a plate for you. You just sit down,' which is a nice touch, because it obviously shows Patriona her whole *concerned* side?

There's a definite big-match tension in the air. At stake is that beautiful little baby sleeping soundly in her pram. There's no point in saying that it's *not* a competition when it obviously is. It's a case of who does Patriona like better – us or the Tuites?

I try to get the conversation rolling. We're talking general pleasantries. I turn to Kennet and I'm like, 'So how did you get out here?'

He's there, 'On ta Deert.'

I look at Patriona and I go, 'He means the Dort.'

She's like, 'Yes, I don't require a translation, thank you.'

It's obvious to me that she's still not over what I said to her on the Stillorgan dualler that day.

Sorcha has her head practically inside the stroller, going, 'Is thatta litta smile, Rihanna-Brogan? Is thatta litta smile for me? Yes, it is! Yes, it is!' basically talking shit, but at the same time just showing everyone how good she is with the baby.

Then she goes, '*Where* is Honor, by the way?' and I'm nearly tempted to tell her to leave her where she is.

Except she stands at the door and storts calling up the stairs to her, going, 'Honor! Honor! We're sitting down to luncheon!'

Luncheon. Even I have to have a chuckle at that one.

We all sit down around the table, but before anyone gets to say anything about why we're all here today, Dordeen – totally out of the blue – goes, 'It's lubbly tat yous two is back thegedder again,' letting Patriona not-so-subtly know that me and Sorcha have had one or two – let's just say – ups and *downs* in our marriage?

It's a low focking blow. But I should have known that they'd try to fight dirty.

Patriona looks at Sorcha, obviously waiting for an explanation – as in, you never said a word about this the last day.

'Yes,' Sorcha goes, 'Ross and I *have* had troubles in our marriage . . .'

'The nanny, wadn't it?'

This, from Kennet.

I end up going, 'It wasn't *just* the nanny,' except I have no focking idea why. It's possibly shock at them going on the actual offensive.

Patriona storts scratching her neck. I don't know why. I think maybe it's just the thought of me dicking the domestic.

Sorcha goes, 'What Ross means is that there were, like, *lots* of factors? One of which was also our age. We were very young when we got married.'

'S . . . S . . . So were we,' Kennet goes. 'We were oatenly noyun teeyun.'

Nineteen. Jesus. I look across the table at Patriona for her reaction – except there *isn't* one? It's the first time I genuinely feel that, for whatever reason, she's actually more on their side than ours.

Dordeen goes, '*We* were teddibly in luff, but.'

And Kennet's like, 'We still eer.'

Then they turn around and kiss each other. They're good, I'll give them that. We've got an actual battle on our hands here. If Sorcha doesn't already realize it, I definitely do. I decide then that I can fight dirty, too. Jerry Flannery has a two-inch-wide bald patch above his right ear to prove that basic point – the hair never grew back, even though we still have a lot of respect for each other whenever we meet.

'Your family seems to be pretty accident-prone,' I go. 'I mean, look at you. You're always, like, tripping over shit or slipping on shit. Either that or shit's falling on top of you. You just strike me as a very careless lot. How can we be sure that this beautiful granddaughter of mine isn't going to be wearing a neck brace before she's a year old?'

Kennet – he's good – he doesn't bat an eyelid. He just goes, 'I c . . . c . . . could ast you sometin s . . . s . . . s . . . simidar.'

I'm like, 'Meaning?'

He looks at Patriona. 'Pooer Ross theer got shot last yee-er – dunno if he m . . . m . . . mentioned that to ye?'

Patriona's face just drops. She seems in genuine shock. And imagine the shit she must see in her job.

She goes, 'You were shot?'

Kennet's there, 'By a couple of big toyum crimiddles – mates of yoo-ers, werdent thee, Ross?'

I'm like, 'The cops never found out who pulled the actual trigger. The main suspect, if you must know, was the daughter of a woman I was, like, *seeing* at the time?'

He laughs. 'Tat's reet. You were trowing the b . . . b . . . boat of tum a length, werdent ye? Ta m . . . m . . . mutter and ta thaughter.'

Fock.

Gerry Thornley often talks about the ebb and flow in the psychic energy of an actual contest. In this case, it's going away from us in a big-time way. Sorcha tries to retake control of the conversation.

'Look,' she goes, 'I don't think we should allow this discussion to degenerate into a character assassination of my husband. I think what we're here to decide is how best to give Ronan and Shadden's beautiful little baby here a life that's full of opportunities and – I know you're not a big fan of the word, Patriona, but I'm going to say it anyway – *wonder*. Be that here *or* in Finglas.'

As she says it, she smiles at Ronan and Shadden down the other end of the table, then Ronan and Shadden smile back and I stort to believe – just for a split-second – that we're capable of turning the tide here.

And, of course, that's when it all begins to unravel.

Patriona storts scratching her neck again, except this time she's actually going at it good, leaving long red claw morks on it. And Honor chooses that exact moment – literally five seconds after the mention of wonder and opportunities – to finally join us.

Straight away, I can see that there's something, like, *different* about her? It takes me a second or two to realize what it is and when I do, I'm too shocked to even open my trap.

'Honor?' Sorcha goes, every bit as stunned as I am. 'What . . . what happened to your hair?'

And Honor, in this little girl voice that I've never heard her use before, goes, 'I cut it, Mommy!'

Except she's not only cut it, she's hacked it nearly all off with the scissors, which she's still holding in one hand, with a big fistful of her once beautiful blonde locks in the other.

Sorcha's like, 'Wh . . . wh . . . why did you cut your hair?'

And Honor – knowing exactly what she's doing – goes, 'Because I'm sad, Mommy! And I thought it would make me happy! Like Daddy when he drinks!'

Holy focking shit.

Patriona goes, 'She . . . cut her own hair?'

She seems in definite shock.

Sorcha's like, 'She's just looking for attention.'

'Hair-cutting is a classic sign of mental or emotional disturbance,' Patriona goes.

That's it, I think. Game focking over.

'She's not disturbed,' Sorcha tries to go.

Patriona's like, 'She certainly *seems* disturbed. Something's clearly upsetting her.'

'I'm just sad in my head,' Honor goes.

Sorcha stands up, as angry as I've ever seen her. She grabs Honor, pretty much bundles her out of the room, then drags her back upstairs, with Honor going, 'Please don't be angry, Mommy! If you lose your temper, it'll be my fault again!' the whole way up to her bedroom.

There's, like, silence around the table – everyone's in pretty much shock – until Dadden eventually goes, 'Jesus, Ine as itchy as fook hee-er,' and storts, like, going at his back and head with his fingers. Enrique, I notice, is scratching himself as well.

'It's possibly hives,' I go. 'The food's obviously richer than you'd be used to.'

Then Sorcha arrives back in the room, all apologies. 'I'm sorry about that,' she goes. 'It's just an attention thing. I'll bring her to Toni & Guy tomorrow. It can still be styled.'

'I'm itchy too,' Patriona suddenly goes, still at herself. 'It's almost like I'm being bitten or something.'

It hasn't escaped my attention that her, Dadden and little Enrique are the three sitting closest to the Christmas tree.

Kennet cops it as well. 'M . . . m . . . must be sometin in tat tree,' he goes – then he has to, like, stand up and make a big focking deal of inspecting it.

Kadden has storted scratching herself now, as – by the way – has Ronan.

'Moy Jaysus,' Kennet suddenly goes, 'it's r . . . r . . . r . . . r . . . riddled, so it is.'

Sorcha's like, 'Riddled?' and then she looks at me expecting an answer. 'Riddled with what?'

He goes, 'F . . . f . . . f . . . fooken fleas or sumthin!' and then he shakes his head in, like, a *disappointed* way? 'Mon, Dordeen – mon, kids – let's geroura hee-er.'

Sorcha stands up and goes, 'You can't just leave.'

'The p . . . p . . . p . . . place is bleaten infested,' he goes. 'Mon, bring little Rihanna-B . . . B . . . B . . . Brogan. Before *she* ends up b . . . b . . . b . . . b . . . bitten. This is no place for a b . . . b . . . b . . . b . . . babby.'

Patriona stands up then. 'Yes,' she goes, scratching herself all over now, 'I think it's best that I go, too.'

There ends up being practically a stampede for the door. Sorcha follows Patriona through the entrance hall, then outside, going, 'I am *so* sorry, Patriona. I *so* am. You haven't seen us at our best today,' and what else is Patriona going to say except, 'I think I've seen enough.'

I'm going, 'Typical Blackrock College,' mainly just to cover my tracks.

Out the Tuites go, roysh, one by one, some of them scratching themselves, all of them with a look of basic disgust on their faces. Ronan looks at me sadly, as if to say, at least you tried, Rosser – that much has to be said, in fairness to you.

I'm like, 'Sorry, Ro,' except he doesn't, like, *answer*?

Sorcha follows Patriona all the way to her Škoda Citigo, still trying to assure her that we're not usually like this, that she shouldn't judge us on the basis of what happened here this afternoon.

But, of course, the worst hasn't even happened yet. I hear the sound of a cor approaching and straight away I know that it's yet more trouble. I've always had, like, a fifth sense for these things.

I spot Lauren's red Fiat Punto making its way up the driveway towards us and I'm too scared, too in shock, too a lot of things, to do the most sensible thing, which is run the fock away.

She pulls up in front of the house, then throws open the door of the cor with everyone still watching. She's already screaming at me before she even gets out.

'You bastard!' she's going, coming straight for me. 'You stupid focking bastard!'

Sorcha ends up having to step between us. Or maybe, being honest about it, I kind of hide behind her.

'Lauren,' Sorcha tries to go. 'Oh my God, this isn't you!'

'Get out of the way!' she goes. 'I'm going to kill him! I'm going to focking kill him!'

Sorcha's there, 'Lauren, calm down. I don't know what you think he's done, but–'

'I'll tell you what he's done,' Lauren goes. 'This afternoon he exposed himself to a seventy-five-year-old disabled man in the wheelchair-accessible toilet of our shop!' Of course, there's fock-all you can say to sweeten that pill.

Kennet and Dordeen both laugh, mainly because they realize that it's game, set, as well as match to them.

I watch Patriona just shake her head, then she gets into her cor – the focking Citigo. By the time she turns the key in the ignition, Sorcha has already turned around and is walking, sobbing uncontrollably, back to the house.

'If we lose our franchise,' Lauren turns around to me and goes, 'I will sue you for every focking cent you have.'

I go, 'Not now, Lauren. Not now.'

I follow Sorcha inside and slam the front door. She's sitting on the stairs – the third one from the bottom – with her hands over her face, crying her little hort out.

Honor is upstairs, going, 'Hillare! *Hill*-are!'

I sit down beside Sorcha and put my orm around her. After maybe a minute of silence, I go, 'She was never ours, Sorcha. Little R&B – she was never ours in the first place.'

She takes her hands away and looks at me. Her face is a mess. 'What are we going to do?' she goes.

I immediately know that she's talking about Honor.

I'm there, 'I don't know – maybe we should be thinking in terms of putting her in boarding school?'

I'm just relieved that she's blaming today's disaster on our daughter pretending to be disturbed, rather than me bringing some kind of plague into the house and taking my mickey out in front of an old-aged pensioner with one leg.

'Boarding school?' Sorcha goes. 'What good would that do?'

I'm there, 'I don't know. But at least she'd be someone else's problem.'

Sorcha shakes her head, looking just about as sad as I've ever seen her, and goes, 'I wouldn't wish her on someone else,' and she seems to really mean it. 'I wouldn't wish her on my worst enemy.'

4.

How Awful!

I'm getting serious filthies from Sorcha's old man. He is not a happy bunny with us crashing his Christmas Day. I'm sure he doesn't mind Sorcha being here. Even Honor, at a push. But I'm the last person he wants to see sitting opposite him, helping himself to seconds of everything and complimenting his wife on her macadamia and pancetta stuffing.

I'm about as welcome here as a focking skin disease, and he's making that much basically obvious.

'Does he have to eat with his hands?' he goes – he doesn't even put the question to me directly. He talks about me like I'm not even in the room?

I'm there, 'Er, it's a turkey leg? How else am I supposed to eat it?'

He actually pretty much explodes. 'With a knife and fork,' he goes. 'Like I'm bloody well doing!'

Sorcha goes, 'Dad, will you please stop picking faults in everything Ross does?'

He's there, 'I'm asking him to please refrain from eating like a Neanderthal at our dinner table.'

'Dad, you've been at him ever since we arrived. Now please, stop. Mum invited us for Christmas dinner while our dining room is being fumigated. We're either welcome here or we're not.'

We haven't really talked about it. About any of it. The house being infested. Honor's little Britney-having-a-meltdown-with-a-scissors routine. Me exposing myself – if you want to call it that – in a wheelchair toilet. But especially losing little R&B. It's, like, too painful for either of us to even go there.

Patriona rang two days after her – let's just say – memorable visit and said she considered it prudent that Shadden should continue to live with her old pair on the northside. Sorcha just went, 'Thank you very much,' and put the phone down. She told me what had been said, then went back to giving instructions to the two dudes from the pest control company.

Sorcha has to sometimes process shit before she's ready to actually deal with it? This feels very much like one of those occasions to me.

I'm looking at Honor. Toni & Guy did their best, but she's ended up with basically a focking crew-cut. Not that she cares. She got what she wanted in the end.

She has her face stuck in her phone, her little thumb working away like a coke mule with an overdraft, her dinner pretty much untouched, except for one orange-infused, bacon-wrapped chipolata, which I watched her take a bite out of, then just, like, discord?

'Come on,' Sorcha goes to her, 'eat your dinner.'

It's literally the second time I've heard Sorcha talk to her since that day.

Honor's like, 'I'm watching my figure,' and she says it in, like, a really sorky way?

'Honor,' Sorcha tries to go, 'your grandmother spent hours preparing this beautiful meal for us.'

And Honor's like, 'Okay – are you deaf or did I stutter?'

While this conversation is taking place, I should add, Sorcha's sister – Archimedes, Archaeopteryx, it could be literally anything – has kicked off one of her kitten heels and is rubbing her foot up the inside of my left leg, which is pretty much a tradition now during Lalor family gatherings.

Hearing Honor trash-talk his daughter pisses Edmund off so much, he decides to have another go at me over why we're even here, ruining his quiet Christmas.

'Six weeks they're in that house,' he goes, 'and already he has it destroyed.'

I'm tempted to remind him that it's not his house any more. But I know this isn't about the actual gaff. I know what he's thinking is that, if it's down to me, his precious daughter is probably going to end up the exact same way – not necessarily full of disease, but basically ruined.

'It wasn't Ross's fault,' Sorcha goes, for some reason determined to see the best in me. 'He bought a Christmas tree in good faith. He was given certain assurances in relation to its health and history. Sadly, those assurances proved to be false.'

He's determined to get her to see me, rather than Honor, as the villain of the whole Patriona Pratshke business. He goes, 'I don't believe for one minute that he got that tree from Blackrock College.' See, he went to school there, which is another reason he's so keen to defend the focking place. 'I could bring the thing up to Alan McGinty as soon as Christmas is over. I'm sure he could tell me immediately if it was one of theirs.'

Sorcha's like, 'You won't. Because we burned it.'

'That's convenient for you,' he goes, meaning obviously me.

'And anyway,' Sorcha goes, 'the house is hordly destroyed. It's, like, one room that has to be sprayed three times over a four-week period. Then it'll be clear.'

He goes, 'It's a pity a spray hasn't been invented yet that could do a similar job on him.'

Sorcha's old dear tries to change the subject. She turns around to Sorcha's sister and goes, 'So how's work been going, Dorling?'

It might even be Archaeopteryx. I'm serious.

The sister rolls her eyes and at the same time shakes her head. She goes, 'I can't believe you're even asking me that. Er, I had to work on Christmas Eve?'

This is in, like, Aldi we're talking. It wouldn't be many people's idea of a fun day.

'Well, lots of people have to work on Christmas Eve,' the old dear goes. 'No one has it easy any more, especially in the current environment.'

Sorcha's there, 'When I had my boutique, I worked – oh my God – every Christmas Eve. It was actually one of our busiest days of the year.'

The sister goes, 'And your point is?'

Sorcha's like, 'My point is that Mum is actually right. This is the first time you've worked since you left college. You've had – oh my God – *everything* handed to you on a plate.'

'Look who's talking. Er, the shop? Er, the house?'

'Excuse me, I worked. Everything I have in my life, I actually worked hord for.'

'Yeah, whatever.'

'Yeah, whatever is right.'

Jesus. They're some focking family.

'Could I get some more of this ham?' I suddenly go. 'It's fantastic, in fairness to you.'

Sorcha's old dear, it has to be said, has always had a bit of a soft spot for me, despite eveything.

'There's some more in the kitchen,' she goes. 'It's already cut. Help yourself.'

Which is what I end up doing. I'm actually shovelling it onto my plate, trying to decide whether to have three or four slices, when my phone all of a sudden beeps in my pocket. It ends up being a text from, like, Grainne.

It's like, 'Hey ross hope ur havin a great xmas, maybe see you soon, grainne x.'

It's hormless enough, roysh, except I'm suddenly thinking, how the fock did she even get my number?

'Who's the text from?' a voice at my shoulder suddenly goes. I end up nearly having a hort attack because at first I think it's Sorcha. It ends up being the sister, though.

I'm like, 'No one,' at the same time quickly deleting it.

She laughs. 'Oh my God,' she goes, 'you're already cheating on her.'

I'm there, 'Actually, I'm not.'

'Your wife's a bitch. I don't care if you are or not.'

'Well, I'm not. And can you possibly stop rubbing your foot up and down my leg under the table?'

'I never heard you complain before.'

'Yeah, no, I'm married to your sister now – in case you hadn't noticed.'

'You were married to my sister before. Like I said, I never heard you complain.'

'Well, these days I'm trying to make an actual go of it. That's the difference.'

She goes, 'Do you want me to pull you off?'

This is, like, totally out of nowhere.

I'm like, 'Excuse me?' wondering does she actually mean here, in her old pair's kitchen, with her mum and dad, and my wife and daughter, literally in the next room.

'Do you want me to pull you off?' she goes, making a grab for the old goody bag.

I end up having to pull away from her with a quick swerve of the hips. I've got a plate of ham in my hand, bear in mind.

'Fock's sake,' I go, 'someone could walk in.'

And that's when she laughs and just says it. 'You might be fooling Mum and Dad, you might even be fooling yourselves – but you're not fooling me.'

I'm there, 'Meaning?'

'There's nothing going on between you two. Come on, I can nearly smell the frustration. From both of you.'

'You don't know what you're talking about.'

At the same time, I'm leaning against the Samsung single-door fridge-freezer.

'She's withholding sex from you, isn't she?'

'No.'

'Until you prove that you can be faithful to her.'

'I told you – that's horseshit.'

'Yeah, no, I think I know my sister. Oh my God, you must be so backed up.'

She makes another grab for the merchandise – this time she gets her hand on it – and at the same time she storts kissing my neck. She's wearing *Classique* by Jean Paul Gaultier, which I have to admit has always done it for me. She sort of, like, guides my right hand onto her left chesticle and goes, 'If she's not doing her job, Ross, there are plenty of girls who'd be happy to do it for her.'

She's suddenly going at my neck like a bird at a feeder.

I give her puppets a good old squeeze, managing to convince myself – because they're implants – that I'm not actually cheating on Sorcha here, that what I'm doing is no worse than feeling up her mother's oven gloves or two focking jelly moulds. I'm not even kissing her, remember. After twenty or thirty seconds, I'm pretty much ready to go off, but then my conscience – yes – suddenly gets to me and I manage to somehow wrestle myself away from her.

'No,' I go.

She's like, 'No?' genuinely surprised at my ability to even say the word in a situation like this, especially with proceedings at such an advanced stage.

I'm there, 'No. Because this is what always happens. Sorcha pisses you off and you end up trying to be with me just to get back at her. Like I said, I'm determined to make a proper go of our marriage this time. And that means possibly treating Sorcha with a bit more respect.'

I walk out of the kitchen and back to the dining-room table, with my meat in my hand. My ham, just to clarify. I can nearly hear the sister seething behind me. I sit down and get stuck into my dinner again.

I can feel everyone's eyes on me. I know that Sorcha's possibly wondering did something happen between us in the kitchen. We were gone a long time? And my face is probably flushed. But I think she possibly also knows that if we're going to make this thing work, she's going to have to learn to trust again.

'Ross got a text message,' the sister all of a sudden goes. 'From someone called Grainne. Merry Christmas with a kiss at the end. He deleted it, but I managed to read a bit of it over his shoulder.'

What a wagon.

Sorcha's old man just sighs, as if his point about me has been somehow proven. Sorcha looks at me, her eyes wide, waiting for an explanation. Of course, I'm such an old hand at telling lies, I can do it without even the need to think.

'It was from Grainne Seoige,' I go, at the same time hating myself, but it has to be done. The two Seoiges were regulars in Sorcha's shop back in the day. Grainne was never out of the focking place. 'She was just wishing us both a Merry Christmas and saying how much she actually missed the shop being there this year. Dublin definitely needs something like it. She'd have texted you directly, but she accidentally deleted your number. There's nothing more to it than that.'

Sorcha smiles, relieved, then – I shit you not – goes, 'Thank you, Ross, for your honesty.'

Lauren hasn't forgiven me for, well, let's just call it the whole taking my mickey out in front of a one-legged old-aged pensioner incident. I can tell from the way she's looking at me across the floor of Kielys. She wanted to set the focking Feds on me. It was actually Christian in the end who covered for me. He hid the security tape and told the Gords that he didn't have the camera set up yet – which, by the way, earned him a formal reprimand from Footlong head office in New York.

That's why I turn around to him and go, 'Dude, I appreciate you covering for me.'

Christian's like, 'Ross, you have no idea of the shit storm you brought down on our heads. They threatened to take the franchise away from us.'

'Yeah, no,' I go, 'that's why I'm saying I owe you one.'

He's being a bit pissy with me, if I'm being honest. It's supposed to be, like, New Year's Eve.

As we're talking, I'm looking around for JP. The sneaky focker has been seeing a bird without telling his mates. Six weeks it's supposedly been going on. She's, like, American and she's called Shoshanna, if you can believe that. It's one of those names – she could be a honey or she could be a hound.

Oisinn arrives back from the bor with fresh supplies. I sink a mouthful straight away.

'Any sign of JP?' he goes, reading my mind.

I'm like, 'Not yet. I'm wondering what she's like.' Knowing JP's history with women, they're generally lookers, but they're always a bit, you know – there's salt in the shaker but no holes in the cap.

Christian goes, 'Did anyone hear from Fionn over Christmas?'

It turns out that Oisinn did.

'Yeah, he rang me on Christmas Eve,' he goes. 'He seems to be getting on great in Uganda.'

Uganda. I'm going to try to remember that name.

'I thought he would have come home for Christmas,' I go.

'He said he was too busy. They're pretty close to finishing that school they're building. Plus, I think he would have found it hard to be here.'

It's his first Christmas since Erika drop-kicked him.

He turns to me then. He's like, 'Any word from Erika?'

I'm like, 'Fock-all. Can you believe that? Didn't even ring Helen or the old man on Christmas Day.'

'She's still in Argentina, though?'

'Yeah, I'm presuming. With that tool. Fabrizio whatever the fock. No one has a number for her. And she hasn't rung in, like, months.'

'Probably scared your old man would try to talk her into coming home.'

'Probably. But, like, Christmas Day. Even just a five-minute call to her old dear. That's cold.'

'But that's Erika.'

'True that.'

All of a sudden, JP finally arrives with Shoshanna – this is at, like, quarter to midnight – and straight away we all end up having to say fair focks. She's a ringer – and I mean a ringer – for Dianna Agron, to the point where you'd nearly think it was her?

J-Town makes the intros. He's like, 'Goys, this is Shoshanna,' and we're all, 'Hey, Shoshanna, lovely to meet you,' air-kissing her and giving her very much the whole JP-has-done-pretty-well-for-himself vibe.

The birds are suddenly flocking around her like seagulls around a vomiting drunk – we're talking Sorcha, we're talking Sophie and Chloe, we're talking Claire from Brayjing.

Sorcha introduces herself while Sophie and Chloe look her up and down slowly, making sure to take in every focking detail.

'Sorry we're late,' JP goes. 'Shoshanna had two clients tonight.'

The girls are all like, 'Clients? Oh my God, what do you do, Shoshanna?'

And Shoshanna – in her American accent – goes, 'I'm a fat whisperer.'

You can imagine the faces on the four birds. Sorcha's like, 'An *actual* fat whisperer?'

She laughs. 'Yes, an actual fat whisperer. I'm fully qualified.'

I'm there, 'Okay, at the risk of sounding stupid here, I'm just going to ask – what the fock is a fat whisperer?'

'Fat whisperers,' Sorcha goes, 'are – oh my God – *huge* in the States. All the celebrities go to them. Kate Hudson has used one. And definitely one of the Kardashians.'

'Yeah, no, but what do they actually *do*?'

'Well, they're like faith-healers? Except they use their energy to persuade fat cells to leave the body.'

She looks at Shoshanna, who nods, as if to say, yeah, no, that's it pretty much in a nutshell. 'We use other methods as well,' she goes, 'like detoxifying wraps and then ultrasound waves to try to break up stubborn fat zones. But yes, it does involve talking to fat cells – but also listening! It's about discerning the emotion of individual cell membranes and discovering how amenable they are to leaving the body.'

I end up laughing in the girl's face. I can't help it. I honestly thought when the economy went tits-up that we'd put this kind of shit to bed. 'Pardon me for saying it,' I go, 'but that sounds like total focking horseshit.'

'Pardon me for saying it,' Shoshanna goes, 'but it sounds like you're very ignorant.'

I think it's obvious from that moment that me and Shoshanna are not going to hit it off.

I'm there, 'I just can't believe that people actually give you money for that shit. Maybe there's hope for this economy after all.'

Garret, who's been hanging off the edge of the conversation, sees this as his opportunity to get in a dig at me. He goes, 'Ross is ignorant, Shoshanna. See, he's never properly travelled. Which is why anything that's in any way spiritual, holistic or alternative to Western precepts, he immediately dismisses,' like that's something I'm supposed to be automatically ashamed of?

The girls all actually tut.

I'm looking at Shoshanna and I'm thinking she's not even that focking thin. Okay, she's no porker, but she could certainly do with aiming a few whispers in the direction of the layer of fat that's hanging over the top of her jeans like a focking pizza crust.

'Well,' the girl tries to go, 'I feel sorry for people who can't open up their minds to new things. I find them actually pathetic.'

I look at JP as if to say, yeah, same-old, same-old. She's a good-looking bird – nice set of bubbles on her as well – but there's a catch. And that catch, as usual, is that she's an iron short of a golf bag.

I'm suddenly the mad one, of course. All the birds are looking at me – including Lauren, by the way, who I at least thought had a brain? – like they feel pretty much sorry for me. All they know about Shoshanna is what she does for a living and suddenly they're all her new bezzy mates. Especially Claire, who only knows her, like, three minutes, but tells her that she – oh my God – so has to come to our next *Downton* night, which she's supposedly hosting at the end of January.

It's, like, five to midnight. We're only out until the year turns, then we're going to have to go and pick up Honor from my old man and Helen's. They're, like, babysitting for us.

'Okay,' Sorcha goes, 'five minutes. New Year's resolutions, everyone, for 2012.'

I'm there, 'I know I say this every year, but mine is to go back playing rugby, even at AIL level, and to possibly do something with Leinster in a coaching slash advisory capacity.'

I catch Garret rolling his eyes. He actually hates rugby.

Claire goes, 'Mine is to finally get Wheat Bray Love up and running,' and she turns to her new best mate to fill her in on the backstory. 'Garret and I have been trying to open an organic bakery for the last, like, nine months. We have a premises and everything, but the banks just will not lend.'

Shoshanna tilts her head and – in this really irritating baby voice – goes, 'Sad story!'

Chloe goes, 'Mine is to lose, like, six pounds,' and Sophie's like, 'Mine is to lose so much weight that people are actually worried about me. Do you remember that time, Chloe, when I was doing pilates, Bikram and Weight Watchers all at the same time, and your dad thought I was terminally ill?'

Lauren goes, 'Mine is . . .' and she suddenly stops and looks at Christian. He smiles and nods, as if to say, yeah, no, go on, tell them.

She's like, '. . . that our baby will be born healthy.'

I punch the air – that's how instantly delighted I am for them. I hang five in the sky for the dude and that ends up turning into a serious hug.

Shoshanna tilts her head and – in the same baby voice – goes, 'Happy story!'

I'm thinking, yeah, that's going to become focking annoying.

The next thing any of us hears is some dude on, like, a microphone giving it, 'Ten, nine, eight, seven, six . . .'

Sorcha comes over and puts her hands on my hips, facing me.

'Three, two . . .'

She goes, 'Happy New Year, Ross.'

I'm like, 'Happy New . . .' but before I've had the chance to finish my sentence, she's thrown the lips on me in a major way.

'Happy New Year!' everyone in Kielys pretty much roars.

I pull away from Sorcha and then I'm saying it – same shit, Happy New Year – to various people around me. I notice that Oisinn is missing.

I'm like, 'Where's the Big O?'

Christian goes, 'He slipped away. Just after Shoshanna arrived.'

I'm like, 'Why?'

He shrugs.

I go, 'Maybe he's got a bird on the go as well.'

I actually hope so.

'Or maybe,' Christian goes, 'he just can't deal with all this optimism.'

I'd hate to think it was that. I would genuinely hate to think it was that.

Sorcha wants to go home. Well, it's not that she wants to go home – it's that we have to collect Honor.

So ten minutes later, after we've said our goodbyes – 'It was so, so a pleasure to meet you,' she goes to Shoshanna – we're in the cor on the way to Ailesbury Road to get our daughter.

'It's lovely to see JP so happy,' she tries to go.

I laugh. I'm there, 'That's where you and I disagree. It's very much a case of back to the drawing board, JP, as far as I'm concerned.'

'Oh my God, Ross, she's so nice.'

'*Sad story! Happy story!* It won't be long before that storts to really piss him off. Hopefully. She was no fan of mine, I don't know if you noticed.'

'Well, I really liked her. I thought she was sweet.'

I bet she did. And I bet her, Chloe, Sophie and Claire from Bray of all places are already scheming to make sure they get the first free consultation out of her. That's before JP drops her like a bad habit.

Calling me ignorant. Jesus.

She pulls into Helen and the old man's driveway.

I'm there, 'It's great news about Christian and Lauren, though, isn't it? A new baby in their lives.'

And then I suddenly stop, roysh, because I feel instantly bad. The critics who say I'm an insensitive prick need to suddenly see this new me?

'I'm sorry,' I go.

She's like, 'It's fine.'

At the same time, I'm thinking, hey, it's nearly two weeks now – it's about time we maybe talked about it.

'Yeah, no,' I go, 'it's just that if things had turned out differently, we'd have a new baby in the house ourselves. In other words, Rihanna-Brogan.'

She shakes her head. 'You were right, Ross. I mean, you tried to warn me. Rihanna-Brogan was never ours. I possibly got carried away with the whole thing.'

I'm there, 'Hey, I'm not denying it was a nice dream. The five of us under the same roof – six, if you count Honor.'

'Living in that big house,' she goes, staring off into the distance, 'it just feels kind of empty, doesn't it? I mean, it's not what I expected it to be.'

I'm there, 'Are you saying you want to move back to Newtownpork Avenue?'

We were talking about possibly renting out the Blackrock gaff.

'No,' she goes, 'I'm just saying that maybe I wanted the house to feel like it did when I was growing up. But it doesn't. And maybe that's because I'm not a little girl any more.'

I nod.

She goes, 'Maybe I was looking for a way to relive my childhood vicariously through someone else. Honor doesn't appreciate things. She doesn't appreciate anything. That's just a fact we're going to have to accept. But I thought maybe Rihanna-Brogan would. That makes me sound – oh my God – incredibly selfish, I know.'

I'm there, 'Or maybe you're just clucky.'

I thought I'd just throw it out there.

She actually laughs. 'I think one child is probably more than you and I can cope with,' she goes. 'Especially when that child is Honor.'

And that's our cue to go in and get her.

The old man meets us in the hallway. I go, 'How was she?' and it says a lot about our daughter that I'm prepared to believe pretty much anything from 'She ran up a two-grand phone bill and flooded the kitchen' to 'She battered Helen to death with a wok and chopped her body up in the bath.'

As it happens, the old man goes, 'She was as good as gold,' except he whispers it to us. 'She tried to stay awake for you. Wanted to wish you a Happy New Year, don't you know! In the end, poor little thing couldn't keep her eyes open.'

Me and Sorcha end up totally confused. We both presume he's talking about Helen. Then he leads us into the living room and there's Honor, in her PJs, curled up in the old man's ormchair, sleeping soundly, with a blanket over her.

I can't imagine how much money the old man had to hand over to her tonight.

I go over to her and pick her up in my orms, She sort of, like, half wakes up and I go, 'It's okay, Honor. We're going home now.'

She puts her orms around my neck and she holds on tight while I'm saying Happy New Year, thanks and goodbye to Helen and the old man. As I'm carrying her out to the cor, I'm pretty sure I hear her go, 'I love you, Daddy,' and, even though she's basically asleep when she says it, it might well be one of the greatest feelings I've ever had in my life.

I'm in literally shock. We're at the UCD underpass before I even mention it to Sorcha.

I'm like, 'Did she say what I think she said?'

Sorcha goes, 'I think so,' but doesn't say anything else. Maybe she's jealous that it was 'I love you, Daddy' and not 'I love you, Mommy.'

Or maybe she's just sad because deep down she knows – just like I know – that tomorrow morning the real Honor will probably be back.

I'm sitting in the Bucky's upstairs in BT2 when I spot Ronan pushing the stroller through women's casuals and my face instantly lights up. I can feel it.

He's like, 'Alreet, Rosser?'

I'm there, 'Alright, Ro. There's your double-shot Americano, as per your text.'

He mustn't be getting any sleep. The first few months can be tough. I remember Sorcha saying that.

I'm like, 'So how is she?' grinning like a big focking gimp in the direction of my beautiful little granddaughter.

'Ine just arthur getting her down,' he goes, which presumably means he doesn't want to wake her again.

I'm like, 'Dude, that's cool. She's just as incredible when she's asleep.'

Ronan smiles at Honor and goes, 'Howiya, Honor?'

And Honor, who used to, like, worship the ground he walked on, goes, 'Hello!' like he's suddenly a stranger, rather than her brother.

I go, 'Is that all you're going to say? You used to give him a big hug.'

And Honor's there, 'I said hello? Hashtag – get over yourself.'

I'm like, 'Fair enough,' and I smile at Ro and throw my eyes upwards, as if to say, it's all ahead of you, kid. Which it probably isn't. If Ronan's daughter turned out anything like mine, there'd be a case to be made for sterilizing the lot of us – to end the family line and save the focking world.

'Honor,' I go, 'why don't you go and play with that little girl over there,' because there's a kid of about her age standing a few feet away, looking like she wants to be her friend. 'I want to have a word with your brother – *mano y mano*.'

'Whatevs!' she goes, shaking her head – everything's a focking problem to her – and then she wanders over to the girl. I hear her go, 'What's your name?'

The girl's like, 'Moag,' which is funny, even I have to admit.

'Oh my God,' Honor goes, 'that's a disgusting name.'

I end up having to agree with her. How do these so-called parents even come up with them? Do they just stuff a load of Scrabble letters in their mouths and spit them at the focking wall? Then whichever ones land face-up – and in that order – that's what goes on the birth cert. Focking ridiculous.

'I haven't had a chance to properly talk to you,' I go, 'since . . . you know.'

I don't think it'd achieve anything to give him a recap of the events of the day.

He's like, 'It's grant, Rosser.'

'At the same time, I want to apologize, Ro. I can't help but feel that it was in some ways my fault. We really wanted you living with us. Jesus, we still do . . .'

'Wadn't to be, Rosser.'

'I know, but . . .'

'Wadn't to be.'

I end up just nodding. If Ronan's learned to deal with it, then I'm possibly going to have to do the same thing.

'By the way,' he goes, 'the christening's next Saherdee.'

I'm there, 'Next Saturday? I'm presuming it's in . . .'

'Saint Canice's. Then back to Shadden's.'

I'm like, 'Yeah, no, I'll be there. I'll definitely be there.'

I'm half listening to my daughter talking to the famous Moag. She's going, 'Who's your favourite out of One Direction?'

Moag's there, 'Em . . .'

'Come on, you have to say someone.'

'Okay, Harry. No, Zayn. No, Harry.'

Honor breaks her hole laughing and goes, 'Oh my God, you actually know their names! That's so lame.'

'What? No.'

'You actually like One Direction? Hashtag – how even old are you?'

God forgive her, she's a little focker.

Ro goes, 'Can I say sometin to you, Rosser?'

I'm like, 'Ro, you can say any shit to me. Jesus.'

'Look, I don't want to hoort yisser feedings.'

'I'm sure you won't.'

'Ine arthur astin Buckets of Blood to be Rihanna-Brogan's godfadder.'

Buckets is his friend who used to work in, like, debt collection. The joke goes that the blood referred to was nearly always his own. The other thing about him is he's a good goy.

I'm there, 'I like Buckets.'

'You're nor offented,' he goes, 'that I dirn't ast you?'

'I'm not offended at all. I've always had a lot of time for Buckets. I couldn't think of anyone more suited . . . Actually, that's not true, so I'm not going to go there. But I have a lot of time for Buckets – I'll say it again.'

'It's just he's veddy down at the moment, Rosser. I think me becoming a fadder is arthur bringing it home to him abour he's own kids – not seeing them and that. Taught this might cheerd him up.'

'Like I said, Ro, I'm totally cool with it.'

All of a sudden, R&B storts stirring. She's awake and she's suddenly not a happy rabbit. From the whiff, I know straight away what's wrong.

I'm there, 'She needs to be changed.'

I notice a slight – I suppose – hesitation in Ro.

I'm like, 'Don't tell me you haven't changed a nappy yet.'

'Once or twice,' he goes. 'But Shadden's altwees been there.'

I stand up, laughing. 'Come on,' I go. 'I'll show you.'

I'm about to tell Honor to come with us, except Moag's old dear – you could nearly cry for the focking kid with a name like that – goes, 'Do you want me to watch your little one while you're gone?'

I'm there, 'Er, yeah, no, that'd be great,' because she seems cool.

At a stretch, you'd say she looks like Sarah McGovern – but that's at a serious stretch.

'They're playing together nicely,' she goes. I'm thinking, she obviously hasn't been listening like I have. 'It'd be a shame to break them up.'

I'm there, 'Yeah, no, cool.'

Me and Ro take R&B down to the baby-changing room and I end up showing him how it's done. I lie the little one down on the table, then I take off the old nappy, while Ronan roots through the bag for the various bits and pieces that are needed. I genuinely thought at this age I'd be teaching Ronan how to put the ball between the sticks from a nearly impossible angle. I didn't think I'd be showing him this shit.

Father Fehily used to say that life is like a grubber kick. You can follow it like an idiot, thinking you know which way it's going to go, then it'll rear up unexpectedly and totally confound you.

I'm like, 'The mopping-up operation, as I call it, is actually the worst of it. Give me one of those wipes there. And never use a Flash wipe, by the way. I made that mistake once with Honor. To this day, I think it possibly explains one or two things.'

Ronan laughs, in fairness to him.

'So,' I go, while he watches the master and learns, 'you're alright, are you?'

He nods. 'Ine grant – like I said to you.'

'And does that include alright for money? Because I could give you however much you need. Five grand? Ten grand?'

He goes, 'Thanks, Rosser. Ine alreet for money, but. Ine steerting work tomoddow.'

I'm like, 'Work? What's this all about, Ro?'

'I have to woork, Rosser – to provide!'

'Yeah, no, that's one way of looking at life. Where are you going to be working, though?'

'Wit one of Kennet's friends.'

He's still watching me – step by step.

I'm like, 'Doing?'

'Removing clamps,' he goes, 'offa keers.'

'So you're working for the actual clampers? Controversial!'

'No.'

'Okay, I don't get it, Ro. Explain it to me. Explain it to me like I'm six. Actually, consider that a general rule with me!'

He laughs. If I was a dinosaur, I'd be a Bantersaurus Rex.

'Keers that are clamped for peerking on private property,' he goes. 'You can ring this mate of Kennet's and he'll get the clamp off for you – for half of what the clamping company cheerge.'

'Ro, that doesn't sound doubly legal.'

'It's all above boward, Rosser. Once you get it off wirout doing addy damage to the clamp, you're moostard. There's a knack to it. A skill.'

I'm thinking, a skill? Jesus focking Christ. It's not the future I had in mind for him.

I'm like, 'What about school? I mean, Ro, you've got brains to literally burn.'

He goes, 'I've also got responsibidities, Rosser,' and of course there's nothing I can say to that. I even admire him for it.

I'm there, 'So that's what you're learning tomorrow, huh?'

'Locky,' he goes, 'this mate of Kennet's, he says there's veddy little to it. Says I'll pick it up in a day or two.'

I just nod, my hort basically breaking for him.

'Well,' I go, 'I can't show you how to remove a clamp, but I can show you how to change a nappy. And that's the end of lesson one.'

He goes, 'Thanks, Rosser,' and he picks up little R&B and puts her back in the stroller, literally happy in her nappy now.

We head back to Bucky's.

I'm possibly already half expecting the scene that greets us. Moag is in tears. The mother – actually, it's doing Sarah McGovern a huge disservice to say this woman is like her – is just sitting there in shock, with her hand literally just slapped across her mouth.

I don't even bother going all the way over because I don't want to know what she's said or what she's done. I just call Honor from a few feet away. I'm like, 'Come on, we're hitting the road!' and then – because it's nice to be nice – I mouth the word, 'Sorry!' to the mother.

She stares right through me, though, like she's traumatized. I've seen that look on the faces of many people who've had the pleasure of meeting my daughter.

Honor walks past us, without a care in the world, stopping only once to shout back over her shoulder at Moag, 'You're a lame bitch. And your hair is focking disgusting.'

I turn to Ronan and I'm like, 'Okay, stort walking, Ro. And just keep looking straight ahead.'

What the fock is *she* doing here?

Sorcha tells me not to make a scene – this is, like, JP's big day.

'My question still stands,' I go. 'What the fock?'

I'm trying to hide my face with my hand, but Sorcha taps the seat beside her and goes, 'This one's free, Fionnuala.'

I'm like, 'For fock's sake!'

This is, like, the Radisson St Helen's, by the way.

The old dear joins us – all smiles. She has a face that'd frighten a trawler captain.

'Fionnuala, you look amazing,' Sorcha goes, letting me down in a big-time way.

She goes, 'Well, I feel fabulous, Sorcha. I've lost seven pounds since Christmas . . .'

I'm there, 'I'd say Butler's Chocolates are letting people go.'

'And a bidding war is raging between four rival publishers for the rights to my new erotic novel.'

I'm like, 'Okay, what erotic novel?'

She's there, 'It's called *Fifty Greys in Shades*.'

Sorcha goes, 'Amazing title, Fionnuala.'

'It's not,' I go. 'It's actually shit. When did you write it?'

The old dear's there, 'I wasn't aware that your permission was required, Ross,' and then she turns around to Sorcha and goes, 'It's about an Active Retirement group from Foxrock and Cornelscourt who go on a two-week trip to Puerto Banús . . .'

'And let me guess,' I go, 'they all stort focking humping each other.'

'Yes, Ross, a number of them do experience a reawakening of their sexuality while they're there.'

'Surprise sur-focking-prise.'

'Oh my God,' Sorcha goes, 'you always have your finger so on the pulse, Fionnuala. Mummy porn is so huge right now.'

I'm there, 'That's easy for you to say – it's not your mummy who's focking writing it,' and then I turn around to the old dear and go, 'Sorry, why are you even here?'

'Well, according to JP's father,' she goes, 'the property market has almost completely bottomed out. It's the time to invest.'

He's possibly right as well. I look around me. The room is rammers. There must be, like, three hundred chairs set out and every single one of them has someone sitting on it. There must be, like, another two hundred people at least standing around at the back.

The next thing any of us hears is the sound of – thinking back to my old man's trial – a gavel banging off wood. I look up at the top of the room and there's JP and his old man, standing behind two – I'm going to say it – lecterns, maybe twenty feet aport.

A hush suddenly descends on the room.

'Ladies and gentlemen,' Mr Conroy goes, 'old friends and new, welcome to the first – and, I hope, first of many – distressed property auction to be hosted by Conroy & Son of Ballsbridge.'

There's, like, a huge round of applause. I forgot how popular JP and his old man were back in the day. Hook, Lyon and Sinker was one of the best-known names in the estate agency business.

JP goes, 'Thank you very much. A total of ninety-five lots will be up for sale today, including fifty-three commercial and forty-two residential properties . . .'

He doesn't seem nervous. I'm possibly more nervous *for* him?

'The first lot, with a reserve price of €700,000, is a street in the town of Drumshanbo in County Leitrim, comprising nine houses – all with a potential to let – and twelve shop units, which currently bring in a combined annual income of €220,000. Shall we start the bidding . . .'

I turn to Sorcha. I'm like, 'They're selling an entire focking street?'

She goes, 'I know. For less than we paid for our house in Blackrock.'

'What the fock were we at?' I go, having one of my real intellectual moments. 'I'm talking about, as a nation?'

Sorcha doesn't answer, because she all of a sudden spots someone over the other side of the room. 'Hey,' she goes, 'there's Shoshanna.'

'Don't focking wave,' I end up having to tell her. 'We might end up owning that pile of shit-bricks.'

'Sorry,' she goes. 'Oh my God, doesn't she look so proud of JP, though?'

'Yeah, she knows him, what, a wet week? I've known the dude for most of my life.'

'Oh my God, it's not a competition, Ross. Oh, by the way, I was talking to Claire.'

'Claire from Bray?'

'Can you not just call her Claire, Ross?'

'I don't think she should ever be allowed to forget where she's from. Much as she'd like to.'

'Anyway, she's having her *Downton* night next week.'

I just shake my head.

'See, this is what I mean. Why does she even have to have one? It's just because you had one. She always wants to be just as good as everyone else. Focking Bray.'

'I know you don't like the place, Ross, but we're going.'

'I'm not going.'

'You are going, Ross. We said that if we were going to try to make this marriage work, we were going to stort doing a lot more couply things.'

'Yeah, as in the flicks. As in, like, meals. I didn't think you meant hanging out in focking Dodge.'

She totally ignores me. She goes, 'Anyway, she's drawn the names out of the hat . . .'

'And let me guess who I got.'

'You got . . .'

'The focking Dowager. Maggie focking Smith.'

'Yes.'

'Rigged. They focking rigged it.'

'Ross, you can't say that.'

'I can say it. They rigged it to get me back for making them the kitchen skivs. Actually, I don't give a fock. It'll be a bit of crack. I'm just going to do it – let them see I'm not orsed. That'll piss them off even more.'

I hear JP give the gavel another whack, then go, 'Sold! For the sum of €820,000,' and there ends up being, like, a round of applause.

Next it's, like, JP's old man's go. They must be taking it in, like, turns. 'Our next lot is an attractive, three-bedroomed, semi-detached house located in a cul-de-sac in a well-established South Dublin suburb . . .'

I'm looking at the photograph up on the big screen, roysh, and I'm wondering why it looks so all of a sudden familiar.

'Well-maintained by its former owners and convenient to shops and all local transport links, it would make an ideal home for a first-time buyer with a young family or a ready-to-go investment property. The bidding will start at €207,000 . . .'

The old dear's hand immediately shoots up, and that's when I suddenly cop it. It's our old gaff. As in, the one in Sallynoggin slash Glenageary that we lived in when I was, like, a kid.

I'm like, 'That's why you're here?'

She has the focking cheek to go, 'I'm perfectly entitled to buy it if I want, Ross.'

Her hand goes up again. Another bid. Someone else obviously wants it. There must be still money in this country, if that's the case.

I'm there, 'I don't give a fock what you buy. I just don't get it. I presume you're going to, like, rent it out. Are you actually planning to live in Sallynoggin?'

'Glenageary,' she tries to go – to me!

'It's focking Sallynoggin,' I go. 'Convenient to shops, it says – yeah, the focking shops in Sallynoggin. You wouldn't even walk to Glenageary from there, it's that far. Don't shit a shitter. It's Sally-focking-noggin.'

Up goes the hand again. She's enjoying herself. You can see it in her big, stretch-morked face.

I'm there, 'I'm sorry. I just have to ask. What the fock? I mean,

I thought you hated that house. I've heard you describe it as your Beirut.'

'My Vietnam.'

'Vietnam, Beirut, whatever. You hated living there. You said the people were not only poor but poor in spirit. And didn't you threaten to pepper-spray some kid who called to the door to collect his sponsored walk money?'

'I didn't agree to sponsor him. He was trying to extort me.'

'He was eight!'

'Well, they start young out there. And *he* was from Sallynoggin.'

Her hand goes up again.

'Which brings me back to my point,' I go. 'Why would you want to own that house, if you associate it with – as you've always said – the unhappiest period of your life?'

'Sold!' I hear JP's old man go, 'to Fionnuala O'Carroll-Kelly for €232,000!'

And that's when she turns to me and – this is, like, word for word? – goes, 'I want to own it, Ross, because I want to be able to look at it every single day and be reminded just how far I've come in my life.'

It's important to be a good loser. You often hear people say that. Father Fehily used to say it was just as important to be a good winner. I know that's a bit rich coming from me, the man who used to pull up his jersey and flash his six-pack to the crowd whenever he scored a try – I used to shout, 'Count them off – they're all there!' knowing that the Muckross and Foxrock girls especially loved it – but there is such a thing as dignity in victory.

Kennet could do with learning that lesson. He hasn't stopped smiling at me since we arrived at the church – gloating basically? Sorcha can sense me getting riled because she keeps squeezing my hand and reminding me that we're in, like, God's house.

The prayers get said. Buckets of Blood and Kadden – the actual godparents – go 'I do' to seven or eight quick questions about Satan and all that shit. Then the priest pours water over R&B's head, the Tuites shout, 'Go on, ya good ting!' while the rest of us simply clap, then it's on to the next of the seven babies being christened today.

It's a bit, I don't know, cold. A bit – I think it's a word – unpersonal? I know that Sorcha's thinking the same thing as me. It's not how it would have been done in Our Lady of Perpetual Premenstrual Tension, as I call it, out in Foxrock.

'Er, can we go home now?' Honor goes. This is, like, afterwards, when we're standing around outside. 'I think I've seen enough of the Third World for one day.'

I laugh. I know I possibly shouldn't – Sorcha definitely doesn't approve – but it's like listening to Frankie Boyle or one of that crowd coming out with shit that you're already thinking but are too scared to say?

'Possibly keep your voice down,' I go to her, 'even though it's a cracking line, in fairness to you.'

Kennet emerges from the church, holding little Rihanna-Brogan in his orms. He cops me and, with a big smile, he goes, 'Ah, there ye are, Ross! Ah, it's g . . . g . . . g . . . great having her living wirrus, so it is. No heerd feedins wha'?' and then he laughs and wanders over to where Dordeen, Shadden, Dadden and Kadden are standing.

'Doatunt lerrim get to ye?' a voice behind me suddenly goes. I turn around and it's, like, Nudger, one of Ronan's many strangely grown-up friends. 'He's a doort-boord, that fedda – a fooken doorty-lookin doort-boord.'

With him is Blodwyn, formerly one of Cardiff's leading shoplifters, but now Nudger's full-time girlfriend. It was me who actually introduced them. I've been there, by the way. I've never been one to kiss and tell, but I rode her like *Frankel* the night before the Heineken Cup final last year and I doubt very much if she's experienced anything like it, before or since.

I catch Sorcha looking her up and down, checking her out, as if she thinks she might have to describe her later. Currents are always interested in exes. It's the law of the jungle.

'Sorcha,' I go, because they've never been actually introduced, 'this is Blodwyn. And Blodwyn, this is my wife, Sorcha.'

'You're his wafe?' she goes, because like I said, she's Welsh. 'You ave may condolence sazz,' and she wiggles her little finger, just to let my wife and whoever else happens to be listening know that I have a small penis. Which I don't, by the way.

She's a class act is Blod.

I spot Tina standing on her own, looking a bit down-in-the-mouth, so I wander over to her.

I'm like, 'No McGahy?'

She's been seeing Ronan's school principal for a long time. He's a complete and utter dick, but I've just about learned to get my head around the fact.

She's like, 'No.'

I laugh. 'He wouldn't even come and see your granddaughter get christened? He just keeps going down and down in my estimation.'

She's like, 'Fook off, Ross. If you moost know, we're fidished.'

She seems a bit crushed by it and I feel instantly bad.

'Well,' I go, 'if it's any consolation, he was a total focking knob. And I'm not just saying that because he banned rugby from Castlerock. So what actually happened?'

She just, like, glowers at me. 'Dat's none of yoo-er fooken business.'

I honestly don't know how I ever went there.

I'm like, 'Fair enough. I just thought, a problem shared and blah, blah, blah.'

She looks across the cor pork at Ronan and I see her mouth the words, 'Call up layhor for yisser tea!' to him.

I'm there, 'What, are you not going back to the gaff?'

She goes, 'I wouldn't go nexter nee-er that famidy for all de muddy in the wurdled,' and off she focking goes.

Hell hath no fury like a something, something, something.

I tip back over to Sorcha. 'Is Tina not going back to the house?' she goes.

I'm there, 'Yeah, no, she's got a strop on. She's also just been red-corded in a big-time way. I was the one who said it was going to end in tears. I just hoped they'd be his.'

The next thing any of us hears is the old man's voice, going, 'God, it's cold,' and I turn around and there he is with Helen, rubbing his two hands together. 'Your mother always said it, Ross. It's a good five degrees colder on this side of the city and she wasn't far wrong.'

I'm like, 'Where the fock is she, by the way?' because there was no sign of her in the church.

'Well,' he tries to go, looking at Sorcha, then at Helen, 'we all know what Fionnuala's schedule is like, don't we? Good God!'

I'm not accepting that.

I'm like, 'She has time to go to, like, property auctions. She has time to buy our old gaff in Sallynoggin.'

He goes, 'No!'

'You didn't hear?'

'No! God, she hated that bloody house! How funny! Anyway, she's also got this new book she's writing. Plus they're, em . . .' and he lowers his voice, so Honor can't hear, '. . . reshooting this movie of hers. I'm not making excuses for her. I'm just saying that she has a lot going on.'

'The only thing that woman has going on is more and more fat on her already humungous orse. She doesn't want to be a great-grandmother. She's ashamed of it. She actually focking told me that.'

Sorcha again reminds me that we're in God's house – or at least the cor pork of it – and I should show a bit of, like, decorum.

I give Ronan a bit of a nod as he straps Rihanna-Brogan into the back of Kennet's cor, then off they drive.

'Are you and Helen going back to the house?' Sorcha goes.

Helen's like, 'Sadly not. I have an appointment with my chiropractor,' because she focked up her back a couple of years ago playing tennis in Fitzwilliam.

She's an unbelievably cool person. I actually hate Erika for what she's done to her.

We hop into Sorcha's cor and we drive to the Tuites' gaff. Honor stares open-mouthed out the window, as we pass a shop van and a burned-out Gorda cor and a boarded-up methadone clinic and some people playing soccer. And then people just generally going about on bikes who are obviously up to no good. Nothing says Dublin drug dealer quite like a man in a hoodie cycling around on a BMX that's far too small for him.

Honor's going, 'Okay, I'm scared now . . . okay, I'm genuinely scared now?'

At traffic lights, I check her Twitter feed, which is something me and Sorcha have got into the habit of doing? In the church, she Tweeted, 'omg i am looking @ THE ugliest baby in the world!' I hand my phone to Sorcha and she reads it but doesn't say anything, just sighs, hands it back to me and looks sad.

The house ends up being focking rammers.

Kennet shouts at me across the kitchen. 'D . . . d . . . do you wanna a bee-er, Ross?' he goes. 'And afore ye ast, we've none of tat p . . . p . . . p . . . piss that you drink,' which he seems to think is hilarious – as do his mates, who all laugh.

He decides to, like, introduce us then?

He goes, ''Tis is Ronan's oul fedda – f . . . f . . . fooken roogby,' and he doesn't mean it in a complimentary way. 'And tis is he's wife. I just say Surrogate because it's the best way to remember,' and then he looks down at Honor and goes, 'And w . . . w . . . w . . . what are you called?'

Honor turns around and – I swear to fock – goes, 'I have no idea what you're saying and no desire to know.'

There's, like, five seconds of pure silence, when you honestly wouldn't know which way it was going to go. Then Kennet just breaks his balls laughing and so do all of his friends and Sorcha says she's going to go and find Shadden, roysh, to give her our present and get Honor out of there before the novelty of her smort mouth wears off – which can happen pretty quickly.

Kennet hands me a can of beer – Lidl's best – and introduces one of his friends to me as Ronan's new boss. He's in, I'd say, his early fifties, with dyed black hair and massive Deirdre Barlow glasses and he communicates almost entirely by winking, clicking his tongue, tapping his nose and going, 'Say nuttin!'

Kennet goes, 'Locky teddles me Roatnan's doin great w . . . w . . . woork, Ross – he's a naturiddle.'

And this Locky dude just winks at me, taps his nose and goes, 'Click, click – say nuttin!'

I suddenly realize that I need to get away from this man before I give in to the temptation to beat him to death with this can of Grafenwalder.

I wander into the living room, where I find Sorcha standing next to Shadden and Ronan and talking them through the various items in the hamper that we brought them as, like, a christening present.

She's, like, pointing through the plastic at each one in turn, going, 'That's a Johnson's Baby 2-in-1 bubble bath and wash combo. That's the L'Occitane Mom and Baby Cleansing Gel that I was telling you about, Shadden. That one there is the Green People Organic Baby Wash and Shampoo – it's, like, an eco-friendly formula of aloe vera, red clover and mandarin. Oh my God, all the midwives recommend it . . .'

While she's saying all this, Dordeen and the three or four friends she's sitting with are just staring at Sorcha, with their big focking dumb mouths open, like she's just taken a shit on the MDF coffee table. Sorcha doesn't even notice. That's one of the lovely things about her. She doesn't cop when people are judging her.

'Do you want a cigarette, Shadden?'

It's one of Dordeen's friends who says it. They're all at it, by the way, the five women – smoking like a Goodyear factory fire.

Shadden goes, 'No, I'm foyen, thanks.'

One of the other friends goes, 'You can go back on tum – sure the babby's borden now.'

Shadden goes, 'No, I've never smoked, so I haven't.'

And the looks she ends up getting. See, that'd be considered acting above your station around here.

Sorcha smiles sweetly, then continues on. 'There's three bottles of Boo Boo Baby Lotion in there – I used it on Honor,' she goes. 'Oh, and that tube there is the Kiehl's Nurturing Baby Cream in vanilla, pear and calming lavender. I thought, oh my God, they have to have the Burt's Bees Diaper Ointment, so I sent off to the States for it, because it's loaded with vitamins A, B, C, up to – I think – E?'

Shadden goes, 'Thanks, Sorcha,' proving that it's not exactly a difficult focking name to master. 'And thanks, Ross,' and she gives us both a really nice hug.

She's a terrific kid. Me and Ro end up exchanging a smile.

The same friend – I think her name's Anita – turns around to Shadden again and goes, 'Are you gonna get Rihanna-Brogan's name tattooed anywhere?'

'No,' Shadden goes, 'I don't like tattoos.'

Again, the reaction – it's like she's just handed a taxi driver a fifty for a ten yoyo fare.

This Anita one looks at Dordeen and goes, 'I don't know where you got her!'

It makes me instantly depressed. Again, I end up having to get out of the room.

I find Nudger and Blodwyn drinking cans with Buckets and another friend of Ronan's called Gull on the stairs. I'm terribly fond of these goys, can I just mention – proving that I'm actually not that much of a snob?

They're talking about, of all things, childbirth. I remember Ronan saying that Buckets was a bit emotional at the moment. He's going, 'I was there when all tree of mine entered the wurdled. No, four. No, tree.'

'Shuren turs nuttin like it,' Gull goes. I've never heard him say much, although they say he opens up when he has a few drinks. 'When eer little Kathleen was borden, I couldn't stop crying in de labour ward. Thee had to nearly ast me to leave. Thee said I was distractin de midwife. Same wit eer Robbie. In fooken bits, I was.'

'I member what you said to me,' Buckets goes, 'de day Robbie was borden. You said dat's it, feddas, Ine goin street. Ine not doin addy mower toyum – de reason bein I doatunt want to miss a midute of me kids' loyuffs.'

Nudger raises his can and goes, 'And you've been as good as your woord, Gull. Feer fooks to ye.'

They all clink cans.

Gull goes, 'It's all a header youse two,' meaning presumably Nudger and Blod.

She doesn't even go, yeah, no, it's still early days. She goes, 'What do you thenk, Noel?' which is instantly funny, because I never actually knew his real name. 'Anoth thare little you or me rennen aboat the place!'

In normal circumstances, I'd actually laugh, or go, 'That's just what the focking world needs!' except this time, roysh, I don't. Because right now I feel incredibly well disposed towards Nudger, Buckets and Gull – and even Blodwyn, the thieving Welsh she-devil. I never really approved of Ronan having actual grown-up friends, especially ones who draw their income from, like, petty criminality? But they've been like three big brothers to Ronan – always looking out for him. I owe these goys in a major way, especially for keeping him on the straight and narrow in the years before I entered his life.

'Yeah, no,' I go, 'on the subject of the whole kids-being-born thing, one of the biggest regrets of my life – aport from telling Warren Gatland that he was a fat-headed muppet who knew fock-all about rugby – is that I wasn't there when Ronan was born.'

Nudger – in fairness to him – goes, 'You're hee-er now. And you've been de best ting dat ebber happened to him – an Ine sayin dat to ye.'

I'm like, 'Keep talking to me like that, Nudger. It's all good stuff.'

'Eeben though,' Buckets goes, 'we taught you were a fooken waste of space at foorst. Do you member him foorst arrivin, Gull. Says I, what kind of a fooken plank is this fedda?'

They all think it's hilarious – which it possibly is.

I'm like, 'Thanks for that, Gull.'

'On a seerdious note,' Nudger suddenly goes, 'ye need to keep an eye on Ro. He needs you now mower than ebber.'

I'm there, 'Are you talking about . . .' and I end up not even having to say Kennet.

'He's a bad piece of woork,' Buckets of Blood goes, shaking his head. 'Shadden's a lubley girdle, doatunt get me wrong. I joost hate seein Ronan gettin heself mixed up in a famidy like dat.'

I'm there, 'We tried to get them out. Me and Sorcha. The social worker decided, for whatever reason, that they were better off here.'

'Watch out for him,' Nudger goes again.

It's at that exact point that a cheer goes up in the kitchen, then Kennet, Dadden, Eddie and Kennet's mates spill out into the hall-way – some of them carrying hammers and crowbors, I can't fail to notice – and there's, like, an air about them that says they're very much men on a mission.

I'm like, 'What the fock?'

'Mon,' Kennet goes, as he morches past us and leads the others out into next door's front gorden. 'Shadden and Roatnan are m . . . m . . . moobin into their new house t . . . t . . . today!'

I head outside with the others. In fact, pretty much everyone – including Ro, Shadden, Sorcha, Honor and all the various, what my old dear would call, wans – drifts outside when they hear the commotion.

Kennet and Dadden – and then the other men – stort prying the wooden boards off the door and the windows on the front of the house. Various neighbours shout encouragement from their gordens. Some of them are going, 'Delighrit for Shadden!' while others are just, like, clapping.

In my total innocence, I go, 'Dude, are they not supposed to wait until the Council tells them they can have it?'

'Ast me b . . . b . . . bollocks, wait,' he goes – because he's had a few at this stage. 'The bleaten Council are f . . . f . . . fooken taken forebber.'

It's, like, Eddie, of all people, who very helpfully explains the legal ins and outs of the situation to me. 'They're probly gonna give it to dem in addyway,' he goes, 'so thee myra swell be in it now.'

I'm like, 'But isn't that, like, squatting?'

'Shuren it takes de Council yee-ers to evict ye in anyhow. Once you're alretty in, de eadiest ting for dem to do is just to fordamize the arrainchmint. That way, at least they're gettin fooken rent our-rov it – stead of chasing you trew the co-erts for yee-ers.'

'Say nuttin,' is Locky's considered legal opinion on the matter.

Kennet manages to get the board off the door and there ends up being a huge cheer, from our crowd and the neighbours.

'Just boot de fooken doe-er dowin,' Dadden goes. 'Me and Eddie will pur anutter one on it – new locks, de lot.'

I look at Ro, standing there, holding little R&B, with Shadden standing beside him, the two of them looking – it has to be said – a bit in shock. What storted out as a christening has turned into a housewarming. And it's still only lunchtime.

I suddenly realize how right Nudger and the others were. Ronan is going to need me more than ever now.

Out of nowhere, Honor's voice suddenly, 'Okay, bored with the povs now! Let's get the fock out of here.'

And I think, finally, something my daughter and I actually agree on.

'We've been driving around for the last twenty minutes looking for you,' I go. 'Jesus focking Christ – Bray is one gene pool in need of a filter.'

I'm letting Garret and Claire see that it doesn't bother me that I'm wearing the same purple, ruffled, floor-length, Queen Mary dress and pillbox hat that Sorcha wore to our *Downton* porty? Yeah, no, I'm just, like, smiling through it, happy to play the handsome villain – the exact same way I dealt with the boo boys back in the day.

Me and Sorcha sit down at the table. I'm wondering what focking muck we're going to be served.

It's definitely a smaller crowd than we had. I recognize Sophie as, I think, Lady Rosamund Painswick – it focking shames me how much I know about that show – and Chloe as Thomas Barrow. Amie with an ie is definitely Miss O'Brien. And Shoshanna, of course, got a seriously handy draw – she's, like, Lady Mary. This was so focking rigged, roysh, because Garret is obviously Robert, the Earl of Grantham, and Claire – I just focking hate Bray – is Cora, the actual Countess. Sorcha, by the way, is Lady Sybil, who just so happens to be Sorcha's favourite character. Then various other Bray friends of Claire's who I don't give a fock about – Les Misérables, as I call them – are various other characters from the show.

There's no sign of the goys, by the way – we're talking Oisinn, we're talking JP, we're talking Christian.

I turn to Shoshanna and I go, 'Where's himself?'

She's there, 'Oh, he's out tonight.'

I'm like, 'Out? Out where? He was supposedly coming here. I spoke to him an hour ago.'

She has the actual balls to laugh. 'He was never coming here,' she goes. 'He's out with Oisinn and Christian tonight.'

I don't believe it. They've focking stitched me up in a major way. Oisinn was supposed to be Lady Edith. JP was supposed to be Ethel Porks. I can nearly see the three of them in Kielys right now, cracking their holes laughing.

Again, I don't let them see that I'm bothered. I just go, 'So what's for dinner? I'd nearly eat a focking baby, I'm that hungry.'

Claire turns to Sorcha – she's always looking for her approval. 'We phoned out for an Indian. We went ahead – I hope you don't mind – and just ordered a load of different dishes. There's a really good Bombay Pantry out here.'

Sorcha says that's cool – which it focking isn't, by the way. At least we went to the trouble and expense of hiring actual caterers. Her and Garret just phoned out. They're a focking disgrace, even to this town.

Again, though, I just stay calm.

There's a ring at the door. Claire goes out to answer it and it ends up being Lauren, full of apologies, roysh, firstly for being late and secondly for the fact that she's ended up having to bring Ross Junior with her. She's, like, carrying him and his little eyes are closed.

'I hope you don't mind,' she goes to Claire – this is in front of everyone. 'The babysitter let me down at the last minute. I was going to cancel, except I've been looking forward to it all week. He's very tired. He'll just sleep.'

'It's fine,' Claire goes. 'Put him upstairs. The bed is made in the box room.'

I laugh. I can't believe I even know people with a box room. I suppose that's another way in which the whole economic downturn thing has affected me.

Ross Junior suddenly opens his eyes and cops me sitting there – dressed as the focking Dowager Countess, don't forget.

He goes, 'Hi, Roth! I like your dreth.'

Oh, for fock's sake.

Everyone laughs, then goes, 'Aaawww!' thinking it's so funny but at the same time – oh my God – *so* a cute thing to say.

I'm like, 'Er, thanks, yeah,' because you have to answer the kid – that's the rule with Lauren. 'It was originally Sorcha's.'

Then he – for no reason – goes, 'My mawmy hath three makthi dretheth. A blue one and a yellow one and a reth one. And they go really nithe with her wedgeth.'

Lauren just stares at me.

I'm like, 'Three maxi dresses – yeah, no, I'm saying that's great. It's good. It's all good like Gielgud.'

Lauren goes, 'Okay, say goodnight to everybody,' and Ross Junior ends up doing exactly that.

He's like, 'Nighth, everyone. Nighth, Roth!' waving at us, as Lauren carries him off upstairs in search of this famous box room.

I reach for the wine – the Bordeaux that cost us nearly forty snots in Mitchell's rather than the four-euro Château Shithole that they're serving – and I give Sorcha a look that says, basically, will you drive us home tonight, because if I'm going to get through this night, I need to get messed up. She gives me a little nod yes, then I pour myself pretty much half the bottle. It's going to be a long night.

'So, Shoshanna,' Claire suddenly goes, just as Lauren comes back to the table, 'how's work going? Garret and I couldn't stop talking about you after we met you the last day. Your job sounds – oh my God – *so* interesting.'

Can I just ask a question? What the fock is Shoshanna even doing here – especially when JP's not? She's only met this crowd, what, once or twice? See, that's Americans for you – over-focking-familiar.

Garret goes, 'I actually got really into the whole area of natural healing when I travelled around Thailand. I read a lot of books about it.'

He's such a focking dick.

'Well, a lot of these techniques,' Shoshanna goes, 'are ancient practices – they go back entire millennia. They're far older than our own so-called medicine,' and she makes those little – I think they're called, like, inverted commas – with her fingers when she says the word medicine.

He goes, 'I met this girl from Kilcoole when I was in, like, Ko Tarutao – which is nice, even though it's bit touristy – and she had her psoriasis cured, literally cured, by this local healer using a paste made from papaya and cardamom and one or two other things and then just heat energy from the healer's fingertips.'

'Happy story!' Shoshanna goes. I pour myself another glass of wine. I'm focking lorrying it into me. 'See, we in the West, we think we're so superior with our – again – medicine, when a lot of the pharmaceuticals that we pay, by the way, way over the odds for over the counter are actually just facsimiles of natural remedies they've been using in the Far East since, like, forever.'

What the fock is JP doing with this girl? She must have four tits or something.

'So,' Chloe goes, 'can I just ask – did you say you just, like, command the fat to leave the body?'

Shoshanna goes, 'That's essentially it. I mean, I do recommend that my patients complement the treatment that I give them with a good diet and exercise regime. It tends to maximize the benefits . . . I can see this guy smirking at me across the table again.'

This goy happens to be me.

'I'm sorry,' I go, 'but how do you know it's not the diet and exercise that's making them lose the weight? I mean, I could say, I don't know, painting your body in creosote and picking your nose and eating it five times a day is great for losing weight when done in conjunction with a good diet and exercise regime. I mean, it's no more ridiculous than what you're telling people. Talking to their focking fat! Are we not, I don't know, cleverer than that – as people?'

She has no comeback to that, except to go, 'Well, if you must know, there is an actual science behind it. Every cell in our bodies, including our fat cells, has an electron cloud surrounding the cell membrane that is believed to affect our consciousness. It responds to outside stimuli – and that includes verbal.'

'I still say you're talking out of your orse.'

'Well, I'm convinced,' Sorcha goes, letting me down in a big-time way.

Chloe goes, 'Shoshanna, I was going to ask you, would it be possible to get a consultation with you?'

Claire isn't happy, of course, with Chloe trying to get in there first. She's like, 'I was actually going to ask her first.'

Shoshanna laughs. 'It's not a problem,' she goes. 'I can see all of you. Just ring me and we'll make an appointment,' and then she looks at me as if to say, yeah, who's talking out of their orse now?

There's suddenly a ring on the door.

'That'll be the food,' Garret goes, then he heads out to get it. When he comes back, he puts the four bags on the table, then goes, 'Ross, one of the neighbours wants to know can you move your car – you're blocking their driveway.'

I stand up.

Sorcha's like, 'Ross, you're not getting behind that wheel. Oh my God, you've drunk, like, the guts of a bottle of wine.'

Garret turns around to Sorcha and goes, 'Do you want me to move it?'

I'm like, 'He's not driving the Lambo.'

Except Sorcha just hands him the keys and goes, 'Thank you, Garret – that's very kind of you.'

I'm there, 'If there ends up being a scratch on that cor . . .'

We all mill into the food, which is incredible, by the way. Everyone says it.

Claire goes, 'There's actually some really, really nice restaurants out here.' See, that's the thing about people from Bray – they're always on the defensive. 'Bray actually has a lot more going for it than it used to.'

There's, like, ten seconds of silence while everyone tries to think of something.

'Oh my God,' Claire goes, quickly changing the subject, 'I thought this was supposed to be, like, a *Downton Abbey* theme night. We haven't talked about the show once. Okay, everyone – favourite lines . . .'

Amie with an ie goes, 'Why must every day involve a fight with an American?'

Everyone laughs. I don't know why. All she's done is remembered a line – she didn't focking write it.

Sorcha goes, 'I've never been called a liberal in my life and I don't intend to start now!'

Sophie's there, 'Who was that?'

Sorcha's like, 'Carson.'

Lauren goes, 'Oh my dears! Is it really true? Last night he looked so well! Of course it would happen to a foreigner. No Englishman would dream of dying in someone else's house – especially someone they didn't know!'

There's, like, more laughter. This ends up continuing – I'm not shitting you – right the way through the meal. Quote after focking quote. And you can imagine me. I'm sitting there in a focking dress – seriously out of my gourd – listening to this shit and thinking, actually for the first time since me and Sorcha got back together, is this it? Is this what married life is like? Because if it is, I'm not sure I'm going to last the pace.

One of Claire's Bray friends – I call all random girls I don't know either 'Fionnuala Hoolahan' or 'Orlaith Hanahoe', mainly because I love saying those names – she goes, 'Don't be defeatist, my dear – it's terribly middle class!'

That gets an actual round of applause. And I'm at the point where I'm actually losing the will to live when all of a sudden the door opens and in walks Ross Junior, in his little pyjamas, going, 'Mawmy – whath thith?'

There's, like, a collective gasp from everyone around the table. Little Ross is waving around – I swear to fock – an actual vibrator.

I'm presuming it's Claire's, because she puts her hand over her mouth and goes, 'Oh! My God!'

No one else knows what to say. Except Lauren. She's like, 'Ross, where did you get that?'

He goes, 'I wath looking at Claireth clothe. She hath loth of jeanth, mawmy.'

Claire's like, 'Oh my God – I am *so* embarrassed!'

Lauren hasn't even taken the thing off him yet, by the way. He's still, like, studying it, with a puzzled look on his little face. He goes, 'Ith it for curling your hair?'

It's only then, roysh, that Lauren snatches it out of his hand. She turns to Claire and she goes, 'I'm so sorry, Claire.'

I'm a bit mashed, bear in mind. I've put away the best port of two bottles of wine. And I go, 'You should be focking sorry. Jesus.'

Lauren – who, remember, isn't exactly my number one fan at the moment – goes, 'Excuse me?'

I'm like, 'Look, I've never been afraid to call it, Lauren. You know that. And I just think it's wrong – him poking around in women's wardrobes. Jesus, he's supposed to be a boy. Why's he even interested in women's clothes? It's not only wrong, Lauren, it's actually a bit focked up.'

I know it's a bit rich, given that I'm dressed as a focking dowager, but my basic point still stands. It's not right.

Lauren goes, 'Oh my God, Ross, you are *such* an arsehole.'

I'm there, 'Hey, you're pregnant, your hormones are doing all sorts of crazy shit and I'm trying to make allowances for you here.'

Sorcha suddenly stands up. 'Okay,' she goes, 'I think it's time we were going?'

Lauren's like, 'Sorcha, get him out of here before I do something I regret.'

I'm there, 'I've been saying it for ages, Lauren, but you didn't want to listen. And I've finally been proved right tonight.'

Sorcha goes, 'I'm so sorry, everyone. Ross, let's go.'

It's, like, mad the way I'm suddenly the villain in all of this? I'm not the one who was waving a focking dildo around at the dinner table, yet I'm the one who's being made to feel like I'm in the wrong.

'I'm supposedly his godfather,' I go, walking out of the room with as much dignity as my mid-heel, pointed brogues allow me. 'I think that entitles me to my views.'

Sixty seconds later, I'm saying pretty much the same thing to Sorcha in the cor. I'm there, 'If Lauren didn't want my analysis, then she shouldn't have asked me to be his godfather.'

We're on the old Herbert Road when I mention this, and we're just coming up to the junction with Bray actual Main Street when the cor comes to a sudden halt. At first, roysh, I think Sorcha is about to put me out – because I've possibly been a bit of a dick – and tell me to make my own way home.

It's only when she goes, 'What the fock?' that I realize that something is wrong with the actual cor? She keeps turning the key and going, 'Ross, it won't stort! Oh my God, it won't stort!'

I tell her to calm the fock down, then I check the dash to see what's wrong. The petrol gauge says the tank is empty.

'How the fock could we have no petrol?' I go. 'I put a hundred yoyos into it yesterday,' and then I stop, roysh, because it all of a sudden dawns on me. 'Focking Garret!'

Sorcha's like, 'What?'

'He drained the focking tank. He said he was moving the cor, but he drained the focking fuel out of it.'

'How would he do that, Ross?'

'He'd have sucked it out using a tube. He's from Bray, isn't he? They learn that before they can read.'

'He's actually from Greystones.'

'Yeah, no, I wasn't aware there was a difference?'

She ends up just shrugging her shoulders. She's like, 'But *why* would he have done it, Ross?'

I'm there, 'Why do you think? To get me back for rigging the draw the last time.'

'Oh my God, are you saying you did rig the draw?'

'Of course I rigged the draw. And this is his revenge. Leaving me stranded in the middle of Bray dressed up as the Dowager Whatever the Fock.'

I'm suddenly sobering up fast.

She goes, 'Well, what are we going to do?'

I'm like, 'Let's just ring the AA.'

'And say what – we've run out of petrol and we're in 1920s fancy dress?'

'Why not? We're covered for that, aren't we?'

'I don't know. Hang on, are we even in the AA?'

'Shit. Now that you say it . . .'

I always forget that it's something you have to actually *join*?

'Oh my God!' she goes, the panic rising in her voice. 'Oh! My God! Oh! My God!'

I'm there, 'Come on, let's not lose it. Let's just come up with a game plan. Which means obviously thinking tactically. Where's the nearest petrol station?'

'There's a Topaz!' she goes. 'On the way into Bray! You know the one?'

'Yeah, no, I do know it.'

'It's definitely a twenty-four-hour one.'

'Great.'

'And it's, like, less than a mile away.'

'Yeah, no,' I go, 'that's not far at all . . . Off you go, so.'

Sorcha's there, 'Excuse me?'

'Babes, I can't walk through Bray dressed like this. I'd be murdered.' It's, like, quarter to midnight and the pubs will be emptying out.

She goes, 'Well, *I* can't walk through Bray like this either.'

I'm there, 'You're at least dressed as a woman,' because I think I mentioned that she came as, like, Lady Sybil. She actually looks well. 'You're just a woman in a very nice frock.'

'You would make me walk through Bray, on my own, at night?'

'I'm trying to think what's the safest option, Sorcha, and at the moment that sounds like it's very much it.'

And that's when she says it, totally out of the blue. 'Maybe I'll ring my dad.'

I'm like, 'Excuse me?'

'I think I'll ring my dad and ask him to come out and get us.'

And she says it like it's a threat. I can just see him now, arriving on the scene with a can of unleaded – the hero of the hour – looking at me in my dress and mentioning to Sorcha yet again what a useless fock she ended up marrying.

I'm there, 'Okay. Okay, I'll go.'

Women know what buttons to press, don't they?

I get out of the cor, shitting bricks, I don't mind telling you. I tell

Sorcha to lock the doors and she asks me to get her a packet of salt and vinegar Hunky Dorys. Then she changes her mind to buffalo and a Double Decker.

I set off in the direction of the Topaz. The dress is floor-length, I think I might have mentioned, and I end up having to lift the hem as I walk, to stop myself standing on it and snotting myself. And of course that ends up drawing a fair bit of attention. That and the stubble – I haven't bothered my orse shaving for a day or two.

I pass whatever that chipper is called opposite the Royal, and that's actually when it storts. I literally haven't walked, like, a hundred yords when I hear the first wolf whistle. It comes from some drunk dude counting his change outside, obviously trying to decide between a bag of chips and the bus home. He's not happy to leave it at that either. He sticks his head into the actual chipper and goes, 'Here, lads, look at the state of this fedda!' and ten or fifteen of them pile outside, with their burgers and their chips, and stort shouting after me, some of them that I'm a fooken pervert who should be locked up and some of them that they'd like to rip the dress off me and ride me.

I've never said a word about Bray that wasn't a hundred percent justified.

I just put my head down and keep walking – the shoes are already focking killing me, by the way – over the Dorgle and towards Super-quinn, keeping the skirt pulled up to just above my ankles, trying not to make eye contact with anyone. I'm actually shitting biscuits.

'Jaysus, Boy George hasn't aged well!' some focking smort orse shouts from the other side of the road.

I don't even look at him. Wouldn't give him the satisfaction. But I'm thinking, Garret and Claire are going to pay for this – and they're going to pay in a major way.

A dog storts to follow me. I'm not making this up. A focking dog. A little Jack Russell who seems to have taken a shine to me.

At the same time, two dudes standing at the bus stop opposite the Mitsubishi centre stort having this, like, debate about the differ-ence between a transvestite and transsexual, which they then try to involve me in? 'Do you still have a mickey?' is the way the actual question is phrased.

On I walk, still trying to keep the hem off the ground, which is sore on the old orms.

I'm passing the – focking hilarious – tackle shop when a cor all of a sudden pulls up beside me. I don't even want to look to see who's in it. But then I do and it ends up being this, like, elderly couple – maybe in their seventies. He's driving and she's in the passenger seat. It turns out that they're, like, kind people.

She goes, 'Do you want a lift?' and I nod, very focking eagerly, I don't need to tell you. She smiles at me. She's like, 'Get in.'

'You shouldn't be out walking on your own,' he goes. 'A woman of your age.'

As I'm opening the rear passenger door, I just happen go, 'You're an actual lifesaver,' and that's when the atmosphere in the cor suddenly changes.

She lets out – not exactly a scream – but a kind of, like, yelp? Then he goes, 'It's a man, Maureen! It's a bloody man!'

I'm there, 'Yeah, no, I'm on the way home from a fancy dress . . .' But I don't get to even finish my sentence.

'You dirty old man!' she goes. 'You filthy, dirty old man!' and off they speed, threatening me with the Gords, the rear door flapping open and closed like a fish's gill.

I take a breath and face into the last hill before the Topaz.

'Mrs fooken Doubtfire!' a woman, who's so mullered she's barely capable of standing, shouts at me from, like, twenty yords up ahead. I decide to cross the road to avoid both her and the dude she's with – her husband slash boyfriend, whose eyes light up when he sees me. There's, like, a fair bit of traffic on the road, though, and it ends up being a few seconds before there's a break in it, by which time the dude – also pissed – has hit me the most incredible slap on the orse and shouted, 'Get up, ya good thing!'

It stings like fock. Now I've got a sore orse and sore feet. But I finally reach the safety of the petrol station.

The focking Jack Russell is still with me, if you can believe that.

The door is locked, so I end up having to go to the little hatch. The dude has a big grin on his face as he's serving me.

I'm there, 'I'm looking for some petrol. To go. Do you have anything to put it in?'

He tells me there's, like, plastic petrol cans at my feet. I look down and there is. He's like, 'Much do you want?'

I'm there, 'A tenner's worth.'

He goes, 'Pay in advance,' and he's dying to say something funny – I can see it. I pay him and he tells me pump four, again with the big smirk on his face.

I go, 'Dude, I've just walked from the focking Herbert Road. I've been called every possible name. Boy George. Mrs Doubtfire. Eddie focking Izzard,' which I forgot to mention. I pick up a can and stort walking across the forecourt to get my petrol. 'Believe me,' I shout back at him, 'there's nothing new or original you could hit me with.'

'Shirley Temple Bar,' he suddenly goes, into the microphone, for the benefit of the three or four other people filling up their cors, 'I said pump four, not pump three.'

Actually, that was new and original. I even think to myself, fair focks, as I fill up the can with ten yoyos worth of unleaded, then hoick up my skirt and face into the waking nightmare of walking back to the cor.

5.

How Ghastly!

Why am I here?

That's the big question I'd like answered. Except the two of them are too lost in conversation to even notice me arriving.

'So what do you think of your friend and mine – Mister Enda Kenny?' the old man's going – this is in, like, The Gables at one o'clock on a Thursday afternoon, by the way – 'Telling the ladies and gentlemen of the World Economic Forum, no less, that we all went mad borrowing. He's changed his bloody well tune, hasn't he, Fionnuala? What happened to, "You're not responsible for this crisis"? Quote-unquote, indeed!'

I pull out my chair and, at the same time, I go, 'Who is Enda Kenny again?' because the name seems definitely familiar.

That at least gets *his* attention? He ends up just chuckling to himself, as I sit down. 'I love that, Ross,' he goes. 'A wry commentary on the futility of trying to stop, by democratic means, the inexorable drive towards a United States of Europe, with Berlin as its beating heart! Political satire, how are you!'

'Yes,' the old dear goes, returning to her menu. 'It's like having lunch with Jonathan Swift, isn't it?'

If that's meant to be a sly dig at me, it's totally backfired on her, because I haven't a focking clue who Jonathan Swift is either.

'What the fock is this about anyway?' I go. 'Why are we suddenly playing happy families?'

The old dear's like, 'Can't you just enjoy a nice lunch with your mother and father without thinking there's some ghastly ulterior motive?'

'Your mother's right, Kicker!' the old man goes. 'We don't do this half enough!'

I don't know why, but it seriously pisses me off that my old pair stayed friends after they broke up. What's so wrong with hating your ex-husband or wife's guts? They just can't act like normal people, even for five minutes. All of a sudden a waitress appears with a bottle of Taittinger NV Brut Réserve and three glasses, and that's when the old dear realizes that she has some serious explaining to do.

'Okay, as it happens,' she goes, 'your father and I do have some news.'

I'm there, 'Continue – I'm all focking ears.'

He goes, 'As and from this morning, Ross, your mother and I are – what's this expression young people use? – *free* agents?'

The old dear's like, 'Our divorce has come through!'

The waitress finishes pouring, then tells us to enjoy it.

I'm there, 'And that's a cause for celebration, is it?'

'Of course,' the old dear goes. 'Your father and I have managed to go our separate ways without bitterness or rancour. We're still terribly fond of each other. We can meet like this and laugh and reminisce about times past. That's something worth celebrating, don't you think?'

'Whatever.'

'And, as your father said, we're both free now to get on with our lives. Charles is with Helen. And who knows, maybe some day . . .'

'Don't say you're going to meet someone.'

'It might happen, Ross. And if it does, you'll just have to like it.'

'It won't happen. Look in the mirror. You're bet-down.'

The old man raises his glass. He goes, 'Shall we have a toast then?'

They can do it if they want. I'm not getting involved.

He goes, 'To you, Fionnuala. You were a wonderful wife. And you're an equally wonderful ex-wife. And I love you very dearly.'

She's there, 'Likewise, Charles.'

I feel like nearly spewing my focking ring up all over the table.

'Speaking of times past,' he goes after they've both had a sip, 'and if you'll pardon the French, Ross here tells me you've bought yourself a little *pied-à-terre*!'

'That's right!'

'Good Lord! I *was* rather under the impression that you hated that house!'

'I did. I mean, I still do. But I figured, what better way of breaking the horrible spell that it cast over that particular part of my life than actually *owning* the thing? That way, I can walk around it any time I like and remind myself just how far I've come.'

'Do you remember the day we moved in, Fionnuala? Ross, you weren't even born.'

'I'd never been in a housing estate before.'

'You said to me – do you remember, Darling? – you said, "Are you telling me there are going to be people . . . living in all these other houses?" '

'Well, it was like Kowloon, Charles!'

'I remember *Strumpet City* was on television at that time. I think you compared it to that!'

They both have a good chuckle at that, whatever the fock it even means.

'Oh,' she goes, 'you and Helen *are* coming to my book launch, aren't you?' and it's suddenly like *I'm* not even *at* the table?

'So-called book,' I go. 'It'll hopefully sink without trace.'

The old man's there, 'Oh, we'll be there – don't you worry about that! Supporting your newest masterpiece!'

The old dear's like, 'Oh and Paris! When are you going to Paris?'

'We fly out tonight,' he goes. 'We're staying at the wonderful George V. The match on Saturday, of course. Can Ireland overcome the disappointment of defeat to Wales last weekend? I know you'll have a view on that, Ross. And is Declan Kidney the man to take us to the next World Cup?'

The old dear's face suddenly lights up. She's there, 'Oh my God, you're going to propose, aren't you?'

The old man just blushes.

I suppose when you spend twenty-something years of your miserable life with someone, that's how well you get to know them.

'Oh, Charles!' the old dear goes.

'Well,' he goes, 'I wasn't one hundred percent sure what the – inverted commas – protocol was in these situations. But you *are* my first wife – as well as the mother of my son and heir – and it would have been rather rude, I think, to let you just read about it in the announcements section of the *Irish Times*.'

'You mean you *are* going to propose?'

'There's not a lot gets past you, Fionnuala! Yes, I intend to ask Helen to become the second, and hopefully last, Mrs Charles O'Carroll-Kelly!'

The old dear goes, 'I have a feeling that one bottle of bubbles isn't going to be enough.'

I suddenly stand up.

The old dear's like, 'Where are you going?' and it's a relief to find out that I'm not suddenly invisible.

I'm like, 'I'm going home.'

'But you haven't even ordered anything. And you haven't touched your Champagne.'

I don't say anything to her. I just turn around to *him* and go, 'Enjoy Paris. I hope you get the result you want,' and then I tip outside.

I end up just sitting in the cor for, like, fifteen, maybe twenty minutes, watching them through the window of The Gables, laughing and reminiscing about shit – the best of focking friends.

I don't know *why* it pisses me off like it does? I know loads of people whose old pairs are divorced. I mean, this is South Dublin we're talking about. Half the kids in Castlerock had rents who lived, like, separately. It's nothing new. It's just *their* old men and old dears cared enough about each other to focking despise each other when it was over.

Where's the sadness in *my* old pair? Where's the regret? How can they just walk away from the wreckage without an actual scratch?

My phone all of a sudden rings. It ends up being Sorcha. 'Oh my God,' is her opening line, 'your daughter was being *such* a little cow to me this morning.'

I'm like, 'Honor?'

'In the cor on the way to school. She wants me to buy her this vintage beaded devoré velvet coat that she saw in a magazine. Twenties speakeasy style is in this year, even for young people. I told her that rewards had to be earned – and she certainly hasn't earned anything with her behaviour recently. She literally yawned in my face, Ross, and said, "Oh my God, you're so boring, I don't think I'm going to be able to stay awake until the end of this sentence." '

'Jesus,' I go. 'That's bad.'

She's there, 'So what's going on? Why did Charles and Fionnuala want to meet you?'

I'm like, 'Their divorce is official from today. They're basically celebrating.'

There's, like, silence on the other end of the phone.

She goes, 'Ross, are you crying?'

I'm there, 'No . . . maybe . . . a little bit.'

'Come home. We'll go for a nice long walk.'

That might be just what I need.

'On Killiney Beach,' she goes.

I'm like, 'Yeah, no, that sounds great.'

Ronan looks at me like I've just used his Bohemians shirt to wipe shit off my alloys. All I said was, 'What's that thing called?'

He goes, 'It's called a jack, Rosser. Have you reedy nebber seen a jack befower?'

I end up shaking my head, just being honest with the kid. He's in genuine shock.

He's there, 'Have you nebber eeben changed a toyer?'

'Again,' I go, 'I'd love to say yes, Ro, but I'm going to have to say no.'

He just shakes his head and laughs. I even laugh. We were born on different sides of life. Deal with it.

So he takes this, like, jack thing and he puts it under this Nissan Almera and he twists this little handle on it and he uses it to literally *jack* up the cor. It's mad the way you can sometimes discover, like, the *origin* of words? In other words, how they actually came about.

There's a dude standing a few feet away, wearing a pair of those Harry Potter glasses that look focking ridiculous on a man of his age. He goes, 'How long is this going to take?'

I mean, *he's* the one who porked on a double yellow line in the first place. I feel like going, 'Yeah, you're getting your clamp removed for thirty snots. If you're not happy, why don't you ring the company that put it on? See what they chorge you – you focking Hogwarts prick.'

Except Ro gets in before me. 'Ten minutes,' he goes. 'Gardenteed, else it's done for free.'

He has a definite way with people. That's another way in which we're different.

This is all happening, by the way, in a little estate of houses off, like, Stradbrook Road. Locky – fock it, I'm just going to call him Say Nuttin – is sitting with a big Polish dude called Marek in a van with 'Clamp Release – €30' on the side, letting Ro do all the work, I can't help but notice.

Still, it's fascinating to just watch him. It's only his third week on the job and already he can do, like, four or five of these an hour.

He uses a thing called a brace to loosen the nuts, then he lifts off the tyre, with the clamp still attached to it.

'How's Rihanna-Brogan?' I go.

He's like, 'She's grant. Still not sleeping, but. She does have teddible coddic.'

'Colic? Honor had that when she was a baby. It's an absolute mare.'

'Me and Shadden are taking it in turdens – you know, to gerrup in the night.'

'Fair focks. You must be wrecked, though, are you?'

'Ah, I'll gerra kip in the vadden in the arthur noon – that's if it's quiet.'

I'm there, 'How's your old dear? How's she coping with the whole being-a-grandmother thing?'

He just shrugs. 'I don't know. Habn't seen much of her since the christenin.'

'You possibly should make more an effort with her, Ro. She's obviously struggling with the whole thing.'

The dude who owns the Almera has the actual balls to look at his watch, then sigh. Ten minutes, he was told. It'll take a wizard of Harry Potter's ability to pull his glasses out of his focking hole if he does that again.

'Won't be long,' Ro just goes.

Like I said, he's able to take shit from people.

I'm there, 'So how's the new gaff.'

'It's grant,' he goes. 'Settled in alreet. The Council is gonna give us the keys on Toorsday.'

Meaning the keys to a door that the Tuites already kicked down nearly a month ago.

I'm there, 'I don't think you're going to need them any more!'

'Well,' he goes, 'they're gonna give us the rent buke in addyhow. Then it's just a mathor of getting all the utter bits and pieces we need. We're arthur getting a cuker, a farridge and a washen machine. And a bed and table and cheers.'

Using a thing that's *like* an Allen key, he loosens something on the underside of the clamp, then there's, like, a crash of metal, as the thing, with the chain still attached, falls onto the road.

I'm there, 'Dude, let me give you some money. Seriously. Wait here. I'll go and get you ten grand.'

He moves the clamp out of the way with his foot, then puts the wheel back in place.

'Rosser,' he goes. 'Ine foyen. Ine looken arthur things meself.'

'Are you sure?'

'Ine shewer.'

I decide not to force the issue. His pride won't let him take his old man's charity – yet another way in which we're different.

I watch him replace the nuts, then tighten them using the brace, then let down the famous jack. It didn't even take him ten minutes by my estimation. It was more like seven. The boy wizard hands him the thirty yoyos and doesn't even say thanks.

That's when we hear the sudden screech of tyres. This white van – a different white van – comes out of literally nowhere and porks diagonally in front of the Almera, blocking it in.

On the side of this van, it says 'South Dublin Clamping' and then underneath – this is taking the major piss – it's like 'Ensuring Sensible Parking since 2005'. A dude in blue overalls gets out.

'Don't you fucking move,' he roars at Ronan. 'You're about to be fucking arrested.'

He is not a happy clamper.

I automatically step in front of my son, ready to protect him in case it turns violent. It turns out, roysh, that there's no actual need. Marek and Say Nuttin get out of the other van. Marek, can I just say, is the biggest human being I've ever laid eyes on. He's built like a cor ferry and he's got biceps like focking bowling balls. He could eat Cian Healy's dinner and Cian Healy would have to just sit there and like it.

They walk over to where we're standing. Say Nuttin says nothing – he doesn't even say, 'Say Nuttin!' because it's Marek who does all of the actual talking.

'What is problem?' he goes, because – like I said – he's from Poland.

The dude goes, 'You're taking the fucking piss, that's the problem. And I'm calling the Guards,' and he shouts to another dude, who stayed in the van, to ring the Feds.

'Guards will do nothing,' Marek goes. 'Is not illegal to remove clamp.'

'Yes it fucking is,' the dude tries to go. 'It's private fucking property.'

Marek's like, 'So is car. Guards will tell you is not criminal matter unless there is damage to clamp. Is there damage to clamp?'

The dude picks it up, roysh, and storts suddenly inspecting the thing, including the chain, trying to find something. There won't *be* anything, though. Ronan's a perfectionist in everything he does.

The dude doesn't say a word, so Marek answers for him.

'No,' he goes, 'there is no damage to clamp. So Guards will tell you what I tell you – which is fuck off, okay? Now move your fucking van out of way or I will fucking turn it over with your fucking friend in it.'

He would as well. He's definitely big enough.

The dude looks at Harry focking Potter then. 'This estate is private property,' he tries to go – which is weak, it has to be said. 'You shouldn't be parking here.'

Harry Potter goes, 'But there are no visitor parking spaces. And I had to call into my sister's house to drop off a prescription she asked me to get for her. She's terminally ill.'

'You still shouldn't be parking here.'

Marek isn't going to listen to any more shit. When you're his size, you don't have to. 'Fucking get in van,' he goes, 'and drive away.'

But before the dude gets a chance to move, some bird – I think she's a little bit like Lea Michele, although not *too* much? – comes over and goes, 'Excuse me, I've been clamped.'

The clamping dude goes, 'Yes, there are double yellow lines marked all over the estate.'

She holds up a piece of paper and goes, 'Erm, is this a genuine offer?'

It's, like, a flier. It says, 'Clamps removed – €30. Inside ten minutes! Guaranteed! Or YOU don't pay!'

Ronan and his two new mates must be following the actual clampers around and putting their ads under the wipers of every cor they do. Even I have to admit that's clever.

The clamper dude – the official one – goes, 'That clamp is the private property of South Dublin Clamping. It can only be removed by a representative of . . .'

Ronan cuts him off. 'It'll cost you nointey if he does it,' he goes. 'Yeah, we'll do it for toorty.'

I'd imagine he's on commission.

The woman's like, 'Great.'

The actual clamper does what Marek told him. He gets back into his van, though not without pointing his finger at Ronan and going, 'You're interfering with a private company going about its lawful work,' trying to put the frighteners on him.

Ro doesn't scare, though. He turns around to the woman. 'Which car is it?' he goes.

She's like, 'The Honda Accord.'

I watch him take his jack and his little toolbox, and, whistling a tune I recognize as Rihanna's 'Only Girl (In the World)', he returns to work. I end up having to just smile. What he's doing, let's be honest, doesn't figure at the end of anyone's rainbow. I mean, he has brains – real brains – and it kills me to think that this might be his future. But at the same, he's providing for Shadden and for their little girl. And I can't tell you how incredibly proud I am of him for that.

I decide to hit the road. But when I turn around, I can see – even from, like, fifty yords away – the little yellow triangle covering the front passenger side wheel of the Lambo.

I pull out my wad and count out three ten-yoyo notes.

'Ro,' I go, 'you might do mine next.'

It wasn't supposed to *be*, like, a boys' night out tonight, but it ended up turning *into* one? The original plan was to watch Ireland against France in Kielys – a few beers – then all go home to our women at the final whistle. But the match ended up being cancelled because, like, the *pitch* was frozen? So suddenly, roysh, with no actual rugby on the TV, it was impossible to gauge what time it was and how much alcohol we had actually put away.

So we've all ended up pretty much shit-faced. Jägerbombs *were* involved, don't you worry about that!

So it's, like, two o'clock in the morning and we're in Eddie Rocket's – we're talking the Rossmeister General, we're talking JP, we're talking Oisinn, we're talking Christian. And we're talking complete and utter shit as well. All four of us.

'I think she could be the one,' JP's going. He's talking about the famous Shoshanna. 'I know it's still early, but I really do think it's the real thing.'

I decide to just level with him. It might be something to do with the drink. 'I'm still not a hundred percent convinced by her,' I go. 'She's no fan of mine, remember. She actually used the word ignorant. And she was still giving me hostile vibes at Claire from Bray's *Downton Abbey* night.'

He goes, 'You do have a way of rubbing people up the wrong way, Ross. I tried to explain to her what you were like. She's American, remember.'

'Well, I hope it did some good. But the jury is still out on her as far as I'm concerned. And I stand by what I said about the whole fat whispering thing. It's a load of focking orse. I might even have to prove it.'

'Ross, don't focking ruin this for me. I really like this girl.'

'I'm just saying, if she pulls the wool over people's eyes for an actual living, you have to ask yourself how you could ever properly trust her. She could be blowing all of us behind your back and you'd never see it in her face.'

'I mean it, Ross. Don't ruin this.'

I'll tell you how, like, unplanned this session was – Christian has got, like, three bags with him full of shopping from Mothercare and the Early Learning Centre. Lauren sent him out shopping for shit for the baby – even though she's still got months to go – and the match was supposedly just a detour for him on his way home. Now it's, like, technically the following day and he's fast asleep on the table with burger sauce on his forehead and in his hair, and his shopping spilling out of the bags at his feet and into the aisle.

'*His* wife's another one,' I go. 'As in, like, Lauren?'

Oisinn's there, 'Dude, I'm discerning a pattern here!'

I laugh. At the same time, I'm like, 'She's going to blame me for the state *he's* in.'

JP goes, 'You *were* egging him on, Ross. Shots were your idea.'

'He's a big boy, J-Town. But *she'll* be onto Sorcha first thing in the morning, blaming me for the fact that she married a man who can't hold his pop. Did you hear what actually happened that night in Bray?'

'I heard Garret stitched you up and you had to walk through the town dressed as the one who looks like Queen Victoria.'

'No, not that. Although that *did* happen – and Garret *and* Claire are going to get what's focking coming to them. Yeah, no, the thing I'm talking about is *his* supposed son – rooting around in Claire's wardrobe. He finds her focking dildo and he brings it downstairs, giving it, "Mawmy, whath thith?" You know the way he talks. Then – I shit you not – he storts waving the thing around the dinner table like some, I don't know, sexually deviant Jedi.'

JP and Oisinn are cracking their holes laughing. I'm good value, in fairness to me.

'Anyway,' I go, 'I just happened to mention that it's wrong. It *is* wrong. A little boy obsessed with women's clothes? I stand by that statement. But Lauren managed to turn it around in such a way that *I* was suddenly the villain – and not Dorth focking Vibrator.'

Again, they laugh. They love it as a line.

I take a bite out of my Classic, then I turn around to Oisinn and go, 'By the way, what's *your* deal?'

He's like, 'What do you mean?' all focking butter-wouldn't-melt.

'Come on, Dude. Disappearing early on New Year's Eve? You were texting someone all night tonight. I've hordly seen you since Christmas. I know when you've something on. So who is she?'

He doesn't even bother denying it. He can't keep secrets from me. I played rugby with him for way too long.

He's like, 'You wouldn't know her.'

I'm there, 'Give me the name and let me be the judge.'

'Her name's Holly.'

'Holly? I rode a bird called Holly two years ago. Does she work for Matheson Ormsby Prentice and have one sticky-out ear and one, like, normal?'

'No.'

'It's definitely not her then. So who is this girl? What school did she go to?'

'You wouldn't actually know her. She's English.'

'English? Where the fock did you meet her?'

'She *lives* here. She's a florist. I dismantled her decking before Christmas.'

'I'd say you did – you filthy fock!'

There's, like, more laughter. I'm definitely funnier with drink on me.

JP gets in on the action then. He's like, 'Why haven't you brought her out yet, for the goys to give her the old once-over?'

Oisinn's there, 'Because it's still early days, Dude. We're taking it slowly.'

I'm like, 'You're completely right, Big O. You don't want to end up whipped – like this pair of saps.'

I think how genuinely happy I'd be if it worked out for the dude. With all the shit he's been through in the last few years – losing everything he owned, being made bankrupt, being made homeless, then the whole cocaine thing – he deserves to be with someone nice.

My phone all of a sudden rings. At first, roysh, I presume it's

Sorcha, wondering why the fock I'm not home. It ends up being my old man, though, ringing from, like, Paris.

I answer it and go outside to talk. I'm like, 'How did it go? Did she say yes or did she tell you go and fock yourself?'

He goes, 'It was a disaster, Ross – of the bloody unmitigated variety.'

He sounds even more mashed than I am.

I'm like, 'What happened?'

'The game was called off,' he goes. 'First time it's happened in twenty-seven years.'

'Yeah, I focking know that. But what happened to you proposing?'

'Oh, well, it was all set up. We were going to the game. I had a good feeling about it. I thought the cold conditions might better suit our chaps. I was planning to pop the question afterwards. I'd booked a late supper for us in a lovely little restaurant I know close to the Palace of Versailles . . .'

'Okay, there's a lot of useless focking detail in this story.'

'We took our seats in the stadium and the next thing there's all this how-do-you-do about the match not being played. I said, why aren't the players coming out? Someone said the pitch was considered unsafe. Frozen bloody solid, it seems. I said, when did they know this? It's been minus something here all week, by all accounts. They could have saved us the trouble of bloody well travelling.'

'So what happened then?'

'Well, I got into a frightful set-to with a member of the Stade de France security staff. "It's all very well you saying come back in March," I said to our friend, "but there's a thing going on in Ireland at the moment called a recession. A lot of people – and, yes, that even includes rugby fans – can't afford to make two trips to Paris in a single spring."'

I'm there, 'Dude, I've a burger and chilli fries going cold inside. Do I take it the upshot of all this was that you didn't actually propose?'

'Well, it just put a blight on the entire evening. I said to our friend, "I want to know, who made this decision? Who is the referee? If it's

Nigel Owens, I demand to know!" Then Helen got upset with *me* for being upset. Didn't speak to me in the taxi the entire way back to the George V. I told her I'd made dinner reservations, but she didn't want to know. Took to her bed.'

'So where are you now?'

'I'm in the hotel bar, chatting with – what's your name again? Maxime! It's Maxime, Ross. And I'll tell you something – he gives bloody good measures.'

I can't believe I'm about to give my old man relationship advice, but I go, 'Dude, go to focking bed.'

He's like, 'But what if Helen's still angry with me?'

I'm there, 'Dude, I always said you were punching well above your weight with Helen. She's in a different class to you.'

'Yes, this I know.'

'But for some reason – it might be some mid-life thing – she's absolutely mad about you. So go and apologize to the woman.'

'Do you really think I should?'

'Go and focking do it.'

'Message received and understood, old scout.'

I hang up on him, then I wander back into Ed's, to discover that Christian has spewed all over himself. It's time he went home. The staff in Ed's are certainly of that view.

Me and the goys manage to get him upright, then I grab his bags of shopping and we walk him to the door. We manage to hail a Jo for him. I tell the driver Booterstown, which is where Christian and Lauren are currently renting. The driver, like, hesitates when he sees the horrendified condition of his passenger, but three crisp twenty-yoyo notes are a pretty persuasive argument.

We manage to get him into the back of the cor, then I put his shopping on the seat beside him. I just happen to look into one of the Mothercare bags, roysh, and I notice that he's bought one of those, like, wireless baby monitors that allow you to hear shit that's going on in your kid's room.

I end up getting this sudden idea – and it's a focking incredible one, even if I say so myself.

I whip the thing out of the bag and I stuff it inside my jacket.

Lauren will go focking ape shit when she finds out it's missing, but they'll both just presume that Christian dropped it somewhere along the way – the little focking pisshead.

I slam the door, slap the roof of the taxi three times, then watch as Christian is driven off into the night.

'What was that you took from his bag?' JP goes.

And I go, 'Nothing. And keep your focking mouth shut if he asks you.'

Sorcha says that Ivana Bacik's latest newsletter arrived today and she thinks that the spoken prayer before each Seanad sitting should be replaced by a period of silent reflection. And I realize that I feel absolutely nothing – as in, I can't even bring myself to be bored by this information.

I go, 'Hey, that's cool, Babes.'

We're sitting in, like, Thornton's, on one of these weekly date nights that Sorcha says are – what was it again? – a vital component in re-establishing trust through actual face-to-face communication.

'I'd love to actually campaign for her,' she goes. 'The next time there's an election. That's if she ever runs in Dun Laoghaire again.'

I'm like, 'Campaign for who, Babes?'

'Ivana Bacik! Oh my God, Ross, are you even listening to me?'

'I am, yeah. I just didn't know if we'd moved onto another subject.'

'No, Ross, I'm still talking about Ivana Bacik. I'm making the point that she believes in – oh my God – *so* many of the things that *I* believe in? An open and inclusive society that welcomes a growing diversity of cultures and lifestyles, grounded on values of equality, tolerance and pluralism.'

I'm trying to look at her wammers down the front of her mint-green Equipment shirt.

'She does amazing work,' she goes, 'especially in the whole area of, like, sexual equality.'

I've never been one, of course, to fail to spot an opportunity. I'm like, 'Speaking of sex.'

Sorcha's there, 'I wasn't.'

'Sorry?'

'I wasn't speaking of sex.'

'Well, you certainly mentioned a word that sounded very like it.'

'I'm talking about sexual politics, Ross. An increase in the number of women in both houses of the Oireachtas. The provision by the State of free or subsidized childcare facilities in order to increase women's participation in the workforce. An end to female genital mutilation . . .'

Jesus Christ. She certainly knows how to ruin a moment. I push away what's left of my Eireyu beef Carpaccio with parsley purée and horseradish cream.

She goes, 'That's what I was talking about, Ross – not sex.'

'Well,' I go, 'since it's come up, what's the deal there? I mean, are we any closer?'

'It's still only February, you know.'

'Jesus, Sorcha, we're back together since, like, the end of October.'

That's, like, three and a bit months of working purely alone. I've the stomach nearly pulled out of myself at this stage.

I'm there, 'I haven't done the dirt on you – just to point that out. I've genuinely changed.'

And that's when I cop her, on the other side of the restaurant, sitting at a table alone, a glass of red wine to her lips. Our eyes meet and I watch her eyebrows go up in, like, recognition. She puts the glass down and gives me a smile and a little wave.

'Who are you looking at?' Sorcha goes.

It's Grainne – the bird from Kielys that night. And Grafton Street that morning. And the text on Christmas Day.

I'm there, 'Er, no one.'

Sorcha has a sly look over her right shoulder. She goes, 'Do you know that girl?'

She looks incredible, by the way. I'm talking about Grainne. If I'm being honest, I'd have to say that Sorcha looks just alright.

I'm there, 'What girl?'

Sorcha goes, 'The one wearing the same Peter Pilotto hella-print silk-blend dress that Jenna Ushkowitz was wearing on the cover of the latest *Grazia*.'

The girl is spilling out of the thing as well. I think I've already mentioned that she's got a fine pair of attention-getters.

I'm like, 'I think I see the bird you're talking about now. Yeah, no, I wasn't looking at her.'

'She looks kind of familiar to me.'

'Maybe to you. I've honestly never seen her before in my life.'

'You smiled at her.'

'I don't think I did, Babes.'

'Yes, you smiled at her.'

'It mightn't have *been* a smile? Yeah, no, there was a caraway seed stuck between my two front teeth. I was trying to free it from the back with my tongue.'

She stares at me like she *wants* to believe me, but past experience is telling her she'd be a focking dope to.

'Anyway,' she goes, 'can we, like, change the subject?'

I'm there, 'Yeah, no, definitely. Did I tell you I ran into Ro the other day? Removing clamps. He has a real knack for it.'

'I heard. I was talking to Shadden on the phone.'

'A definite knack. And when I say knack, I don't mean . . . I suppose that's obvious. Poor little Rihanna-Brogan has colic.'

'Yeah, Shadden said. Poor little thing.'

Grainne's *with* some dude. He comes back from the can and sits down opposite her. He's, like, a fattish dude with thinning hair, which he's obviously trying to hide by, like, brushing it backwards to try to give it more volume, then big red focking cheeks as well. It never ceases to amaze me how low girls are prepared to set their sights. She's Heineken Cup. He's AIL. It amazes me and it kind of angers me at the same time.

Grainne gives me another sly little smile and *he* obviously notices, roysh, because he says something to her and she, like, shakes her head, and then – a bit like Sorcha – he has a big paranoid look over his shoulder.

I quickly look down. The waitress is clearing away our plates.

Sorcha, I notice, ended up horsing her celeriac velouté with brioche croutons, which is a shame, because I was going to, like, *ask* her for some?

'So Claire is seeing her next Tuesday,' Sorcha goes. 'Then I'm the day after that.'

I'm like, 'Who? Sorry? What?'

She hates when I stop listening to her. At first, roysh, I just presume she's back talking about Ivana focking Blahface.

'I'm talking about Shoshanna,' she goes.

I laugh and just shake my head. I'm like, 'Not this nonsense again. You're worse than JP. At least he's getting something out of her.'

'You can snigger all you want, Ross. But you heard what she said the last day – a lot of people in the States are storting to believe that fat whispering is an actual *science*?'

There's money in unhappiness. That was one of the first lessons my old man learned in business.

Grainne's dessert arrives, I notice. They're, like, way ahead of us. A chocolate something or other, with two spoons. They're obviously sharing.

'Look,' I go, 'I just hate seeing you with someone who doesn't deserve you.'

Sorcha's like, 'With someone who doesn't deserve me? Ross, what are you talking about?'

Shit.

I'm there, 'Er, what I mean is, I don't want to see you get taken for a ride.'

'We're hordly being taken for a ride. She's giving us our first consultation for free . . . Ross, do you want to go over and sit with that girl?'

I'm like, 'Sorry?'

She goes, 'That girl behind me. You seem far more interested in her than in anything I have to say.'

'I'm not.'

'Ross, you can't take your eyes off her.'

I'm like, 'Babes, believe me – you're definitely imagining it. It's genuinely all in your head,' and then I go, 'What did you order for your main again?' just to change the subject.

She goes, 'The magret of duck with girolles, braised red cabbage and morel sauce,' except she says it kind of *warily*? I've still got a huge job ahead of me trying to properly win back her trust.

She raises her glass to me and goes, 'Anyway – Happy Valentine's Day.'

And I lift mine, thinking, Valentine's Day? When the fock is that?

'I know I'm twenty-four hours early!' she goes and I can suddenly relax. I've still got time to get online and get Tesco to deliver her a bunch of whatever-the-focks first thing in the morning.

She leans across the table with her lips primed for a kiss. The Rossmeister obliges. It doesn't go unnoticed by Grainne. And the fact that it doesn't go unnoticed by Grainne doesn't go unnoticed by the dude she's having dinner with. He's suddenly looking over his shoulder at me again.

'Ross,' Sorcha goes, 'I do appreciate it, you know.'

I'm there, 'Appreciate it? As in?'

'As in, I know how difficult the last few months must have been for you – just abstaining.'

'I've got balls like a focking Bengal tiger, Babes. And that's not exaggerating.'

She laughs. 'Well,' she goes, 'you won't have to wait much longer.'

I'm there, 'Are you serious?'

'Yes, I'm serious.'

'Is that a promise?'

'Yes, it's a promise. I think I'm nearly ready.'

That means tomorrow. Of course it does! It's, like, Vally's Day! I'll make my move the second the Tesco truck disappears down the driveway.

Oh, fock! *He's* suddenly coming over. He's got a face on him as well. He's not happy. I try to pretend that we're, like, deep in conversation about something else.

I'm like, 'So tell me a bit more about this Ivana person. She sounds pretty amazing.'

Sorcha – all delighted – goes, 'Well, she acted as Junior Counsel in

196

the Katherine Zappone and Ann Louise Gilligan versus the Revenue Commissioners case . . .'

Except the dude is suddenly standing over our table.

'Excuse me,' he goes. 'Why do you keep looking at my fiancée?'

I'm thinking, fiancée? This is a girl who was offering it to me on a plate a couple of months ago.

I'm there, 'I don't keep looking at her.'

I *could* hang her out to dry – except that would mean having to explain the entire backstory to Sorcha, and I'm not sure she'd believe that I was the innocent porty and Grainne was the one who was basically gagging for *me*?

'She says you've been looking at her all night,' he goes. 'Do you think you know her from somewhere?'

'No.'

'Because she says she doesn't know you.'

'She doesn't.'

'So why the interest in her?'

I should focking deck him, except I don't think Sorcha would be impressed. The dude sounds like he's from Cork, by the way. I don't think I *need* to add anything to that?

I'm there, 'Dude, believe me, I've no interest in her.'

He goes, 'So why do you keep staring?'

I look over at Grainne. She mouths the word, 'Sorry!' to me.

Women's tongues are the deadliest weapons of mass destruction ever created.

'I haven't *been* staring,' I try to go.

He's like, 'She says you have. Are you saying she's lying?'

He's clearly one of these insecure dicks. I might just deck him anyway and accept the consequences.

I'm there, 'I'm saying she's imagining it. I'm saying it's all in her head.'

Then I suddenly notice the way Sorcha's looking at me and I remember that those are the exact same words I used to her not two minutes ago.

'Well, can you please stop,' he goes. 'It's making her uncomfortable.'

I'm there, 'It's making you uncomfortable, you mean,' because I can't resist it.

What a knob end.

He's like, 'It's making both of us uncomfortable,' and then he strolls back over to his table.

'Can you believe that?' I go, just shaking my head. 'The actual nerve of people.'

I don't need to look at Sorcha's face to know that I won't be getting sex from her tomorrow. Or any time soon.

'I said to the chap, "It's all very well you telling us to come back in March. But there's a thing going on in Ireland at the moment and it happens to be called a recession."'

I'm there, 'Yeah, no, you told me this. On the phone. When you were mullered.'

'I said, "A lot of people – and that even includes rugby fans – can't afford to make two trips to Paris in a single spring." And it's true, Ross. The Squeezed Middle, they're calling these people. Oh, they exist.'

This is us in, like, Dubray Books on Grafton Streeet, at the launch of *Fifty Greys in Shades*.

The shop is full of *her* mates. We're talking Delma and all the veterans of her various campaigns over the years to keep poor people out of the ports of the city that she likes and keep them in the ports of the city that she hates.

There's enough *Chanel No. 5* in the air to chloroform a bull.

I'm there, 'So I take it you didn't pop the question in the end?'

He has a look over his shoulder. Helen's around here somewhere and he doesn't want her to hear.

He goes, 'Had to put the plan on ice, regrettably. Well, the whole business cast something of a pall over the weekend. Bloody referee. It'll have to be another time, I'm afraid.'

Helen is all of a sudden behind us. I try to cover up for the old man by going, 'I heard *he* got completely wankered and made a focking holy show of himself in Paris.'

Helen laughs. She's always been a massive, massive fan of mine.

She's like, 'Oh, he was just upset. I kept telling him, never mind the match, just think of your heart.'

I'm there, 'Sensible advice.'

I'm skulling the free wine, by the way. I wouldn't even be here if I wasn't in the doghouse with Sorcha. She's still pretty pissed off about what happened in Thornton's and she made it pretty clear that getting back into *her* good books meant coming with her to the launch of my old dear's *bad* book.

Marriage is about compromise. It's an unfortunate fact of life, but there you have it.

Right at this moment she's giving out yords to Honor, who has spent the last fifteen minutes tearing the final page out of every book in the thriller and mystery section. It's the kind of behaviour that'd strike you as being both incredibly clever and incredibly disturbed. I don't know whether to fear for her or for the rest of the world.

Sorcha arrives over to us, shaking her head, which is all any of us can really do.

'Your mum looks amazing in that dress!' she happens to go.

She's standing at the other end of the shop.

I'm there, 'I disagree. I think she looks like Steve Borthwick in drag.'

'Ross, it's a Joanne Hynes.'

'My analysis still stands. I think she looks focking raddled and that's me being totally unbiased.'

All of a sudden, the old dear steps up to the lectern. There's, like, a huge round of applause, led by my old man, who shouts, 'Bravo! Bravo, Fionnuala!' His lack of bitterness and hatred for his ex-wife, *I* think, has actually scorred me for life.

There's suddenly silence. The woman is obviously going to read. But first she pauses, roysh, presumably for dramatic effect, but she does it for, like, way too long and ends up totally tearing the orse out of the moment.

'Get on with it!' I shout. 'Don't be always looking for attention!' and various people shush me.

She goes, 'Herman was emptying the sand from his espadrilles into the bathroom sink when the knock on the door came. He considered not answering. He didn't want company – not at this moment. The argument on the beach with Mr Loughran had taken a lot out of him. And at 82, he knew he had to think of his heart. But the knocking persisted. He went to the door and answered. Isolde was standing there in a Marks and Spencer's tangerine T-shirt with matching cropped towelling pants, looking up at him over the top of her reading glasses. "Hello, Mr Chistman," she said. Herman nodded and acknowledged her with a formal: "Mrs Kendall".'

I'm thinking, Herman? Where the fock does she even get the names? I'm looking around me, roysh, and people are obviously into it, lapping up every line.

Sorcha – who reads actual books – turns to me and goes, 'Her characters are – oh my God – so well drawn.'

'Herman opened the door wider,' the old dear goes, 'as an invitation to Isolde to enter. "I came to see if you were okay," she said. "I know Mr Loughran upset you." They had argued badly. Voices were raised; the Saviour's name invoked. The row was over the Seniors Got Talent singing contest that was due to take place in the commissary the following night. Herman was going to be Roy Orbison. He said it first. But then Mr Loughran announced that he was going to be Roy Orbison, too. Roy Orbison! It seemed so trivial now! But there was a history of bad blood between them. Mr Loughran was from New Foxrock. Herman would have considered it more Deansgrange and he was never slow in reminding people. They could never be friends.'

Sorcha shakes her head. 'She builds the tension – oh my God – so well.'

'Isolde smiled. "There is a solution," she said. "You can both be Roy Orbison. You can do 'Candyman'. And Mr Loughran can do 'Blue Bayou'."

'It was a simple solution. Herman had been too worked up to see it. "That man," he said, "he gets under my skin. That's not even real Foxrock he's from."

'Isolde touched his forearm absently. "Come on, Mr Christman," she said. "You remember what Dr Goswami said about your blood pressure." Herman recoiled – from the pain of sunburn rather than shyness.

"'Sweet merciful hour!' Isolde exclaimed. "Your poor arms! We need to put something on them." She disappeared into Herman's bathroom and returned a moment later with a bottle of after-sun. She squeezed some into her hand, warmed it between her palms, then touched Herman's arm with it, in light, tentative touches at first, but then more fully, with gentle, loving strokes . . .'

My phone all of a sudden rings. It's the *Hawaii Five-O* theme tune. I check out the screen and it's from, like, a withheld number. Various people turn around to me and tell me to either switch it to silent or to step out of the shop. I tell them to go and fock themselves, then I answer the phone and wander outside onto Grafton Street.

I'm like, 'This is Ross O'Carroll-Kelly. If you're ringing from a call centre somewhere in India, hang up now before I get angry.'

It's a thing I sometimes do.

'Ross,' a girl's voice goes, 'it's Grainne.'

I'm like, 'Grainne?' and I laugh as I'm actually saying it. 'You've some balls ringing me after what happened in Thornton's.'

'Ross, I'm ringing to apologize.'

'What, for hanging me out to basically dry?'

'Look, Desmond can be really, really possessive. He asked me why I kept looking over at your table. I panicked and said it was because *you* kept staring at *me*.'

'He's called Desmond, is he? You never told me you had a fiancé the night you basically offered it to me on a plate.'

'We got engaged two weeks ago.'

'You're marrying the dick. And yet a month ago you were prepared to cheat on him with me?'

'So?'

'Yeah, no, I'm just trying to establish it as a fact.'

'I told you I wanted to be with you, Ross. I don't think I could have made it any clearer than I did.'

'Even if that meant risking your relationship?'

It's flattering, that's all I'm saying.

She goes, 'I'd love to see you. I *want* to see you.'

I'm there, 'Grainne, that's possibly not a good idea.'

'Even if it's just a drink?'

'I'm not sure it'd just be that. As in, I don't think I could trust myself,' because I am seriously gagging for it at this stage. I'd get up on a crack in the curtains.

'Okay,' she goes. 'I might send you a picture of my breasts, though – my way of saying sorry.'

I laugh, roysh, presuming she's joking.

She's there, 'You can save them to your phone – a permanent reminder of what you could have, if you change your mind.'

I'm there, 'I'd better go. Might see you around.'

She's like, 'Bye, Ross.'

I tip back into the bookshop. The old dear's still reading. And things are obviously storting to hot up.

'There was a change in the current between them,' she goes. 'There was no point in denying it. Herman felt a tectonic movement in an area that had long been inactive. "It's important to look after your skin," Isolde said, trembling now, "especially at our age," and she quietly chastised herself for sounding so gauche: it seemed like such an affront to the moment. Herman leaned closer to her. He was aware of her smell now. Olay Anti-Wrinkle Targeted Treatment Serum and Fox's Glacier Mints.

'Their lips joined. Herman felt suddenly strong and vital, the same way he'd felt when first they met, on Kildare Street, the day they helped force a Government U-turn on the issue of means-testing medical cards for the over-70s. Isolde felt two sets of fingers tug against the elasticated waist of her cropped towelling pants and, in an instant, she knew what it was to be a teenager again.'

The old dear looks up, looking incredibly pleased with herself. I'm suddenly deafened by the applause.

At that exact moment, my phone beeps. It turns out to be, like, a text from Grainne with, like, a photograph? I open it up and my jaw nearly hits the shop floor. It's a picture of her, obviously standing in front of the mirror, blowing me a kiss, with her ginormous Milk Duds on full display.

I'm in shock. We're talking, like, *genuine* shock? But then not so shocked that I forget to save the picture to my phone.

I'm listening to Shoshanna through the door of her so-called treatment room. She's going, 'There's a thing that I like to say. The body always tells the truth – it's the mind that makes up lies.'

Claire from Bray is such a suck-orse. 'That's an amazing quote,' she goes.

And Garret is even worse. He's there, 'That's not only true. It's actually true on a lot of different levels.'

Another serious focking spoofer who's going to get his comeuppance today.

The clinic – if that's what we're agreeing to call it – is in Donnybrook Village, upstairs, two or three doors down from Terroirs. It's set up to look and feel like an actual spa. I'm in, like, the waiting area and it's all white sofas and mood lighting and candles that smell of basil and mandarin and possibly pomegranate and the soundtrack to *The Piano* playing softly in the background and full-length mirrors tilted backwards at an unflattering angle, presumably to make clients think they're fatter than they actually *are*?

I'm listening through a crack in the door as Shoshanna gives them both the spiel.

'I had a girl who came to me,' she goes. 'I'm not going to say her name because confidentiality is obviously very, very important in my business . . .'

That's hilarious. I've just read her focking client book from cover to cover.

She goes, 'But this girl was eighteen stone. And when she came to see me, she had tried literally everything to lose the weight. Exercise. Every diet in the book. She could never lose more than four or five pounds and then it would go back on again almost as quickly. She said to me, "Shoshanna, all of my friends are in happy, stable relationships," and she was in tears when she said this. "I'm so fat I'm never going to find anyone nice." *Sad* story! Right? But she did my programme. She followed the steps, like I told her, while I whispered away all of those bad fat cells. Three weeks ago, she was a svelte ten stone when she married a really, really nice guy. He works for PricewaterhouseCoopers. *Happy* story!'

'Oh my God,' Claire tries to go, 'that's an amazing story. It's also, like, inspirational.'

Shoshanna goes, 'I've given you probably an extreme case. The vast majority of my clients are girls like you, Claire, who want to lose weight in specifically targeted areas.'

'Well, with me,' Claire goes, 'it's my legs. I've tried walking, weights, the cross trainer, the bike – they just, like, *refuse* to tone?'

That's actually true. She's got focking thighs like Richie McCaw.

'The reason,' Shoshanna goes, 'is because of recalcitrant fat cells that have to be persuaded to leave the body. And that's a process we're going to hopefully start today. Now, like I said to you on the phone, the first consultation *is* free. After that, it's two hundred euros per consultation. I recommend that you do at least ten, as well as an hour of rigorous exercise a day and that you cut fat, sugar, wheat, dairy, carbohydrates, red meat and alcohol from your diet.'

That leaves, what, chicken, fish and vegetables? Any focker could lose weight eating chicken, fish and vegetables and exercising for an hour a day. What a focking chancer – this is a bird who called *me* ignorant, can we all just bear in mind?

'Okay,' Shoshanna goes, 'if you've finished your herbal tea, I'm going to bring you into this room here, weigh you and calculate your body's water and fat content. Garret, do you want to come with us?'

He goes, 'Yeah, like I said, I'm really into the whole area of natural healing.'

They disappear out of the treatment room and that's suddenly my cue.

In I go.

I know I probably don't have long – maybe a minute or ninety seconds at the most. I look for somewhere to put the speaker from

Christian and Lauren's baby monitor. At first, roysh, I stick it up under the heat mat on top of the treatment bed, except there ends up being, like, a bulge, which Claire would definitely feel. So then I get down on my hunkers and stort feeling around underneath. And that's when I find it – paydirt! On the underside of the actual bed itself, there's, like, a leather pocket thing. I higher the speaker volume up as loud as it will go and then I stuff it in there, making sure the bit that the actual sound comes out of is sticking out. I don't want my voice to be muffled.

I tip out of the room, just as Shoshanna brings Claire and Garret back in.

Shoshanna's giving it, 'Now, Claire, if you could just lie on the treatment bed there, on top of the heat mat, we can begin your session.'

'Oh my God,' I hear Claire go, 'it's really hot, isn't it?'

'It's that heat that's going to instruct the metabolism to switch to fat-burning mode.'

There's, like, a whole rigmarole to be gone through before the actual whispering can begin. Various motors and engines turn on and off at, like, sixty-second intervals. From, like, following the commentary, I discover that Shoshanna is cupping Claire's cellulite – whatever the fock that even means – then rolling it.

Again, from following what's being said, Shoshanna then wraps Claire from head to toe in bandages, and paints her – I shit you not – with this, like, herbal paste, the formula for which is a secret, Shoshanna says, although from the smell that's drifting through the crack in the door, I'd say it's Doritos hot salsa dip and if it's not, it's something very like it.

Then she puts a rubber suit on her – I'm guessing it's like one a frogman would wear? Then she puts a heated blanket on top of her.

I end up having to be patient, roysh, because that takes forty minutes, then Shoshanna – the focking bluffer – puts a pair of plastic focking trousers on the girl, which inflate and deflate, giving the lymphatic system a good workout – these are *her* words, by the way – and draining toxins from the body.

I pass the time staring at my photo of Grainne's juicers and eating two packets of Monster Munch that I found in Shoshanna's bottom drawer.

Then the noise dies down and it's suddenly showtime.

'Okay, Claire,' she goes, 'now we've come to the actual whispering part of the session.'

I hear Garret go, 'Can anyone do it, Shoshanna? In other words, can anyone influence the behaviour of fat cells with just their voice?'

Shoshanna's there, 'Only if you have a strong intuition.'

'It's *actually* fascinating,' he goes, the dick.

'When I concentrate, I can literally hear the emotion trapped inside each cell membrane. That's something to remember. Sometimes the fat cells are just being stubborn in refusing to move and they need to be spoken to in a firm way. But quite often they actually want to be released. They just don't know how to go about leaving the body.'

'So they have to be almost given directions?'

'That's exactly it. Claire, I want you to visualize your body's meridian system.'

Claire's like, 'My what?'

It's Garret who ends up answering. 'Your channels of awareness,' he goes. 'Remember that Australian girl we met in Phu Quoc who knew loads about Chakra?'

'Exactly,' Shoshanna goes. 'We all have an invisible energy flow circuit. Can you visualize yours, Claire?'

'I think so.'

'What colour is it?'

'Does it have to be, like, a primary colour?'

'It can be any colour.'

'I'm going to say *feldgrau*.'

'*Feldgrau*?'

'No, fandango pink.'

'Either of those is fine. Let's say fandango pink, then. Now keep visualizing all that good energy flowing through you, nourishing every corner of your body . . . Now repeat after me. I love my beautiful, slim, toned legs.'

I end up having to put my hand over my mouth to stop myself from laughing.

'I love my beautiful, slim, toned legs,' Claire goes.

Shoshanna's like, 'Again. I love my beautiful, slim, toned legs.'

'I love my beautiful, slim, toned legs.'

All of a sudden, roysh, Shoshanna – without any hint of embarrassment – goes, 'Okay, Claire, I think your body is ready to talk to me now. So I'm going to listen to it, okay?'

'Okay.'

'I'm going to listen to your fat cells and find out what they have to say.'

I hold the microphone port of the baby monitor to my lips and in a low whisper I go, 'Feeeeeed meee!'

It's Garret who actually reacts. He's like, 'What the fuck?'

Shoshanna goes, 'Garret, try not to break Claire's concentration.'

He's like, 'Did you not hear that?'

'Hear what?'

'I thought I heard . . .'

'What did you hear?'

'I don't know. Nothing.'

Shoshanna suddenly storts shouting then, like the priest out of *The Exorcist*. She puts on a good performance, you'd have to say that for her. She's giving it, 'What do you want? What do you want? What do you want?'

So I go, 'Fooooood!'

I say it exactly like E. T. would. And that's not just me patting myself on the back. It's incredibly clear as well – fair focks to Christian – no static or anything.

'Okay,' Claire goes, '*I* heard it that time.'

Garret's like, 'Does it ever happen that – okay, this is going to sound ridiculous – but that the fat cells actually talk back?'

What a dope.

You can tell that Shoshanna's thinking, no, because the entire thing is total horseshit and I'm taking you for a pair of focking mugs. But she doesn't say that, of course. Instead, she goes, 'It might have been the leather – you must have shifted your weight, Claire.'

I do it again. This time, I go back to, 'Feeeeeed meee!'

Again, it's pure E. T.

'That wasn't the leather,' Claire goes. 'Oh my God, that was an actual voice.'

Shoshanna's there, 'What do you want?' except this time I can hear the genuine *panic* in her voice? 'What do you want?'

I take, like, a deep breath and I scream into the thing. I go, 'I WANT A BIG MAC FOCKING MEAL!'

The next thing I hear is, 'Aaarrrggghhh!!!' as the three of them stort screaming their lungs out. Yes, *three* of them – Garret included, screaming like a focking ten-year-old girl at a horror movie.

They're genuinely terrified. It's one of the funniest things possibly ever.

The next thing, roysh, the three of them come running out of the treatment room. Shoshanna first, in her long white coat, her face the exact same colour, going, 'No! No! Please no!' Then Garret, shouting, '*Aum Namah Shivaya! Aum Namah Shivaya!*' which turns out to be some focking mantra he picked up on his travels that's supposed to ward away danger. Then Claire, wrapped up like a mummy and covered in dip, with a rubber suit on her and a pair of inflatable focking trousers, going, 'Oh my God! Oh my God! Oh my God!'

I'm actually in convulsions of laughter. They focked with the Rossmeister and now it's payback time.

They're so scared for their lives that they don't even notice me, sitting on Shoshanna's desk with the other end of the child monitor still in my hand, holding my side with my other hand, trying to catch my breath, wondering is it possible to actually die from laughing.

They run right through the reception area, down the stairs and out onto Morehampton Road. And I can still hear their screams a full five minutes later.

If they ever make Staring People Down an Olympic event, my daughter will bring glory to this country. She already has *me* beaten. I'm pretending to read the label on a bottle of San Pellegrino just to avoid having to make eye contact with her.

I'm going, '*Acqua Litinica Alcalina,*' just basically babbling. 'It's mad, when you think about it, all the different foreign words there are.'

Her mother is made of sterner stuff.

'Honor,' she goes, 'you can stare at me like that all day and all night for all I care. I am not buying you those shoes. Firstly, because they cost six hundred euros. And secondly, because you haven't done anything to deserve them. I am frankly disturbed by some of the things you've been writing on Twitter.'

'Oh my God, you are such a sappy bitch,' Honor goes, under her breath, but loud enough for us to *both* hear?

She knows that Sorcha's not going to make a scene – not in the Horvey Nichs Ground Floor Café, where she's a regular. Instead, she just goes, 'Honor, you used to be such a lovely little girl,' trying to work a bit of psychology on her.

And that's when – totally out of nowhere – Honor goes, 'Is that why you tried to swap me?'

Sorcha's like, '*Swap* you?'

People are listening in – other diners, basically.

'You tried to swap me for that other baby. The one that Ronan had with that skobie girl.'

'We weren't trying to *swap* you.' She looks around, embarrassed. Horvey Nichs is Horvey Nichs.

She goes, 'Yes, you were!' except she actually *shouts* it? 'You tried to swap me because you didn't want me any more! You didn't want me any more because you hate me!'

'Honor, eat your duck terrine.'

'No. I don't even want to sit with you!'

'Then go and sit at another table. We're just about tired of your unpleasantness anyway.'

'I will then!'

She ends up just doing it as well. She leaves her duck terrine where it is, but picks up her phone and her glass of orange and mango juice and moves to a vacant table, three or four tables away.

'I know you think I'm being hord on her,' Sorcha goes, 'but she's going to have to learn.'

I *don't* think she's being hord on her? I don't think she's being hord enough. I just happen to have my phone in my hand and I notice a brand-new message in Honor's Twitter feed. It's like, 'My mother is a sad and hopeless bitch.'

I decide not to tell Sorcha about it.

Instead, I go, 'I must give JP a shout back. I've had, like, six missed calls from him this morning. My guess is he's pissed off about a certain little stunt I pulled in Shoshanna's place yesterday.'

Sorcha's there, 'I wouldn't be surprised if he *is* pissed off. I heard what you did, Ross.'

'It was fully deserved. It was nothing I can't stand over.'

'You know Claire was pretty much traumatized? It took Garret a good three hours to calm her down.'

'That's hilarious. He was the one doing most of the screaming when I left them.'

'They want an apology from you.'

'They'll be waiting. They had it coming to them.'

'And Lauren's not happy with you either.'

'Lauren's never happy with me these days. I'm putting that down to the changes that are going on in her body. And that's me being charitable.'

'You stole her baby monitor.'

'Borrowed it. Jesus Christ, the baby isn't even due for another four months.'

'It wasn't *for* the baby. It was for little Ross.'

I laugh. I'm like, 'Excuse me?'

'He's been having nightmares,' she goes. 'They want to make sure he's okay after they put him to bed.'

'He's been over-mothered,' I go. 'That's the kid's only problem. They'd want to send him to Blackrock on a Saturday morning. Or even Old Belvedere. Get him playing rugby. Make a man of him.'

My phone all of a sudden rings on the table.

Sorcha's like, 'Is that JP again?'

I check. It is. I decide I can't go on avoiding him forever. He's already ringing every, like, half hour. So I answer it, at the same time deciding to try to, like, brazen it out.

'Dude,' I go, 'tell me that wasn't one of my finest comedy moments.'

'Fock you,' he just goes.

I'm like, 'Whoa, whoa, whoa . . .'

'I spent the entire night with Shoshanna in Vincent's.'

'Vincent's? As in, the hopsital?'

'She was suffering from shock. What you did was very focking dangerous.'

'Well, that'll teach her not to mess around with things she doesn't understand.'

He suddenly goes, 'Dude, I'm focking finished with you.'

I'm like, 'Whoa! You don't mean that.'

'I do mean it. You can consider our friendship – such as it was – at an end.'

I'm there, 'Dude, take that back! Dude, take that back!' except he's already hung up.

Sorcha is suddenly looking at me, her eyebrows raised, obviously wondering how it went. 'He thinks he might need a bit of time,' I go. 'That focking Shoshanna. She strikes me as one of those girls – you know the type – she can't go out with a guy without trying to turn him off all of his mates. It's disappointing, that's all I'm going to say. I'm going to go up and pay the bill.'

We've been trying to get the attention of a waitress for the last, like, five minutes. I go up to the counter, passing Honor on the way. She calls me an orsehole under her breath but I don't respond. I wouldn't give her the pleasure.

Our lunch is seventy something snots, which is alright. I end up flirting with the waitress, who looks a little bit like – I'm going to say – Caggie Dunlop. Three or four times, she goes to take the money from my hand, except I keep pulling it away at the very last second. It's a thing I've been doing for years. Women who work in pubs and restaurants love it.

I finally let her have it, give her a wink and tell her to keep the six snots change for herself. Then I turn around, roysh, to be greeted by a sight that, even from twenty yords away, I know straight away spells trouble.

Sorcha is talking to – oh, fock – Grainne Seoige. As in the Grainne Seoige.

I *should* go over and break it up. They usually spend the first two or three minutes of every conversation talking in Irish, basically trying to outdo each other. I could get in there while it's still *conas* this and *agus* that. But I don't. I make the fatal mistake of hesitating and, just from reading their facial expressions, I can nearly pinpoint the exact moment when Sorcha thanks her for her lovely text message on Christmas Day and Grainne Seoige asks her what the fock she's talking about.

They're both looking suddenly confused and I have to turn away from them, back to the counter, just to buy myself a minute to come up with an explanation. Except my mind is a blank. I'd normally fancy my chances of lying my way out of any situation. But I'm just too out of practice.

By the time I turn around again, Grainne Seoige has focked off and Sorcha – shit, shit, shit – suddenly has my iPhone in her hand and is obviously going through my messages. So much for all those date nights that were supposedly about re-establishing trust. Again, just from the look on her face, I could pretty much tell you the exact moment that she finds it – the photograph of the *other* Grainne with her Milky Moos out.

She stares at it for a long time. I should go over and tell her that it's okay, that it's all been just a huge misunderstanding. Except I'm pretty much frozen to the spot. All I can do is watch this look of, like, disappointment come over her face, then her eyes fill up with tears, then she closes them and sucks in her lips and she thinks what a fool she was to think that her useless fock-up of a husband could ever change.

What happens next is pretty unexpected. She stands up. She doesn't even look at me, bear in mind. And she just runs out of the Horvey Nichs Ground Floor Café.

I take off after her. She's got a good headstort on me, but I was always pretty fast on my feet, and by the time she reaches the back door of the shopping centre, I've closed the distance between us to maybe twenty feet.

I'm going, 'Sorcha! I can explain!' but she doesn't want to hear it.

'How could you do it to me?' she's roaring and crying at the same time. 'I would have trusted you with my life!' and she just keeps running in the direction of the red cor pork. It's only as we're passing Molton Brown that I suddenly remember Honor, back in the restaurant. I think, shit, and I end up having to stop.

Still, I've a good idea where Sorcha is headed – where she's always gone when I've screwed her over in the past. Into the orms of her old man.

I go back to Horvey Nichs.

'Oh, the drama!' Honor goes, in a really sarcastic voice.

I'm there, 'Come on, we're going.'

'I think I'll stay, thank you. I might have dessert.'

'Please,' I go. 'I'll buy those shoes that your mother wouldn't let you have.'

She doesn't even blink. 'I also want a pair of fish-scale metal cuffs,' she goes. 'They're by Deepa Gurnani.'

'Okay, those as well. Come on – please.'

She follows me out to the cab rank next to the cinema. We jump into the first cor and I go, 'The Beacon South Quarter.'

The entire way there, I end up rehearsing what I'm going to say – she was the one who came on to me, she was gagging for it, I meant to actually delete that picture of her jobbers – hoping against hope that it'll be enough to put her mind at ease.

But then *he'll* already be in her ear with his focking told-you-sos.

The taxi pulls up outside. I just throw a load of random money at the dude and jump out, dragging Honor behind me. The elevator takes for-focking-ever. When we reach the floor and the doors finally open, I can already hear Sorcha talking in that sad, little-girl-lost voice with which I'm way, way too familiar.

I step out into the corridor. Sorcha is still standing at the door. Her old man is going, 'Darling, please come in.'

She's going, 'No.'

I actually shout, 'Sorcha, I have no idea how that photograph even got in my phone.'

And that's when events take what would have to be described as an unexpected turn. Sorcha looks her old man in the eye and goes, 'I will never forgive you for this. Never!'

And like probably you, I'm thinking, okay, what the fock? I'm possibly still in shock, though.

I go, 'Sorcha, I was every bit as surprised as you were to open that text message and see those things staring out at me.'

Without even looking at me, she goes, 'It was my dad, Ross.'

I'm there, 'Excuse me?'

She knows how famously slow I am on the uptake, so she explains it to me. 'The girl in the photograph. I knew I recognized her that night in the restaurant. Her name is Grainne Gish. Her father is Aidan Gish, a private investigator who did a lot of work for my dad when he worked in family law . . .'

He doesn't deny it. He says fock-all in fact.

'I remember her now, from Alex. She was an amazing debater . . . She tried to set you up, Ross. *He* tried to set you up. My dad.'

I'm suddenly thinking, of course! All that, 'How could you do it to me? I would have trusted you with my life,' when she was running through Dundrum Town Centre. She was talking about her old man.

I'm there, 'You set me up?' directing my question at him.

He doesn't even answer me. He looks at Sorcha and goes, 'He's going to let you down, sooner or later. I preferred that it should happen sooner, so you could get on with your life. I'm not going to apologize.'

Sorcha's there, 'You set out to wilfully destroy my marriage.'

'To stop *him* destroying your life.'

She goes, 'I meant what I said. I never want to see you again. Ever.'

It's a day for big statements. First JP, now her.

She turns her back on him and walks to the lift. Honor follows her, going, 'I so love being a member of this family!'

I'm left standing face-to-face with the supposedly great Edmund Lalor, who tried to fock me over but ended up getting focked over himself. I should feel some sense of satisfaction. But I don't.

I go, 'Grainne said a lot of nice things to me about my rugby. Are you telling me all those lines were fed to her?'

He looks at me like I'm a big brown curler that won't flush away. Then he goes, 'Get the hell out of my sight.'

6.

How Dare You!

Ronan's got a black eye and it's a real beauty. It's not *only* black? The thing is swollen to, like, the size of a golf ball and I'd be pretty surprised if he can even see through the actual slit.

I'm there, 'Who did that to you?'

He's like, 'Dudn't mathor, Rosser.'

This is, like, standing at his front door.

I go, 'I beg to differ.'

Even the thought of someone hurting my son. It's like when I look at photographs of Pippa O'Connor marrying Brian Ormond – it sends me into a blind rage.

I'm there, 'Tell me who it is and they will be decked. One thing will automatically follow the other.'

From the kitchen, I can suddenly hear the sound of a baby – I'm presuming Rihanna-Brogan – crying.

'I'd bethor get that,' he goes. 'Mon in.'

I go in and follow him down to the kitchen. They've done quite a bit with the place since I was here last. There's, like, corpets on the hall floor and on the stairs and there's, like, a forty-eight-inch plasma screen TV on the wall, which is turned to Sky Sports News, as I presume it is twenty-four hours a day.

Ronan picks little R&B out of her Moses basket and goes, 'Ssshhh!' as he gently bounces her up and down in his orms.

'No Shadden?' I go.

I don't know why, when I hear a baby cry, I automatically wonder what the mother's doing. It's probably just sexism.

'She's next doe-er,' he goes.

I'm there, 'I'm surprised she didn't hear her squeals *from* next

217

door – then come racing in to find out what was wrong with her baby.'

He goes, 'We had a row.'

I'm there, 'You and Shadden? Don't tell me *she* gave you that eye.'

I'd be genuinely surprised. The girl couldn't weigh much more than a packet of biscuits.

He goes, 'No, she fooken didn't,' his pride all of a sudden hurt.

I hold out my orms. 'Here,' I go, 'give her to me,' and Ronan hands over little R&B, then I stort rocking her in my orms, I suppose, *soothingly*?

I'm there, 'When was the last time you slept?'

He goes, 'Two nights ago.'

I'm like, 'Two nights? Jesus, Ro, no wonder you two are at each other's throats if you're not getting any sleep.'

'She cries all night, Rosser.'

'I presume we're talking about Rihanna-Brogan.'

He nods. 'Still the codic.'

I end up having to shake my head. 'So much for K . . . K . . . K . . . Kennet and D . . . D . . . D . . . Dordeen helping out. Useless focks.'

Little R&B stops crying within, like, thirty seconds of me taking her from him. There's no doubt I have a way with people, male and female, young and old.

'So do you want to tell me who blackened your eye?' I go.

He can't even look at me. He spends so much of his life cracking on to be a hord man that it must be difficult for him to admit any sign of weakness.

I'm there, 'I'm going to presume it was a clamper.'

He nods.

I'm like, 'What about Marek? Is he not supposed to protect you?'

'He oatenly woorks tree days a week,' he goes.

'What, so for the other two you're on your Jo Malone?'

'Ine not *on* me owen. I've Locky wit me.'

'You mean Say Nuttin? I wouldn't trust him to make a salad out of a bag of focking lettuce. That's it, Ro, you're getting out of that job.'

'Ine not, Rosser. I caddent.'

'What do you mean you can't?'

'I need to woork. To suppowurt Shadden and the babby. I've biddles to pay. I've debts.'

I'm like, 'Debts?' instantly sensing that something's not right here. 'What kind of debts could you have?'

'I bodied muddy,' he goes and he won't even meet my eye when he says it. 'All this stuff dudn't come for free, Rosser,' and he gestures to the fridge and the cooker, and the plasma screen TV on the wall and the net curtains that he seems to have been in the process of hanging when Rihanna-Brogan kicked off.

Net curtains. I could nearly weep for the kid.

'How much did you borrow?' I go.

He doesn't *want* to tell me? But I end up just staring him out of it until he does. 'Torty grant,' he eventually goes.

I'm there, 'Thirty grand? Jesus Christ, Ro, why didn't you just come to me? I'd have *given* you that.'

He goes, 'I toalt you, I ditn't *want* you to give it to me. I want to stant on me owen two feet, Rosser.'

It's, like, his famous pride again.

I'm there, 'Ro, everyone admires what you're doing – especially me. It's not an ideal situation. I think we've all established that. But you're making the best of it. You're putting food in the mouths of your baby and her mother. You're putting – okay, it's not exactly *my* taste? – but net curtains on their windows. Look, Ro, I'm not the brightest crayon in the bunch. I don't need to tell you that. There's fock-all going on in my head except two clowns driving around in a clown cor parping the horn . . .'

He laughs, in fairness to him.

'I'm as thick as they come. But I've lived long enough, Ro, to know this much for sure – you should never be too proud to ask for someone's help. Okay?'

He nods, roysh, then I just smile at him and I'm like, 'Now, you go upstairs and get some sleep.'

He goes, 'But whor about . . .'

I'm there, 'I'm going to bring her out. Let you get some rest.'

I put her into the stroller, very gently, then I clip her in. Ronan ends up just staring at me in genuine awe. He's there, 'Thanks, Rosser.'

I'm there, 'There's a lot of people in this world who love you, Ro, and I'm at the top of that list. All you ever have to do is ring me. Or even text me.'

He sets off up the stairs then. He looks totally wrecked. He stops when he gets, like, two or three steps from the top.

He goes, 'Shadden wants to orcanize a famidy portrait.'

I'm there, 'Okay.'

'All the diffordent genorashiddens. Me two granddas and me two grandmutters. You and me ma. Sorcha. Kennet and Dordeen. Shadden and her brutters and sisters. Honor and Rihanna-Brogan.'

That's some rogues' gallery.

I'm there, 'Yeah, no, I get the idea. When's it happening?'

'Couple a weeks. In some stutio Shadden's arthur foyuntin.'

'I'll be there, Ro. Don't you worry about that. Now go and get some sleep.'

Sixty seconds later, I'm pushing my granddaughter through one of North Dublin's roughest council estates – when the local residents association has the word continuity in its title, you know you're in a trouble area – and I'm thinking about the unexpected twists and turns that life sometimes takes.

Tina answers the door in her nurse's outfit. It does fock-all for me. She's cured me of that particular fetish for life. I probably should point out that she actually *works as a* nurse? There's nothing kinky going on.

I'm like, 'Hey.'

She's there, 'What the fook do *you* want?'

'Swearing like a drunken stevedore in front of your own granddaughter,' I go. 'You're a class act, Tina, there's no doubt about that. Are you not going to ask us in?'

'No,' she goes. 'Ine just arthur comin off de night shift. Ine going to me bed.'

I'm there, 'Ronan has a black eye. I thought, as his mother, you might want to know.'

She does seem upset, in fairness to her. She's like, 'Who gave um a black eye?'

I'm there, 'He was unclamping a cor – totally legally, by the way – and I'm presuming he got a box in the face. Now *I've* got a question that I wouldn't mind answered. Who lent him money?'

'Soddy?'

'He borrowed thirty Ks off someone to buy shit for this little one and for the house. That's why he's *having* to work?'

She's like, 'Tooorty grant?' except she actually roars it. It's more money than she's probably ever seen.

I'm there, 'Yeah, no, he told me that figure himself.'

'Toorty fooken grant?'

'Calm down, Tina. I get that it's a lot of money to someone like you. But if you keep shouting, you're going to wake Rihanna-Brogan and we don't want that. Look, even I can make a reasonably intelligent guess as to who lent it to him. But I don't want to put pressure on the kid.'

Tina goes, 'Shadden's fooken da,' like she's already beating him to death with one of her shoes in her mind.

I'm there, 'That's who I was actually going to say, although I might have phrased it differently.'

'He's a muddy lenter.'

'Is he?'

'Among udder tings.'

In my total southside naivety, I end up going, 'Well, let's just hope he's not chorging him interest – given that Ronan's pretty much port of his family now.'

Tina ends up totally losing it with me. She's like, 'Of cowerse he's cheergen him intordest. It's not Fox fooken Rock, you know.'

If there was ever a line that summed up this port of the world, that's it. I'm sure it's on the Finglas coat of orms. *Il nisi Fox fucking Rockio* – or whatever it'd be.

'I'm going to pay him off,' I go.

Tina's like, 'Who?'

'Who the fock do you think? K . . . K . . . K . . . Kennet.'

'It'll be toorty grant and twice that again in intordest. I toalt um not to get mixed up wit dat famidy.'

'Tina, you're shouting again. You need to chill. If it's ninety Ks, it's ninety Ks. I'll find the moo. I don't want to see him spending the next ten years of his life working for Say Nuttin. I'm still hoping he'll go back to Castlerock in September.'

'He woatunt be goin back to Castlerock.'

'Excuse me?'

'Thee doatunt want him back.'

'Whoa, whoa, whoa! He was the brightest kid in his class. He sat his Junior Cert a year early.'

'He's arthur havin a beebee.'

'So?'

'Thee said he'd be a modally codduptible influence on the utter students.'

'Could you possibly tone down your accent, Tina? Did you say a morally corruptible influence?'

'Yeah.'

'It's all beginning to make sense now. Is this why you broke up with McGahy?'

'It wadn't Tom's decision to meek. It was the bowerd of maddigement.'

'Of which McGahy is a member. I'm taking it that he didn't speak up for Ro and that's why you red-corded him.'

She goes, 'I doatunt have to explayun me personiddle life to you or addyone else!' and she slams the door in my face.

I'm walking in the door and I'm on the phone to – of all people – Fionn. He's ringing from, like, Ublah-blah, filling me in on what's been happening in his life – some of it interesting, some of it dull as shit, but I'm at least making all the right noises.

He's there, 'Last weekend we put the roof on the school,' meaning presumably the one he's been helping to build, between classes, according to his blog.

I laugh. I'm like, 'Manual labour, Fionn? I'm worried about you.'

He laughs then.

I miss him. It's not gay to admit it.

He goes, 'I'm pretty much a qualified bricklayer now. There were many times when I was standing there with the sun baking down on me and a trowel in my hand, thinking, what would Ross say if he could see me now?'

I'm there, 'I'd be more concerned about what your old pair would say. They didn't send you to the most expensive school in Dublin for you to end up with brick dust under your fingernails.'

He laughs, even though I'm not actually joking.

'So,' I go, 'what's this supposed country even like? Do they have, like, rugby over there?'

He's like, 'No, it's all soccer.'

I'm there, 'Yeah, no, I'd have guessed that alright, just looking at the pictures on that blog of yours.'

'But I'll tell you something really exciting,' he goes. 'Father Fehily taught in a school about thirty miles from where I'm teaching.'

'Really?'

'On the other side of Mbale.'

'I didn't know he was there before.'

'He spent four years in Africa after the war. He was in Botswana for three, then he was here for one.'

I'm suddenly confused. I'm there, 'Is Africa not, like, a country itself?'

'No, it's a continent,' he goes, 'made up of fifty-four different countries.'

See, I'd love to, like, *know* loads of shit? I'm definitely going to try to improve my mind – be a little bit more like Fionn in that way – maybe even this summer. Just set aside a week to learn just loads and loads of different facts, then try to actually remember them.

Can you imagine me suddenly spouting all this, like, *new* stuff? Africa is a continent made up of, whatever he said, fifty-four, fifty-six countries. People would be going, 'Okay, Ross, where is this shit even coming from?'

It'd mean a lot of work, but I'd love to impress people.

I go, 'There's been no word from Erika,' and I don't know why I mention the fact. He went away to supposedly forget about her and there *I* go, dragging him back to that scene in Donnybrook Church nearly a year ago, when she tore the poor focker's hort clean out of his chest and took off with that Fabrizio showjumping fockwit.

All he says is, 'Erika will be fine, Ross. People who prioritize their own happiness over everyone else's generally are okay,' and I'm just thinking how much other shit he could say about her, but he doesn't.

There's a lot of ways in which I'd like to be more like Fionn.

I'm there, 'So are you ever coming home – even for a holiday?'

He goes, 'I'm hoping to get back next month. It'll be just for a few days. Anyway, I'd better go. I think my money's about to . . .'

The line goes suddenly dead.

It's only after we're cut off that I become suddenly aware of the smell. I recognize it straight away as *Maison Martin Margiela* – a perfume that has always done it for me and that Sorcha generally only puts on her when she wants something.

I'm suddenly like one of the focking Bisto Kids, following the waft through the hallway and up the stairs to – as it happens – our bedroom. I push the door, except she's not in there – although laid out on the bed, I notice, is the navy-coloured lace appliqué silk slip she bought from Victoria's Secret the last time she was in the States.

There's, like, a trail of pink rose petals leading into the *en suite* bathroom. I follow it. And that's where I find my wife, in a Jacuzzi full of bubbles, surrounded by so many candles you'd swear Westlife were about to shoot a focking video in here.

'Hey,' she goes, smiling at me. She looks incredible in the flickering light.

I'm like, 'Hey.'

I've suddenly got a stick on me that could conduct a symphony orchestra.

She goes, 'Are you getting in?'

This is at, like, ten o'clock in the morning, bear in mind. I've only just dropped Honor off at school. There's, like, two glasses of red wine poured and she's already milled into hers.

This must be my reward for managing to resist Grainne. I'm nearly wishing her old man was here to see it. Off come the clothes and I slip straight into the Jacuzzi, lying down at the opposite end, the one with the taps. I'm there, 'Okay, tell me if I'm misreading the signals here, but does all of this mean . . .'

She shushes me and tells me not to ruin it by speaking.

You know me. I'm a gentleman in a lot of ways. So no, I'm not going to give you the full blow-by-blow account of what ends up happening next, other than to say that the second we dry off and Sorcha gets into that silk slip, we stort going at each other like two cats in a bag, with me showing her three or four little tricks she's been missing since the separation and her f-ing and blinding like a paratrooper.

When the show's over, we end up lying there for, like, an hour or more in the whole post-sex glow. At some point, I go, 'So what did you think?' and I'm sort of, like, playing with her hair, which she's always loved.

She's there, 'I think . . .' and then she lets her voice just trail off.

I'm like, 'Go on, Babes, what?'

'I think you were single for far too long, Ross.'

'What do you mean by that?'

'That stuff you were saying while we were making love.'

'Okay, what in particular?'

'Well, *Lein! Ster! Lein! Ster! Lein! Ster!*'

'Okay. And you're saying that didn't do it for you?'

'No, Ross, it didn't do it for me.'

'See, any little pointers you can give me like that as to what you want me to do less and what you want me to do a lot more of would be great.'

'Excuse me?'

'Well, I'm just making the point that different girls like different things, don't they? That's the lesson. That *Lein! Ster!* thing was massive about a year ago.'

She ends up totally flipping. She's like, 'I'm not one of your little tarts, Ross! I'm not one of your one-night stands.'

I'm there, 'I know.'

'I wanted you to make love to me like you're my husband, not some porn-star.'

'And I'm accepting that. I'm just saying, we're only, like, rediscovering each other's bodies, bear in mind. Remembering what turns the other one on and blah, blah, blah.'

'Kissing your biceps and saying, "Welcome to big school!" is also something you could drop from your routine.'

'Okay, that's gone too. Like I said, it's all about finding things we're *both* comfortable with?'

A lot of birds *do* love that *Lein! Ster!* thing, by the way – it was especially popular, I remember, after we beat Northampton last year.

Sorcha goes, 'Aport from the talking, it was very nice, Ross,' which I suppose *is* a compliment.

I'm there, 'Yeah, no, I'm sorry the show was over so quickly as well. You deprive me for months and that's what going to happen.'

She goes, 'Ross, what would you think of us renewing our vows?' and she says it out of literally nowhere.

I'm there, 'Renewing them? What does that actually involve, Babes?'

'It involves us reaffirming the promises we made before God when we got married.'

It already sounds expensive.

I'm there, 'Are we talking, like, a second wedding?'

She goes, 'It's *like* a second wedding – except it's *not*?'

'Er, okay. Would it involve, just for instance, buying a new ring?'

She laughs. 'No,' she goes. 'We'd use our original rings.'

Shit. I couldn't even tell you where mine is.

'In fact,' she goes, 'that's when I'm going to go back to wearing mine. And I was thinking we could actually do the whole thing here.'

'Here?'

'This summer. We could have the ceremony in the gorden – oh my God, can you imagine! – in a morquee, overlooking the bay. You and me, Ross, making a public declaration of our love with our closest friends and the people who *actually* love us as witnesses.'

I get this, like, sudden insight into what this is possibly about.

'Your old man,' I go. 'Will he be invited?'

She's like, 'No. Obviously I want Mum there and even my sister. But that man is not welcome.'

It's just as I suspected.

She's there, 'What would you think of Saturday, the sixteenth of June as, like, a date for it?'

'The *sixteenth* of June?' I go. 'That's . . .'

She's like, 'What?'

I was going to say it's the day of the second test between Ireland and the All Blacks, except I manage to stop myself in time.

'. . . that's all good,' I go. 'That's all I was going to say.'

It'll be an early morning match. I'll still get to see it.

She's like, 'We also have to decide on a priest to do the actual ceremony.'

I'm there, 'Again, I'm easy.'

'I was thinking of Father Seamus.'

'Father Seamus who's, like, a friend of your old man's?'

'He's a friend of our entire family, Ross.'

I'm there, 'Sorcha, are you sure this isn't about just making a point?'

She goes, 'It *is* about making a point. It's about making the point that we love each other and we're mature enough this time to actually *honour* the commitment we first made to each other eight years ago?'

'I'm talking about you making a point to your old man. His favourite daughter – the apple of his literally eye – getting remarried and the dude's not invited. That's a serious kick in the dash-and-two-dots.'

'Oh my God,' she goes, 'I can't believe that it's, like, you of all people *defending* him?'

And to be honest, I can't believe it either. A lot of people are probably thinking, that's incredibly big of you, Ross, and a real mork of the kind of man you are but never get credit for actually being. Don't get me wrong, though – I hate Sorcha's old man more than I hate, I don't know, famine. But I also understand a little bit about the bond between a father and his daughter. I remember when Sorcha took Honor away to live in the States, it nearly killed me not being able to see her every day. I probably wouldn't care so much now – I'd be glad of the focking break – but back then it was genuinely the worst thing that ever happened to me.

'I'm not defending him,' I go. 'He's a dick. I told you that a long, long time ago and I'm happy to say I've been proved right. It's just, I don't know, you told him you never wanted to see him again. All I'm trying to say is that never is a long time.'

She's there, 'He sickens me. Oh my God, he asked someone to try to seduce you.'

'I know.'

'She sent you a picture of her actual breasts.'

'I know.'

'And not once did you waver.'

'Hmmm.'

'My mind is made up. I don't want him at our wedding.'

'Wedding?'

'Did I say wedding? I meant vow renewal.'

In they walk. They make the cast of *Tallafornia* look like focking royalty. Kennet and Dordeen, Dadden and Kadden, Eddie and Shadden, then Ronan, still with his black eye, carrying little Rihanna-Brogan. Kennet and Eddie are wearing their surgical collars and the rest of them are decked out in their finest sportswear – except for Ro and Shadden, who've at least made the *effort*?

Matthew is the photographer's name and his face lights up when he sees them. Photographers love faces with a story behind them and this is a family that's been around a few corners.

Honor goes, 'Oh my God,' out of the corner of her mouth, 'it's like the Chamber of Horrors in Madame Tussauds!' and I laugh and go, 'Good one!' at the exact same time as Sorcha goes, 'Honor, don't be rude.'

The old man is straight over to them, of course. It's always been one of his biggest failings that he doesn't see the badness in people. Him and Kennet, as it happens, shared a landing in Mountjoy when my old man was sent down for paying bribes to secure land rezonings, soliciting bribes to deliver land rezonings, tax evasion and sixteen or seventeen other things. They apparently hit it off and the old man considers it a lovely coincidence that they are now bonded by blood.

He's like, 'There he is! Kennet Tuite! As I live and breathe!'

And Kennet's there, 'Ch . . . Ch . . . Ch . . . Cheerlie, me owl mucker – h . . . h . . . how ta hell are ye?' and it's all, like, hugs and backslaps and shoulder squeezes.

'And this is the famous family!' the old man goes. 'Oh, he talked about you all the time when we were – as they say – on the inside. It was, "I'm going straight, Charlie, and I'm doing it for them!" and so forth.'

Kennet does the introductions and the old man – I swear to fock – remembers something about all of them.

He's like, 'Dadden! Oh, yes! You were the famous footballer! You had trials with – who was it?'

Dadden's there, 'Dagenham and Redbridge.'

'Dagenham and Redbridge! Quote-unquote! And is this their badge you've got tattooed on your neck?'

'No, it's ta Depeertment of Soshiddle Welfeer.'

'Oh! *How* interesting!'

Sorcha wanders over to Shadden and Ro. Ten seconds later, of course, she's got Rihanna-Brogan in her orms and she's going, 'Hellooo, Rihanna-Brogan! Hellooo! Are you going to talk to me? Are you going to say hellooo?' and making the usual shite-talk. I hear Shadden mention – again – colic and early teething and one or two other problems and Sorcha tilts her head and pulls every sympathetic face in the playbook.

I turn to Honor and I go, 'Will we go over and see your little niece?'

And Honor's like, 'No, thank you.'

'Are you sure?'

'Er, do *you* need your *ears* syringed?'

'No, my ears are fine.'

'So then you're just slow.'

God, she focking hates me.

I watch the photographer look through his lens, then make little adjustments to the various lights he's got scattered about the place, either making them brighter or dimming them down or changing the direction that they're, like, pointing. We're going to be photographed standing in front of, like, a white background apparently.

'Hello,' this voice behind me suddenly goes. I turn around, roysh, and I literally can't believe my eyes. In fact, it's probably only the whiff of gin off her breath that convinces me that I'm *not* hallucinating?

I'm there, 'I didn't think *you'd* show your face.'

She goes, 'Family is the most important thing in the world to me, Ross,' and she pats Honor on the head like she's testing the heat of a hob with her hand.

She's like, 'Hello, there.'

Honor goes, 'Hi,' with an equal lack of interest.

The old dear surveys the room – although mostly she surveys the Tuites. She looks at anyone who earns less than two hundred Ks a year as a potential mugger.

'Well, they certainly make an interesting study,' she goes. 'Although a study in what precisely, I'm not so sure.'

Honor goes, 'They're like the Chamber of Horrors in Madame Tussauds,' and the old dear breaks her balls laughing. It's, like, not even fake laughter. For once it's actually *genuine*?

She's there, 'That's a good one, Honor. Oh, that *is* a good one.'

I'm like, 'So come on, out with it. Why are you here?'

She tries to go, 'I told you, Ross, I'm very much a family person.'

Except I'm just like, 'You want something from me. You might as well tell me, so I can tell you to go fock yourself now.'

She sighs, roysh, then she goes, 'Will you go on *Miriam Meets* with me?'

I'm like, 'Go fock yourself.'

'Ross, please.'

'This is to plug your so-called book?'

'It's part of my publicity schedule, yes.'

'What even is *Miriam Meets*?'

'It's a radio show in which Miriam O'Callaghan interviews two people – at least one of whom is a well-known Irish personality – about their connection through love, friendship or family.'

'Why would you want me on that? I hate your basic guts and I'd have to end up saying it.'

'Oh, come on, Ross, we both know that's not true. We have far more in common than you've ever cared to admit.'

'Why don't you ask one of your mates? From the Move Funderland to the northside campaign? Or Ban Poor People from the National Gallery?'

'Angela gets too nervous doing anything like that and Delma's in St Kitts.'

'My answer is still go fock yourself.'

'Look, Miriam asked for you specifically, if you must know.'

'Did she?'

I've always had a major thing for Miriam O'Callaghan. That's from, like, way back.

'She said, "What about your son – the one who was a wonderful, wonderful rugby player?"'

'Did she? She actually said that about my rugby?'

I love a compliment. But after the whole, like, Grainne thing, I'm determined to never be suckered again.

'Yes,' she goes, 'she's a big fan of yours, Ross.'

I'm like, 'Okay, I'll do it,' thinking, at the very worst it's an opportunity to flirt my hole off with Miriam and put a few facts about my old dear out there in the public domain. 'So go on then, family person – are you not going to go over and meet your great-granddaughter? Three months old, by the way.'

She goes, 'I *was* about to, thank you very much,' and then she switches her fake smile to full-beam and walks over to where Sorcha, Ronan and Shadden are standing, going, 'So this is my beautiful great-granddaughter! Who's been keeping us apart all this time?'

The photographer – this Matthew dude – suddenly claps his hands together and goes, 'Okay, five minutes, everyone. Are we still waiting for anyone?'

'Yeah,' Kennnet goes, 'm . . . m . . . m . . . moy peerdents.'

231

I'm there, 'Yeah, no, plus Tina and her crew,' and it's, like, speak of the devil, because suddenly in they walk – we're talking Tina, her old pair and her brother Anto, who I haven't seen in literally donkeys. He was the transition year student I exchanged homes with back in the day as port of the effort by the Jesuits to get us to see how the other half lived. He robbed everything in our gaff that wasn't soldered to the floor, while I rode his sister and made her pregnant with Ronan. But then, you know all that.

I'm there, 'Anto, how the hell are you?'

He's like, 'Howiya?'

I say the exact same thing to Tina and her old pair and they're like, 'Howiya?' as well.

Anto just stares Kennet out of it and goes, 'Look at dat fooken scoombag.'

Seriously, if someone like Tina's brother gives you a bad character reference, then you know you're a worthless piece of shit.

Tina turns around to me and goes, 'Did you talk to um?' meaning Kennet.

I'm like, 'Not yet, no.'

She goes, 'Fooken when then?' the absolute chormer that she is. I look over at him and he's reminiscing with my old man about characters they both knew in prison – 'I'll t . . . t . . . t . . . tell you who's arthur getting t . . . t . . . t . . . teddible strung out . . .' – and I just think, hey, there's no time like the present.

I tip over and go, 'Kennet, can I've a word in private?'

He's like, 'Er, yeah, no woodies.'

I find a quiet corner and he follows me over. He's like, 'So what's th . . . th . . . thrubbling ye, Ross?' with the usual big grin on his face.

I'm there, 'Did you lend my son money?'

He's like, 'B . . . B . . . B . . . Becka peerden?'

'You focking heard me. Did you lend Ronan moo?'

'Tat'd be between me and Roatnan. C . . . C . . . Cloyunt confidentiality, knowmean?'

'You *did* lend him money. Thirty Ks. I know it for a fact.'

'Soddy, what's it to do wit you in n . . . n . . . n . . . nanyhow?'

'What it has to do with me is that he's my basic son.'

232

'Look, it's an exp . . . p . . . p . . . p . . . p . . . pensive bidiness set-ting up a howum. I toalt um the muddy was there if he wanted to boddy it. Ine oatenly helping the fedda get a steert.'

'Well, I don't want to see him throwing away his future to pay off some focking loan shork.'

'Who are you c . . . c . . . cawden a loaten sheerk?'

'I'm calling you one. A focking scumbag one. You might fool my old man, but you don't fool me. What kind of interest are you chorging him?'

'Tat's b . . . b . . . b . . . between me and ta c . . . c . . . cloyunt.'

I'm there, 'How *focking* much?' and he suddenly knows I'm not in the mood to be dicked around here.

Sorcha, the old man, Ronan and one or two others look over.

Kennet goes, 'Tree hundoort percent ober ten yee-er.'

I'm like, 'Don't give it to me in percentage terms. Give it to me in basic English. How much is he going to have to pay you back?'

He's there, 'Noyunty – on top of ta orichinal toorty. And watch who you're cawden a scoomback, by the way.'

'Don't threaten me. I've decked a lot bigger than you, you sad focking streak of human misery. That's a hundred and twenty thou-sand euros – is that what we're saying?'

'You tell me. You're the fedda went to the p . . . p . . . posh school.'

'A hundred and twenty is what I make it. I'll give it to you?'

He's like, 'Becka peerden?'

He can't believe that someone could lay their hands on that kind of money without holding up a cash-in-transit van.

I'm there, 'You heard me. I'll get you the hundred and twenty.'

Sorcha's storted talking about putting the Newtownpork Avenue gaff on the morket for the last couple of weeks. This is what I'll do with my whack from it.

'You c . . . c . . . caddent *do* tat,' he goes.

I'm like, 'What do you mean I can't do that?'

'A schedule of p . . . p . . . p . . . payments was agreeyut.'

'Whoa, horsey. You lent him thirty Ks – when? – a month, two months ago? I'm offering you a hundred and twenty Ks pretty much straight away. And you're *still* saying no?'

'Roatnan's a long-teerdem investment. He's m . . . m . . . more vaduable to me in debt.'

Suddenly, it's my turn to go, 'I beg your pordon?'

He has the balls to even smile at me. He'll be lucky if I don't deck him right now on the spot.

'Roatnan nebber sees he's w . . . w . . . wages. Locky pays me direct for he's seervices. Then I thrun Roatnan enough m . . . m . . . muddy for him and Shadden and ta babby to lib on.'

'You've got him focking enslaved,' I go, 'like the dude in *Oliver!* I can't remember who it was who played him.'

Matthew all of a sudden claps his hands together and tells us all to gather in front of the white screen. Everyone does what they're told and then suddenly it's only me and Kennet who they're all waiting on.

'Hee-er,' he goes, turning his back on me, 'you could have a chat wit ta finanshiddle reggalater – aldo I reckon he's bicker fish to f . . . f . . . froy.'

He ends up having a good chuckle to himself, then he walks over to where the others are huddled together and steps right into the front of the shot, with one orm around Ronan and one orm around Shadden, holding the baby.

I stand at the very edge, next to Sorcha and Honor, who makes a point of *not* looking at the camera? She's busy Tweeting. I look over her shoulder and it says, 'omg im doing a photo shoot for combat poverty!!! #ItchyAllOver.'

Sorcha squeezes my hand and goes, 'Hey! Is everything okay?'

I nod. I'm like, 'Yeah, no, it's *all* good.'

The old man goes, 'Oh, Kennet! Who would have believed that our old friend Fate would throw us together like this again?'

And Matthew's there, 'Okay, everyone . . . smile!'

JP answers on the third ring.

'Oh, you're finally picking up,' I go. 'I've been ringing you for three focking weeks. Am I to take it that you finally see the funny side of what happened?'

He's like, 'The funny side?'

I'm there, 'Dude, you didn't see the three of them on Morehamp-ton Road. They'd totally lost it. Screaming and crying. Claire from Bray thought it was like that scene in *Alien* – a focking monster was going to burst out of her stomach. You'd have definitely got a laugh out of it, if you weren't – I'm going to say it – sexually involved with one of the three.'

He goes, 'Why do you keep ringing me, Ross?'

I'm there, 'Jesus, I can't believe you'd ask me that. Dude, I'm one of your best friends.'

'No, you're not. I told you I didn't want anything to do with you.'

'Yeah, no, you were angry. I just presumed you'd take a few weeks to sort your head out, then we'd go for pints and you'd even laugh about it. I'm babysitting at the moment, but I could certainly do scoops tonight.'

There's, like, five seconds of silence and that's when I realize that the dude has actually hung up on me. I can't even begin to tell you how hurt I am in that moment.

I wander out to the hallway and I have a quick listen to what's happening upstairs. They say that, don't they? You should always make an effort to know what shit your kids are up to. Honor is having, like, a playdate with her friends Georgette and Allison with two Ls, as well as the famous Ross Junior, who wasn't supposed to be port of the original line-up, but Sorcha asked Lauren to go shopping with her to find a dress for this whole vow renewal thing. Her and Lauren have really become bosom buds since Erika focked off.

Upstairs, they're playing – get this – day spa! The last I saw of them, Honor was going through all of Sorcha's lotions, potions and mixed emotions, giving Georgette and Allison the full makeover treatment.

I can hear them now – you know what kids are like – arguing over who's going to be which Kardashian.

Georgette's like, 'No, I want to be Kim.'

Except Honor's going, 'No, you have to be Khloé!' which is obvi-ously just her being a wagon, roysh, because Khloé isn't the best of them – I think everyone would accept that.

Georgette's there, 'I said I wanted to be Kim first!'

But Honor's like, 'Er, it doesn't *matter* who said it first? You're no Kim Kardashian, Georgette. Hashtag – look in the mirror.'

She's *being* a bitch? But at the same time, she *has* a point. Georgette's not going to win a lot of beauty pageants in her life and it's probably better all round that she hears that now.

I tip down to the kitchen and switch on the Nespresso. I'm still in a bit of shock over the way JP spoke to me. I pop a Ristretto capsule into the machine and I think about all the shit we've been through over the years – as, like, *mates*?

Of course then I end up just ringing him back.

He answers by going, 'We've an auction starting in five minutes. I don't have time for this shit.'

I'm there, 'Dude, you and me have a long history. This isn't the first time I've focked you over. I've been doing it to you for years. Not just you – Fionn, Christian, Oisinn. All of you. I don't understand this reaction.'

'Ross . . .'

'No, Dude, let me finish. This is a girl who called *me* ignorant, can I just remind you? Well, *I'm* not *her* biggest fan, let me just say. Even setting aside the fat whispering. All that, "Sad story! Happy story!" You couldn't listen to that for the rest of your life. You'd end up topping yourself.'

There's, like, five or six seconds of silence and I'm beginning to think he's maybe hung up on me again, when suddenly – totally out of left-field – he goes, 'She's pregnant, Ross.'

I'm there, 'Pregnant?' and, at the same time, I'm thinking there seems to be a fair bit of it about at the moment, between her and Lauren.

'Wait a minute,' I suddenly go, 'are you saying that it's yours?'

He's like, 'Yes, it's mine. And do you know the damage you could have done by giving her the fright that you did?'

I'm there, 'Okay, firstly, congratulations – that's if you're happy about the situation. Secondly, you can't hang that on me. I didn't know she was pregnant?'

'You didn't ask.'

'Dude, you're reaching a bit there. Seriously. She's given you an ultimatum, hasn't she? She's turned around to you and gone, "It's him or it's me."'

He doesn't say shit. He doesn't need to. His silence is enough.

He goes, 'I've got work to do,' and then he ends up hanging up on me again.

I knock back my coffee, with my feelings, I suppose, *conflicted*? On the one hand, I'm delighted for the dude. He'll be an amazing dad. He used to be an estate agent – imagine the focking bedtime stories he'll make up.

But at the same time I feel – I'm going to be honest here – *betrayed*? How was I to know that Shoshanna was up the Ballyjames? And what I also can't help thinking about is the number of times I stood by JP down through the years – including when he thought he wanted to become a priest and including when he then decided to go into repossessions instead. Even on the rugby field. He was possibly one of the best full-backs to ever play the game at schools level. But a lot of that was down to the fact that he had me to protect him. I'm thinking about the amount of punishment I took for him on the field.

And I'm thinking how we all swore – we're talking me, JP, Christian, Fionn and Oisinn – back when we were fourteen and discovering drink and girls for the first time, that we would never, ever fall out over a woman. Whatever happened to that promise?

I decide to go and check on Honor and the other three. I tip upstairs, at the same time comforting myself with the notion that the dude will eventually come round. I push Honor's door and I go, 'Sorry, kids, I just wanted to check was everything . . .'

I end up not even finishing my sentence, roysh, because I can tell that something is instantly wrong. Instead of there being, like, three girls and a boy in the room, there's suddenly four girls. I'm thinking, okay, what the fock is going on here?

I end up spending, like, twenty seconds looking from one to the other before I finally cop what's happened. Honor has dressed Ross Junior up as Kim Kardashian.

Jesus Christ.

He's wearing Honor's favourite Little Black Dress and – I'm not exaggerating here – his own bodyweight in foundation, nail vornish, lipstick and eyeliner. His hair is in braids. Honor has even stuck him in a pair of her high-heel shoes.

'Roth,' the kid goes, 'I'm wearing make-up and a dreth.'

I'm like, 'Okay, what the fock?' because it's all I can basically think to *say*?

Allison with two Ls goes, 'It wasn't us,' meaning her and Georgette.

Honor looks at me and just shrugs. 'He wants to be a girl,' she goes, 'so I made him into a girl.'

Ross goes, 'Roth, Honor let me wear her pretthy dreth.'

It's at that exact moment I hear the sound of tyres on the gravel outside and I know that this isn't going to be my day.

Honor smiles at me and goes, 'Oh, no!' pretending to actually give a shit. 'Mommy is home! What will Lauren say when she sees Ross looking like this?' and it's a horrible moment, roysh, because I realize that she actually did this just to land me in the shit. She's possibly never going to forgive us for trying to bring Rihanna-Brogan into the gaff. Or stop blaming us for her not becoming the new Saoirse Ronan. And this is a sign of how much she despises me.

She's there, 'Oh my God, what are you going to do, Daddy?' being a definite bitch.

I realize that I have to think fast here.

I go, 'Okay, where are the cucumber wipes?' knowing that I've got about thirty seconds to scrub my godson's face clean and come up with a plausible explanation for him wearing a dress.

Honor's like, 'Cucumber wipes?' pretending she's never heard of them.

I'm there, 'Don't act the innocent, Honor. You know what I'm talking about. The wipes your old dear uses to remove her make-up in the evenings.'

She goes, 'I don't think she has any left.'

Honor has hidden them, in other words.

I hear the front door open, then Sorcha shouts, 'Ross, we're home!' and it echoes through the house. 'Are you upstairs?'

Shit.

Ross goes, 'Roth, I have my nailth varnished. Roth, I have prethy nailth.'

There's, like, a hundred little bottles and tubes and whatever else scattered all over Honor's bed. I'm picking them up one by one and reading what they are, looking for something, anything that sounds like it might have, I don't know, *cleaning* qualities?

But at the same time, I can hear footsteps on the stairs – two sets of footsteps, then Lauren's voice going, 'I still love the second dress you tried. It was, like, classic without being *too* weddingy weddingy?'

And Sorcha goes, 'It's definitely between that and this, like, Jenny Packham gown I saw online.'

And I think, Fock. It's too late.

Suddenly, Sorcha has pushed the door and she's looking around the room with a confused face, obviously thinking the same thing as me five minutes ago – okay, how did three girls and a boy turn into, like, four girls?

Lauren works it out more quickly. She goes, 'What the hell have you done!' and she's looking straight me, holding – I only realize later – a lipstick and an atomizer bottle full of *Liu* perfumed shimmer powder by Guerlain.

I'm still trying to think of something to say when Ross Junior goes, 'Look, Mawmy, I'm a girl! I'm a girl, Mawmy! I'm a girl!'

I'm about to go, 'Er, it wasn't, like, *me* who did this? It was actually Honor?' but I end up not even getting the words out.

Lauren walks over to me and slaps me hord across the face. As in, like, *really* hord? To the point where it'll end up being red for, like, a *day* or two? Then she turns, grabs Kim Kardashian Junior and just, like, storms out of the room, then downstairs and out of the house, with Sorcha following her, apologizing for my – yes, *my* – behaviour.

Honor laughs a really evil laugh.

'Hillare,' she goes, looking straight at me in, like, a challenging way. 'Oh my God! *Hill*-are!'

It's often occurred to me that the essential difference between men and women, when you boil it right down, is that men see things in black and white, while women see things in starless night and cottage cream, anthracite and slipper satin, or Périgord truffle and cosmic focking latte.

Just to, like, bear this out, Sorcha is showing me two identical pieces of white cloth and asking me to express, like, a preference. And given that I haven't had my first coffee of the day yet, she might as well be asking me to choose between two different ways she blows her focking nose – in other words, it's not something I really *give* a shit about at, like, ten past seven on a Monday morning?

'That one there,' I go – because you have to pick one, don't you? She's like, 'The tailor's chalk?'

'Definitely – if that's what it's called.'

'Last night you said you preferred the Stowe hoar.'

Why the fock are you asking me again then? That's what I want to say. I don't, though. I go, 'Yeah, no, I've had a chance to sleep on it now, Babes, and I'm definitely preferring the other one.'

'The tailor's chalk?'

'Yeah, definitely. It's amazing what a night's sleep will do. What's all this about anyway?'

'I told you last night, Ross. I'm trying to choose the tablecloths for our vow renewal banquet.'

'Yeah, no, I forgot.'

'Oh my God, there's, like, *so* much work to do between now and June.'

'Work, as in?'

'The morquee! The flowers! The dress! The save-the-dates! The colour theme! The music! The invitations! The decorations! What are we going to give people to eat, for example? What readings are we going to choose?'

'I don't mind taking a back seat for all of this, Babes.'

'I was thinking iced mint green tea, followed by chilled English pea soup with crème fraîche, blackberry walnut salad with lime ginger vinaigrette, herb panzanella with tomatoes and husk cherries and then frozen affogato for dessert.'

'Sounds good to me.'

'It's, like, summery-summery. And for the reading I was thinking something from Ecclesiastes.'

'Hey, I'm a fan.'

'And speaking of which, we're going to see Father Seamus the week after next. He's on the parish trip to the Holy Land at the moment.'

'I'm going to say fair focks.'

'Did you wake Honor?'

'I did, yeah.'

'And?'

'She buried her head under the pillow and told me she hated me fifteen or sixteen times.'

'She's really not a morning person.'

'She's not too hot in the afternoons or the evenings either, Sorcha. I don't think her being a bitch was ever a time-of-day issue, to be fair.'

Sorcha hands me my coffee and smiles. She goes, 'I think this thing we're doing is, like, *so* a good idea, though.'

What she's talking about is us – as in, like, me *and* Sorcha – dropping Honor to school together in the mornings, as opposed to Sorcha doing it three or four days a week and me doing it one or two. She says that Honor needs to become acclimated to being in a two-parent family again and the more things we do – the three of us together – the more happy and secure she will feel in her changed environment.

Sorcha reads possibly too many books.

She goes, 'When are we going to tell her, by the way?'

I'm there, 'Tell her what?'

'About us renewing our vows.'

'Do you think she'll give a fock one way or the other?'

'It's a huge thing for her, Ross. I'm beginning to think that a lot of Honor's behavioural problems relate to insecurity. I've been reading some books . . .'

'I thought you had. I definitely picked up on one or two signs.'

'No, Ross, let me finish. I've been reading some books and I've come to the conclusion that watching her mother and father separate must have – oh my God – *so* fractured her trust in adult role models. Seeing us reaffirm our commitment to each other in front of our families and friends – *and* obviously God – can only help repair that fracture and make her feel more, basically, *stable*?'

'Babes, she dressed Christian and Lauren's little boy up as a little girl just to land me in the shit. There's something seriously wrong there. I took a slap across the face for it – and you let me, by the way.'

It's still a sore point with me. Sorcha never told Lauren that it was actually Honor.

She's like, 'I know you think I should have defended you, Ross. You weren't the one in the wrong. I'm just tired of Honor being seen as the villain all the time. Oh, and I know you and I always joke about her being a little bitch, but we're actually going to stop saying that, because it's not nice.'

'Even though it's true?'

'Our friends hear us talking about our daughter like that and, like, they think *they* can talk about her like that? She doesn't need people hating on her. She needs love and she needs security and it's up to us – as, like, her parents? – to give it to her.'

Sorcha steps out into the entrance hallway and shouts up the stairs, 'Honor! Honor, dear!' in, like, a proper Julie Andrews voice. 'Come and have some breakfast with Mommy and Daddy!'

See, I wouldn't see this as the actual way to go. Father Fehily used to tell us this old African saying that to give in to a bully is to feed a lion your chickens in the hope that the focker will eat you last.

I'm there, 'Did I tell you that JP's going to be a father?'

She goes, 'Oh! My God!'

'Yeah, no, that explains why he couldn't see the funny side of that whole Shoshanna thing. He said she could have lost the baby.'

'Oh my God, that's a bit horsh. You didn't know she was pregnant.'

'Exactly. Thanks for the back-up, Babes.'

'Not that I'm defending what you did. I still think it was appalling. Claire and Garret are still waiting for you to apologize, by the way.'

'They're going to be waiting a long focking time.'

Sorcha then remembers something. There was a letter for me. She collected the post from Newtownpork Avenue yesterday.

'Here,' she goes, pushing it across the breakfast table to me. The envelope is brown, which is always a sign of trouble. I stort tearing it open.

'I forgot to ask you,' she goes, 'what happened to Ronan's eye? It was all black when we were doing the photo the other day.'

I haven't actually told her about Ronan becoming Kennet's slave. Maybe it's because I don't want her to worry or maybe it's because I'm ashamed that I let it happen.

'He, em, got a bang playing soccer,' I go.

She's like, 'Soccer? That's like, oh my God!'

I'm like, 'Ooohhh, shit.'

Sorcha goes, 'What's wrong? Who's the letter from?'

'I've been called up for focking jury service.'

Sorcha takes the letter from me. 'Oh my God,' she goes, 'you are *so* lucky.'

I'm like, 'What?'

'I would love to be on a jury. I've been reading loads of Ivana Bacik's cases recently. I'm, like, obsessed with the woman. And with the whole, like, *legal* thing? You *are* doing it, I presume?'

'I am in my focking hole.'

'Ross, it's your duty as a citizen.'

'Fock that. I'll get the old man to write them a letter saying, I don't know, Ross broke both of his legs playing the game he loves – the game of rugby. Actually, that's exactly how I'll get him to phrase it. "The game he loves – and the name of that game is rugby." I genuinely love it as a turn of phrase.'

All of a sudden, Honor walks in and the kitchen dorkens. Or seems to. She sighs. At nothing. Just sighs as if the world and everything in it bores her.

'Good morning!' Sorcha goes, all chirpy and enthusiastic, like the woman on the Kotex ad telling the world how happy her focking sanitary towels make her. 'Will you have half a baked grapefuit or are you just going to have muesli?'

Honor goes, 'Okay, do you remember I told you about outdoor voices and indoor voices? Hashtag – lower the volume.'

Sorcha's there, 'Don't be like that, Honor – your father and I have some news for you.'

She's like, 'I already know this is going to be lame.'

'We're renewing our vows!'

She laughs. 'What vows?'

'Our wedding vows.'

'Er, *how* old are you two again?'

'And I was going to ask you if you'd do me the honor of being my flower girl?'

'Oh my God – puke!'

'Honor, I thought you'd be excited.'

'Oh, yes, Mommy, believe me, I'm totes emosh.'

Miriam O'Callaghan introduces us as 'Fionnuala O'Carroll-Kelly – novelist, screenwriter, style icon, philanthropist and, I think it's fair to say, humanitarian' and – this is the bit that really grinds my gears – 'her son, Ross'.

As in, she doesn't say anything *about* me? She doesn't mention that George Hook said, 'This kid attacks the gain line like no Irish player has for a generation,' or that Tony Ward said, 'Provided he lives his life right, he will make the Irish number ten jersey his own for a decade to come.'

Yeah, no, that *all* gets swept under the corpet.

Miriam looks great, though. I'll say that in her defence. She goes, 'You're both very welcome to the show.'

She has a way with people – of really putting you at, like, your *ease*?

The old dear goes, 'Thank you, Miriam. I listen to it every week. Even when I'm in California – my L.A. life, as I like to call it – I never, ever miss a show.'

Miriam's there, 'Oh, thank you so much, Fionnuala!' and then she turns to me. 'So, Ross, what was it like growing up with this amazing mother? Actually, I'm going to use the word Supermom, because she is *all* of these things. A multimillion-selling author? A mother? An activist? A fashionista? A screenwriter? A fundraiser? A wonderful pianist and singer? We're going to hear her play, I hope, in a moment. A model? A voice on behalf of the vulnerable in our society? What was *that* like, Ross, growing up with this extraordinary, extraordinary woman as your mother? For instance, what are your earliest memories of her?'

I'm there, 'I would sum it up, Miriam, by saying the smells of *Eternity* by Calvin Klein, extreme sexual frustration and the fistfuls of fresh mint she used to chew on to try to hide the smell of drink off her breath.'

The old dear continues on smiling, pretending she's not hurt by it. Miriam is more than a bit taken aback, though. She's trying to see around me, to someone sitting at the mixing desk through the glass, obviously thinking, okay, why didn't my researchers tell me that this is a dude who isn't afraid to consistently call it?

I go, 'One thing I will say in her favour, though, is that later on, when I was playing rugby, I never once came up against a forward – however big, however ugly – who scared me. That was because, as a baby, I always had that focking face there bearing down at me in my pram, like something Tim Burton would draw in a bad mood.'

The show is being pre-recorded, by the way, and I'm praying they don't cut out all of my really cracking lines.

Miriam turns around to the old dear and goes, 'Er, maybe we'll lighten the mood a little with our first piece of music. Fionnuala, will you *play* something for us?'

The old dear gives this, like, embarrassed laugh – 'Oh, you're terrible, putting me on the spot, Miriam!' – trying to pretend it *wasn't* all prearranged? She has the focking sheet music in front of her.

'Come on, Fionnuala,' Miriam goes, 'I've heard you play *and* sing many, many times and you have a fantastic voice.'

The old dear hops up from the desk and runs for the piano like she's just been told there's a bottle of Beefeater hidden inside it.

She storts tinkering, tinkling, whatever you want to call it, with the keys, while doing this big, ridiculously long-winded introduction to the song.

'Miriam,' she goes, 'it's a very difficult time for a great many people out there at the moment. The world as we knew it has changed. There's no point in denying that reality. A lot of the old certainties have gone. People I know, people we all know, have lost their jobs, their homes, their fortunes, their sense of themselves . . .'

I make a big yawning sound into the microphone.

'I myself personally have known difficult days. I've known years of struggle. And this much I've learned from my own travails. We *will* get through this. We will get through this as a country and we will get through this as people. This is a song that has always inspired me when life feels like an uphill struggle, as it often does. It's called "Living in These Troubled Times".'

'Maura O'Connell,' Miriam goes. 'From *A Woman's Heart*! I *love* this song!'

I'm disappointed in Miriam, it has to be said. I thought there'd be a lot more flirting with me across the table and a lot more ripping the pistachio out of my old dear's new book. I pick it up off the desk just as the so-called singing storts – she sounds like a donkey being sexually assaulted with a vinegar bottle.

Miriam has her eyes closed and a smile on her face and is just, like, rolling her head from side to side in, like, appreciation – pretend appreciation, obviously.

I open *Fifty Greys in Shades* at, like, a random page and it's a scene – I shit you not – involving a character called Ace, who's described as 'an octogenarian from Monaloe Park in Cabinteely – a demon at the dominoes table and a devil between the sheets'. For the sake of decency, I'm not going to describe to you what actually happens in this scene, other than to say that he ends up throwing this seventy-four-year-old woman called Agnes a bone while she's straddling him on the bidet with the water jets on full.

I'll spare you the details.

And even worse, roysh, the old dear has managed to work all these – I'm presuming – *dominoes* terms into the story? As, like, sex-ual innuendos? We're talking pivot. We're talking shuffle. We're talking doublet. We're talking spinner. At one point Agnes fingers Ace's pips, while *he* stares admiringly at her open end.

Do we not have a thing called censorship in this country?

The old dear finishes, thanks be to fock, and returns to the table. Miriam gives her a huge round of applause – she's a lovely woman, in fairness to her – then goes, 'And can I just say that while you were performing there, Ross was glued – and I mean *glued* – to your new number one bestselling book, *Fifty Greys in Shades*, which is available, as they say, in all good bookshops.

'Now, Fionnuala, before we go on to talk *about* the book, as well as all of your other wonderful successes, tell me first about this fine young man sitting beside you here. Because he's your only child. And I'm sure that when you look back on your life, reflecting on all of your extraordinary successes, Ross must rank as your one overall crowning achievement.'

The old dear – I swear to God – goes, 'Oh, no . . . no, I wouldn't say that at all, Miriam.'

I can't even begin to tell you how suddenly hurt I am by that. It's like I've been kicked in the stomach. I go to call her a hatchet-faced pronk, but the words won't come out.

'Ross hinted at it there at the top of the programme,' she goes. 'We've never had much of a relationship. We've certainly never had what you might call the conventional Irish mother–son relationship. Even now, there's very little between us in the way of warmth or affection or anything like that.'

This is good radio and Miriam instantly knows it. 'And whose fault *was* that?' she goes. 'Was it, would you say, a combination of perhaps the two of you?'

The old dear's like, 'Oh, no, Miriam – it was entirely down to me.'

I am literally stunned into silence. All my basic life, I've been waiting for her to admit that and now the moment is finally here.

She goes, 'You mentioned in your introduction, Miriam, all the various things I've done. Author? Yes, I've sold thirty-seven million books worldwide. Fundraiser? Yes, I've responded to nineteen natural disasters on four continents and the person I'm most often compared with is Adi Roche – I hope I did *something* to ease people's suffering. Style icon? Look, if clothes look fabulous on me, then they look fabulous on me. But a mother? No. I can't accept any credit for that. My record at mothering – if you want to call it that – is the single biggest blot on the copybook of my life. My only *real* failure, some would say. But an unforgivable one, because it was the most important job I was ever given to do.'

Miriam goes, 'But, Fionnuala, surely you're being hord on yourself.'

I reach across the table and touch Miriam's hand. 'Let her talk,' I go. 'This is all good shit. Trust me.'

The old dear's like, 'I was a reluctant mother. I don't think I'm trampling on Ross's feelings – *or* telling him anything particularly new – by saying that children never figured in my life plan. But once Ross came along, well, my life plan should have gone out the window. Like everyone's does. It was time for me to step up. Like I did when 138,000 people were killed by the Bangladeshi Cyclone in 1981. Like I did after the Aremero tragedy in Colombia in 1985 – 23,000 innocents, Miriam. Like I did after the Chernobyl thing, although it's Adi who's most associated with that and good luck to her.

'The point I'm trying to make is that I could organize a charity coffee morning or tray-bake sale like no one on Earth. I could empa-thize with these poor children in Mexico and in Ethiopia and in Cambodia and in, em . . . I've forgotten what country Chernobyl is in – it'll come back to me. I could empathize with these poor, often starving, orphan children whom I'd never met before. And yet I couldn't connect with this little baby – who was my own flesh and blood, remember – whose cries for attention and love and, yes, occasionally food went unanswered by a mother who was up to her elbows in self-raising flour and just self-importance.'

Fock me. I'm floored by this, can I just say? I genuinely didn't think she was going to open up like this.

'Were you depressed?' Miriam goes. 'Do you think you were suf-fering from perhaps post-natal depression?'

'Oh, undoubtedly!' the old dear goes. 'Oh, of course! But that's not an excuse, Miriam. I just didn't want the responsibility. I was cold. I was withholding. And Ross grew up resenting me for that. And quite frankly I don't blame him.'

I'm there, 'These are genuinely lovely things to hear, by the way.' And I mean it.

The old dear's like, 'But will I tell you the really wonderful thing to come out of this, Miriam? When I see him now with his own son and daughter. And his granddaughter. He became a grandfather just before Christmas. He's so wonderful with them. So caring. So giving. So full of love. He really would do anything for them . . .'

I immediately think of Ronan. Then, a few seconds later, I think of Honor.

She goes, 'Ross's father, Charles, is the same, of course – a wonderful man and a wonderful father. But the irony in all of this is that I think Ross learned how to be a good parent from watching his mother be a completely disastrous one. He learned how to do it by first learning how *not* to do it, if you see what I mean.

'So you can sit there, Miriam, and tell me that I've written books, saved lives, worn a Marlene Birger Malagasia blazer with Clesenzia tapered pants to the recent I.F.T.A.s and – as one magazine put it – proved that rich velvets in Gothic hues scream seduction, but what I would say back to you is this: I would much rather have done nothing with my life and been a good mother. And I would give up everything I own tomorrow just to be able to say that I was even half the parent my son is . . .'

Oh, shit. My eyes are storting to tear up here.

'I love him very dearly, Miriam. I don't know if he loves me. It's all very complicated, but it's a mess of my own making. But when I see him with his son and with his daughter, I am in awe. And even though we've never been friends and we probably never will be, I admire him – genuinely admire him – more than anyone I've ever known.'

Jesus focking Christ.

Miriam looks at me. She's like, 'Are you okay, Ross?'

I just nod.

She's there, 'You're very emotional, I can see. Do you want to introduce *your* first piece of music, a song that you said always reminds you of your mother whenever you hear it,' and she looks down at her notes. '"Fat Girl" by Niggaz Wit Attitudes.'

I'm like, 'Don't play that . . . don't play it . . . please.'

She goes, 'Do you want to choose a different song?'

I'm there, 'I was only focking around. Yeah, no, a different song, definitely. I'll come up with something,' and then I turn to the old dear. 'We did have *some* good times.'

'Of course we did!'

'I'm saying my childhood wasn't, like, *totally* bad? We had laughs, didn't we?'

'Yes, I'm sure we did.'

Neither of us manages to come up with anything specific.

I'm there, 'Right, laughs. I think what I'm saying is you shouldn't be kicking the shit out of yourself over the way you raised me. You didn't do that bad a job. And, yeah, no, when it comes to the whole admiration thing, I definitely admire you.'

'Do you?'

'I wouldn't go so far as to call it awe. But, yeah, no, you write those books, for example. I mean, they're not *my* thing, but they seem to sell by the skipload, for whatever reason. Looks-wise, I personally think you're raddled – you know that – but all these fashion magazines seem to think you're some – I don't know – rare beauty. And they're *in* that industry, so they know a thing or two about a thing or two. Then all the charity stuff. Don't think I wasn't proud of all that.'

'Really?'

'What did you raise for, like, Somalia that time?'

'One hundred and eighty-six pounds, before expenses.'

'Oh. I thought it was actually more than that. But even so, how many lives did that save? A lot would be my guess.'

The old dear smiles. I'm not going to spoil a beautiful moment by saying what she looks like.

A trout suffocating in jam.

And even though I know I'm going to regret this, I surrender to the moment and I end up going, 'That thing a minute ago when you said that you didn't know if I, like, focking loved you or whatever. Well, I'm just letting you know – focking blah, blah, blah – that those feelings, obviously from my point of view – again, blah, blah, blah – are, I suppose, very much there for me as well.'

She puts her hand on top of mine. She goes, 'After everything I put you through, Ross, I can't tell you what an unexpected but beautiful thing that is to hear.'

It's a moment – there's no denying that. Something tells me I don't want to be in the focking country when it goes out on radio, though.

Miriam goes, 'Do you want to choose another piece of music, Ross? A lot of people like *"Non, Je Ne Regrette Rien"*?'

The old dear goes, 'No . . . play "Fat Girl".'

And she continues on holding my hand, while I dry my eyes with my other hand, and we end up listening to the entire song, the two of us just staring into each other's eyes and smiling and wishing things had been maybe different but knowing that we wouldn't be the people we are today if they had been.

Sorcha's old man can't bring himself to even look at me. He has some set of sphericals, you'd have to say.

'I'd like to speak with my daughter,' he goes, staring at a point basically six inches above my head.

I'd be perfectly within my rights to shut the door in his face after what he tried to pull. Except I don't. Because it's nice to be nice – especially knowing how much it pisses *him* off.

'Edmund,' I go, 'step in out of the rain there. I'm glad you're here. I was going to give you a bell about that Jacuzzi upstairs. Do you know how to change the massage function?'

He doesn't answer. That's how he's choosing to play it, see. Just blank me. Pretend I don't exist.

Sorcha steps out into the hallway. She's been in the kitchen all morning, putting the save-the-dates in the envelopes. She's like, 'Ross, who's at the . . .' and then she cops him standing there and ends up totally flipping. She goes, 'I told you I didn't want to see you again and I meant what I said . . .'

He goes straight on the offensive then. He steps past me into the house going, 'You've had your say, young lady, now let me speak.'

Young lady. I can't believe I was *actually* feeling sorry for this knob end.

He goes, 'I'm not here to apologize,' making sure to get that out there early on. 'I'm here to tell you that I'm disappointed in you.'

Sorcha's like, '*You're* disappointed?'

I laugh. I can't help it. This focker hires a bird to see how ready and willing I'd be to cheat on Sorcha – *she* texts me a shot of her lemons – and he has the balls to try to claim, I don't know, the moral *high* ground?

'Yes,' he goes, 'I'm disappointed. With the choices you've made. With one choice in particular. Everything that has gone wrong in your life can be traced back to the moment you met this . . . fool of a man!'

I say fock-all.

Sorcha's like, 'What's gone wrong, Dad? What – in your view – has gone wrong in my life?'

'Well, your career for a start.'

'What career?'

'Precisely.'

'Excuse me, I ran a fashion boutique, which *Image* magazine named as one of the twelve best places to shop in Dublin.'

'And what happened to becoming Ireland's first female Attorney General?'

'Oh my God, I was, like, eight years old when I said that.'

'Or a human rights lawyer?'

'So I chose a different path in life. You're disappointed because I didn't become a human rights lawyer?'

'I'm disappointed that you surrendered all those ambitions you had to spend your life with him and his daughter.'

'*His* daughter?'

'Yes, *his* daughter.'

'Honor is my daughter as well.'

'I don't see anything of you in her. Obnoxious little brat. Oh, believe me, she's all him.'

He's out of order. The princess complex she definitely got from *their* side of the family.

Sorcha ends up going totally bananas. She's like, 'Don't you dare speak about my daughter like that! Don't you *dare*! And don't you *dare* come to *my* home and start criticizing my whole life! What about you? What about the choices *you've* made? You gambled everything you had – your savings? your security? this *house*? – and poor Mum has ended up living in some rented box in the middle of an industrial estate. Let *me* tell *you* something, Dad – *I'm* disappointed in *you*!'

It's a massive, massive thing for Sorcha to say and all three of us immediately know it. It's, like, a genuine *game* changer? Sorcha and her old man, bear in mind, have hardly exchanged an angry word in thirty years.

Not that I ever thought their relationship was healthy. I have this theory that no matter how much you love your old pair – even if you think the world of them and they think the world of you – at some point, preferably in your teens, you need to tell them to go and fock themselves.

Get it out of the way early would be my basic advice.

– *Mum?*

– *Yes, Son?*

– *Go and fock yourself.*

– *Oh. You've never spoken like that to me before.*

– *Well, it needed to be said . . . Dad?*

– *Sorry, Son, I'm just re-grouting the floor tiles in the bathroom.*

– *Don't stop on my account. I just wanted to tell you that you're a prick and that you should definitely go and fock yourself.*

You show me someone who's never said that to their mother and father and I'll show you a relationship that isn't built on anything.

Sorcha's old man turns to go. Sorcha follows him to the door, going, 'If you must know, we're renewing our vows. We're asking Father Seamus to do it. And I don't want you there. Mum is invited. And my sister. But you're not welcome.'

He smiles, I think the word is, like, *grimly*?

He goes, 'I watched you make the biggest mistake of your life once. That was difficult enough. I have no desire to see you do it again.'

And then he's gone. Sorcha closes the door after him. I'm expecting, like, tears, except there *aren't* any?

I'm there, 'Are you okay?'

She goes, 'I can't believe he said those things about Honor and my boutique.'

'If you ever want me to deck him, I will – just say the word.'

'Especially about Honor. I know she has her moments, Ross, but I'm actually, like, *tired* of listening to people run her down?'

'Yeah, no, I suppose.'

'And run *you* down.'

She walks over to me and we end up, like, hugging. It's actually alright. She goes, 'Ross, let's draw a line.'

I'm there, 'Okay. What kind of line are we talking?'

'A line under the past. Everything that happened before – girls you may or may not have been with while we were together – I don't care about any of that any more. All I care about is the future. The future with you. But no more lies, Ross. No more cheating.'

'Yeah, no,' I go, 'I'm pretty sure I can handle that.'

The old man is on the phone.

'Ross!' he goes.

I'm like, 'Yeah, there's no need to make such a big focking deal about it.'

'Helen and I just heard you on *Miriam Meets*.'

'Like I said . . .'

'The way you and your mother spoke! To tell each other you loved one another on national radio like that.'

I wish he'd stop focking reminding me. I'm already nearly regretting it. I was too embarrassed to sit and listen to the show with Sorcha, which is the reason I've spent the last hour just driving aimlessly around the whole Dalkey and Killiney area.

Sorcha's rung three or four times, by the way – probably to say the same kind of shit as my old man.

'Oh, it gladdened my heart to hear you two getting along so well,' he goes. 'Well, Helen will tell you, I've been blubbing like a big, bloody well idiot for most of the last half an hour. I've always said it,

you see – said it to Hennessy a thousand times – that Ross and Fionnuala have far more in common than they probably realize.'

I'm like, 'Okay, yeah, can we possibly *change* the subject now?'

He laughs and goes, 'Yes, of course!'

By this stage, I've pointed the Lambo in the direction of – this is
going to sound focked up – but *Sallynoggin*? I've decided to go back
to the old gaff, half out of boredom and possibly half out of nostal-
gia. All of the shit that came out during the interview with Miriam
has got me wondering if I've, like, *misremembered* my childhood –
even though I know I've just made that word up.

I go, 'We did have some good times when I was a kid, didn't we?'

The old man's like, 'Oh course we did! I could probably even give
you five or six instances if I sat down and thought about it for long
enough. But they *were* there – rest assured!'

'It's, like, hord to remember specifics, though, isn't it?'

'Well, it's a long time ago. Wait a minute, didn't you once . . .'

'What?'

'No, my mistake. That was a TV programme I was thinking
about.'

I take the turn into our old estate.

I'm there, 'It doesn't matter anyway. By the way, did you write
that letter for me?'

He goes, 'What letter?'

'The one about my jury service – the one telling them to go and
fock themselves.'

'Oh, yes! It went out with the post on Friday. That was a lovely
turn of phrase – I must congratulate you. *Broke his two legs playing
the game he loves – and the name of that game is rugby!*'

'Yeah, no, I don't know where it even came from. It just struck
me as being really, really good.'

'That would be inspiration, Ross!'

Out of nowhere, I hear myself suddenly go, 'What? The? Fock?'

The old man's there, 'Is everything okay, Ross?'

'What number did we live in again?'

'When?'

'When we lived in the Noggin.'

'Careful! Your mother would still insist on calling it Glenageary, you know! Especially now that she's once again the proprietress!'

'Dude, shut the fock up. What was the actual door number?'

'It was 27.'

'It's gone.'

'What? Kicker, where are you?'

'I'm sitting in the focking cor outside where our old house used to be.'

'*Used* to be?'

'That's what I'm trying to tell you. It's not even there any more.'

I hang up on him. I get out of the cor and I walk slowly to where my childhood home once stood. All that's left of it is, like, a giant crater in the ground. It's genuinely like something out of a science fiction movie.

If M. Night Shyamalan was directing my life, this would be the moment when I find out that my past never actually existed.

'It's gone,' a voice behind me goes.

I turn around. It's an old woman – obviously one of the neighbours – with a little mutt on a lead.

I'm there, 'Where? How?'

'The lady had it knocked down and taken away,' she goes, 'brick by brick.'

It takes a good twenty seconds for that to sink in. I hop back into the cor again and stick its nose this time in the direction of, like, Foxrock. You can't blame me for wondering, what the fock?

Ten minutes later, roysh, I'm pulling up outside the old dear's gaff. I don't bother my orse knocking on the door because during the drive a mad idea occurred to me as to what she might have done. You see it on, like, *MTV Cribs* all the time. We're talking, like, rappers and American footballers who want to be reminded every day – like my old dear said – of how far they've come.

I walk around the side of the gaff, then I end up just stopping and staring in basic silence. Because I was right. She's had our old house in Sallynoggin slash Glenageary knocked down and completely rebuilt at the bottom of her gorden.

All I can do – I told you – is just stand there with my mouth open, shaking my head. It's brilliant and at the same time totally insane. She's like a Bond villain or something – Drax or one of those mad focks.

I turn around, roysh, with the intention of walking back to the cor. But for some reason I decide to pop in and – whatever – say hello.

I reach for one of the French doors leading to the kitchen and I'm sliding it across when I suddenly notice something. It's actually a weird thing to notice, but there are, like, two sets of breakfast dishes on the table. We're talking two plates, two side plates, two glasses, two cups and saucers, two knives, two forks – blah, blah, blah.

Meaning she has company.

There's another plate of what I immediately recognize as the old dear's eggs *en cocotte* with bacon and Gruyère turned upside-down on the floor. Beside it, I notice, is her dressing gown, then her slippers, then another dressing gown. Staring through the glass, I follow this trail of clues across the kitchen floor to the other end of the kitchen, where I notice . . .

Jesus *focking* Christ.

Where I notice . . .

I can't even say it. I can't even take it in. It's like I'm having one of those, I don't know, out of body experiences – watching myself watching, if that makes any sense.

My old dear is . . .

I can't say it.

My old dear is being ridden bug-eyed by some big fat dude.

There. I said it.

He has his back to me. *She* has hers up against the double doors of the Zanussi fridge-freezer, her legs wrapped yoga-style around his enormous waist, holding on to him like a shipwreck victim to a life-buoy, combing her fingers through his curly blond hair, her mouth all over his, bouncing up and down on him like a jockey on a horse with fright.

It's already the worst day of my life and the worst of it hasn't even happened yet.

I slide open the door and I go in. I don't know what focking possesses me, but that's what I do. Maybe I have some idea of what the

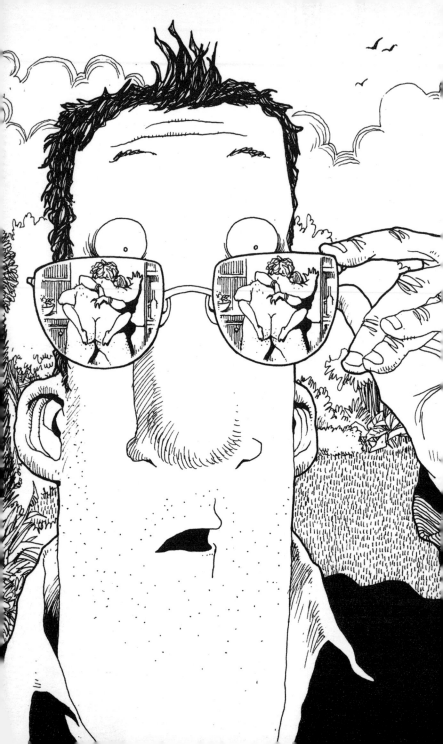

deal is here. You always hear that word subconscience used, don't you?

Suddenly, I'm standing in the kitchen, staring at *his* big flabby orse as he continues on rattling her scaffolding. She's suddenly going, 'Keep . . . doing it . . . Keep . . . on doing it. Don't you dare . . . finish . . . Don't you . . . finish without me . . .' her head back and her eyes shut tight like a dog that's too constipated to go.

I clear my throat, loud enough for *her* to hear. *He* doesn't seem to. I'd say his ears are focking ringing from *her* screams.

She at least has the decency to *act* shocked?

'Oh, Jesus!' she goes when sees me, at the same time trying to dismount. 'Oh, Jesus! Oh, Jesus!' trying to cover her Charleys, like she thinks it's possible to still emerge from this with her dignity intact.

He senses then that something is wrong. He turns his head and that's when I suddenly realize that I know the man who's pounding my old dear up against her own side-by-side, American-style fridge-freezer.

It's Oisinn.

7.

How Beastly!

Sorcha says I must have been mistaken. She says that I – oh my God – *have* to have been? And I end up losing it with her a bit.

I'm like, 'Sorcha, I think I know what Oisinn's orse looks like. I played rugby with him for long enough.'

She's there, 'I'm sorry, Ross. I'm just saying there might be an explanation for it.'

I'm like, 'There *is* an explanation for it. They're hord at it. My old dear and one of my so-called best friends.'

'I don't believe it, Ross.'

'I don't believe it either. But I know what I saw . . . Jesus, he was going at her like a bull at a gate.'

'Okay, way too much information, Ross. I think I can get my head around this *without* the visual reference points?'

'I think I'm going to hurl. I think I'm going to genuinely hurl.'

'Did they say anything? Did *you* say anything?'

'No, like I said, I saw them through the French doors. Well, I saw *her* – getting her jollies up against the fridge. Off what I *hoped* was just some random fat dude she picked up in Buck Whaleys.'

'Why did you go in, Ross?'

'What?'

'If you knew that Fionnuala was having sex in the kitchen, why did you go in?'

'I don't know. But it's a good job I did. Otherwise I would never have caught them in the act.'

'So what happened then?'

'I told you. I saw *his* orse. I stood in as a second row a good few times back in the day. I know it like I nearly know my own. Then *she* saw me. Opened her eyes and saw me. And *he* turned his head and looked straight at me. He said my name. He was like, 'Ross . . .' and I could tell – I swear to fock – that he was about to say that it wasn't what it looked like.'

'Well, what else *could* it have been?'

'Nothing! It was *exactly* what it looked like! Jesus, he was bouncing her up and down hord enough to knock her focking fillings loose.'

'*Ross!*'

'I was like, "Fock you! Fock the two of you!" and then I walked out of there. I still keep hoping that it's, like, a dream I'm going to wake up from.'

'Did they follow you?'

'No – can you believe that? I'm telling you, I doubt if they're even ashamed.'

I'm lying on our bed with, like, a cold compress against my forehead. Sorcha shakes her head. *She* at least has the decency to go, 'Oh my God, what is Fionnuala thinking?'

I'm there, 'Yeah, no, that'd also be *my* point? I mean, there she was on the radio this morning – you heard her – finally admitting what a bet-down, gin-soaked, sea-donkey of a mother she was to me growing up. And she even had me thinking, okay, this is something we can actually build on.'

'Oh my God, the age difference alone has got to be, like, twenty-five years?'

'Yeah, no, try thirty-five. She's always trying to lose a decade of her life, but she's not getting away with it any more.'

'And Oisinn . . .'

'Exactly. Oisinn, who, two years ago, I persuaded to come back to Ireland. Oisinn who was all, "Oh, Ross, I don't know where I'd be today – probably dead – if it wasn't for you coming over to Monte Corlo and bringing me home. Hero of the hour – blah, blah, blah." Where is all of that now?'

My phone all of a sudden rings. The screen says it's Oisinn. It's, like, his fifth time ringing me in the last hour.

Sorcha goes, 'Are you going to answer that?'

I'm like, 'No,' and once again I kill it.

'I still can't believe he'd do it to you, Ross.'

'Yeah, well, certain things are storting to add up for me. *Him* slipping away from the pub early on New Year's Eve? He was obviously heading for Foxrock to throw *her* a bone. I even asked him if he had something on the go. You know he had the balls to tell me it was some florist called Holly?'

'Didn't Fionnuala once work as a florist?'

'She focking did actually.'

'And maybe he said Holly because they were first with each other – as in *with* with? – at Christmas time.'

'Why are you trying to make it sound romantic?'

'I wasn't.'

'They were first with each other – as in *with* with – at Christmastime. That's what you just said. It's not romantic, Sorcha.'

'I know.'

'It's sick and depraved.'

'That's possibly a bit over the top.'

'Oh, is it? Well, how would you like if it you walked into the kitchen and caught me bailing into *your* mother?'

That would never happen, by the way. Her old dear isn't great – even though she *has* an alright body and has always been a major backer of mine.

'Again, Ross, you don't have to keep painting pictures for me, okay?'

'I'm just saying, Sorcha, I don't think you'd just stand there while we were pulling up our trousers and go, "Oh my God, random! When were you first with each other – as in, like, *with* with?"'

I suddenly stand up and I throw the cold compress down on the bed.

Sorcha's like, 'Okay, where are you going now?'

I'm there, 'I'm going to see what my old man thinks of this.'

'But what can *he* do about it?'

'He can hopefully talk some sense into the twisted hag.'

'They're divorced.'

'So?'

'So Charles has his life now and Fionnuala has hers. He's not going to tell her what she can and can't do.'

'Oh, isn't he?' I go, at the same time throwing on my jacket. 'We'll see about that.'

I step out onto the landing, or the passageway, or whatever we're agreeing to call it.

'You know, just once,' I go, 'just once, I would love to know what it feels like to be port of a normal family.'

As I pass Honor's room, she goes, 'Join the club, Daddy dearest! Join the club!'

I hop into the Lambo and I head for Ailesbury Road. It's, like, a Sunday lunchtime, so there's fock-all traffic, except for people coming from probably Mass. The whole way there, I'm thinking, yeah, no, you're going to wake up any minute now and realize that it's all been basically a nightmare.

A horrible thought hits me as I'm letting myself into the gaff. What if the old man and Helen are also going at it? I don't think I'd ever recover from the shock of that. But then I think, yeah, no, *they've* got more actual sense.

I wander down to the kitchen, except it ends up being empty. The table is set for two. They're having, like, duck foie gras with Melba toasts and there's, like, two glasses of Champagne also poured. There's no recession in this house – that much is pretty much obvious. I stuff a load of foie gras between two pieces of toast and shove it into my mouth, washing it down with one of the glasses of Champagne, then the other.

I hadn't realized how badly I needed a drink. It's possibly even a bit of delayed shock.

I look out the window. The old man and Helen are in the back gorden. Fully clothed, I'm happy to report. They're, like, walking hand in hand back towards the house, deep in conversation.

The old man opens the back door for her and I hear him go, 'They're saying more than half of the country still hasn't paid this household charge. The Government badly mishandled it, of course.

You mark my words, it won't be long before Fianna Fáil are riding high in the opinion polls again,' and I'm thinking, yeah, go on, you focking silver-tongued chormer.

Helen's delighted to see me, in fairness to her. *He* seems disappointed, though, as if I'm suddenly, like, *interrupting* something?

He goes, 'Ross? Oh. Um, if it's about your car insurance, just leave the giro slip on the table in the hall and I'll pay it in the morning,' trying to get rid of me quickly.

I'm there, 'It's not *about* my cor insurance – although that *is* due, now that you mention it. It's about your ex-wife carrying on like a sick, deranged . . .'

'Ross,' the old man has the balls to go, 'this really isn't a good time. Helen and I were just about to sit down to a – quote-unquote – *romantic* lunch.'

I'm there, 'A romantic lunch? Yeah, no, I heard one or two of your lines there. Fianna Fáil and the focking household chorge. I really don't know how you keep your hands off him, Helen.'

Helen laughs, to be fair to her. I *am* good value.

She goes, 'I'll set another place for you, Ross,' and she heads off down the other end of the kitchen to get a plate and a glass and some cutlery for me.

The old man storts whispering to me then out of the side of his mouth. He's all, 'I don't wish to be rude, Ross, but do you think you might consider leaving and coming back later?'

I'm there, 'No, Dude – because this is important.'

'Well, so is this, as it happens.'

'Like I said, this is about the old dear and what a focking disgrace to humanity she is.'

He practically snarls at me then, which is very unlike him. He goes, 'For heaven's sake, Ross, I was about to propose!'

I'm like, 'Propose?'

'Yes! After the disaster of Paris! Second time lucky! That's what this was all about!'

'I didn't know.'

'Thus the foie gras. Thus the . . .' He all of a sudden stops. He goes, 'Where's the Champagne gone?'

I'm there, 'What Champagne?'

'I filled two glasses before we went outside.'

'I drank them.'

'You drank them?'

'Yeah, what's the big focking deal? You've still got two thirds of a focking bottle there.'

That's when he says it. 'Ross, there was a diamond ring at the bottom of one of those glasses.'

That comes as something of a surprise to me, as you can imagine. I'm like, 'Excuse me?'

He goes, 'Yes! A diamond ring!'

'Jesus Christ! What the fock did you put it in there for?'

'It was supposed to be a surprise.'

'Well, it *is* a focking surprise, I can tell you that much.'

'Helen was supposed to hold the glass to her lips and see it resting at the bottom. How the hell could you swallow a diamond ring and not notice?'

'I don't know. I was eating toast and foie gras at the same time. Jesus, it couldn't have been a very big diamond.'

'It cost sixty thousand bloody euros!'

Helen is suddenly back with my plate and my glass. She goes, 'What cost sixty thousand euros?'

The old man's there, 'Oh, nothing. Just, em, a car I was considering buying.'

Helen sits down and tells me to tuck in.

'So,' the old man goes, 'what was so important that you just *had* to call in here this morning?'

He's all pissy with me now for ruining his morning.

I'm there, 'The old dear . . .'

'Fionnuala!' he goes. 'Oh, we both enjoyed you on the radio this morning, didn't we, Helen?'

I'm like, 'Well, I called into the gaff about an hour ago and caught her having sex with Oisinn.'

'Good Lord! Well, why are you telling us this?'

I honestly can't believe his reaction. Or lack of.

'That doesn't shock you?' I go. 'Oisinn, as in *my* best friend?'

He's there, 'Whether I'm shocked or not, Ross, what your mother gets up to in her private life is entirely *her* business.'

Helen at least *tries* to say the right thing? She's there, 'You must feel terribly betrayed, Ross.'

I turn to the old man. I'm there, 'See? That's what I would call a normal person's reaction to that news. Helen, I honestly don't know what you see in this loser. I really focking don't.'

The old man tries to go, 'Ross, your mother and I have remained dear friends, despite the divorce. But I'm not entitled to make pronouncements about whom she sees. It's nothing to do with me . . . Did you clear up the mystery, by the way?'

'What mystery?'

'The missing house, of course! I was telling Helen – a case worthy of Poirot!'

'She had it knocked down, the mad bitch, then rebuilt – brick by brick – in her focking gorden.'

'In Foxrock?'

For some reason, this seems to engage him more than the *other* news?

I'm there, 'In Foxrock, yeah.'

'She would have required planning permission for that?' he goes. 'Do you know is she just going to seek retention?'

I end up totally losing it with him then. I'm there, 'It's funny, it didn't actually come up when I was watching her being focking rutted stupid-faced against the fridge – a fridge that *you* paid for, can I just remind you?'

Shit. I'm actually going to vom here unless I stop remembering it.

The old man goes, 'Who paid for the fridge is immaterial, Ross. Your mother told you – I heard her with my own ears – that one day she'd move on and you'd have to come to terms with the fact.'

Helen goes, 'But one of his own friends, Charles. That's what's upsetting Ross.'

'Well,' he goes, 'maybe if he didn't come blundering unannounced into other people's homes when they were trying to enjoy a moment of quiet bloody privacy . . .'

I'm there, 'I honestly can't believe your reaction. You should have heard the noises coming from her.'

Okay, I'm definitely going to hurl if I don't stop thinking about it.

He goes, 'Well, I for one am not going to judge her, Ross.'

I'm there, 'That much is obvious.'

'Your mother has needs like the rest of us . . .'

'Dude, don't say that.'

'Needs that have to be satisfied . . .'

'Jesus Christ.'

'She's a very sensual woman, your mother.'

It comes out of me like a focking volcano erupting, all over their romantic breakfast for two. Helen actually screams.

I'm like, '*Bllleeuuurrrggghhh!!! Bllleeuuurrrggghhh!!! Bllleeuuurrrggg hhh!!!*'

Up it all comes. We're talking the foie gras and Melba toast. *Bllleeuuurrrggghhh!!!*'

We're talking the fresh fruit kebabs and the eggs Florentine that Sorcha cooked for us this morning.

'*Bllleeuuurrrggghhh!!!*'

We're talking the two packets of Chipsticks and the Snickers I bought from the Texaco on Rochestown Avenue when I was randomly driving around this morning.

'*Bllleeuuurrrggghhh!!!*'

And then, finally, with one last push, marinated in a foam of Champagne and stomach acid – '*Bllleeuuurrrggghhh!!!*' – one of the biggest diamond rings I have ever seen in my life.

It hits the table with a pretty much *thud*?

Suddenly, the three of us are just sitting there, looking at it, winking up at us from the middle of this multicoloured mess of foul-smelling puke.

Helen goes, 'What . . . what is that?'

The old man shakes his head and goes, 'What is it they say about the best made plans of mice and men?'

I'm there, '*Bllleeuuurrrggghhh!!!*' except there's fock-all coming out now. It's just, like, dry *retching*?

268

'Oh, well,' he goes, 'if this is how it is to be, then this is how it is to be,' and he pushes back his chair and at the same time drops down onto one knee.

'Helen,' he goes, 'it would make me the happiest man in the world if you were to agree to be my wife.'

'*Bllleeuuurrrggghhh!!!*'

I'm asked if the name Dechtire Ní Conchobhair means anything to me. It honestly doesn't. Could be the capital of Mongolia. Could be a sexually transmitted disease. Could be Harry Potter's geography teacher.

Actually, now that I think about it, I might have been with a bird called Dechtire Ní Conchobhair back in the day.

'She went to Coláiste Íosagáin,' Sorcha goes. 'She plays the horp. She has beautiful red hair. Her grandfather was involved somehow in the drafting of the Constitution.'

Shit. I definitely remember her.

I'm there, 'Before you say another word, Babes, you and I were on a break at the time.'

Sorcha laughs. Luckily, she thinks I'm joking.

We're in the cor, by the way, on the way to collect Honor from school.

She goes, 'Anyway, I rang her last night – Ciadhla Nic Airt gave me her number – because I was thinking about what we were going to do in terms of, like, *music* for the day? I knew Dechtire was in this – oh my God – *amazing* string quartet with Gormlaith Ní Dochartaigh, Muirgheal Ní Muireadhaigh and Rionach Nic Giolla Mhaoil.'

Jesus Christ. She might as well be talking Wookie for all I understand of that last bit.

I'm there, 'Yeah, no, keep talking, Babes, I *am* listening.'

'In terms of the music, I was thinking there should definitely be, like, a theme of all the songs that *mean* something to us? "Don't Know Much" by Linda Rondstadt and Aaron Neville. "A Whole New World" by Regina Belle and Peabo Bryson. "Still the One" by Shania Twain. "Kiss Me" by Sixpence None the Richer. "Save the

Best for Last" by Vanessa Williams. "After All" by Cher with Peter Cetera. Okay, cheesarama, I know, but they're, like, *our* songs?'

I honestly couldn't whistle one of them for you.

I'm there, 'Keep going, Babes.'

She's like, 'Well, that's obviously for the reception. But we're going to need, like, different music for the actual ceremony – especially for when I'm walking up the aisle.'

'There is an aisle?'

'Of course there's an aisle. Why wouldn't there be an aisle?'

'I don't know. It just sounds very, all of a sudden, *weddingy*?'

'We're reaffirming our vows, Ross. It *is* weddingy.'

'Yeah, I suppose.'

'See, I was thinking in terms of something, like, Irish and definitely *traditional*? I mean, I love "She Moved Through the Fair" – the Sinead O'Connor version from, like, *Michael Collins*? But like I said, I was talking to Dechtire – oh my God, she's *so* nice, she lives in, like Kilternan – and she thinks that because it's a renewal rather than an actual wedding, we should go for something with more personality – as in, like, more *individualistic*?'

'What are we talking about here?'

'Well, she said on the phone that she could actually compose something specifically for us. It'd be, like, *Sorcha and Ross's Theme*? That's what she'd even call it.'

I go, 'Wow!' at the same time thinking, this is going to cost a focking orm and a leg.

She's like, 'She wants to meet us, though.'

I'm there, 'What?'

'Yeah, she says she would never compose a piece for a couple without actually meeting them first and getting to know a bit about their personalities.'

Fock. This is not good news. Look, I won't go into the ins and outs of it. Let's just say that it did not end well between me and Dechtire Ní whatever the fock.

I'm there, 'It all sounds a bit over the top to me. Could you not just meet her and give her a little flavour of what I'm like? The good shit obviously.'

Sorcha ends up losing it with me. 'Ross,' she goes, 'I'm organizing everything for this vow renewal. I haven't asked you to do a thing, except meet Father Seamus with me next week and now this.'

It's definite emotional blackmail.

'Okay,' I end up going, 'I'll do it.'

There's always a chance that Dechtire has forgotten me – or at least what I did to her.

I turn right into the cor pork. The school is already emptying out. The barristers and the whatever-elses of tomorrow.

'Oh, by the way,' I go, 'the old man and Helen got engaged yesterday. I thought I'd just mention it to you, because *he's* obviously going to be going around making a major deal of it.'

Sorcha goes, 'Oh! My God! That is *amazing* news! I am *so* happy for them! Helen was like a second mother to me growing up and they are – oh my God – *so* cute together as a couple!'

'Well, I still say she could do better for herself. I know that's me being biased, but I think she's way too good for him.'

'So how did he propose?'

'What?'

'How did he produce the ring?'

'Er . . . he didn't actually say.'

'Well, if I know Charles, there'll be some – oh my God – so, so romantic story involved. I'm sure we'll all hear it in time.'

The back door of the cor opens and in Honor climbs.

Sorcha goes, 'How was your day, Dorling?'

Honor's like, 'I'm too tired to invest, thank you. Can you drive?'

I suddenly feel like Morgan Freeman in what's the film?

I'm just about to move off when I notice Ann Tilson – as in, the mother of Honor's little friend Georgette – waving to me in a way that tells me she wants a word.

Honor cops her, too.

'Ignore her,' she goes. 'Or better still, run her over, the stupid bitch.'

Sorcha goes, 'Honor, has something happened?' at the same time winding down her window to hear what the woman has to say. 'Hi, Ann. Is everything okay?'

Ann's like, 'Georgette is very upset about some of the things Honor has been saying about her on Twitter.'

'What kind of things?'

'All sorts of things. Hurtful. She calls her Khloé. She has a lot of the other girls doing it as well.'

Sorcha goes, 'Okay, what am I missing here?' and I'm definitely picking up a sudden *defensive* vibe from her?

'I think she means Khloé Kardashian,' I go, just trying to move things along.

Ann's like, 'That's right. Khloé Kardashian.'

'She wouldn't be the pick of the family,' I go. 'I think that's what the actual *slagging* is?'

Ann, I should mention at this point, has a definite thing for me. She made the mistake of telling Sorcha at the blessing of the Madeleine Sophie Prayer Room that she thought I was very handsome and Sorcha has never trusted her since that day.

'It's just that Georgette is very hurt by it,' Ann tries to go.

She's being very reasonable, it has to be said.

Honor pipes up, from the back of the cor, 'Okay, do you *have* mirrors in your house?'

Sorcha's like, 'Honor, please let me deal with this, okay?' and what I presume Sorcha is going to say is that we'll talk to our daughter, sit her down and explain to her why she can't say shit like that about other kids on Twitter, maybe cut her phone credit back to ten euros a day as a punishment.

Instead, roysh, Sorcha goes, 'Ann, why are you coming to me with this tittle-tattle?'

Ann's like, 'Tittle-tattle?'

I end up chuckling, but only because I like it as a word.

'Yes,' Sorcha goes, 'tittle-tattle. Honor said this and Honor said that.'

Ann's there, 'It's affecting Georgette very badly. She's falling behind academically because of it.'

Academically. She's focking six.

I go, 'Maybe it was a misunderstanding,' just trying to keep the peace here. 'Maybe Honor meant one of the other sisters – there's a lot of them, isn't there? – one of the decent-looking ones. Who else is there? They're all Ks, aren't they?'

There's no way Honor would make that mistake, though. She knows that family better than she knows her own. She certainly spends more time with them.

'I *said* Khloé,' she suddenly goes, 'and I *meant* Khloé.'

Ann probably already realizes that she's not going to get any change out of Sorcha here, so she goes, 'I am not going to stand by and allow my daughter to be cyber-bullied.'

Sorcha's like, 'Did you say cyber-bullied? Because that's quite a loaded term to be throwing around the place. Some would say it was even slander.'

'Do you ever look, even out of curiosity, at what she writes?'

'I don't need parenting tips from you, thank you.'

'Maybe you do. I've heard stories from quite a number of other mothers as well. And they don't paint a very pretty picture of your daughter.'

Sorcha practically explodes. She goes, 'Then why do you keep bringing Georgette over to our house for playdates?' and she screams it. Her face is red and her eyes are literally popping. 'You don't need to answer that! It's so you can lech over my husband! Drive away, Ross! Just drive!'

Which is what I end up *having* to do?

As we join the queue of cors waiting to pull out onto the Lower Kilmacud Road, Honor looks up from her iPhone and she goes, 'Nice work, Mom!'

There's a new sub on the Footlong menu for Easter – we're talking spiced lamb meatballs with mint yoghurt and thyme. It sounds focking revolting, but I tell Christian I'll try one anyway.

I want to support the dude.

He goes, 'Are you going to pay for this one?'

I'm like, 'Excuse me?'

Lauren has changed him, and I don't mean in a good way.

'It's just that the last three times you've eaten in here,' he tries to go, 'you haven't paid.'

I'm there, 'Dude, I told you to stort a slate for me.'

'And I told you we don't operate slates.'

'Then how the fock are you supposed to keep track of what I owe you?'

He throws his eyes skyward – the tight focker – then slices a wholegrain roll in half, we're talking lengthways, and storts buttering the thing with a definitely heavy hort.

I'm there, 'Dude, I could do with a bit of support here, if you wouldn't mind.'

He goes, 'So you keep saying.'

'Er, yeah, two days ago, can I just remind you, I caught one of my so-called best friends nuts-deep in my old dear. I'm just saying that a bit of back-up would be appreciated.'

'I'm making you a sandwich, aren't I?'

'Yeah, with a focking face on you. You're taking all the good out of it.'

Something suddenly occurs to me then.

'Hang on,' I go. 'When did *you* first know?'

He's there, 'Know what?'

'About Oisinn and my old dear.'

'I didn't. Not until you told me five minutes ago.'

'Are you sure?'

'Jesus, Ross, don't stort getting all paranoid now.'

He spreads the spiced lamp meatballs and the rest of the shit on the roll.

I'm there, 'Sorry, Dude. My head – as you can imagine – is melted with this thing.'

'Hi, Roth!'

Ross Junior has just walked in. As has Lauren, who's really, like, noticeably pregnant at this stage. She's only got, like, three months to go.

I'm there, 'Hey, Ross Junior, how the hell are you?' and Lauren, who still thinks it was me who dressed him up as a girl, jumps straight on my case.

She goes, 'He's not Ross Junior.'

I'm like, 'Sorry?'

'His name is Ross. It's not Ross Junior. The Junior implies that we define our son in relation to you, which we most certainly don't.'

Jesus. There's a focking pair of them in it.

I'm there, 'I know you're not my biggest fan in the world these days, Lauren, and there's a lot of things – some of them chemical – possibly contributing to that. But I'm going to ask you to go easy on me today.'

Christian puts my sandwich on the counter and goes, 'He's had a bit of a shock.'

Lauren goes, 'What, you walked in on your mother having sex with Oisinn?' and she says it like it's no major deal – like it's the kind of thing that happens to us all two or three times a week.

I'm like, 'Who told you?'

She goes, 'I just spent the last two hours with Sorcha.'

I remember now. She was helping her choose, like, the invitations and the stationery for the renewal. Lauren has a good eye for that shit.

She turns around to Christian then. She's like, 'Make sure he pays for that sandwich.'

I reach into my pocket and whip out a fifty, which I slap down hord on the counter.

I'm like, 'Satisfied?'

She goes, 'Take what he owes for the other three out of that.'

I'm there, 'I thought you weren't keeping a slate?'

Lauren's like, 'I don't see what your issue is anyway. I said it to Sorcha. They're both consenting adults?' and I don't know if she's saying it deliberately to *rile* me?

I'm there, 'What, my mother and my friend? And I'm not allowed to be upset by that?'

And that's when she hits me with it – right between the eyes.

She goes, 'You slept with Christian's mother, didn't you?'

What happened between me and Christian's old dear is something that never gets mentioned between me and Christian. It's a bit like the Amlin Challenge Cup. We can't deny its existence as a fact, but neither of us ever wants to get into it.

I'm there, 'What happened between me and Christian's old dear was different.'

She's like, 'How was it different?'

'Because she was vulnerable and in a bad place mentally and I took full advantage of that fact. This is worse when you think about it. Because Oisinn and my old dear know *exactly* what they're doing.'

'Roth!' Ross Junior suddenly pipes up – I'm just going to continue on calling him that. 'We're having a borbecue for Mawmy'th birthday and Thaddy saith I can have a bounthy cathel.'

I'm there, 'Yeah, no, that's great news – they can be a lot of fun.'

'Ith going to be a printheth cathel.'

I don't even answer that. I wouldn't even know how to begin. I just sink my teeth into my Holy Week Melt and stare straight ahead.

It's then that I notice a sudden shift in the air in the shop – you could almost call it, like, a tightening of the *atmosphere*? Someone walks through the door and Christian's face drops. It's like something out of a Western. Even Lauren looks suddenly concerned.

I turn around and there – speak of the devil – stands Oisinn, bold as brass – the focking nerve of him to even show his face in public ever again.

'Ross,' he goes. 'Can I have a word?'

I end up turning on Christian then. I'm there, 'How did *he* even know I was here?'

Christian goes, 'Ross, you're here every lunchtime.'

That's actually true. I don't acknowledge that, though. I just put my sub down, brush straight past Oisinn – giving him the shoulder-nudge of a lifetime, can I just say? – walk through the door and out onto Chatham Street.

He follows me, going, 'Dude, please . . . Dude, give me a chance to explain.'

I just keep on walking.

It's as I'm passing The Corkscrew that I end up losing it and just turning around and roaring at him. I'm like, 'We played rugby together!'

He can't even look me in the eye when I bring that up. He just stares into the window of the shop – there's a special offer on the Cantine de Falco Primitivo 2010 – and goes, 'I know.'

I'm like, 'Rugby! There was a time when that used to mean something.'

'Dude, it still does. Look, the last thing I ever wanted . . .'

'. . . was for me to walk in and catch you riding my mother like Rocco Siffredi?'

I possibly watch too much porn.

I'm there, 'So how long has it been going on for?'

He has the cheek to go, 'What?'

'You're going to make me actually say it? You and her. And I want an honest answer. You owe me that.'

'Since just before Christmas.'

'So that's where you slipped off to on New Year's Eve, was it? You probably did the dirty deed with her that night as well, did you?'

'Ross . . .'

'I'm just trying to imagine what it'd be like to have sex with my mother. Like waving a hotdog in the O2, I'd say.'

'Jesus, Ross . . .'

'And Holly, the famous florist that none of us got to meet – you just made her up, I'm presuming?'

'You asked me for a name and I panicked. I just said the first thing that came into my head.'

'Well, I'm glad for her sake that she doesn't exist. It'll spare her ever having to find out what a total snake in the grass her boyfriend is.'

'I'm sorry, Ross.'

'So you should be. I was the one who went and got you, do you remember that?'

'Yeah.'

'I couldn't stand the thought of you being out there in the world on your own, maybe thinking of possibly *topping* yourself? Focking months I spent looking for you. Ringing around, like the dope that I am. People saying to me, "If the dude wants to hide from the world, why don't you just let the dude stay hidden?" And I was like, "Because this is a goy who I respect and love like an actual brother."'

Yes, love. I'd no focking qualms about saying it either. It didn't even seem gay.'

'Ross,' he goes, right out of left-field, 'I'm lonely.'

I'm there, 'Lonely?' because it's such a random thing to hear from another goy. 'What the fock are you talking about, lonely?'

He's like, 'Lonely. What do you think I mean? I look at you and – you know – you're back with Sorcha. Two kids. Christian has Lauren. Second baby on the way. JP has Shoshanna now. About to become a father for the first time. Look at me, Ross. Jesus Christ, I'm thirty-three this year and I'm still on my Tobler.'

I'm there, 'You're one of the lucky ones.'

'I'm not,' he goes. 'That's just some shit people say. It's horrible being alone, Ross. It's just . . .'

His eyes stort filling up. Fock. He has me actually feeling sorry for him here.

He goes, 'Father Fehily used to say that loneliness was the most insidious form of mental illness there was. Look out for it in people – do you remember he said that? Because it eats you from the inside out and it's difficult to see what's happening until it's too late.'

I'm there, 'Dude, you're hordly on your Tobler. You've loads of mates.'

He shakes his head, like it's obviously not enough for him.

'Every night, Ross, I go back to my old bedroom in my mum and dad's gaff and I go to sleep in my old bed on my own. I've still got a poster of Gillian Anderson on my wall. Remember her? It's like something from a lifetime ago. And Teri Hatcher. Look, it doesn't bother me that I'm back living with my old pair. I honestly never think about what I used to have and what I don't have any more. I don't care about that shit. What I miss is . . . human focking contact, man. I lie in my bed and I think, I just wish I had someone here beside me, just to say, "How was your day, Oisinn? That bad, huh? Never mind – there's another one tomorrow, you know?"'

Shit. The tears suddenly stort to *really* flow. I love Oisinn too much to ever want to watch him cry.

'You could do with losing a bit of weight,' I go. 'I'm just making that comment.'

He laughs through his tears. He's like, 'Thanks, Ross.'

'You've got an orse on you like a focking rhinoceros. At least that's one thing you and her have in common.'

There's, like, five or ten seconds of silence, then I go, 'Dude, I might possibly one day forgive you for this. But you've got to tell me that it's over.'

Un-focking-believable – he goes, 'I can't, Ross.'

'You can't? You're saying you're going to continue seeing her?'

'Yeah.'

'I honestly thought you were coming here to tell me that it was a mistake – biggest mistake of your life – but it was over now and blahdy blah.'

'I like her, Ross. I *really* like her.'

I end up totally losing it – there on Chatham Street. I'm there, 'You're not *allowed* to focking like her. This is my focking mother we're talking about. I mean, what the fock do you expect me to say here? "Yeah, no, go for it, Dude"?'

'I'm just telling you how I feel.'

'Well, I'll tell you one thing, don't expect her to ever feel the same way about you. The woman is incapable of actual feelings. I can tell you that from personal experience.'

'I didn't come here looking for your forgiveness, Ross. Okay, I never meant for you to see what you saw on Sunday morning. But I'm not going to say sorry to you for feeling the way I do about Fionnuala.'

'This is too focked up for words. I'm still convinced that I'm going to wake up and it will all have been, like, a nightmare.'

He goes, 'I wanted to offer you this,' and he sticks out his hand – again, un-focking-believable – expecting me to just *shake* it?

I'm there, 'Sorry, what the fock is that?'

He's like, 'The hand of friendship.'

'Dude,' I go, 'your wingman status has been revoked. As a matter of fact, I wish you'd go away again and stay focking lost this time.'

★

Ronan answers on the seventh ring. He must be working, roysh, because the first thing I hear, before he even says a word, is the sudden crash of metal – obviously like a clamp hitting the ground.

Another satisfied customer, I'd imagine.

He's like, 'Awreet, Rosser.'

I'm there, 'Alright, Ro? Working away, yeah?'

'I am, yeah. Ine bolloxed, so I am.'

'Really?'

'The little one's still not sleepin great.'

It breaks my hort. He should be in school. He should be looking forward to his summer holidays. Instead of . . .

I'm like, 'Any more hassle?'

He goes, 'What do you mean?'

'I mean, any more black eyes?'

'Oh. Er, no.'

'Marek looking after you, is he?'

'He is, yeah. Here, I have to go, Rosser. Ine arthur gettin calt to anutter job.'

Father Seamus turns out to be a cool goy. He's a massive rugby fan and a massive fan of mine. They're one and the same thing, a lot of people would say.

All he wants to talk about, while I'm horsing into the Viscounts, is whether Declan Kidney should have gone after the disappointment of the Six Nations and whether Leinster are capable of winning a third Heineken Cup.

He even goes, 'When I was watching Ireland lose at Twickenham, I thought, why isn't Charles O'Carroll-Kelly's young chap out there?'

It's a genuinely lovely thing to hear.

'A variety of reasons,' I go.

'It wasn't in His plan for you.'

'It wasn't in Warren Gatland's or Eddie O'Sullivan's either. I'm not bitter, though, even though I could be.'

He smiles and pours us all more tea. 'Well,' he goes, 'may I say how nice it is to see you both reunited. Your father told me, Sorcha, there had been some trouble in the marriage.'

'That's actually why we wanted to talk to you,' Sorcha goes. You should actually hear the accent. It's comical. 'Ross and I are – like you said – reunited after a definite rough patch in our marriage. And we wanted to, like, restate our commitment to each other by basic-ally renewing our *wedding* vows?'

Father Seamus looks from Sorcha to me and then back to Sorcha again. It's like he's confused or some shit.

'*I* can't help you renew your wedding vows,' he goes. 'What I mean by that is the Catholic Church doesn't believe in it. The vows you took were for life, weren't they?'

Sorcha's there, 'Yes, Father.'

He's like, 'Then there's no need to reaffirm them. God doesn't require it of you.'

But such is her confidence in her debating skills, Sorcha is con-vinced that she can argue God around. That's what six years at Mount Anville would do for your self-belief.

'With respect,' she goes, 'I think what we're trying to say in renewing our vows is that – oh my God – we both made *mistakes* in our marriage? A lot of that was possibly down to our age when we made the commitment the first time around. But we're older now and we believe in that commitment more than we ever did – so much so that we want to restate it. And also to emphasize to God and our family and friends the *now* aspect of our marriage? In other words, how much we've grown together, despite being aport, what we've learned, how much our love means today and how it's still an enduring light that hasn't been extinguished.'

Father Seamus looks a bit, I don't know – *overwhelmed* might be the word? I'd imagine God is up there scratching His head as well.

'Those sentiments are all very well,' he goes, 'but, like I said, I can no more perform a vow renewal than I can perform a Church of Ireland service, or walk into the Mosque in Clonskeagh and lead the call to prayer. It's not within my remit to do it.'

'Well, they do it in the States.'

'They do a lot of things in the States, I'm told. Look, I'll tell you what – what if I agree to bless your marriage?'

'You're allowed to do that?'

'I'm allowed to bless anything within reason.'

He really is a sound dude.

Sorcha goes, 'Would Ross and I be allowed to restate our commitment to each other in the form of, like, promises?'

He's there, 'Yes, but it wouldn't be part of a religious rite, if you see what I mean,' and then he looks down at Sorcha's hand and goes, 'You're not wearing your ring.'

'Excuse me?'

'Your wedding ring. You're not wearing it, I notice.'

'No, I was going to put both of my rings – including my engagement ring – back on after we've reaffirmed our vows. It's sort of, like, *symbolic*?'

'You see, this is exactly what I'm talking about. You shouldn't think of this as a second wedding. You're not remarrying in the eyes of God.'

'Yes, I've taken your point on board, Father. Are we allowed to, like, read something from the Bible?'

'Oh, I would never discourage anyone from doing that!'

'There's a line that I – oh my God – love in the Book of Ecclesiastes. *Though one may be overpowered, two can defend themselves.*'

'Ecclesiastes 4:12,' he goes, then he stands up out of his chair. 'I'll go and get my Bible.'

On his way out of the room, he goes, 'What date have you set for the blessing, by the way?'

Sorcha's like, 'The sixteenth of June.'

He repeats it to himself a couple of times, then he suddenly remembers something. 'You do know Ireland are playing the All Blacks that day?' he goes.

I'm there, 'Er, really?'

'It's the second test.'

'God, I don't know how that slipped my mind. It's on early, though. We'll know the result by then.'

'Yes, that's true.' Then he goes off to get his Bible.

'We are *not* calling it a blessing,' Sorcha goes, the second he's out of the room.

I'm there, 'You heard the man, Sorcha. In fairness to the dude, I think he's pulling out all the stops for us.'

'The stationery has already been printed,' she goes. 'We're calling it a vow renewal and that's all there is to it.'

I spot her through the window of her usual, The Gables, wrapping her big, shiny, Space Hopper head around a piece of their coffee cake, and at the same time laughing. She looks like a focking hippopotamus eating its own face at gunpoint.

I can't resist the temptation to go in.

She's sitting in the window – no shame – chatting, as it turns out, to Niamh Horan from the *Sunday Independent*, who's got, like, a notebook in front of her, and there's also, like, a digital recorder on the table between them.

As I'm approaching, I hear the old dear go, 'Yes, there is someone special in my life at the moment, but it's still early and, well, I'm not ready to announce it in the pages of my favourite Sunday newspaper just yet!'

'You scabrous focking sea monkey!' I shout.

That gets pretty much everyone's attention. They look up from their spiced beef couscous and their prawn and crayfish pil pil.

I go, 'I'll tell you who her someone special is, will I? It's Oisinn Wallace!'

Niamh goes, 'The fragrance guy?' obviously knowing her stuff.

I'm pretty sure I tried to be with Niamh at Pippa O'Connor's either twenty-first or twenty-fifth, except she told me she'd too much sense.

I'm there, 'That's right. He also happens to be thirty-five years younger than her – oh, and did I mention, also one of my best friends?'

She's like, 'What?'

'Oh, yeah,' I go. 'Check the record books. We played on the same Senior Cup team – me at obviously outhalf, him at hooker. Not that you'd know it from the way he's stabbed me in the back. I walked into the house a couple of Sundays ago and caught the two of them doing the nasty-nasty up against the fridge. Put that in your story. You can use that as a direct quote.'

The old dear has to try to turn the whole thing around then.

She's all, 'How dare you moralize with me! With the way *you* carry on? I'm a single woman and I am free to see whomsoever I choose.'

'*Whomsoever*? That's not even a word. And you're supposed to be a writer?'

She looks at Niamh then. 'And the age difference is twenty-five years, by the way, not thirty-five.'

I go, 'Yeah, ask her for her birth certificate – no one's ever focking seen it.'

The old dear's there, 'Well, since you've put his name into the public domain, Ross, yes, it *is* Oisinn Wallace.' She smiles at Niamh, who I definitely still fancy in a big-time way. 'It's been going on since Christmas. He treats me very well and he makes me very happy. He's been through a lot, as you know, financially. And I've been through quite a lot emotionally. And we're just good for each other. Spiritually, psychically, whatever you want to call it. We fit together.'

I'm there, 'I can only presume it's your money he's after. And I hope he gets it – every focking penny. You dog.'

'Would it be fair to say,' Niamh goes, 'that you've experienced a similar sexual renaissance to some of the characters in *Fifty Greys in Shades*?'

I'm like, 'Don't even think about answering that.'

The old dear just smiles and goes, 'No, I think I've always been a very sexual person. I've always had something of a lascivious side to my personality, which I think has probably always been present in my writing. And, yes, it's always been difficult for my son to accept. I think my books and some of my life choices have embarrassed him over the years. But that's who I am. I have needs and I have desires and I'm unapologetic about that.'

I'm there, 'I can't believe you're saying this shit on the actual record. You're a disgrace.'

'Ross,' she goes, 'you really must grow up. I told you – do you remember? – that one day I was going to meet someone and you would have to accept that.'

'Yeah, and you said that *knowing* that you were jumping one of my oldest friends at the time.'

'I appreciate that it's difficult for you, Ross.'

'What, to walk into the kitchen and catch the two of you at it like porn stors? Nice of you to say that.'

'Well, if you didn't barge into my home uninvited on a Sunday morning, then you wouldn't have had to look at us.'

She has the cheek to actually smile at me. So I look back at her, roysh, like she's something nasty-smelling that I've just found on the sole of my good Dubes.

'You're dead to me,' I go. 'You're genuinely dead to me.'

Like I said, there's always the possibility that Dechtire Ní Conchobhair won't remember me or what I did to her. But to be on the safe side, I tell Sorcha that I'm going to stay in the cor.

She won't hear of it, though.

'It's supposed to be a piece of music that encapsulates *our* relationship – in other words, our personality together, as, like, a couple?' she goes. 'That's why she wants to meet both of us.'

'I still say she's tearing the orse out of it a bit. I don't know what's wrong with *"Pie Jesu"*. Here, we could see if we could get that bird who won the Eurovision to sing it.'

'Eimear Quinn?'

'Eimear Quinn. She lives around somewhere. I am the voice and blah, blah, blah.'

God, I'd love to get off with Eimear Quinn.

'Ross,' Sorcha goes, 'come on,' and she gets out of the Lambo and I have no choice, of course, but to follow her to the front door. I pull my baseball cap down low and I pretend to be scratching my nose when the door is answered, just to cover half my face and stop the girl from instantly recognizing me.

'Dechtire?' Sorcha goes, completely overdoing the 'eeeccchhh' sound, so that it sounds like she's about to focking gob.

Dechtire's like, 'Sorcha!' and they, like, shake hands and whatever else.

She's just alright looks-wise, but she's no Freya Mavor.

Sorcha goes to work straight away on establishing the connection. You know what birds are like. 'It was actually Ciadhla Nic Airt who recommended you to me,' she goes. 'And I'm also friends with Muirgheal Ní Muireadhaigh, who I know is in the same string quartet as you. I don't really know Rionach Nic Giolla Mhaoil that well, although we *are* friends on, like, Facebook.'

Dechtire goes, 'Oh my God, how do you know Ciadhla Nic Airt?'

'Oh my God, she's actually a really, really good friend of mine – her parents lived on my road growing up. And she's also so, so good friends with another friend of mine – Aodamar Nic an Tuile? I think she was in your year. And Eabha Ní Shé.'

'Eabha Ní Shé was in my year, but Aodamar Nic an Tuile was a year ahead, even though we were all – oh my God – really good friends. So if you know Ciadhla Nic Airt, you must also know Siofra Ní Uirthile, Tiarna Nic Uilgeagoid and Treasa de Poire.'

'I do. And Clar Ní Riada.'

'What about Sile Ní Mhurchu?'

'Not that well. But I was in Irish college with Naoise Blennerhasset and Miryam Nic Mhathuna.'

I swear to fock, it's like listening to Chewbacca trying to argue his way into a pub pissed.

'Oh my God,' Dechtire goes, 'I was actually really good friends with Naoise Blennerhasset in primary school, although not so much in secondary. She was more part of the Richeal Mhic Uaid and Eilís Nic Chochlain crowd . . . Aine Ní Ghallchóir, Ide Ní Bhroin, Dearbhla Nic Amhlaoibh, all those.'

For fock's sake.

I end up listening to about ten minutes of this focking gobbledegook before Sorcha thinks to even introduce me. 'Oh,' she finally goes, 'this is my husband, Ross. Like I said to you on the phone, Dechtire, we've decided to reaffirm our commitment to each other by renewing our vows.'

'Hello,' Dechtire goes, looking at me for the first time. 'Oh . . . hello.'

She definitely remembers me.

Fock.

Even Sorcha cops the sudden flicker of recognition in her eyes.

She's like, 'Have you two met before or something?'

I'm there, 'I'm, er, struggling to place the girl – and that's me being honest.'

Dechtire goes, 'We were with each other,' and from the way she says it, it's pretty obvious that it's not among her most treasured memories.

Sorcha's like, '*With* each other? As in, like, *with* with?'

I'm there, 'Yeah, like I said, Sorcha, we were on a break.'

'I thought you were joking. When was this?'

Dechtire's there, 'Years ago.'

I'm like, 'Well, I hope you've one or two nice memories of what happened,' trying to hurry the conversation along. 'Now, on to the famous *Sorcha and Ross's Theme!*'

'You're a focking arsehole,' Dechtire goes.

I'm like, 'I think we should agree to disagree on that point. And I think we'd all be better off letting bygones be bygones.'

'You're a focking . . . arsehole. Do you know how many years I've waited to say that to you?'

'Look, I think we've all done a lot of growing up since those days. I know I certainly have.'

Sorcha's like, 'Okay, what actually happened between you two?'

Dechtire shakes her head and laughs, like she can't believe that I've actually shown up on her doorstep, under these circumstances, all these years later.

She goes, 'I went back to his house . . .'

Sorcha's like, 'Which house?'

Shit.

'I don't know,' Dechtire goes. 'It was somewhere in Blackrock.'

Sorcha's like, 'Blackrock?' and then she turns to me. 'Are you saying this was, like, *while* we were married?'

'Like I said . . .'

'Do not say we were on a break. Do not say that again.'

'Fair enough.'

'Where was I when this was happening?'

I take a breath. There's no point in lying to her. She did offer me an amnesty on all past crimes, just so long as I didn't lie to her in the future.

'You were in London,' I go, 'at some – I don't know – *protest*?'

She's there, 'The one outside the Thai embassy? The one calling on Thaksin Shinawatra to end the ivory trade?'

'Yeah, no, it might have been that one alright.'

'Oh my God, you encouraged me to go away for that.'

Dechtire, who's obviously very bitter about the whole experience, goes, 'Well, he couldn't wait to get rid of me the following morning. Actually, he tried to get rid of me the night before – about ten minutes after we had sex – except I just refused to leave.'

I'm there, 'Sorcha, you said we'd draw a line in the sand? Anything that happened before a certain date I was basically off the hook for?'

She's entitled to be shocked, though.

'So the following morning,' Dechtire goes, insisting on telling the whole boring story, 'I had an episode with my breathing. I suffer pretty badly with asthma. And I asked Ross to get my Ventolin inhaler from my handbag downstairs. So he went off, came back and he said it wasn't *in* my bag?'

Sorcha's there, 'Ross, what did you do with it?'

She knows my M.O.

'He put it in the bin,' Dechtire goes.

I'm like, 'I didn't put it in the bin. I hid it, if you must know – in the hot press.'

Sorcha's like, 'Oh my God! I *found* a Ventolin inhaler in the hot press.'

'There's my proof then that I didn't fock it in the bin.'

We still haven't been invited inside, by the way.

'Meanwhile,' Dechtire goes, 'I'm having an asthma attack. Ross says there's a pharmacy in Blackrock village that's open at, like, eight o'clock on a Sunday morning.'

I'm there, 'I had to think fast. My wife was coming home that morning.'

'You told me you were divorced.'

'Well, you just seemed determined to hang around all day like the smell of cabbage.'

'So out we go to Ross's car and we head for the village. Oh, yes, he holds my hand while he's driving and he keeps saying to me, "Don't you die! Don't you dare die! Not now that I'm developing genuine feelings for you."'

I look at Sorcha. I'm there, 'It was just a line, Babes. I didn't mean a word of it.'

'We pull up outside the pharmacy,' Dechtire goes, 'and Ross tells me to go in – he's just going to park the car.'

'I think we've all heard enough at this stage.'

'And that was the last I ever saw or heard from him . . . Oh, apart from the wheel-spin he performed as he drove away.'

'In fairness,' I go, 'that was just to let you know that I was out of there. I didn't want to think of you hanging around the village for hours wondering was I coming back. Especially in your condition. It was my way of saying, look, we both enjoyed ourselves – there were no losers last night – but now you've got to get on with the rest of your life.'

No one says anything for a good, like, thirty seconds after that. I look at Sorcha. She seems – I don't know – lost in *thought*?

'Babes,' I eventually go, 'this all happened, like, years ago.'

She's there, 'Did you do it in our bed?'

I'm there, 'Thankfully, no.'

'We did,' Dechtire goes. 'It was a big double bed in the front bedroom.'

I'm there, 'Okay, then, we did do it in our bed. But again, Sorcha, you did agree to an amnesty as far as the past was concerned. Forgive and forget – blah, blah, blah.'

She's there, 'I know. It's just . . .'

She doesn't finish her sentence. My guess is that she's thinking about what her old man said. Whatever about forgiving and forgetting, actually trusting me not to return to my old ways – riding all around me and acting the serious *playah* – is going to be hord for her.

Sorcha turns to Dechtire and goes, 'Can you, like, still compose something for us?'

We're still standing on the focking doorstep, bear in mind.

Dechtire shrugs and goes, 'This is my job. I'm a professional.'

Sorcha's there, 'So do you need to know anything else about us?'

And Dechtire's like, 'No, I think I know everything I need to know.'

I don't believe it. I don't *focking* believe it.

I hand the letter to Sorcha and I ask *her* to explain it to me – the Attorney General who never was.

She throws her eyes over it and goes, 'They're refusing to excuse you from jury duty.'

I'm there, 'Yeah, no, that's what I *thought* it said? And do they give, like, a reason?'

'It says, *See attached document*,' and she turns to the following page, which she then reads. 'Ross, did you go through all of this?'

I'm there, 'No, I saw where it said *exemption declined* and I kind of flipped and handed it to you. What does the second page say?'

'It's a letter you sent them in 2003 – the last time you were called for jury service.'

'I vaguely remember that. Yeah, no, I was supposed to be going to Australia for the Rugby World Cup.'

'You told them that you'd just had both of your legs amputated.'

'Did I?'

'That's what you said in your letter.'

'They kept that – the sly bastards.'

'Well, you can see their dilemma, can't you, Ross?'

'I can't actually.'

'Well,' she goes, at the same time laughing, 'they're obviously dubious about your claim that you broke your leg playing rugby – the game you love – when you had both of your legs amputated nine years ago.'

I end up just shaking my head.

'Imagine,' I go, 'they actually kept that letter. You'd have to wonder about some people, wouldn't you?'

We're standing at the deli counter in Wilde & Green in Milltown. Sorcha loves their pimiento-stuffed Spanish olives.

'So the upshot of all of this is what?' I go.

She throws her eyes over the first page again 'The upshot,' she goes, 'is that you have to report for jury duty on Monday, 28 May, at 10 a.m.'

I'm there, 'Sly bastards. Seriously.'

She grabs the olives and we turn away from the counter. And that's when we see them. Four of them – we're talking Ann Tilson and three other mothers from the school – walking towards us with an air of definite purpose about them.

Sorcha picks up on it straight away, because under her breath she goes, 'Okay, *what* is this going to be about?' and you can tell she's already gearing up for a fight.

I don't recognize the woman who obviously elects herself as the spokeswoman of the little group. She goes, 'We'd like a word, please.'

She's, like, the definite horsey type. Green Barbour jacket, jodhpurs, knee-high boots. Big cranky Protestant head on her. I'd definitely ride her.

I'm there, 'A word?'

Actually, Sorcha says it at the exact same time as me.

We're both like, 'A word?'

'Yes,' the woman goes, 'about your daughter.'

Sorcha's there, 'Okay, first of all, who even *are* you?'

'My name is Judy Hemmel. I'm Allison's mother.'

'Okay, I don't even know who that is.'

'And I'm Lucy Winckworth,' this little mousy one with glasses and a big focking serious face goes. 'I'm Jessie's mother.'

And then the other one, who's like a thirty-something-year-old Diane Keaton, right down to the white turtleneck sweater, goes, 'And I'm Suzanne Lamar, Alex's mother.'

She's one of those women who you just know would be absolutely filthy in the sack.

Sorcha turns to Ann and goes, '*Really*, Ann? You put this little group together, did you? To, what, tell me what a horrible little girl I've raised?'

'Our children are being bullied,' this Lucy focking Winckworth one goes.

Sorcha's like, 'Okay, why are we having this conversation here?' *Here* happens to be next to the cupcake counter, although I think she means Wilde & Green. 'As a matter of fact, how did you even know we were here?'

'We tried to talk to you at the school,' the big Protestant-looking one – Judy Hemmel – goes. 'But you drove away.'

'Oh, so you actually *followed* us here? You're *admitting* that? You're admitting to basically stalking?'

Suzanne – the filthy one – goes, 'We wanted to talk to you because *our* daughters are being victimized by *your* daughter.'

'Did you say victimized?'

'Yes, I did say victimized. She's bullying our children.'

Now, if it was up to me, roysh, at this exact point I would just agree with them. I'd be inclined to go, 'Yeah, no, who are you talking to? She makes *our* lives a focking misery as well,' because she actually does. I was trying to watch Leinster beat Clermont Auvergne in the semi-final of the Heineken Cup yesterday – I was, like, making tactical notes in my book, as you do – and she was just, like, throwing peanut M&Ms at my head, going, 'Oh my God, you really think you're a coach! Hillare!'

You do get used to it. But at the same time, there's no point in denying what our daughter basically is. And Sorcha – I think I've mentioned before – did that Certificate in Mediation course in the Smurfit School, so she should know better than to say what she says next, which is, 'Our daughter is not a bully. Does it not strike you as – oh my God – a bit hypocritical that you're now the ones victimizing *her*?'

I mean, that's hordly going to take the heat out of the situation.

'She wrote on Twitter that Allison looks like a horse,' Judy goes. She's actually quite horsey-looking herself, I think I said. 'Good luck at Cheltenham, Allison – that's what she Tweeted recently. That was just one of many. Every time she sees her, she neighs at her. Allison comes home from school every second day in tears.'

Lucy's there, 'She calls my daughter Jessie Wankworth. On Twitter and to her face. She wrote it on the cover of all of her schoolbooks. Oh, and Jessie had this One Direction folder that she loved. Honor scribbled over all of their faces and told her that liking them was lame. Jessie won't even listen to their music now.'

'She told Alex that they were dead,' Suzanne goes. 'She said they'd all been killed in a car crash. Alex came home in tears. And Honor's also been following her around the playground, apparently, throwing M&Ms at her.'

'Finished?' Sorcha goes.

Ann's there, 'There are other parents with similar stories – especially about Twitter.'

'Oh, I'm surprised you didn't round *them* up as well, Ann. Or maybe you're waiting until I'm in Donnybrook Fair. You're going to ambush me when I'm at the cheese counter.'

If I had to choose what order I'd do them in, it'd be Suzanne, then Judy, then Lucy, then Ann.

'Your daughter,' Lucy goes, 'is making a lot of children's lives miserable. Do you ever look at her Twitter account? Have you seen the hurtful things she writes about people?'

Sorcha's like, 'Oh my God, I can't believe we're even *having* this conversation? Girls can be bitches – maybe you all need to learn that basic fact. I'm sure your daughters are no angels.'

Suddenly, roysh, out of nowhere, Judy produces this piece of paper – just, like, A4 paper? – except folded over in three. She, like, hands it to Sorcha, who opens it up, going, 'Okay, *what* is this?'

It's definitely a day for letters.

'It's a cease and desist demand,' Judy goes.

Sorcha's like, 'Excuse me?'

'A letter from my solicitor asking that you tell your daughter to cease and desist from such behaviour that is detrimental to the mental well-being of our children.'

I go, 'For fock's sake – is that not a bit heavy?'

'Well, I tried to talk to you about it in a reasonable manner, but you weren't interested.'

The next thing any of us hears is just, like, a rip, then another, then another. Sorcha is tearing the letter to pieces. When she's ripped it and ripped it and ripped it again, she drops all of the bits on the floor, while the four women just stand there staring with their mouths basically open.

Then off she walks. What can I do but shrug and follow her?

'I wouldn't be a hundred percent sure that was the right way to handle it,' I go, when we're standing at the checkout. 'A lot of that shit they said sounds true. I've had some of that treatment myself. I mean, you've read some of the shit she's said about *us* on Twitter.'

But Sorcha's like, 'I'm going to protect our daughter, Ross. I'm not going to let her become a victim.'

Ronan looks like crap. And I'm saying that as his father. He's pale. His shoulders are slumped. The spork he used to have in his eyes has been replaced by just this distant stare. He's got far too much on his plate for a kid of his age.

'How's work?' I go, even though I'm sure I know the answer. Borderline criminality is pretty much recession-proof.

'Floyen,' he goes. 'Woorked sixty hours last week.'

Sixty hours. A boy of just turned fifteen. All to pay that stuttering fock for the price of a few kitchen appliances and a half-decent stroller. I could nearly punch the wall.

'I like this one,' Shadden goes.

They've called out to the gaff to show us the proofs of the famous family portrait we got done.

She's like, 'Rihanna-Brogan is de image of you in dis one, Ro-Ro. Look at de way she's looking at you as well. Jaysus, she adores you, so she does!'

She's right about his daughter being a ringer for him. I can definitely see our family in her face. She'll break horts, there's no denying that.

Sorcha is sitting with her at the piano, showing her how to play

'Frère Jacques'. She's going, 'Watch what notes I'm hitting, Rihanna-Brogan. Sing along with me. *Frère Jacques. Frère Jacques. Dormez-vous? Dormez-vous? Sonnez les matines. Sonnez les matines. Ding, ding, dong. Ding, ding, dong.*'

While she's singing, R&B storts just slapping the keys with her hand in no particular order. That's not me being critical. She's still only five months old.

'Good girl!' Sorcha goes. 'Oh my God, I think we've got a little Mozort on our hands here, have we? Hab we godda liddew Mozort on our hands?'

It's too early to make those kinds of claims, but Ronan and Shadden both laugh and it makes me think of how things might have been. Then I look down at the photographs, spread out across the dining-room table, around which me, Ronan and Shadden are sitting. I'm looking at *him*, at Kennet, smiling, no, actually grinning, giving my old man the rabbit ears in one or two, laughing at us all.

'Are you goin to the match?' Ronan goes.

He means the Heineken Cup final this weekend. It's Leinster against Ulster at Twickenham. All the shit he's got on his plate and he still remembered. He's such a great kid.

I'm there, 'Wouldn't miss it for the world, Ro.'

He goes, 'All the boys goin over as well, are thee? Christian and the rest of them.'

'Yeah, no, Christian's not sure if he can, JP's new girlfriend has poisoned his mind against me and Oisinn, well, I might as well tell you now because it's going to be all over the *Sunday Independent*, he's riding your grandmother.'

His jaw just drops – Shadden's, too.

'Honor and I are going to go with him,' Sorcha goes. 'We're going to make a day of it. Ross is going to go to his match and I'm going to take Honor around London to see all the sights – Harrods, Alexander McQueen, the big Stella McCortney store in Mayfair. Plus, I'm hoping to pick up my dress for the renewal – it's going to be a Jenny Packham gown.'

Shadden goes, 'Jaysus, I'd luff a weekend like dat.'

I'm there, 'Come *with* us, why don't you? The three of you!'

Except Ro goes, 'Ine woorking, Rosser.'

'On a Saturday?'

'Saturday. Sunday. Every day.'

I pick up a photograph and I stare at K . . . K . . . K . . . Kennet again and I realize that what I feel for the man is literally hatred.

It's, like, quarter to nine on Saturday morning and we're sitting in the deporture lounge, waiting to board, and I'm just watching old YouTube clips on my iPhone – Rob Kearney's two tries against Cordiff, Cian Healy's against Clermont Auvergne, then just a five-minute highlights reel of Drico's best bits in blue – and everything feels suddenly right with the world.

I even go, 'Can I just say something here? This team has brought me more happiness than I don't know what.'

Honor looks up from her own iPhone and goes, 'And you're telling us this *why* exactly?'

I'm there, 'I'm just making the point, Honor, that I could be, like, *bitter*? Had the cords fallen differently, I might have been playing against Ulster this afternoon. It didn't work out for me. But I still love this team like a basic family. Actually, that's what they are to me. They're, like, a second family.'

Honor goes, 'Oh my God, I'm *so* embarrassed for you.'

'Don't be embarrassed for me, Honor. I'm calling it – something I've never been afraid to do.'

'Okay, I'm actually embarrassed for *me*. Hashtag – can you please stop talking now?'

'Fair enough.'

Sorcha looks up from the iPad then. The three of us are glued to our screens. We're some family. 'I've finished the invitation list,' she goes. 'I want to send them out first thing on Monday morning.'

'I hope my old dear's not on it.'

'What?'

'I'm serious, Sorcha. The woman is focking dead to me. I told her that.'

'Oh my God, I couldn't imagine us reaffirming our commitment to each other without Fionnuala being there.'

'Well, what about your old man? Is he on the list?'

'No.'

'Well, then, it's the same for me with her. So it's no to my old dear and no to your old man. What about *your* old dear – will she come without your old man?'

'I don't know. I think she's still hoping that he'll come around to the idea of us being back together and that he and I will patch things up.'

'But you're saying you don't think either of those things is going to happen?'

'No.'

She deletes my old dear from the list.

'Oh,' I quickly go, 'no Oisinn either.'

Sorcha's like, 'Ross, you've been friends since . . .'

I'm there, 'I gave him a chance to end it, Babes – whatever the fock it is that's going on between him and my old dear, the tramp. And he said no, he was going to continue it on. So now he can fock right off. And I'll tell you something else, I don't want JP and Shoshanna there either.'

'Ross, come on!'

'I'm serious. Telling me he's finished with me over something that was intended as an amazing focking joke. I said it from pretty much day one that Shoshanna was one of those birds who tries to turn goys against all of their old mates just so they can have them to themselves. I hate birds like that.'

She deletes Oisinn, JP and Shoshanna from the list.

She's like, 'Oh my God, are *any* of your friends going to be there?'

I go, 'Christian.'

'Well, you're skating on very thin ice with Lauren at the moment.'

'Hey, she has issues with me that she needs to sort out in her head. And *he* needs to man up. I mean, where is he this morning? Leinster are playing in a Heineken Cup final and he has to stay home because his wife's up the spout.'

'She's in her final trimester.'

'I never heard anything so stupid.'

'I'm just saying, Ross, you could probably stop antagonizing her . . . Okay, so who *do* we have? Charles and Helen. My sister. Maybe my mum, but probably not. Then, like, Chloe, Sophie and Amie with an ie. Claire and Garret, obviously . . .'

'Ronan and Shadden.'

'Ronan and Shadden . . . Oh my God, is that it?'

'No, there's got to be more than that.'

'Who? Who else?'

'Errr . . .'

All of a sudden they make, like, the pre-boarding announcement – anyone with infants or anyone requiring special assistance and all the usual blahdy blah.

Honor jumps up and storts heading for the gate, with me and Sorcha trailing after her and carrying her various bits of cabin baggage, like we're her – I don't know – valets. By the time we catch up with her, the air-hostess checking the boarding passes is telling her that she'll have to sit down again and wait until her seat row is called – which Honor isn't a hundred percent happy about, given the way she's, like, *glowering* at her?

I'm like, 'Okay, what seems to be the issue here?' Ever the diplomat.

The woman – perfectly reasonably – goes, 'Only parents with small infants are entitled to pre-board, I'm afraid,' and you know the Aer Lingus staff – they're lovely, even if you'd only ride two out of every five of them. 'And you're not a small infant. You're a lovely big girl, aren't you?'

I can't actually believe what I hear next. Honor – out of the side of her mouth – goes, 'Fock you, you patronizing bitch.'

The air-hostess hears it. I said it was out of the side of her mouth, but it was definitely still loud enough for her and the rest of the cabin crew to hear. I see them all, like, looking at each other with their basically open mouths, then our air-hostess turns back to me.

'Sorry,' she goes, 'what did she just say to me?'

I can nearly hear Sorcha's body tensing up beside me.

I'm there, 'It's actually just a line from a song. I don't know if you've ever heard of Cee Lo Green?'

She's no fool, though. We've made an enemy. And she's suddenly not happy with where we're standing. 'I have to keep this area clear,' she goes, no even eye contact with us any more. 'You're blocking people who are trying to board the aircraft.'

Sorcha goes, 'I hope you don't mind me saying it, but I think you're being a bit officious.'

Oh, shit. You know when you can just *sense* an atmosphere suddenly souring?

'Being a bit what?' the air-hostess goes.

See, a lot of them would only have two honours in the Leaving Cert and some kind of tourism and travel course.

'Officious,' Sorcha goes. 'It means asserting your authority in an unnecessarily forceful or *petty* way?'

People are suddenly looking. I'm thinking about obviously the match.

'Let's all just take a deep breath,' I go. 'Let's not say anything we'll regret.'

Honor goes, 'I told you, she's a bitch,' and then – I swear to fock – she looks the air-hostess in the eye and goes, 'Have you ever wondered what your life would have been like if you'd been given enough oxygen at birth?'

There are literally gasps from the other passengers. I smile and throw my eyes skyward and try to pass it off in a kids-say-the-darndest-things kind of way. It's a good ten seconds before the air-hostess gets it together to say anything. And when she does, it's not good.

She's like, 'You're not getting on this plane.'

Sorcha's there, 'Excuse me?'

'This girl is not getting onto the plane. She's being rude and abusive.'

'You were the one being rude.'

Fock.

'Please step away from the gate!' the woman goes.

Sorcha's like, 'We will *not* step away from the gate.'

She raises her voice slightly. 'Please step away from the gate,' she goes, 'or I will call security.'

We end up having to do what we're told. Except we only move, like, a few feet to our right. Sorcha has got, like, literally tears in her eyes. I'm quietly shedding one or two myself, if I'm being honest. Her and Honor were only going shopping. I'm the one who's going to miss the focking Heineken Cup final.

Sorcha insists on hanging around – in full view of everyone – for another five minutes, going, 'Oh my God! Oh! My God!' at regular intervals, hoping that this might somehow change their minds, until eventually a big dude in a yellow bib with a walkie-talkie comes over to us. He doesn't even have to say anything. He just, like, smiles sadly at me – like a dude who understands, except his hands are tied – and we end up having to just leave.

We're walking back through Duty Free and Sorcha – at the top of her voice – is like, 'I'm going to write a letter – oh my God – the *second* we get home.'

I'm there, 'I wonder could we have possibly handled that a bit better, though?'

'Are you saying you were on that woman's side?'

'I don't want to think of it in terms of sides.'

'She called our daughter rude . . . and something else.'

'I think it was abusive.'

'Rude and abusive.'

Honor suddenly has her phone in her hand – okay, when is it ever anywhere else? –and she goes, 'I'm making sure – oh my God – *everyone* on Twitter knows what a bitch that woman is. Did you see her make-up? Hashtag – pancake Tuesday.'

I suddenly stop.

Sorcha and Honor keep walking. But when they finally realize that I'm no longer with them, they both turn around.

Sorcha's like, 'What's wrong?'

I'm there, 'Yeah, no, I think you were right.'

'Excuse me?'

'That woman was bang out of order.'

'I'm going to definitely write a letter.'

'Is a letter enough, though?'

'What do you mean?'

'I had a focking ticket for the Heineken Cup final. I'm going to go back and have a serious go at her. And I'm *talking* serious?'

Sorcha's like, 'Ross, don't do anything stupid,' as I'm turning away from her. 'We don't want to end up on a No Fly List.'

Five minutes later, I'm back at the gate.

At first, roysh, I end up just, like, staring at the air-hostess, who's suddenly all smiles again, not a care in the actual world. I'm just standing there thinking, how focking dare you try to keep me from supporting the team that I've followed through thick and sometimes thin.

I morch straight over to her with my head down and I hand her my boarding cord. Luckily, she doesn't recognize me.

'Have a nice trip,' she goes.

I'm like, 'I will.'

Sixty seconds later, I'm buckling myself into my seat, thinking that – in a lifetime of being a complete and utter shit to Sorcha – this is one of the worst things I've possibly ever done. In an hour, maybe two, she'll work out what's happened and realize that I'm not coming back. And maybe, given time, she'll understand why I did what I did and she'll possibly forgive me. Or maybe she won't.

But this I have to say in my defence. I love Leinster. Right or wrong, they're my team. And, unlike my daughter, unlike my old dear, unlike my friends and my family, they've never, ever let me down.

Sorcha ends up working it out quicker than I expected. By the time I land, I've got, like, six voice messages from her. I decide not to listen to them – I genuinely don't want guilt getting in the way of my enjoyment of the day – although I do read three or four of the seventeen text messages she also sent, while I'm in a Jo on the way to actual Twickenham.

The first one is like 'OMG!', which is predictable enough, but the second one is like 'You do realize I have your match ticket?'

Shit.

That's actually true. See, my original match ticket was for the seat next to Oisinn's, but there was no way in this world that I was using that. So Sorcha went online and paid – I'm pretty sure – a grandington for a new one, which – according to the third text I read – she has now torn up and put in the bin on the way back to the Terminal Two cor pork.

I ask the taxi driver to drop me off at The Misty Moon. I'm think-ing, yeah, no, I'll just buy another one – there's always a few spares knocking around. This is Leinster, bear in mind, not Munster.

I walk into the pub and there ends up being a massive cheer. I hate patting myself on the back, but I'm actually a bit of a hero to the Leinster faithful and the vibe is very much one of, 'The Ross-meister is here – it's banter o'clock!'

I'm handed a pint of the wonder stuff by a dude called Barry O'Crohan, who was on the S in Clongowes the first year I sat the Leaving Cert. We were, like, sworn enemies on the field. Even if I saw him now, in Kielys, say, on a night out, I'd probably call him a dick or a cock and nudge him with my shoulder as I walked past him to try to, like, spill his pint. But that's the lovely thing about fol-lowing Leinster – it brings people from different backgrounds together in peace and, I suppose, *hormony*?

'Who'd you come over with?' Barry wants to know. 'Are you on your Tobler?'

He's with, like, six or seven other Clongowes heads, most of whom I recognize. I decide, fock it, I might as well tell them the story. I'm a hero to a lot of these goys and they love hearing about the shit I get up to.

'You did *what*?' Barry ends up having to go.

I'm there, 'Yeah, no, my daughter was mouthing off – she's a focking nightmare – so we were borred from the flight.'

'And on the way back to the cor pork, you made an excuse, you doubled back and you got on the flight without telling your wife?'

I end up just laughing. I suppose it *is* funny.

'Hey,' I go, 'that's a sign of how much I love my team.'

That gets a cheer and a round of high-fives and one or two of the Clongowes goys just smile and shake their heads and go, 'He *is* a legend,' and that must be difficult for them to admit.

'Legend or not,' I go, 'the only problem is that I now don't have a ticket. It was in Sorcha's carry-on bag.'

'We'll get you a ticket,' Barry goes, then he turns to one of the others. 'Traolach, give Ross that ticket, will you?'

Traolach whips it out and goes, 'I couldn't think of anyone better to have it.'

I put my hand in my sky rocket, except Barry tells me not to be stupid. They don't even want money for it. Like I said, that's just what it's like when you're with The Ster. It doesn't matter what school any of us went to – could be Blackrock, could be Terenure, could be Michael's, could be Gonzaga – for those few hours, we're all basically the same.

Anyway, to cut a long story short, six or seven pints and however many hours it is later, I fall out of The Misty Moon and stort making my way – on my ownio – to the ground. The atmosphere is electric and the banter between the Leinster fans and the Ulster fans is pretty intense.

I'm making my way down the road, minding my own business, when all of a sudden I hear my name being called. I turn around, roysh, and it ends up being JP and Oisinn – the two of them thick as thieves.

I go, 'Oh, look, it's my mother's boyfriend. Or are you, like, my stepdad?'

The interview with my old dear is going to be in tomorrow's paper and I'm already dreading the fallout.

'Come on, don't be like that,' it's JP who goes.

I'm there, 'Oh, *you're* back talking to me, are you? Well, lucky me. It's because *she's* not around, isn't it? The focking fat whisperer! A focking ridiculous person, by the way, who *you've* managed to get up the spout!'

He doesn't have any answer to that.

'Look, Ross,' Oisinn tries to go, 'we still have your ticket if you want to . . .'

'Sit with you two? Dude, I'd rather be boiled in my own spit.'

JP suddenly explodes. I think they've both had a skinful, just like me. 'We thought we'd let the past be the past,' he goes, 'with the day that's in it. It was Oisinn's idea. But you're not big enough, are you? You don't have the character.'

Off he stomps, with Oisinn following. Two dicks. No, actually, a dick and a snake.

I don't know if it's, like, the drink, but I get a little bit sad then, thinking about how we were all together in Edinburgh when we beat Leicester and how we were all together in Cordiff when we beat Northampton. A lot can change in, like, a year. I think about the twelve months I've just had. Discovered a grandmother I didn't know existed. Watched her die. Inherited a mansion. Got back with my wife. Became a grandfather. Took my yoghurt chucker out in front of an old man in a wheelchair. Saw my old pair get divorced. Saw my old dear getting ploughed by one of my friends. And by the time I get home, my marriage could be possibly over again.

So I'm thinking all these, like, really deep thoughts as I'm making my way into the ground, roysh, and I end up so lost in my own little world that I fail to notice that I've been stitched up by Barry O'Crohan and the other Clongowes goys. It's only after I climb up the steps into the stand that I realize – with a fright that almost empties my lunch out of my orse end – that my seat is in the Ulster end.

That thing I said about how, when we follow Leinster, we're all the same? It doesn't apply to Clongowes. They're *always* dicks. And actually, now that I think about it, so are Blackrock, Terenure, Michael's and Gonzaga.

I don't even *need* a steward to point me to my seat. I can already see it. One tiny little empty space in this, like, ocean of white jerseys.

I realize that I can do one of two things here. I can split now and watch the match in, like, The Misty Moon or some other local battle cruiser. Or I can face down the hostile crowd like I used to back in my Senior Cup days.

You can probably imagine the crack among the Ulster fans when I stort shuffling my way along the row of people to get to my seat in my Leinster colours and the blue-and-white jester hat that I'd be pretty famous for.

It's like, 'Och, look at this wee jawker' and it's like, 'Yee lawst, son?' and all the rest of it.

It's all good-natured slagging – *banterus maximus*, it has to be said – until some focking giant sitting in the row in front of me turns around to see what all the crack is about and happens to notice what I've done to my jersey. After the quarter-final victory over Cordiff, as a mork of confidence that another European Cup was in the basic bag, I asked Sorcha to go ahead and sew the third stor above the Leinster logo. Some people might see that as possibly arrogance. The six-foot-focking-ten dude sitting in front of me is certainly of that view.

'*Thray* stores?' he goes. 'Whay have yee got *thray* stores?'

I'm there, 'My, er, wife sewed the other one on,' quietly shitting it. 'Not that I'm being a grass.'

'But yee've only won tea.'

'Yeah, no, that's just a sign of my belief in this team.'

That's when he goes, 'Teak it off yee! Noy!'

I'm like, 'Take it off?' looking around me for at least someone with a bit of sense. 'I can't take it off. I'd focking freeze to death.'

'You're nat sitting thor wearing a jorsay with thray stores on ut,' he goes. 'Sumple as thot.'

Another dude beside me goes, 'Ay'll give yee somethun tea wore, son. Dee as he says – yee cawn't wore thot if yee're gonna sat with us.'

The teams are already out on the field. With chants of, 'Off! Off! Off!' from a hundred or so Ulster fans ringing in my ears, I end up having to peel my Leinster jersey off me – the jester hat's long gone, by the way – and just sit there, as the match storts, naked from the waist up.

The dude beside me hands me something. It's an Ulster jersey.

I go, 'Dude, I don't mean any disrespect to your people, but I will not wear those colours.'

He just nods and goes, 'Lat me knaw if yee cheenge yeer maind.'

Ruan Pienaar puts Ulster ahead with a penalty and I'm shivering and looking down at my goosepimply orms and thinking I might actually die here.

'It's the cawldest Mee on rackard,' someone behind me helpfully points out. But still I refuse to take the jersey they keep offering me.

Can you imagine what it would do to my reputation if a photo-graph ever came out?

It's not long before Leinster stort to weave their magic and get their off-loading game going and Sean O'Brien scores a try after we win a turnover on the Ulster twenty-two. Johnny kicks the extra two, and from that point the result is never in doubt. The only ques-tion is whether I'll be dead from exposure by the time Leo Cullen becomes the first man to lift the cup three times.

My body is so cold, you could hang a couple of wet duffle coats off my nipples. But still I refuse to wear the white of Ulster.

It has to be said, you can hear the growing respect among the supporters around me, not just for Leinster's performance – we end up running in, like, five tries – but also for the resilience of their sixteenth man. They're, like, alternating their comments about the match – 'Breeno Thraskell's pleen ite of his skan' – with lines about me: 'Hoy's *he* stell alave?' and 'Loves his team, fear plea tea hom.'

They're even giving me nips out of their hipflasks and telling me I'm a hordy mawn.

The final whistle eventually goes. My muscles are, like, frozen solid and I'm too stiff to even punch the air. The dude in front of me hands me back my Leinster jersey. 'There yorr,' he goes. 'Thray stores. See, noy yee've earned thom.'

A woman behind me – in fairness to her – goes, 'Ay've navver seen support lake thot. Teak a boy, son. Teak a boy.'

They literally applaud me out of my seat.

I'm actually still shivering when I get back to Heathrow and a feeling of dread comes over me when I realize that I now have to face Sorcha. I sit at the bor in Terminal One, my hands wrapped around a hot whiskey, and I try to come up with a story.

She answers on the third ring, already in tears. Or maybe she's been crying since this morning.

I go, 'Babes, I went to give the air-hostess a piece of my mind – like we agreed – but, by the time I got to the gate, she was actually getting onboard. So I followed her onto the plane and I told her I thought she was bang out of order – you'd have actually been proud if you'd heard me – but the next thing I knew the doors were closed and I was told to take my seat.'

'I can't believe it,' she goes, seriously sobbing now. 'I can't believe this has happened.'

She obviously hasn't bought it.

I'm there, 'Sorcha, we'll get over this. It's a blip – especially when you compare it to some of the shit I've done in the past.'

She goes, 'Ross, I'm not crying because you went to the match. I had a phone call this afternoon. From Mount Anville. They don't want Honor back at the school. She's been expelled.'

8.

How Interesting!

Sorcha says she can't help thinking about something Jackie Onassis once said. That's one of the things about Sorcha. You sit down to talk to her about one specific thing and the conversation could go literally anywhere. It means you always have to be concentrating on what she's actually saying.

'Jackie Onassis?' I go. 'Okay, give me the quote.'

'She said that if you bungle raising your children, then whatever else you do in your life doesn't matter very much at all.'

'Okay, do we know if that's an exact quote, though?'

'Yes, Ross, it's an exact quote.'

'Well, all I'll say in answer to that is that they didn't have Twitter in Jackie Onassis's time. And then to quote what you said that day in Wilde & Green – because it was actually very good – girls are bitches.'

Sorcha shakes her head. We're sitting on our bed. She's been crying for, like, an hour.

'Ross,' she goes, 'I said that because I was trying to evade my responsibility for the way Honor has turned out.'

I'm there, 'Jesus, you sound like you think that *you* might be somehow to blame.'

'I am! Oh my God, of course I am! I've failed, Ross! Like Jackie O said, I've bungled raising my daughter.'

I'm there, 'Well, I still say we've no major questions to ask ourselves. Neither of us.'

It has to be said, being totally selfish for just a minute, the one major upside of Honor being expelled from school is that it's taken the heat off me. The disappearing trick I pulled at Dublin Airport this morning hasn't even been mentioned.

Sorcha dries her tears with her open hand. She goes, 'I'm just remembering the day she storted in the school. All the hopes and dreams and aspirations we had for her. Do you remember?'

'Er, *refresh* my memory?'

'The European Youth Parliament? The Sacred Heart Committee? The choir?'

'Oh, yeah.'

'We *all* learned how to sing *bel canto*, Ross.'

'I know. I know.'

'And now that's all gone. She's never going to have any of that.'

I'm presuming that being focked out of the primary school means they're not going to want her when she's old enough to join the secondary.

'Look,' I go, 'there's other schools.'

It sounds weak, I realize, like telling a Leinster fan that there are other teams. No, there aren't. Not when you've loved The Ster.

Sorcha laughs in, like, a *sad* way?

'Who's going to want her?' she goes. 'Seriously, Ross? Who – after spending, like, five minutes in our daughter's company – is going to think that she has anything to offer a student body other than nastiness and hurt?'

'She's still young. I'm just playing devil's avocado here. She might have other shit to offer later on.'

'Do you really *believe* that?'

I don't even answer. I have to admit, it's hord to see it now.

I'm there, 'Do you know what I still don't understand? Why weren't we told that she was being a bitch? Surely there should have been, like, warnings. I was a dick myself at school, so I know the drill. Letters home threatening suspension, we'll have to call the Gords if it happens again – blah, blah, blah.'

'There *were* letters,' Sorcha suddenly goes. She looks away as well when she says it.

I'm like, 'Excuse me?'

She's there, 'There were letters and there were phone calls.'

'And, what, you ignored them?'

'Yes, I ignored them.'

'Jesus Christ, Sorcha.'

'Ross, please don't be angry with me.'

'What did these letters even say?'

'I don't know.'

'You're saying you didn't even read them?'

'I thought that we – as in, like, you and I – could get to the root of what was making her act the way she was acting ourselves. And I suppose . . .'

'What?'

'I felt guilty.'

'What do you have to feel guilty about?'

'What Honor said that day,' she goes. 'We tried to bring another baby into the house, Ross. We tried to *swap* her,' and then she bursts into tears – we're talking, like, *serious* sobbing here?

I put my orm around her. I'm there, 'But we weren't trying to swap her, Babes. And anyway, Honor was out of control long before Rihanna-Brogan was even born. No, I stand by my original statement that we've been pretty much model parents.'

She goes, 'Have we, though?'

'I'm saying yes.'

'Ross, for most of her life we've been separated.'

'Lots of parents split up.'

'But I'm wondering did we possibly spoil her – be it consciously or unconsciously – to, like, *compensate* in some way?'

'You know my view, Sorcha. It's impossible to spoil kids. I'm on the record as saying that.'

'And, well, look, I don't want to sound like I'm getting at you, Ross, but the way you speak to your mum and dad . . .'

'What about it?'

'Well, it's the same way that Honor speaks to us.'

'You're not suggesting that it might have had an impact?'

'Maybe.'

'Look, you're letting your imagination run riot, Sorcha. Some kids – no matter what you do for them – just turn out bad. Honor's one of those. We just have to accept it.'

'I just read her Twitter account. Oh my God, the things she's written, even in the last two days . . .'

'Anything about me?'

'About you, about me, about girls in her class, about celebrities. It was an insight into what's going on in her head, Ross, and, let me tell you, it was – oh my God – terrifying for a parent to read.'

'What specifically did she say about me, though?'

'She said you were pathetic, you were brain-dead, you were a loser. She talked quite a bit about your rugby tactics book . . .'

'Okay, I get the picture.'

There ends up being a minute or two of silence then. It's, like, we've talked the whole thing out and there's nothing else to say except, what happens now?

Sorcha goes, 'What happens now?'

I'm there, 'Would Loreto Dalkey take her?'

'What do *you* think, Ross?'

'Yeah, no, what about Andrew's then?'

'Look, with her reputation, no good school is going to take her. Which leaves us with only one option.'

'Don't send her to school?'

'That would be illegal.'

'Okay, what then?'

'We'll have to send her to a non-fee-paying national school.'

She says it just like that, like it's *not* a major deal? But she must also see the shock on my face, because she goes, 'Okay, what alternative *is* there?'

I'm there, 'What about, I don't know, a tutor?'

'She's not having a tutor,' she goes.

'I don't mean one who's a pushover. I'm talking about a serious ball-breaker. She doesn't even have to be good-looking if you're worried about me possibly coming onto her.'

'Ross, Honor is not being home-schooled. Because that would be to reward her for what she's done and that would send definitely conflicting signals. I certainly don't think the way to correct her anti-social behaviour is to remove her from contact with people. I actually think the opposite.'

'Sorcha, if you go in there and tell her that she's being sent to a non-fee-paying school, she will shit seven colours.'

'So let her! Ross, we've tried every other approach with her. We've tried to reason with her. We've tried to understand her. We've tried to be her friend. Maybe it's time we acted like actual parents. As a matter of fact . . .'

She suddenly jumps up from the bed.

I'm like, 'What are you doing?'

'Come on,' she goes, 'Sister Bernardine used to always say there's no better time for action than now.'

I have no idea, by the way, who the fock Sister Bernardine is. But I follow her out of the room and along the passageway to Honor's room. She opens the door and in we go.

Honor, without even looking up from her iPhone, goes, 'Yeah, have you ever heard of knocking?'

Sorcha doesn't say anything. She walks over to her and, like, snatches her iPhone out of her hand. 'Your phone and computer privileges have been revoked. And that's what they are, Honor. Privileges, given to people who know how to use them in a civic and responsible way.'

Honor laughs and goes, 'Oh my God, you are so lame!' cracking on that it doesn't actually bother her – and maybe it actually *doesn't*? She turns on me then. She's like, 'Oh my God, nice move at the airport, Dad!'

I'm there, 'Don't try and twist this around and make it about me. It's about you getting expelled from school for basically bullying.'

'Yeah, whatever.'

Sorcha then morches over to the little desk where Honor's laptop sits and she, like, closes it over and picks it up. 'I'll be back for the TV,' she goes.

I think the TV might be a step too far, although I don't say anything. Honor just laughs anyway. Doesn't give a fock.

She's like, 'Oh my God, do you really think I'm bothered? Hashtag – pah! thetic!'

Sorcha – no effort to, like, sugarcoat it – goes, 'And next week,

Honor, your father and I are going to start the process of trying to find a national school that will take you. An actual *national* school?'

Honor just shrugs. She goes, 'I don't care.'

And the most shocking thing of all is that she seems to genuinely *mean* it?

It's the headline that really pisses me off. It's like, 'I'm fifty-five – but I feel half that!'

If they were talking about stones rather than years, there'd at least be some truth in it.

Then underneath, it's like, 'Author of *Fifty Greys in Shades* phenomenon says young love has taken years off her life.'

I wish that was literally true.

The only upside is that at least there's no photograph of the two of them together. I really don't think I could have kept my eggs Benedict down.

Sorcha storts reading it over my shoulder. She at least has the decency to be shocked by it. 'Oh my God,' she goes, 'what is Fionnuala thinking?'

I'm there, 'She's not thinking. She's off her head on prescription tablets and, I don't know, turpentine, or whatever the fock her tipple of choice is these days.'

'I mean, this thing with Oisinn, it's obviously not going anywhere.'

'Do you not think?'

'Ross, it's a fling – a silly fling.'

'I can't tell you what a relief it is to hear you say those words.'

'But why is she telling the entire country about it? That's what I don't get.'

'It's pretty obvious, isn't it?'

'No.'

'To piss me off.'

'I don't think she'd do that, Ross.'

'You didn't see the look on her face that day in The Gables. Talking about needs and pleasures and at the same time licking her teeth.'

'The whole thing is just, like, oh my God!'

'That's exactly what it is.'

'And also – I'm not being a bitch – but I wouldn't have worn those shoes with that dress. I would have worn something maybe fuchsia, which offsets turquoise without, like, *upstaging* it?'

'Keep saying that kind of shit to me, Sorcha, because it definitely helps.'

I stort reading the actual story then.

It's like, 'Irish bonkbuster queen Fionnuala O'Carroll-Kelly has a new romantic tale to tell – involving herself!

'The stunningly attractive author has been celebrating the phenomenal success of her latest book, *Fifty Greys in Shades*, with a brand-new beau – who is almost half her age!

'Fionnuala (55) revealed this week that she has been cosying up with Oisinn Wallace, the 33-year-old former fragrance designer and property magnate, who was declared bankrupt last year with debts and liabilities amounting to more than €700m.

'She admitted this week: "The sex is fantastic! He makes me feel half my age!"

'The couple met through Fionnuala's son, Russ, a one-time Irish rugby hopeful, who played on the same team as Oisinn at Castlerock College in the late 1990s . . .'

Russ? Focking Russ?

'Oisinn developed the fragrance *Eau d'Affluence* for Hugo Boss and later invented and successfully marketed a range of scented holy waters, before losing everything in the property crash.

'According to a source, "They can't keep their hands off each other. Any room in the house, it doesn't matter. They're at it all the time. I don't know where they get the energy!"

'*Fifty Greys in Shades* is already a worldwide publishing phenomenon, selling almost 700,000 copies in its first few weeks of publication. It tells the story of an active retirement group from South Dublin who go to Puerto Banús one summer and find themselves possessed by a renewed sexual vigour.

'The book has been praised for daring to grasp the thorny issue of seniors sex. In one scene, ninety-four-year-old Sally Smiles from Clonkeen Road mistakes an Ecstasy tablet for her arthritis medication and has intercourse with an Israeli tour rep 70 years her junior.

'So is it a case of art imitating real life? Fionnuala laughed off the suggestion this week. "No, I'm not as old as Sally Smiles thankfully – and Oisinn isn't as young as Gideon Ben Basat!"

'She added: "Right now, we're just enjoying each other. We love each other's company. We laugh a lot. Which isn't to say it's not a physical relationship, because it very much is. It's very, very much physical."

'Fionnuala was previously married to the businessman and disgraced former Dun Laoghaire–Rathdown County Councillor, Charles O'Carroll-Kelly, who served a three-year prison sentence for corruption. They divorced earlier this year. Her first "adult" novel, *Criminal Assets*, was a partly autobiographical account of her marriage.

'Asked how her son, Russ, had taken the news of her romance with his former teammate and friend, Fionnuala said, "He'll just have to accept it. I'm a very sensual woman and I have desires and needs – just like the characters in my books!"'

I end up just seeing red. I don't know if it's being called 'Russ' by a girl I went to the trouble of making a move on, or if it's because it's out there now – the story – and I'm going to end up getting text messages left, right and centre from people who've been waiting to have something on me for years, especially fockers from the likes of Mary's, Michael's and Belvo.

I suddenly throw the *Sunday Independent* on the floor and jump to my feet.

Sorcha's like, 'Oh my God, where are you going?'

I'm there, 'To see *her* – where do you think?'

'I thought you told her she was dead to you.'

'I'm still entitled to tell her that she's a focking disgrace to humanity. I might even have a look down the back of her sofa – see can I find the decade she keeps losing out of her focking life.'

Sorcha goes, 'Well, just make sure you knock this time. I don't think you could take another shock like the last one, Ross.'

I drive to Foxrock in, like, a blind rage.

There ends up being, like, no cor in the driveway, but I ring the bell anyway, remembering Sorcha's warning. It *would* possibly kill me to see that again. After three or four long rings, it's obvious that no one's home.

I'm about to get into my cor and go home again when I suddenly remember something. My wedding ring. It's in my old room. I remember focking it into a drawer after Sorcha told me that our marriage was one hundred percent definitely over.

I stick my key in the door and I let myself in.

I can feel *his* presence in the gaff pretty much straight away. His black Helly Hansen Voss jacket is hanging on the coat stand in the hall. I can smell *John Paul Gaultier II*, which is what he nearly always wears. On the little table beside the front door is his copy of *Leo Cullen – A Captain's Story*, which he's obviously still reading. He's only on page 212 – six months after storting the focking thing. I'm a famously slow reader and I had it finished in two weeks.

I'm obviously a bigger fan.

I trudge up the stairs to my room. I pass *hers* on the way. The door is open. I just happen to give it a shove and I go in. I don't know why. I just do. I have a bit of a mooch around the room.

I notice Oisinn's Leinster training jersey in a ball on the floor. She won't be happy with that. She used to give out yords to me for not putting my shit in the laundry basket. Hopefully there'll be a humungous row and she'll finish it with him or he'll finish it with her.

There's, like, a programme on her dressing table for something at the Bord Gáis Energy Theatre last week. *Tristan und Isolde*. The greatest operatic achievement of all time, it says. So-called. There's, like, two tickets tucked inside. She's obviously storted bringing him out to shit – showing him off.

Then I think, yeah, no – *that's* what's in it for *him*. It suddenly dawns on me. All that talk of loneliness was basic horseshit, even though he almost had me feeling sorry for him that day on Chatham Street. It's all about the Cora Venus. *He's*, like, bankrupt and *she's*, like, *loaded*? It makes total sense that he'd want to be with someone

318

with actual moo, regardless of what she looks like – a camel shitting a gallstone, by the way – and regardless of who gets hurt in the process.

I think about maybe wrecking the room, just to make a statement, but then I think, fock it, no. Just get your wedding ring, Rossmeister, then – like the Good Shepherd – get the flock out of there.

I go into my old room. I find my ring and I stick it in my pocket. I notice that the door of my old wardrobe is open, so I have a look inside. And that's when I see the box.

It's a box I've honestly never laid eyes on before. It's just, like, an ordinary cordboard one, the kind you'd pick up in Superquinn or Donnybrook Fair for your bits. But it's full of books and that's what makes me suddenly suspicious. Because I've never owned a book in my life – I borrowed the Leo Cullen one from Ryle Nugent – and I'm proud to say I hopefully never will.

I lift it and carry it over to my old bed, then I stort fishing the books out. They're all obviously my old dear's. It's all *Riders* by Jilly Cooper and *Lethal Seduction* by Jackie Collins and blah, blah, blahdy-blah. The same kind of filth she writes basically. What's, like, weird about these books, though, is that they all have like, Post-it notes stuck in them or the corners of pages turned down. I flick through one or two and I notice that she's got, like, sentences – and sometimes entire *paragraphs*? – morked with a yellow highlighter pen.

It immediately strikes me as odd.

I pick one up – it's called *Jew Make Me Feel So Young* by Josephine Ashmore – and I open it at just a random page. There's, like, a paragraph highlighted and it's like, 'Yossi pulled Lucille close and pressed his young mouth against her cracked, ninety-four-year-old lips. She felt his hands – hard and firm from two years of compulsory military service – explore her grey whorls of hair and his tongue forcibly occupy the territory of her mouth. She tasted potato bourekas and stuffed vines leaves on his breath. He tasted Campbell's Homestyle Chicken Noodle Soup and Steradent Active Plus on hers. He slipped her cardigan from her shoulders and her blood heated to boiling point as it fell to the floor.'

I close the book and I can suddenly feel all of my hairs standing on end.

I race back to my old dear's room. She has a copy of *Fifty Greys in Shades* on her bedside locker. Of course she does – that's how seriously into herself she is. I pick it up and stort, like, riffling through it, my hands literally trembling with excitement.

Eventually, I find what I'm looking for – the bit where Sally Smiles from Clonkeen Road gets ridden bow-legged by Gideon Ben Basat. The old dear had the actual balls to read it out on *Miriam Meets*.

It's like, 'Gideon pulled Sally close and pressed his young mouth against her cracked, ninety-four-year-old lips. She felt his hands – hard and firm from two years of compulsory military service – explore her grey whorls of hair and his tongue forcibly occupy the territory of her mouth. She tasted potato bourekas and stuffed vines leaves on his breath. He tasted Campbell's Homestyle Chicken Noodle Soup and Steradent Active Plus on hers. He slipped her cardigan from her shoulders and her blood heated to boiling point as it fell to the floor.'

I laugh. She focking robbed the line. I literally run back to my old room.

I stort opening all of the books and reading other lines that are morked.

In one – *Members Only* by Anna Pryce – there's, like, a paragraph that goes, 'The night had been a rollercoaster ride, not a cheap, three-dollar trip either, but a double-double dipper, full of neck-breaking shunts, loop the loops and breathless highs and lows. She couldn't remember how many times she'd exploded in orgasmic ecstasy.'

The old dear used that line – I focking remember it – in *Criminal Assets*.

There's another one – in *The Games People Play* by Emily Corroon – and it's, 'Just his touch was sufficient to reduce her to a quivering, babbling, moist mess.'

She used that in *Legal Affairs*.

It's actually hilarious. My old dear has made an entire career for herself out of ripping off lines from other writers. Hundreds of them. No, thousands. And not just lines either – we're talking entire, like, *plots*? *Hungry for Naan* by Nirawan Chettri is the story of an English grandmother who goes to India and – this is a direct quote from the back – *blossoms sexually*. That's almost the exact same storyline as *Karma Suits Ya* – another book that the old dear supposedly wrote herself.

She's a focking fraud.

I pack them all back into the box as quickly as my shaking hands will let me. Then I close the lid and carry it downstairs and out to the cor. I throw it in the boot, then I head for home, happy in the knowledge that I finally have the power to destroy, once and for all, that sexually depraved, Martini-swilling, pot-bellied grunt, who, for thirty-two years, has had the balls to call herself my mother.

'What would you think of us writing our own vows?' Sorcha goes.

I'll say this for my wife – she picks her focking moments. I'm standing outside the Dublin Circuit Criminal Court in the pissings of rain when she rings.

I'm like, 'Our *actual* vows? As in, like, what we're going to say to each other on the day?'

She goes, 'Exactly.'

'Are there not, like, websites you can get that shit from?'

'Yes, but I just think it'd be nice to have something a bit more, like, *personal*? We've been through – oh my God – *so* much as a couple that it would be *so* a lovely thing to exchange vows that reflect our actual history.'

'I've an idea. Why don't you scribble something down and I'll give it the yay or nay. I'll probably love it. You're good at that kind of shit. Words and blah, blah, blah.'

'Ross, they won't be *our* vows unless we write them together. Let's schedule some you and me time over the next week or so and decide how we're going to word our pledges.'

'Er, fair enough.'

'The other thing I was going to ask you was what would you think of us showing, like, a video segment from our original wedding video on, like, a big screen?'

'Er, cool.'

'Even, like, a slideshow of photographs from our happiest times together – holidays, the debs, the Leinster Schools Senior Cup final, other celebrations, when Honor was born – with again all of, like, *our* songs in the background. "A Page is Turned" by Bebo Norman. "Lost in Space" by The Lighthouse Family. You can do it using, like, iMovie.'

'Yeah, no, that's cool. There's some photographs of the schools cup final on my laptop.'

'Okay. So how are you feeling about your jury service? Oh my God, I was so proud watching you leave this morning, Ross – going off to do your civic duty!'

'I'm still trying to think of a way out of it. If you get a call from a hospital to say I've had a focking stroke, don't panic – it'll be me just faking it.'

'Or,' she goes, 'you could do what Erika did when . . .' and then she suddenly stops, roysh, like she's already regretting *saying* anything?

I'm there, 'What did Erika do?'

She goes, 'Actually, forget it, Ross. You'd better go in. It's five to ten.'

I'm there, 'Sorcha, tell me!'

So she takes a breath – actually sighs, more than anything – then decides to fill me in. 'Look, she was called up a few years ago. Obviously she didn't want to do it. So she said a few things within earshot of one or two of the barristers, and maybe even the judge, that made them think she wouldn't be a fair and impartial juror.'

'What kind of things?'

'She said she thought that poor people should be chemically castrated.'

'She really does believe that, in fairness to her.'

'Well, she deliberately said it loud enough to be heard when they were selecting the jury. So she wasn't picked. She was having breakfast in Brown's Café half an hour later.'

I laugh.

I'm like, 'That's exactly what I'm going to do.'

Breakfast in Brown's sounds great. I can decide which newspaper to leak the story of my old dear's secret disgrace to over chorizo scrambled eggs and coffee.

'Anyway,' Sorcha goes, 'I'd better go, too. I'm meeting Father Seamus this morning, just to run through a few things ahead of the big day. Oh, by the way, he said he might be able to help us find a school willing to take Honor! Isn't that amazing?'

'It's all good like Gielgud, Baby. Look, I'll text you the second I get out of this bullshit.'

So in I go. The place is, like, rammers – people milling about, barristers and judges and criminals. I show my letter to a woman at a desk and I'm sent down a corridor, through a door, across a courtyord, through two more doors, along another corridor, then finally into a room not much bigger than a school classroom. It's, like, full when I get there – we're talking maybe a hundred ordinary shmoes, some of them sitting but most of them just standing around.

I'm obviously the last to arrive. Every set of eyes in the room turns to see me and, at the top of my voice, I go, 'Does anyone know if it's safe to pork the cor around here? It's just there seems to be a lot of scumbags out there . . . focking scum . . . scum of the earth.'

No one answers me. They all just turn back to the front of the room. But I think my point is made.

There's, like, a dude with a clipboard then, who storts reading out names and telling people to go immediately to court number this and court number that. Mine ends up being the tenth or eleventh name called. This bird – who could look like Laura Haddock if she did something with herself – morches a group of maybe twenty of us through, like, a warren of corridors towards, presumably, the courtroom where the trial is going to take place. Every time we pass someone – again, at the top of my voice – I go, 'He's guilty . . . She's guilty . . . He's definitely guilty . . . Sometimes you can just tell by the look of these fockers . . . Guilty! Jesus, look at the way he's dressed . . .'

We're finally led into a courtroom. There's, like, two barrister dudes there already waiting for us. We sit down, then in walks the judge and we have to all, like, stand up again, just for focking him.

When there's, like, silence in the courtroom, I turn to the dude beside me and go, 'Everyone on this side of the city looks like a possible killer to me,' and I say it loud enough for everyone in the room to hear. I'm on, like, a serious roll now. 'I think I'd definitely have to class myself as racist against northsiders.'

The judge asks us each to stand up and say our name in turn. When it comes to me, he asks me to repeat it, then writes it down, which at first I think must be a good sign.

Then the two barristers stort calling out names and telling people that they can go home.

It's like, 'Vincent Tiernan – you're excused,' and it's, 'Ursula Downs – you're excused,' and there's no, like, reasons even *given*?

I realize that I'm going to have to ramp up the act here, otherwise I'm going to end up on the jury. I rub my hands together and go, 'I hope it ends up being a nice easy case. Someone from a real scumbag area. Send them down, no matter what. God, I love the power.'

It's like, 'Catha Considine – you're excused.'

It's like, 'Martin Brannock – you're excused.'

I go, 'I'm on the record as saying that we should just build an electric fence around areas like Finglas and Coolock. It'd save us the cost of jailing these fockers later on.'

It's like, 'Tina Saurin – you're excused.'

It's like, 'Emeka Ibrahim – you're excused.'

Shit. I look around me and do a quick head-count. There's, like, fourteen of us left. Which means if it's a jury of twelve, there's only, like, two more who are going to get out of this.

I go, 'All I'll have to do is hear the focker's accent and my mind will be made up straight away about whether he's getting life or not.'

It's like, 'Redmond Gallagher – you're excused.'

It's like, 'Colm Caulfield – you're excused.'

I don't focking believe it. I'm in. What the fock do you have to do or say to convince these fockers that you're, I don't know, prejudiced? I'm turning around to my – I genuinely don't believe it – fellow focking jurors and I'm going, 'I don't need this in my life right now! I literally don't need it!'

There ends up being a bit of chatter between the two barristers and the judge, very little of which I understand, but the upshot is that the trial of whoever the fock it's going to be ends up being deferred for another week.

The judge goes, 'Please be here in court at 10 a.m. on Tuesday, the fifth of June,' and then, just as I'm standing up to go, he's like, 'Ross O'Carroll-Kelly,' like he's suddenly got something that he wants to say to me *specifically*?

I'm like, 'Er, yeah?'

He goes, 'Whose colours are they?'

I look down at my jersey. I'm like, 'You mean this? It's Leinster.'

Jesus, I thought a judge of all people would have known that.

He's there, 'Leinster will not be playing in my courtroom next week. You might consider wearing something more befitting of the occasion.'

I've never heard of a saint called Aileran. Sorcha says she hadn't either, but she Googled him and he definitely exists. And he must have been one of the good ones if they're naming actual schools after him.

'Saint Aileran's National School in Ballybrack,' she goes. 'That doesn't sound too bad, does it?'

I'm there, 'Well, it's not Mount Anville, though, is it? You can't say it in a fock-off kind of a way. "No, you will not put me on hold! I went to Mount Anville!" '

'Unfortunately,' she goes, 'we don't have that option any more. Look, she doesn't *have* to go to this one. Father Seamus just very kindly arranged for us to meet with the principal, Riobard O'Fathaigh.'

'Riobard O'Fathaigh? Jesus Christ! Is it, like, a *gaelscoil*?'

'No, but they place a very strong emphasis on the Irish language and heritage. Which I think is – oh my God – so important. I do think multiculturalism is important as well. But so is learning about your own culture – and that's not racist.'

'I honestly wouldn't know what was and what wasn't any more. Ballybrack, though! Fock.'

'Well, Father Seamus speaks very highly of Mr O'Fathaigh. He's a big believer in discipline apparently, which is exactly what Honor needs. And it's also co-ed.'

'Does that mean boys *and* girls?'

'Exactly. I think she might actually benefit from being schooled in, like, a *mixed* gender environment?'

'Er, yeah, whatever you think, Babes.'

We're, like, sitting at the kitchen table, where we've been for the past, like, two hours, supposedly writing our vows to each other. Mine haven't been going well.

'How are you getting on?' Sorcha goes.

I'm there, 'Errr . . .'

She grabs my rugby tactics book and turns it around so she can read it. She looks, I don't know, *puzzled* – if that's not too random a word to use.

She's like, 'Ross, what's this? What have you spent the last two hours writing?'

I'm there, 'It's just . . . I don't know.'

'Jonathan Davies. Manu Tuilagi. Ross, what are all these names?'

'It's the Lions squad I would pick right now if I was the coach and the tour to Australia was this year rather than next.'

'Ross, you're supposed to be writing a pledge to me for our renewal! It's only, like, two weeks away!'

'I'm not in one of my deep-thinking moods, Sorcha, and that's me just being honest. I can't just turn it on and off.'

'Okay, will I read you what I've written?'

'Yeah, do.'

'It might give you one or two pointers.'

'Yeah, no, I'm saying go on.'

'Okay. My dearest Ross. You are my beloved husband, my best friend, my chief support, my guiding star, my confidant, my ballast, my compass. You are my north, my south, my east, my west. The first thing I think about in the morning and the last thing I think about at night. Eight years ago we made a pledge before God, our families, our friends and all those whom we hold dear, to love one another for life. And today my heart rejoices as we celebrate that promise, which has only grown stronger as we've travelled along life's turbulent path together. As Tom Cruise said to Renée Zellweger in the movie we went to see on one of our very first dates together, and which we both still love, you complete me. Even if our years together have included some rough patches, I never stopped believing that. And that is why it makes my heart brim over with happiness to re-dedicate my life to you today, to thank you for helping me to become the person I am today, to promise that I will always be beside you as your loving and devoted wife and to pledge that I will always give you the very best of me. I love you with all my heart. And I always will.'

Sorcha has this way of occasionally just flooring me.

I'm like, 'Jesus . . . Fock . . .' It's all I can think to say.

She goes, 'It's still pretty rough at the moment.'

'Sorcha,' I go, 'that's unbelievable. If you say that to me on the day, I'll . . . I don't know what I'll do. I'm not going to be able to write something like that.'

I look at what I've spent the last two hours doing. The words, 'Fock off, Chris Ashton, you absolute wanker!' leap off the page at me in underlined capitals.

Sorcha goes, 'You will, Ross.'

I'm there, 'I genuinely won't be able to follow that, though. Unless I have one of my famous deep moments between now and the big day. It's a while since I've had one actually.'

There's all of a sudden a ring at the door. I get up and I go outside to answer it.

It ends up being Sorcha's old dear. She looks horrendous. I think I've said before that the woman is anything but a looker. But what I mean this time is that she looks like she hasn't slept in days.

I'm there, 'Come in, Mrs Lalor. Are you okay?'

She's like, 'Yes, is Sorcha home?'

I go, 'Yeah, come in.'

She follows me down to the kitchen. Sorcha sees straight away that something's wrong. She's like, 'Mum?'

They've got one of those my-mum's-my-best-friend relationships that would be big out this direction.

Her old dear just bursts into tears. Sorcha throws her orms around her, going, 'Oh, Mom! What's happened?'

I hope she's left Sorcha's old man. That would be funny.

I go, 'I'll, er, go upstairs and see what Honor's up to,' because I've never known how to handle seeing people cry.

'No,' the woman goes. 'Stay, Ross. This affects you, too.'

She pulls out a tissue and cleans up her face.

Sorcha goes, 'You're not coming, are you? To see us renew our vows?'

Her old dear shakes her head.

'It's fine,' Sorcha goes. 'He's your husband. You have to stand by him.'

'We're leaving,' her old dear all of a sudden goes.

Sorcha's like, 'Leaving?' automatically in shock. 'What are you talking about? Where are you going?'

She's there, 'London. Your father's made up his mind. He's going to file for bankruptcy in the UK.'

'How long will you be gone for?'

'A year or two. I don't know for sure.'

'Oh my God.'

'That way he can start over, you see. Come back and practise law again. Maybe buy a little house somewhere. It's not been good for him stuck in that apartment . . .'

Her voice cracks.

'. . . knowing he's lost his daughter and his home to you, Ross. And I'm sorry, I don't mean to hurt your feelings.'

I'm there, 'Hey, it's cool.'

'That virus of an individual,' she goes. 'That's what he calls you.'

'Well, we all knew he wasn't a backer of mine.'

'He just doesn't see that there's anything left for him here. And I was wondering, Sorcha, if there was any chance . . .'

Except Sorcha all of a sudden cuts her off. She's like, 'Oh my God, I hope you're not asking me to apologize?'

'Not apologize, no. Just – I don't know – see if you can't reach some kind of accommodation, where it's not necessary for anyone to say sorry? You did that course, Sorcha, in the Smurfit school. There must be a way.'

'He tried to destroy my marriage, Mum. I don't see why I should be the one reaching out to him.'

'I know.'

'I actually *want* an apology?'

'I understand.'

'So when are you actually leaving?'

'The fifteenth of June.'

'The fifteenth of June? Oh my God, that's, like, the day before we renew our vows!'

'I know.'

'He's doing it to cause – oh my God! – *the* maximum upset.'

'Please don't think that of him, Sorcha. He just didn't want to be here when it happens. He said he couldn't watch you do it.'

'And you still think it's possible to fix this?'

The mother shakes her head, like she's finally resigned to it.

'No,' she goes. 'He's too stubborn. You're both too alike. But I couldn't forgive myself if I didn't at least try.'

'Can I ask you both a favour?'

Sorcha's there, 'Mom, I'd do anything for you specifically.'

'Your sister's going to have nowhere to live.'

I wish someone, just once, would use her focking name.

The mother goes, 'I mean, when we leave the apartment. She can't come to England with us. She has her job in Aldi.'

Sorcha's there, 'She can live here,' and then she looks at me.

'I'm like, 'Er, yeah, whatever.'

'I'm so sorry,' Sorcha's old dear tries to go, 'to be missing your big day.'

Sorcha's like, 'I understand. I totally do.'

'Make sure to send me lots and lots of photographs.'

'I will.'

She smiles sadly at her daughter then. 'He'll come around,' she goes. 'It'll just take time.'

Then she focks off.

I turn around to Sorcha and I go, 'Are we definitely sure it's a good idea, your sister coming to live here?'

She looks at me like I'm possibly mad. She's like, 'We have plenty of room, Ross.'

Room, of course, is not the issue. When that gorgeous little fun-bundle is stalking around after you, wearing half-nothing and flashing those fantastic cupcakes of hers, there isn't a house in the world big enough to hide in. Making vows is actually the easy bit, I realize. Keeping them is about to become a whole lot horder.

Claire says there's a real buzz about Bray at the moment and I laugh openly in her face. I watch Garret stiffen – like he's *thinking* of throwing a punch? – except he wouldn't have it in him. There's more meat on Stella McCortney's conscience. He *knows* he'd be decked.

We're in Christian and Lauren's – the gaff they're renting in Booterstown – for, like, Lauren's birthday borbecue. The gorden is rammers. It's the second day of June, the sun is splitting the skies, there's a smell of burning flesh in the air and everything seems right with the world.

So why does *she* have to keep bringing up Bray?

'I'm just making the point,' she tries to go, 'that there's a real, like, civic spirit in the town at the moment because of the whole London 2012 thing?'

'Oh my God, Katie Taylor!' Sorcha goes. 'I *so* hope she wins gold. She is *such* a strong role model for women everywhere.'

Claire's there, 'And talk about uniting an entire town!'

I go, 'Yeah, wouldn't you know that as soon as Women Fighting became a recognized sport, Bray would produce an Olympic champion in it.'

It's a cracking line – genuinely funny. But Claire tells me I'm a wanker and Garret just goes, 'Agreed,' like he's at a focking board meeting or something. But at that point I'm already walking away – off to see how Christian's getting on with those steaks.

I could eat a nun's orse through a convent fence.

'Lauren looks like she's about to pop any minute,' I go, friendly hand around the shoulder. 'You must be excited.'

He's like, 'Counting the days.'

I can't tell you how good it is to see my best friend this happy. I say that to him as well.

He goes, 'It just feels – I don't know – like my life is finally coming together. That sounds weird, I know. Two years ago, I was the project manager of a Las Vegas casino, living in a three-million-dollar condo overlooking the strip. Now I'm living in a rented house in Booterstown and managing a sandwich shop . . .'

I'm there, 'That's some comedown alright. Jesus.'

'But I'm happy, Ross. I've honestly never *been* happier?'

'That's children for you,' I go. 'Here,' and I hand him a can of the Dutch master and we do, like, a toast.

Those steaks are taking their focking time.

'What about you?' he goes. 'Lauren told me about Honor.'

I'm there, 'Are you talking about her getting banned from a flight or expelled from school?'

'Well, both. I mean, is there any chance Mount Anville will take her back?'

'Not a chance in the world.'

'Fock.'

'She's a little horror, Christian. I hate saying that about my own daughter, but she's a good advertisement for not having kids.'

At that exact moment, I notice Sorcha snatch something out of her little hands. This is Honor's new thing – stealing other children's iPhones, so she can get on Twitter. She's obsessed.

I hear Sorcha go, 'Give that phone back to Myrna this instant!'

Myrna is the daughter of this seriously hot friend of Lauren's called Lisa Manning, who I got off with once or twice back in the day. She's a little bit like Bérénice Marlohe, except she makes this gorging sound with her mouth when she kisses, like a dog that can't get the food into his mouth quick enough. I'm not sure why that's relevant.

Honor gives Sorcha the finger.

Sorcha goes, 'I'm not reacting to that, Honor, because I know that's all you're looking for.'

Christian watches this little scene, too. He goes, 'What are you going to do?'

I'm there, 'We've got an appointment to meet the Principal of Saint Something or other, first thing Monday morning.'

'Where is it?'

'Ballybrack.'

'Jesus.'

'I know. But we don't have a lot of options. She's turned into a serious piece of work. By the way, did I mention I'm doing focking jury service?'

'I thought you wrote them a letter?'

'They didn't buy my excuse.'

'You should do what Erika did a few years ago.'

'I tried that as well. I put on a serious show for them. But they still ended up picking me.'

He laughs. I end up having to laugh then.

I'm there, 'I mean, what the fock are they thinking, putting *me* on a jury? I'm one of Ireland's stupidest people. That's well known. The only thing I've ever been able to concentrate on for more than, like, five minutes is rugby. I'm not capable of following an actual trial. You'd genuinely have to wonder what this country is coming to.'

Suddenly, I hear, 'Hi, Roth!'

My godson is shouting at me from the inflatable princess castle, where he's playing with the rest of the girls.

I'm there, 'Hey, Ross. Come over here. I brought you a present.'

He comes bounding over. He *is* a great little kid. The other thing is something he'll hopefully grow out of.

'Roth,' he goes, 'my mawmy ith wearing a makthi dreth from Reith and timeleth ethpadrilth!'

I'm like, 'Never mind all that! Here!' and I hand him a little something I picked up for him this morning in Elvery's on Stephen's Green. A little thing called a rugby ball.

He looks at it – I shit you not – like I've just handed him roadkill and said it was lunch.

Lauren suddenly waddles out of the house, in her maxi dress, yes, and her timeless focking espadrilles. I don't even get a chance to wish her a happy birthday. She just goes, 'I don't know why you brought that thing. He has no interest in sport.'

Ross Junior turns around – this is a direct quote – and goes, 'What ith it, Mawmy?'

And Lauren – again, exact words – is like, 'It's not important. Come on, let's go and find your friends, Myrna and Lucy.'

She hands the ball back to me. My jaw is practically on the ground. Christian obviously doesn't want to get into it, roysh, because he makes an excuse about needing more sausages and just, like, slips into the house.

Sorcha wanders over to me. I'm spinning the thing in my hands, just staring into space.

She goes, 'Ross, what would you think of giving out little packets of flower seeds as favours at the renewal – just as a symbol of, like, nurturing?'

She suddenly notices that I'm upset.

She's like, 'Ross, what is it?'

I'm there, 'My godson. I showed him the rugby ball we bought him and he didn't know what it was. He didn't know what it was, Sorcha. He didn't recognize a standard Gilbert.'

'He did spend the first three and a half years of his life in the States, Ross. Rugby isn't a central part of life over there like it is here.'

I end up just shaking my head. That isn't the real reason and she knows it. I'm there, 'When I remember the player his father used to be. Brian O'Driscoll named Christian Forde as one of the five best centres he'd ever played against.'

'I remember you cutting that interview out of the paper.'

'That was Brian O'Driscoll saying that, Sorcha. Jesus Christ, I'm filling up with tears even thinking about those words.'

Sorcha tells me not to get upset, then she says she's going inside to use the toilet.

I can't let it go, though. Christian and Lauren put me in chorge of this kid's spiritual well-being – and as far as I'm concerned, that includes rugby.

I find him literally cycling around on Myrna's pink Dora the Explorer classic dual-deck tricycle.

I'm there, 'Ross, come over here a minute,' and I stand him on the grass behind the – Jesus Christ – inflatable princess castle. 'Just stand there,' I go.

I'm still spinning the ball in my hands.

He's like, 'Whath are we thooing, Roth?'

The little lisp *is* cute, even though it does become seriously focking annoying after about thirty seconds.

I'm there, 'No questions, Kid. Just get ready to catch this thing when I throw it to you, okay?'

He goes, 'Okay.'

I step back maybe twenty yords away from him. I ask him if he's ready and he nods. That's the thing – he definitely nods. Then I send a pass spinning through the air towards him. He doesn't even move. I swear to fock. He just stands there, watching it speed towards his head.

The ball hits him, hord, on the forehead and he goes down like the proverbial sack of Maris Pipers.

I've never been so disappointed in my life. One of the things that made his old man a truly great centre was his handling. It didn't matter what kind of ball you gave him, he would control it and he would make something of it. His son has none of that. No reflexes whatsoever. Like I said, I'm disappointed.

But that disappointment turns to worry when little Ross doesn't immediately get *up*? I possibly put too much force behind the ball – that's just the competitor in me. I'm like, 'Ross? Ross, come on, up – we'll give it another go,' except he still doesn't stir. That's when I realize that he's out cold.

My first thought is obviously, 'Oh, shit!' and my second – I'm not proud of this – is, 'I wonder could I just step away here and deny all knowledge of this?'

That's how terrified I am of his mother.

But in the end, I do the right thing. I go, 'Lauren, come quickly – Ross has just fallen off Myrna's tricycle!'

Luckily, the ball bounced off his head and into the shrubbery, so it's nowhere to be seen.

Every conversation suddenly stops. Lauren screams, while Christian runs the length of the gorden and picks up his son, who I'm relieved to notice *is* actually conscious, although a bit groggy.

The kid goes, 'It wath too fatht, Daddy! He threw it thoo fatht!'

I quickly go, 'Ah, he's babbling now. It's possibly concussion.'

Lauren goes, 'Concussion? How hard did he hit his head?'

'Pretty hord. He went over the handlebors. Dora the focking Explorer, huh? It's all hormless fun until someone gets hurt.'

'Mawmy,' the kid goes. 'I can thee thpoth.'

Lauren goes, 'He needs to lie down,' and the two of them bring him inside – Ireland's most pampered kid – and put him to bed.

Everyone looks at each other, going, 'Poor little lad!' but thankfully no one saw what happened and I end up being treated as a bit of a hero just for having alerted Christian and Lauren to it. Lisa Manning's husband – Myrna's old man – asks me if I'm okay and hands me a beer and I end up adding a few details to the story, with me seeing it happen almost in slow-motion and trying to catch the kid before he cracked his head off the ground. He goes, 'You did good!'

'He did *amazing*!' Lisa goes – and she gives me a huge hug.

Not to be outdone, Aoife Bass – this serious honey who's in, like, Lauren's book club – comes over to me and goes, 'The way you handled that was, like, oh my God!'

I'm there, 'In a situation like that, the adrenalin just takes over. You do what you have to do.'

Someone else slaps me on the back and goes, 'You the man, Ross!' and I couldn't tell you how long it's been since someone said that and how good it feels to finally hear it again.

Hilariously, the famous Lisa ends up taking over the borbecue and finishes cooking my steak.

Lauren and Christian don't show their faces again for a good, like, fifteen minutes. When they do, Christian mouths the word, 'Thanks,' to me from across the gorden, while Lauren – fair focks to

her – actually comes over to me and goes, 'I don't even want to con-template what might have happened if you hadn't been there, Ross. Thank you.'

I'm there, 'Hey, I can be a nice goy, Lauren.'

She smiles at me. It's not often that happens either. She goes, 'Maybe I should acknowledge that a lot more than I do.'

Half an hour after that – with the food eaten – we all end up having to go inside, because it storts to piss. That's the thing about the weather. It can change very suddenly. And it's not just the weather either.

We're all, like, packed into the kitchen. I end up chatting to Lisa's husband about the first Ireland v New Zealand test next weekend. He agrees with my analysis that Ireland have a decent chance of winning one of the three matches – possibly the second – even though he went to a GAA school himself and knows very little about the game beyond the stuff he hears *other* people say?

JP and the famous Shoshanna show their faces then. Late. She's really showing now, however many months she has left. *He* doesn't even look at me. He falls into a conversation with some random dude about – get this – the referendum on the European Fiscal Compact Treaty, while Shoshanna hears the story about Ross Junior's accident from Claire and Amie with an ie, cocks her head to one side and, in the usual baby voice, goes, 'Sad story!'

There's, like, no sign of Oisinn. He's probably too busy having sex with my old dear. His girlfriend. It's too focked up for words.

I tip over to One F, who's telling a group of, again, randomers about a conversation he had once with Bonnie Tyler, who it turns out is a massive, massive Welsh rugby fan. One F is a legend to me. He wrote some of the best orticles that were ever written about me back in my playing days.

'Derek,' I go, 'can I've a word?'

He's like, 'What's up?' – you know the way he talks.

'Are you still writing for that focking rag?'

I often buy it – just to read *him* – but I still like to give him a hord time about it.

He goes, 'Yeah.'

I'm there, 'I've got a story, if anyone in there is interested.'

'It's not another Ross comeback story, is it?'

'No, it's not another Ross comeback story. This is about my old dear. Tell someone in the newsroom to give me a bell. I've got something that will destroy that bitch once and for all.'

The four or five people he was telling his Bonnie Tyler story to seem a bit shocked by that. But then, they've never met my old dear.

I need to piss. There's someone *in* the jacks in the hall, so I end up having to trudge up the stairs to use the one up there – something that's becoming a bit of a theme with Lauren and Christian.

I have a quick wiz. I'm on my way back downstairs and I'm, like, passing little Ross's room – singing a One Direction song to myself, weirdly enough, because I've a fair few drinks on me – when all of a sudden I hear him call my name.

He's like, 'Roth! Roth!'

I stick my head around his door. I'm there, 'Hey, little goy – how are you feeling?'

He goes, 'Much bether now, thank you . . . Roth, why dith you throw the ball ath me?'

I'm there, 'Er, I *didn't*? You snotted yourself on that little girl's bike, remember?'

'No, you thold me to thee if I could catch the ball, then you threw it at me thoo hard!'

He's like Celine Dion. It's all coming back to him now. I just think, fock it, I might as well say what I have to say here.

'I wouldn't have classed that as too hord,' I go. 'That was just an average pass.'

He's there, 'Ith hith me on the head!'

'But you didn't even move! You didn't even move, Ross! And much as I hate saying this, I was actually disappointed in you. Genuinely disappointed. Your old man was one of the best centres ever to play the game in Ireland.'

'Roth, my mawmy ith wearing a makthi dreth and timeleth ethpadrilth.'

'Jesus, will you quit saying that shit? Why are you so obsessed with women's clothes? It's not normal is what I'm saying.'

'She hath thix makthi dretheth.'

'It doesn't matter a fock to me how many focking maxi dresses she has. And it shouldn't matter a fock to you either. You've turned into a sissy, Ross, and I'm saying that as your godfather.'

'Whath a thithy?'

'It's when you're a boy but you act like a girl. You don't want to get the shit kicked out of you in school, do you?'

'No.'

'Then try and act more like a boy – that's all I'm saying. Boys aren't interested in, like, dresses and what their mothers are wearing. They're interested in shit like rugby.'

'Roth, you threw the ball ath my head!'

'I didn't throw it *at* your head. You just have zero reflexes, that's all. And by the way, don't you dare tell your mum and dad that I focked the ball at you.'

'Why noth?'

'Well, because *they'd* be as disappointed as I am by your lack of rugby-playing ability. They genuinely would. Your old man's nickname used to be Velcro Hands. And your old dear saw him play many times. So tell them you fell off the bike, okay?'

'Okay.'

'Dora the focking Explorer.'

'Okay.'

'Jesus, I bought you that ball as a gift. I'll see you later, okay?'

'Okay. Bye, Roth.'

'Bye.'

I tip down the stairs, thinking, that's the lovely thing about kids. They do listen. All he needed was a strong voice to tell him to get his nose out of his old dear's wardrobe and stort getting interested in the kind of shit that boys *should* be interested in?

I mean, I bought him a little Leinster jersey for his birthday and I haven't seen it on him once.

That will hopefully change now. I'm actually in good form as I tip back down to the kitchen. I walk in and go, 'Okay, it's beer o'clock – who's got a cold one for me?'

There's, like, silence in the room. Every single set of eyes is looking directly at me when I walk in. Lauren, I notice, is crying and Christian is doing his best to comfort her. Sorcha looks pretty much in shock.

Something has obviously happened.

I look at all these faces, staring at me in just, like, *shock*? Christian. Lisa Manning and her husband. JP. Shoshanna. Claire from Bray. Garret. One F. Amie with an ie. All of Lauren's friends and all of Christian's. Everyone.

I'm like, 'Sorry, what's the focking story?'

And then I hear it. A little voice coming from across the kitchen. It's like, 'My mawmy hath thix makthi dretheth.'

And that's when I remember the baby monitor in Ross Junior's room.

Honor laughs. She's the only one. 'Oh my God,' she goes. 'Hillare!'

I turn around and, without saying a word, I head for the door. Because sometimes you just know when a porty is over for you.

Mr O'Fathaigh turns out to be one of these, like, really *serious* headmaster types? Bald, except for two giant tufts of grey hair on either side of his head. Loves his GAA, you can tell from the cut of him. Thorn-proof sports coat with leather patches on the elbows. And never happy. The kind of focker who smiles first thing in the morning to get it over with for the day.

I'm taking an interest in all these posters that he's got hanging on the walls of his office, which, by the way, is colder than a nun's left knocker and smells of bleach and old sick.

I'm like, 'Okay, what's this one then – the one with all the writing?'

He goes, 'That's the Proclamation of Independence!' like it should have been somehow obvious to me.

Sorcha goes, 'It was read by the 1916 Volunteers, Ross, of the GPO.'

I'm lucky she's still talking to me after what happened in Christian and Lauren's on Saturday. I suppose she needs today to go well.

'What, the GPO in town?' I go.

She's like, 'Yes, the one on O'Connell Street.'

I shake my head. 'It's mad, isn't it, how you can walk around and there's all this, I don't know, history around you that no one knows about. Not that I make a habit of going over that side of the river.'

He just, like, stares at me, obviously taking me for an idiot.

'Ross,' Sorcha goes, 'maybe you should come and sit down.'

Which is what happens. I'm conscious of not letting her down again, so I end up just joining them – Mr O'Fathaigh sitting on one side of the desk and me and Sorcha on the other. Honor, by the way, is outside the door. The dude wanted to interview the two of us alone – although it's Sorcha who seems to be asking most of the questions.

She's there, 'I'd be very interested in knowing what, like, subjects you teach?'

She's wearing her Alexander Wang cigarette-leg trouser suit with a white shirt by Saint Laurent and Pigalle 100 pumps by Christian Louboutin. I personally think she's overdressed.

Ballybrack is Ballybrack.

'Irish,' Mr O'Fathaigh goes. 'English. Mathematics. History. Geography. Nature. Art.'

There's, like, silence then. Sorcha is obviously waiting to hear more. There's suddenly nothing else coming, though.

'So that's, what, the *core* curriculum?' she goes.

He's like, 'No, that's the curriculum.'

Silence again. Outside, I can hear the screams and shouts of children at play. Except they're not the kind of voices you'd normally associate with southside children on their lunchbreak. They're, like, louder and – I think it's a word – *coarser*? And the names that are shouted. Marty. Natalie. Dunner. Saoirse. Tooler.

A ball suddenly hits the window. It's an actual soccer ball. We've entered into a whole new world here.

Sorcha goes, 'So you don't offer subjects like French or Mandarin?'

He's like, 'Mandarin. Like they speak in China?'

'Yes.'

'No.'

'Is there ballet?'

'No.'

Sorcha nods, roysh, and makes a note of it in her little Mont Blanc portfolio pad. 'And what about extra-curricular activities?' she goes. 'Do you have, like, a Peace and Justice Committee or a Year-book Editorial Board?'

She's overplaying her hand here. I know it. She knows it. And Mr O'Fathaigh definitely knows it, because he goes, 'The point of today was that *I* would interview *you*, not the other way around.'

He doesn't seem the type of dude who'd take a lot of shit. He has what looks like a letter in his hands. He throws his eyes over it. 'Your daughter was expelled from her last school,' he goes. 'Is that correct?'

'Well,' Sorcha goes, 'I'd prefer to say that, educationally, it just wasn't a good fit.'

He's here, 'Yes, expelled for bullying.'

He obviously knows the full story. I just go, 'Yeah, bullying,' because there's no point trying to shit the dude. Sorcha looks at me, though, like I've just betrayed her – betrayed them both.

'She comes with quite a reputation,' he goes and then he sort of, like, smiles to himself. He's definitely heard one or two stories, you can tell that much. 'So let's put this notepad of yours away, shall we? You have to send your daughter to school. That's the law. But no fee-paying school is going to take her now. That's why you're here. Oh, don't worry, it happens two or three times a term – well-to-do parents wind up here, asking us to take their problem children.'

'She's not a problem child,' Sorcha goes.

'She certainly won't be as long as she's here. I can assure you of that. But to answer your question, no, we don't have a Yearbook Editorial Board. And we don't have – what was the other thing?'

'A Peace and Justice Committee.'

'We don't have a Peace and Justice Committee either. What we do have is a leak in the roof of the assembly hall where last week somebody stole the lead from above our heads and an overrun on our annual budget, which the Department of Education wishes to speak to me about, except I haven't been taking their calls. Do you understand me?'

'Yes.'

'This isn't Mount Anville, Mrs O'Carroll-Kelly.'

'I do realize that.'

'Your daughter has been banished from the world of Peace and Justice and Yearbook Committees. So don't patronize me by taking notes in front of me and pretending that you have options. I agreed to *consider* enrolling your daughter in this school because Father Seamus is an old family friend. No other reason. Now show the girl in.'

That's put Sorcha back in her box.

I stand up and go outside for her. She's just sitting there, her little thumb still working away – it's, like, a nervous tic she was left with after we took the iPhone from her.

I go, 'Honor, Mr O'Fathaigh wants to see you.'

I notice that his secretary has been crying. She's, like, mopping her eyes with a piece of tissue. I don't even *want* to know what my daughter said to her.

Honor follows me into the office, sighing, rolling her eyes and dragging her feet. Before Mr O'Fathaigh gets a chance to open his mouth, Honor fixes him with a look and goes, 'How did you end up as headmaster of such a knacker school? I'd say your mum and dad must be *rul* proud!'

Mr O'Fathaigh literally explodes. He brings his fist down hord on the desk and he's like, 'Don't you *dare* address me unless you are asked a direct question!'

I jump. Sorcha jumps. I have never seen another human being look so angry. And the most incredible thing happens then. Honor shits it. I have honestly never seen my daughter frightened of anything until that moment.

'Okay,' she goes.

'You don't say, "Okay",' he screams at her. 'You say, "Yes, Príomhoide"!'

She's like, 'Yes, Príomhoide!'

I look at Sorcha and I know we're both thinking the exact same thing. This place seems perfect.

The dude sitting in front of me says it's going to be, like, a fraud case and he says it like he's *excited*? He even rubs his hands together and I think, how little would you want to have going on in your life to get worked up at the idea of sitting on, like, a jury? Listening to two barristers, who are on serious squids, going, 'The goy didn't do it!' and 'Er, yes, he actually did!' and 'No, he focking didn't!' for, like, a week – which is how long we've been told the trial is going to last – and then having to decide who made the best case at the end.

What a serious waste of my focking time.

What's worse is there's nothing to even look at in the courtroom. The jury is made up of, like, eight men and four women. Three of the women are, like, married – we're talking forties – and possibly even fifties-plus. The other is my age, but she's as ugly as they make them. She's called Bernadette and she's from, like, Tipperary. She's one chunky monkey too, with thick black hair like steel wool, a big agricultural voice and teeth like a box of Wedgwood China that was sent through the mail and has been kicked across the floor by every focking postal worker who handled it along the way.

She also has this really annoying habit of storting sentences with the words, 'Ah, leds!'

She latches onto me right from the off – it's pretty clear that she fancies me – choosing the seat right next to mine and going, 'Ah, leds! Thet was some show you put on the lest dee!'

I'm there, 'What do you mean?'

'All thet stuff about scumbags and making your mind up about a fella on the basis of his eccent. Ah, sure, leds! You didn't expect to get awee with thet!'

'Well, as it happens, I actually believe a lot of that stuff. All of that stuff. I've also always been a big believer in the proverb that there's no smoke without fire. Any focker who finds themselves in court chorged with a crime, I'd send them down on the basis that, even if they didn't do one particular thing, they probably did something else – and they'd almost certainly go on to do even more.'

I end up getting shushed by the dude in front of me, who thinks he's in the focking cinema or some shit.

Bernadette has a root around in her bag and she pulls out a pair of humungous glasses, which she then puts on. There is literally no good news about this girl.

There ends up being a bit of a hush in the courtroom then, while the accused arrives in. I don't even bother looking at him. I end up just staring at this bird who's, like, scribbling notes in the press box and who's a ringer for Katrina Bowden, except with mosquito stings instead of proper actual breasts. I smile at her, but she doesn't smile back.

I'm already bored and the thing hasn't even storted. I check my phone for text messages – still nothing back from Christian. He's going to need a day or two more to forgive me, I reckon.

Like I said, I have zero interest in even being here. My plan is to just, like, space my way through the entire case, occasionally pretending to take notes – I might have a crack at my vows, or even pick my dream XV for the first test against New Zealand – and then just go along with whatever seems to be the general feeling at the end, whether it's guilty or not guilty.

I don't owe these fockers any more than that.

It's only when the dude is being sworn in that I finally look at him. And that's because I realize – with a fright that almost causes me to shit Weetabix in my boxers – that I actually know the accused.

He goes, 'I sweer to tell ta t . . . t . . . t . . . troot, ta whole t . . . t . . . troot, and nuttin but ta t . . . t . . . t . . . troot.'

Shit the focking bed.

I actually say those words out loud. I'm like, 'Shit the focking bed!'

And it's only then that Kennet cops me. He's as shocked to see *me* sitting *here* as I am to see *him* standing *there*, although the look of surprise on *his* face quickly turns into something else – the look of a man who knows an opportunity when he sees one.

'Kennet Tuite,' the judge goes, 'you are charged with conspiracy to defraud Capital Insurance of €175,000 by staging a bogus traffic accident on the Old Airport Road, Cloghran, County Dublin, between 10 p.m. on August 25, 2009, and 4 a.m. on August 26, 2009. How do you plead?'

I suddenly remember him mentioning the case he had coming up. It was before Christmas. When he was giving out to Dadden and Eddie for not wearing their collars that day in the gaff.

Kennet's like, 'Not g . . . g . . . g . . . guilty.'

At the same time, roysh, he can't stop looking at me and grinning. And to be honest, I can't stop looking at him. I'm *not* grinning, though? I think I'm still in possible shock.

The judge suddenly picks up on the vibe. He looks at Kennet and goes, 'Are you acquainted with any member of jury?'

Kennet doesn't even bat an eyelid. He's like, 'N . . . n . . . n . . . no, Your Honour.'

It doesn't cost him a moment's worry to lie to the actual court.

The judge looks over in my general postcode then. 'And is any member of the jury acquainted with the accused?'

I could say something. I *should* say something. His daughter and my son have a kid together. That's all I'd have to say. No one's fault. Just one of those coincidences. I'd be sent home and that would be that.

But just as I'm about to open my mouth, I hear a cough come from the direction of the public gallery. I look across and it ends up being Dadden and Eddie, staring me down in what would have to be described as a *threatening* manner?

So I end up saying nothing. I shake my head along with the other jurors. No. Never met that stuttering fock before in my life.

And the trial begins.

The case against Kennet is outlined to us. Some time on the evening mentioned, acting with person or persons unknown, he staged a fake traffic accident in which he claims to have received a whiplash injury to his neck. This barrister dude, who walks up and down in front of the jury box, says the prosecution will *prove* that the accident was stage-managed and that the accused's subsequent claim to have been injured was both spurious and fraudulent.

Then it's Kennet's barrister's turn. He does the whole walking up and down in front of us thing as well. He says his client is an honest family man, a father of six, who, if anything, is the real victim here – the victim of a callous multinational insurance corporation that has already refused to pay out compensation to which his client is legally entitled, despite making billions of euro from premiums every year.

I'm sitting there, listening to this shit, thinking, okay, just say something! There's still time! Shout something! Do it now! You wanted an out, now here it is! Kennet Tuite is no honest family man! He's as crooked as a seven-euro note! And I should know because I'm practically related to the focker!

But, again, I don't say anything. And then it ends up being too late anyway, because it's Kennet who suddenly stands up and goes, 'Parding me for the inteduption, Your Em . . . Em . . . Em . . . Eminence. But I would like to s . . . s . . . s . . . sack me baddister.'

There's, like, gasps in the courtroom. And his barrister doesn't look a happy rabbit, it has to be said. He definitely didn't expect this, judging from the way his mouth is suddenly flapping open and closed.

'You wish to seek new legal representation?' the judge goes.

Kennet goes, 'Yes, I do,' and then he turns to the barrister. 'Ine soddy, Bud, it's n . . . n . . . n . . . nuttin personiddle against you.'

'You've left it very late in the day,' the judge goes.

Kennet's like, 'Ine entitled, but, ardent I?'

'Yes, you're entitled to change your legal counsel at any point. Do you have someone . . .'

'Ine gonna r . . . r . . . r . . . represent meself, so I am.'

'And are you aware of the rules and protocols relating to individuals representing themselves before the court.'

'N . . . N . . . No, Your Eminence.'

'Of course not. That's why you're referring to me as "Your Eminence". You are going to be given a booklet. I want you to read it today and familiarize yourself with the rules. I will adjourn the case until ten o'clock tomorrow morning.'

'Ah, leds!' Bernadette goes. 'Heff day!' and then she turns around to me and – with the self-confidence of a girl who's mysteriously under the impression that she looks like Florence Brudenell-Bruce – she goes, 'Do you want to get a bisha lunch?'

I notice that Dadden and Eddie are just, like, staring at me from the public gallery.

'With you?' I go. 'Yeah, no, I don't focking think so.'

I see the two boys climbing out of their seats at the exact same time as me.

I get out of that courtroom as fast as my feet will carry me. I get out onto the quays and I stort literally running back towards town. I don't even need to look over my shoulder to know that they're immediately behind me.

'Fooken grab him,' I hear one of them go. I'm pretty fast on my feet, though – you know that much about me – and I manage to put a bit of distance between us by the time the Ha'penny Bridge comes into view. I'm thinking, if I could just get over the other side of that. But then I forget to look left as I'm crossing Capel Street and I end up getting creamed by a Seat Toledo. I literally go over the bonnet and the roof and I hit the ground with a crack.

Jesus! My focking tailbone.

Dadden and Eddie are straight on top of me, dragging me to my feet and reassuring passers-by that I'm fine and that it's *nuttin to woody about* and that I'm their brother – which is an obvious lie, even from the way we're dressed.

They pull me into the doorway of a pub and Eddie – still holding onto me – rings Kennet and tells him where we are.

'Don't woody,' Dadden keeps telling me, 'we're just gonna have a woort wit ye.'

Two minutes later, Kennet arrives on the scene, holding a rolled-up copy of what I presume is the booklet on court protocols that the judge was banging on about.

'Mon, we'll have a thrink,' Kennet goes. 'M . . . M . . . Mon, it's only a thrink!'

It's obvious that I have no choice in the matter. I follow them into this seriously dodgy-looking pub. He orders double whiskeys for him and the two boys – this is, like, twelve o'clock in the day we're talking – and then he turns to me and goes, 'What do you call tat p . . . p . . . piss you thrink again?'

I don't even answer him. He already knows. He just likes slagging it off. He laughs, then orders me a pint.

'Well,' he goes, 'what a fortuitous s . . . s . . . s . . . set of circum-stances, wha?'

I'm there, 'No – because I'm going to tell the judge the truth tomorrow.'

'You won't be teddin the judge addything tomoddow,' he goes. 'You fooken w . . . w . . . woatunt, do you hear me?'

'Are you threatening me?'

'Ine not trettnin addyone. Ine just . . . Look, Ine just aston you to see tings from m . . . m . . . moy point of view here. Ine looken at f . . . f . . . fooken jail toyum – am I right, feddas?'

Eddie and Dadden both nod.

He goes, 'Thee've got a lot on me – inclooten CCTV of me woorkin a nightclub doe-er when I was apposed to be c . . . c . . . crippled wit me neck. I've p . . . p . . . previous for tis as well. Ine lookin at tree to foyuv years here.'

I'm there, 'So what do you expect me to do?'

'You're on the fooken jewery! Use yooer influence. Alls you've got to do is convince a few of the utters tat Ine n . . . n . . . not gid-dlety. Tat ters a reasondibble d . . . d . . . doubt – knowmsayin?'

I laugh. *I'm* suddenly in a position of power over *him* and I have to say, I like the sudden feeling.

'I don't owe you a focking thing,' I go. 'What, after what you've done to my son?'

He's like, 'Okay, wh . . . wh . . . what do you waddent?'

I'm there, 'From you? Nothing.'

'Ta muddy I lent to R . . . R . . . Roatnan . . .'

'What about it?'

'It's wiped. If I get off.'

'Are you serious?'

'T . . . T . . . Toorty grant.'

'Plus the interest?'

'Plus the inthorest. Ters no f . . . f . . . f . . . fooken debt if you can keep me ourra jail. How's tat?'

'And he won't have to work for Say Nuttin any more?'

'Who?'

'Locky, or whatever the fock he's called. I don't want my son removing wheel clamps for a living. He could do anything. He's got actual brains. And I want him back at school.'

'I'll s . . . s . . . s . . . square it wit Locky, so I will – *if* you can get me off.'

'Dude,' I go, 'you've got yourself a deal.'

9.

How Splendid!

Sorcha asks me what I think of the idea of a God's knot instead of a unity candle and I tell her I love it. That's become my stock answer, in fact, every time a question about the vow renewal slash blessing gets asked. I've stopped even listening. If she asked me what I thought of doing it in a mankini, with a patch over my eye and a focking monkey on my shoulder, I'd tell her I loved it.

'He doesn't know what a God's knot is,' Honor pipes up from the back of the cor.

She's a serious shit-stirrer.

I give her a filthy in the rearview mirror. She's sitting there in her uniform – snot-green is the only way you'd describe it – with her little thumb still working like mad, pressing invisible buttons, writing imaginary Tweets, presumably about how much she hates her parents for sending her to a national school.

'A God's knot,' Sorcha goes, 'is a cord of three strands – a white one representing the bride, a purple one representing the groom and a gold one representing God. And the idea is that we braid the three strands into a plait to symbolize the union of husband, wife and God.'

I'm there, 'Yeah, no, I love it.'

'It ties in with the whole Book of Ecclesiastes thing. *A cord of three strands is not quickly broken.*'

Honor goes, 'Oh my God, could you two *be* any lamer?'

Sorcha doesn't respond.

But I go, 'So are you looking forward to your first day in your new school?' and I'm being a total bastard, I admit it. 'They have a girls' soccer team and monthly headlice inspections.'

'I know what you're trying to do,' she goes.

'What am I trying to do?'

'You're trying to get a reaction from me. Being sent to a knacker school is my punishment and you need to see that it bothers me. Which it doesn't, by the way.'

It might be the mention of knackers, but Sorcha suddenly remembers something.

'Oh my God,' she goes, 'what time do you have to be in court?'

I'm like, 'Ten o'clock.'

'Oh, you've loads of time. You haven't even told me what the case is about yet.'

I end up saying the first shit that comes into my head.

I'm there, 'It's, em, treason.'

'Treason?' she goes. 'Oh my God, that's, like, *so* random! Oh, by the way – major goss – do you know who else is in court this week?'

'Who?'

'Shadden's dad!'

I end up nearly wrapping her cor around a focking lamp-post, I get that much of a fright.

I'm there, 'Er, really? How do you, em, know that?'

She goes, 'I was talking to Shadden. He's on trial for, like, *insurance* fraud? Not quite as exciting as treason, though! Is it a man or a woman, Ross?'

'I'm, er, not supposed to talk about the case, Babes.'

'Oh, okay. I didn't think of that.'

'Yeah, no, we've all been warned to never, ever speak about it, not even to our wives. Even after it's over. It's heavy shit.'

'Sorry, Ross, I didn't mean to pressure you.'

Honor goes, 'Boring!'

Sorcha stares out the window. After a few seconds of silence, she suddenly remembers something else. It's often the way with women.

'The morquee is arriving on Tuesday of next week,' she goes. 'I wanted it up a good few days before the actual ceremony, just so I can, like, decorate it at my *leisure*? We did agree on Regency Grey and Nordic Spa for the colour scheme, didn't we?'

'We did.'

'I just think it'll look – oh my God – *so* amazing. What do think of the idea of hanging, like, ribbons or streamers in those colours from all of the trees in the gorden?'

'I love it.'

Honor laughs. 'Yeah, just remind me,' she goes, '*how* old are you two again?'

Sorcha's there, 'Do you really love it, Ross, or are you just saying that?'

I'm like, 'Yeah, no, I do.'

Five seconds of silence and then there's something else.

She goes, 'You need to speak to Christian, by the way.'

I'm there, 'Christian? Why?'

'Over those things you said to Ross Junior.'

'Oh, that.'

'*So* funny,' Honor goes. '*They'd be as disappointed as I am by your lack of rugby-playing ability.* Oh my God, you are so brain-dead.'

I try to think of something to hit her back with, but my mind isn't quick enough.

Sorcha's like, 'I haven't been able to bring myself to face Lauren. And they still haven't RSVP-ed.'

I'm there, 'I'll, er, go and see him at lunchtime today.'

'You really need to, Ross. I genuinely don't know if they're even still *talking* to us?'

'I've an hour for lunch. Look, I'll peg it across town and see him in the shop. I'll square it, don't worry.'

The playground is full of kids, running mad, kicking balls – the round variety – and walking around in, like, packs. Even the girls. It's a tough school. You can tell by just the atmos.

Everything seems to stop when we pull up in the old Mercury Mariner Hybrid. Three hundred kids instantly stop playing and just stare at this fancy-shmancy compact crossover SUV – one of the best in its class – and this little South Dublin princess suddenly in their midst.

I get out and open the back door for her. I'm about to say something not very nice to her, like, 'Don't come home pronouncing your th's as d's or some shit like that!' But then I happen to look at her little face and I recognize something in it that I've genuinely never seen before.

Fear.

'Don't make me go in there,' she suddenly goes, giving me the big Sacred Hort of Jesus eyes, which I can never resist. '*Please*, Daddy.'

Every instinct I have wants to tell her, okay, stay in the cor, we'll go home – the three of us – and try to come up with another plan. But Sorcha is stronger than me. She always was. She gets out of the cor and goes, 'Come on, Honor – school.'

Honor – with tears in her eyes – is like, 'I don't want to go in there. I want to go back to Mount Anville.'

Sorcha goes, 'I'm afraid that's no longer an option, Honor. You ruined it for yourself. But you do have to go to school. That's the law. Now come on, out of the cor.'

She obviously doesn't want to be seen to be blubbing in front of the other kids, roysh, so she turns her sad face into an angry scowl.

She goes, 'If you make me go in there, I will never, ever forgive you.' She looks from Sorcha to me and then back to Sorcha again. 'I mean it,' she goes. 'I can be an even bigger bitch.'

'Out of the cor,' Sorcha goes, although I can tell from her voice that she's only being tough because she *has* to?

We walk into the school building – kids, teachers, parents, all staring at us wide-eyed and open-mouthed, like we've just arrived from another planet. Which is probably what the Vico Road *is* to them.

We run into Mr O'Fathaigh in the corridor. There's no, like, welcome to your new school or any of that shit. He just goes, 'I'll show you to Miss Ní Bhroin's classroom,' without even looking at Honor, then he leads us down a corridor that reminds me of a hospital corridor, with a cold, tiled foor and brick walls painted mental-institution magnolia.

We turn right into a classroom. Miss Ní Bhroin turns out to be a looker, which I didn't expect. I hear an Irish name and I automatically think she's going to be a boiler, but Miss Ní Bhroin looks like Alison Brie, except with black horned-rim glasses and stupendous cans.

Mr O'Fathaigh says something to her in Irish and I end up just zoning out and looking around at what is going to be Honor's classroom. There's, like, paintings hung around the walls – work the kids have obviously done in ort class – and I can't help but notice that they're shit. There's a crucifix and a poster showing all the different types of trees there are in Ireland – a lot more than I would have presumed – and another poster demonstrating how to perform CPR and other basic first-aid procedures.

'*Suí síos,*' Miss Ní Bhroin looks at Honor and goes, pointing to the desk immediately in front of her. She's obviously heard the stories herself.

A bell rings, then the classroom fills with noise. Kids comes chorging in from the corridor outside. They walk past us and one or two of the girls try to talk to Honor. It's all, 'What's your name?' or it's, 'Do you like One Direction?' and I hear one of the boys – a heavy-boned kid with a bowl haircut and definite attention-deficit issues – go, 'Fooken poshie!'

'I'll see you at two thirty,' Sorcha goes.

Honor just looks at her and she's like, 'I hate you,' and then she looks at me and says the exact same thing. 'I hate you.'

We walk back to the cor in silence. I put the key in the ignition and Sorcha storts sobbing as we're driving away. Neither of us says anything until maybe ten minutes later, when we're passing what used to be the Killiney Court Hotel and Sorcha goes, 'Ross, pull over.'

I'm there, 'What's wrong.'

She's like, 'Pull over!'

Which I do.

Sorcha gets out of the cor and she storts just really sobbing – then, in between sobs, dry retching. This is on the side of the road, just up from the Dort station. Sobbing and dry retching and sobbing some more with the sadness of knowing that all the dreams she had for our daughter have died.

You'd have to wonder what that stuttering focker is playing at, deciding to represent himself. If he insists on cross-examining every witness, we might all still be here at Christmas. Which might actually *be* the plan? To d . . . d . . . d . . . drag it out for so long that we all stop giving a f . . . f . . . f . . . fock whether he's guilty or not – then we let him walk, purely on the basis that we all just want to get on with our lives.

You wouldn't put it past him.

The door of the court opens and in he walks, wearing – I shit you not – an actual suit, which is black and about, like, three sizes too big for him. 'Ah, leds,' I hear Bernadette go.

She's moved seats, by the way, since I knocked her back yesterday. She's now sitting directly in front of me, having buddied up with two of the other women jurors, one of whom – Irla – looks a bit like Judi Dench, while the other one doesn't look like anyone. She's just a dog called Sandra.

Anyway, after a bit of blah, the prosecuting counsel – you'd be surprised how quickly you'd pick up the terms – calls the first witness.

Hilariously, it turns out to be Say Nuttin.

The focker steps up to the witness box and he gets sworn in. He's wearing the exact same suit as Kennet, I notice, except *his* actually *fits* him? Came from the same source, would be my guess. So focking hot you'd need oven gloves just to do up the buttons.

The prosecuting dude goes, 'Can you tell the court what exactly you witnessed on the Old Airport Road in Cloghran on the evening of August 25, 2009?'

Say Nuttin goes, 'Yes. I was thriving along the Old Airport Road in Cloghran at just arthur half eleven. I passed a thruck with a load of baddles on it that was peerked in the heert showulter. In anyhow, the next thing I see is there's anutter keer in me rearview middor. Just as it was passing the thruck, all these baddles fell off the back of it into the path of this particalur keer, which then had to sweerve out of the way to avoid being hit.'

'How many barrels?'

'Fower or foyuv.'

'Four or five. And what happened to this car?'

'It crashed into a three.'

'It crashed into a tree! Can you tell the court what you did then?'

'I pult in. You would, woootunt you? I taught to meself, this fedda's obviously been hoort. I ren to the keer, pult the doh-er open and thragged the poo-er fedda out.'

'And who was it?'

'It was Kennet theer.'

'Mr Tuite?'

'That's reet.'

'Can you explain to the court, Mr Loughran, your relationship with Mr Tuite?'

Kennet jumps to his feet. He's like, 'Objection!'

The judge – who obviously isn't one to take shit – goes, 'On what grounds are you objecting, Mr Tuite?'

'I know what he's getting at wit tat question, Your Em . . . Em . . . Em . . . Eminence.'

'Is there a point of *law* on which you wish to object, Mr Tuite?'

'Er, no.'

'Then I suggest you sit down . . . Mr Loughran will answer the question.'

'The fedda happens to be a ferrent of moyen,' Say Nuttin goes.

The barrister is like, 'Come, come, Mr Loughran! He's more than a friend, is he not? You're godfather to his eldest son. He's god-father to your only daughter. Would it not be more accurate to describe him as your *best* friend?'

'I suppose it woot, yeah.'

'So how did you feel when you discovered that the man whom you so bravely pulled from the wreckage of his car – the man whom you'd almost watched die – was in fact your best friend?'

'I was shocked, so I was.'

'Of course you were! By the coincidence of it as much as anything!'

'Begga peerden?'

'Two cars on a deserted stretch of road late at night. The driver of one is involved in an accident. The driver of the other is the only witness to that accident? I'm just wondering did it strike you as an extraordinary coincidence that you should both happen to be on that stretch of road at that time of night?'

'I suppose it did.'

'A coincidence or a convenience?'

'Soddy?'

'Does your account of what happened not stretch credulity?'

'No.'

'I put it to you, Mr Loughran, that it was *no* coincidence that you happened to be on that stretch of road, for you were there with a common purpose, which was to stage-manage an accident with the intention of defrauding an insurance company out of a lot of money. And that you were a full and active participant in this attempted fraud . . .'

'*Objection!*' Kennet goes. 'Mr Loughran hasn't been ch . . . ch . . . cheerged in relation to any croyum.'

'Overruled,' the judge goes, I suppose, *wearily*? 'The witness will respond.'

Say Nuttin is like, 'You're wrong, so you eer.'

The barrister's just there, 'I put it to you, Mr Loughran, that you were not – as you claim – driving innocently along the Old Airport Road when Mr Tuite's car ran into a tree. You were in fact on the back of the beer truck, freeing the bolt that sent the barrels crashing into the road, and that this occurred some minutes *after* Mr Tuite drove deliberately into a tree.'

'You're wrong.'

'Is that not a more reasonable explanation for what happened that evening?'

'No.'

'No . . . further . . . questions.'

Kennet gets to his feet again. The funniest thing of all – I actually laugh out loud when I see it – is that he hooks his two thumbs into his ormpits, like you see lawyers do in movies and on, like, TV?

I don't know if he's trying to look the port or just rip the piss. Either way, it's pretty focking hilarious.

He's like, 'I have one or two questions,' he goes, 'if it should p . . . p . . . p . . . please, M'Lud?'

'Ah, leds,' I hear Bernadette go, 'who does he think he is – Rumpole of the Beeley?'

Sandra laughs.

The judge goes, 'You don't require my permission to question the witness.'

He's like, 'Very good, Your Eminence,' and then he turns to Say Nuttin. 'You are – are you not? – M . . . M . . . Mister Anthony Joseph Loughran of 397 C . . . C . . . C . . . Constance Markievicz Teddice, D . . . D . . . D . . . Dublin 11?'

'That's reet,' Say Nuttin goes.

'Perhaps you would c . . . care to tell the co-ert whedder or not you were born on ta eighth day of September in n . . . n . . . n . . . noyenteen hundoord and sixty.'

The judge interrupts. He's there, 'I think the court can accept the witness's bona fides with regard to his name, address and date of birth. Can you proceed with a line of questioning that is perhaps germane to the case at hand?'

'Yes, Your Eminence.'

I'm still wondering what he's actually playing at. It's possible that he's doing what Skerries Community School used to do on the rugby field back in the day – in other words, drag everyone down to their level so that the entire thing becomes, like, a total joke. If that *is* the case, it's a serious miscalculation. There's more than a few *tuts* coming from the jurors around me. Stephen, this dude sitting to the right of me, was hoping for, like, a juicy murder, instead of this obvious charade. I'm already wondering how the fock I'm going to persuade them that this joker is actually innocent.

'Now, Mr Loughran,' Kennet goes, 'on the n . . . n . . . noyt in question, you were comin from D . . . D . . . Dublin Earpowurt.'

'That's reet.'

'Can I ast you what you were doin at Dublin Earpowurt?'

'I was thropping the brutter off. He was going to Majorca with a bunch of feddas to play golf.'

'A bunch of feddas who were going off to play a b . . . b . . . b . . . birra golf. Veddy good. And do you know why *I* happened to be on ta Old Earpowurt Rowut on tat f . . . f . . . fateful noyt?'

'Yeah, you were thropping off a couple of feddas off as well.'

'A couple of feddas who happened to be on ta s . . . s . . . s . . . sayum golf thrip to Majorca?'

'Yeah.'

'So thee were f . . . f . . . f . . . floyun out at ta exact sayum toyum?'

'Thee were, yeah.'

'So we boat thropped feddas off, at roughly the sayum toyum, to catch the exact sayum fleet dat a loata feddas we know from F . . . F . . . F . . . Finglas were getting, cos thee'd be big golfers. Den we throve the sayum rowut back to Finglas. Tat's not too m . . . m . . . much of a coincidence, is it?'

'I wootunt of taught so, no.'

'No foorter questions, Your Eminence.'

Next, roysh, the prosecution calls Patrick Gillen, the driver of the beer truck. Same shit – he gets sworn in and all the rest of it. He's a big sweaty dude with, like, a neck beard and a massive gut hanging like a focking awning over the band of his trousers.

The dude from the prosecution side goes, 'Can you tell us, in your own words, what happened on the night of the alleged accident?'

The goy goes, 'I was heading for the M1, heading north, when I pulled in. I always take my breaks – half an hour for every four hours of driving – and that particular spot on the Old Airport Road would have been a regular stopping-off point for me. That night, yeah, I remember it well. I heard something on the back of the truck.'

'Some *thing*?'

'Some *one*. It had to be some *one*. Because I heard them unlock the bolt.'

'The bolt holding in place the barrels that you were transporting?'

'That's right.'

'Did you get out to investigate?'

'Not immediately. But then I heard this crash.'

'What was it?'

'A few of the barrels had been pushed off the back of the truck onto the road.'

'Pushed? How can you be sure they were pushed?'

'Because I was parked on the flat. The barrels were stacked on top of each other – they were only stacked three-high. Even with the bolt off, it would still need someone to give them a shove to knock them off the truck.'

'So what happened when you did get out?'

'I saw Mr Loughran standing in the hard shoulder on the other side of the road.'

'And what did he say?'

'He said there'd been an accident. A car had swerved to avoid the barrels and had crashed into a tree.'

'Did this surprise you?'

'Yes.'

'Why?'

'Well, because I didn't *see* a car.'

'You didn't see a car?'

'No.'

'You didn't see Mr Tuite's car approaching from the opposite direction in the moments before the barrels mysteriously slipped their moorings and fell from the truck?'

'No.'

'A red Renault Mégane, bought second-hand three days before the incident . . .'

'I didn't see it. Well, I did see it when I got out of the truck. It was crashed into a tree.'

'You saw the aftermath?'

'Yes.'

'But no accident?'

'No.'

'Quite a difficult thing to miss, one would have imagined?'

'Yes.'

'You didn't see it swerve dramatically off the Old Airport Road to avoid this *avalanche* of barrels, then crash into a tree just twenty yards from where you were sitting?'

'No.'

'You must have heard something then?'

'I didn't hear anything.'

'You didn't hear a car horn sound?'

'No.'

'What about the screech of tryes? Surely you heard the screech of tyres?'

'No.'

'The crash of metal and glass?'

'No.'

'You saw no accident?'

'That's right.'

'You heard no accident.'

'That's right.'

'And the most reasonable explanation for that – am I correct in saying, Mr Gillen? – is that there was no accident?'

'Yes.'

'Thank you, Mr Gillen. I have no further questions.'

Kennet gets up – again with the thumbs in his ormpits. It'd make great TV.

'Mr Gillen,' he goes, 'you w . . . w . . . woork long hours, do you?'

The dude's like, 'Yes, I do.'

'Very t . . . t . . . t . . . t . . . toyerden work, I'm imagine – th . . . th . . . thriving up and down the mothorways of Arelunt?'

'It's tiring, yes. But, like I said, I always take my breaks.'

'You moost of been wrecked that noyt, but. Had it b . . . b . . . been a long day?'

'No. As a matter of fact, I'd only been driving an hour.'

'An hour? This wadn't long befower m . . . m . . . midnight, but.'

'Yes, I was working nights.'

Kennet nods and goes, 'I see! I see! I see!' and then, roysh, this look of sudden confusion comes over his face. You can tell he's putting it on. He's like, 'T . . . t . . . t . . . tat's fuddy.'

The dude's like, 'What's funny?'

'No, it's just what you were s . . . s . . . s . . . sayin there about only bein woorkin an hour. Ine just wontherin, you know . . .'

'What?'

'Why you felth ta need to take a break?'

I can instantly see where he's going with this. So can the other jurors. Four or five of them are suddenly scribbling away on their pads.

'I ast you,' Kennet goes, 'if you were t . . . t . . . toyred and you said no. Do you member?'

'Yes, I do.'

'Fuddy den tat you f . . . f . . . f . . . felt ta need to stop. *Ine* puttin it to *you* tat you *were* toyered. And not oatenly tat – you were s . . . s . . . sleeping in ta heerd showulter. Ine goin to ast you a question. And beard in moyund that you *eer* under oat. Did you sleep in ta thruck?'

'I wasn't asleep when your car supposedly . . .'

'Tat's not ta question Ine arthur aston. Did you sleep in ta thruck?'

'Yes. I hadn't slept well that afternoon. And, yes, I had a very short nap. Five minutes – ten, at the most.'

Kennet just nods. He's good. He might play the fockwit, but he's nobody's fool. I think back to the day that Patriona Pratshke came to visit us and he danced around her like Jason focking Robinson. He's a master in these situations. I don't know how I could have doubted him.

'B . . . b . . . but you were awake,' he goes, 'when the baddles f . . . f . . . fell off ta thruck? Tat's what you're clayumin?'

'Yes, I was.'

'W . . . w . . . woyut awake?'

'Wide awake, yes.'

'What keer was Mr Loughran thrivin on ta noyt in question?'

'Excuse me?'

'He throve p . . . p . . . past you just a few seconds befower I did.'

'I didn't see his car either.'

'It was a black P . . . P . . . P . . . Peugeot 206.'

'It wasn't on the road.'

'It wadn't on ta rowud? Maybe it was. Mayve you joost doatunt remember it because you were f . . . f . . . f . . . fast asleep?'

'I wasn't fast asleep.'

'So answer me tis den – what *was* ta last keer to p . . . p . . . p . . . pass ta thruck before ta baddles fell?'

'I . . . I . . . don't remember.'

'You doatunt remember?'

'No.'

'You remember that *I* ditn't past you and tat Mr Loughran ditn't past you. But you doatunt remember who did?'

'No, I don't.'

'Because you were ourrof it.'

'I wasn't.'

'Ine puttin it to you that you weer. You doatunt know if moy keer passed you – tat's ta troot. A f . . . f . . . f . . . flatbed thruck could have thriven boy with fooken Beyoncé naked on ta back of it and you wouldn't have kn . . . kn . . . kn . . . known a ting. Because you were asleep at ta wheel.'

'That's not true.'

'Ine puttin it to you, Mr Gillen, tat what woke you up was ta baddles hitting the growunt. Ta baddles that blew off ta thruck arthur you didn't secure ta boawult properly. Ta stordee about someone loosening ta bowult, you eeder threamt it or you m . . . m . . . m . . . made irrup to s . . . s . . . s . . . save your job, because you'd be sacked utterwise. Am I reet?'

'No!'

'Am I reet?'

'No!'

'No foorter questions.'

Lunchtime possibly wasn't the wisest time to drop in unannounced on Christian and Lauren. The queue is all the way down to Pasta Fresca and I end up again having to run an angry gauntlet of customers, who think I'm trying to, like, skip the line.

I'm there, 'I'm on jury service, if you must know, and it's an important case. I'm entitled to focking skip you.'

I've a big smug grin on my face, of course.

There's a few shouts of, 'Focking dickhead!' and 'What a focking asshole!' but I'm an old hand at blanking out negativity. Any number ten worth his place will tell you that it's a skill.

I wouldn't mind, I don't even want to eat – although if I was offered anything I wanted off the menu as, like, a peace offering, it'd be a steak and cheddar melt with a lorge Coke.

From the moment Christian sees me, though, it's obvious that I'm not going to be walking out of here with him accepting my apology and me wrapping my face around a great-tasting and nutritious roll. The first words out of his mouth, in fact, are, 'Get the fock out of here. I never want to see your focking face again.'

Everyone in the shop suddenly looks at me, including the staff. He's got about eight working for him – most of them Chinese. You'd have to say fair focks.

'Dude,' I go, holding up my hands, in fairness to me, 'I want to apologize if I was out of order that day at the borbecue. I genuinely forgot about that child monitor you had. If I could turn back the clock – blah, blah, blah.'

'I will never forgive you,' he goes, pointing a twelve-inch ciabatta at me, 'for those things you said to my son.'

There's no sign of Lauren, thanks be to fock.

I'm there, 'Okay, try to see things from my point of view, Christian. He had genuinely no idea what a rugby ball was or what to even do with it. I was upset – especially knowing the player that you were – and I acted.'

'You told him he was a sissy,' he goes, his voice steadily rising. 'You told him that me and Lauren would be ashamed of him if he couldn't play rugby. You told him he was going to get the shit kicked out of him in school . . .'

There are, like, gasps from people in the shop. I genuinely didn't expect this.

He's like, 'You threw a rugby ball at my son and you knocked him out cold.'

I'm there, 'What kid of four can't catch a ball?'

'And then you pretended he fell off his bike,' he goes.

'What an absolute prick,' some dude behind me goes.

I decide I'm not going to stand here and just take this. I'm entitled to, like, defend myself. 'It wasn't *his* bike?' I go. 'It was Myrna's bike. And that's my basic point. He's too interested in, like, girls' things.'

'Don't you dare tell me how to raise my son,' he goes – again, with the ciabatta. 'You haven't done such a great job of raising your own.'

I'm there, 'Excuse me?' because there are two areas of my life where I would consider myself above criticism. As an outhalf and as a father.

'Your son had a baby at fourteen,' he goes. 'Your daughter was expelled from school for bullying. At six! You've raised a promiscuous teenage father and an obnoxious little bully who nobody – and I mean *nobody* – can stand the focking sight of.'

'Dude, you're coming dangerously close to saying . . .'

'The apple doesn't fall far from the tree, Ross.'

It's, like, a genuine blow to hear that out of the mouth of my best friend. It's a serious slug in the guts.

I go, 'I came here today to try to make peace. And to find out why you haven't RSVP-ed yet.'

The next thing I hear is, like, Lauren's voice go, 'I'll give you our RSVP.'

She's standing at the top of the stairs, holding a tray piled high with, like, paper cups and sandwich wrappers that she's obviously just cleared from the tables.

My hort is suddenly beating like a kick drum.

She drops the tray and comes down the stairs at a speed that I wouldn't say is recommended for a woman who's eight and a half months pregnant. She reaches the bottom of the stairs and, without even pausing, grabs a breadknife off the counter, one of those ones with the seriously serrated edge, and runs straight for me, holding it at shoulder-height, actual *Psycho*-style.

I have no choice but to turn and make a run for it.

She chases me out the door, going, 'This is our RSVP! *This is our focking RSVP!*'

She's totally lost it.

I run in the direction of Grafton Street with Lauren in hot pursuit, years of anger with me finally coming to a boil. We pass the flower-sellers and I end up slipping on some spilled water and Lauren is nearly close enough to put that blade between my shoulders. She actually tries. She brings it down and I can nearly feel it whistle by, about five millimetres from my actual spine.

I suddenly kick then – I think you all know about my famous kick – and I put some distance between us. But I don't stop running or looking over my shoulder until I'm back in the safety of the Dublin Circuit Criminal Court.

The afternoon is filled with, like, technical evidence, very little of which I end up following. I'm too distracted. Too hurt by what Christian said. I honestly think that if Lauren had managed to plunge that knife into my back, the pain wouldn't have been as bad as the pain of being told that the way my kids turned out is down to basically me.

Something Something or other is in the witness box. He's, like, a scene of accident investigator – we're talking, like, forensic? – and he's pretty much saying under, like, cross-examination that Kennet's story is a crock of shit.

'In your expert opinion,' the prosecuting barrister goes, 'at what speed was Mr Tuite's vehicle travelling when it struck the tree?'

The dude's there, 'I would estimate that it was somewhere between five and ten kilometres per hour.'

'Five and ten kilometres?'

'Yes.'

'And were the brakes applied before the impact?'

'There was no evidence to suggest that the brakes were applied prior to the impact, no.'

'Rather unusual, wouldn't you say?'

'Yes, I would. In normal circustmances, in the case of a crash like the one described in the accident claim form, there would be some evidence of hard braking . . .'

'A tyre mark on the road, for instance?'

'Yes. There would also be signs of what we call rapid deceleration. Evidence of the ground being torn up by the wheels of the car suddenly locking.'

'There was none in this case?'

'No.'

'Was it your conclusion then, from studying the evidence, that the defendant simply drove his car into the tree at a steady speed of between five and ten kilometres per hour?'

'That was my conclusion, yes.'

Bernadette turns around and tries to catch my eye to find out what I'm making of it. I'm barely even listening. All I can think about is how angry Christian seemed with me. Lauren trying to stab me with a breadknife is one thing. She's always had her reservations about me. I'd have nearly expected her to do it at some point. But Christian has never, ever spoken to me in that way, even when I rode his mother.

'So,' the prosecuting barrister goes, 'was the damage sustained to the front end of Mr Tuite's car consistent, in your opinion, with the speed at which it was travelling when it impacted with the tree?'

'No,' the dude goes.

'No?'

'No. As a matter of fact, a lot of the damage was, in my opinion, legacy damage.'

'Legacy damage. Do you mean damage that was done to the car prior to the accident?'

'I mean damage to the car that certainly wasn't sustained in the accident.'

'Thank you. No further questions.'

Kennet stands up. The thumbs go in the ormpits again. 'I hab one or two,' he goes.

It'd nearly be funny, if I didn't have to convince a majority of my fellow jurors that the fockwit is innocent.

He's like, 'J . . . J . . . Joost a momemt ago, you toalt ta co-ert tat moy keer was thriven at between f . . . f . . . f . . . foyuv and ten kilometres an hour when it hit ta three.'

'That's right.'

'Dat was yooer opinion – idn't dat ta w . . . woord you used?'

'In my opinion – yes.'

'So it's joost an opinion?'

'It's an educated opinion.'

Kennet laughs.

'An educated opinion?' he goes. 'Perhaps you'd be g . . . g . . . g . . . gooth enough to tell the co-ert what exactly an educated opinion is.'

369

The dude turns to the jury box. 'One that's based on thirty years of experience and expertise in the area,' he goes.

Ouch. The stupid focker badly misjudged that one. He goes scrambling through his notes then, to try to find something to hit the expert back with.

I go into a bit of a daydream again, thinking how much can change in such a short time. A few months ago, I genuinely believed that I had, like, the best friends in the world. We said we'd never let shit come between us. We'd been through too much, both on and off the rugby field, to ever let that happen. Mates forever was what we agreed. And now I've lost them all. We're talking JP. We're talking Oisinn. We're talking Christian.

'How m . . . m . . . m . . . mooch muddy,' Kennet goes, 'do you eern in a yee-er?'

'Objection!' the prosecuting barrister shouts. 'How is that relevant to his testimony?'

'I'll t . . . t . . . t . . . tell you how it's redevant to he's testimody when he answers ta question.'

'I'm going to allow it,' the judge goes. 'The witness will answer.'

'Last year,' the expert dude goes, 'something in the order of two hundred thousand euros.'

'Noice m . . . m . . . m . . . muddy.'

'I work hard, Mr Tuite.'

'Oh, Ine sh . . . shewer you do. How much of your muddy comes from tis koyunt of w . . . w . . . woork?'

'I don't understand.'

'P . . . p . . . proving – or *thrying* ta prove – dat ceertain accidents ditn't really happen?'

'All of it.'

'All of it?'

'Yes. I investigate fraud. That's what I do.'

'How intoresting! And who p . . . p . . . p . . . pays ye?'

'Insurance companies.'

'Inshewerdence companies? Inshewerdence companies like ta one that refused to p . . . p . . . pay out on moy clayum?'

'Well, yes. I work for them.'

'Can you repeat tat for ta co-ert.'

'I work for them. I'm here as their witness. I didn't think there was any doubt about that.'

Kennet turns around and gives the jury a knowing smile. I don't know what the fock he thinks he's just proved. But no one on the jury seems to think it's anything. In fact, they're all just exchanging confused looks.

Kennet goes, 'No f . . . f . . . f . . . foorter questions, Your Grace.'

It could be any time. It could be, like, nine o'clock on Saturday. Could be three in the afternoon. Could be even, like, Sunday. Seriously. I wouldn't be surprised if I slept right through. That's how wrecked I am. Four days of a criminal trial and the stress of wondering how I'm going to persuade an entire jury that Kennet didn't do something that he clearly focking did. And then all the shit with Christian and Oisinn and JP and Honor. It's the best night's sleep I've had in a long time.

I hear voices downstairs. Sorcha's, obviously, because she's not in the bed beside me. And a man's voice that I don't instantly recognize. At first I wonder is it her old man. Has he had, like, a change of hort about me and decided to come to the renewal after all? But then I hear Sorcha coming up the stairs and she's going, 'Ross is going to be, like, oh my God when he finds out you're here!' and I realize that it definitely couldn't be him then.

Sorcha pushes the door open and goes, 'Ross, you have a visitor.'

I'm like, 'Who is it?'

She's there, 'It's a surprise! He's in the kitchen!' and then she disappears again to go and check on Honor – who isn't talking to us, by the way. Sorcha collected her after her first day of school and Honor – after fifteen minutes of just staring into space – went, 'They give out *free* milk!' Since then, it's been nothing but the silent treatment.

I throw on my Cantos and my Leinster training top and tip downstairs. The dude is sitting at the free-standing island, looking tanned and well – for *him* anyway.

It's Fionn.

'Look who's back from Umbongo!' I go.

He laughs. Same old Ross, is the vibe – he'll never change. He gives me a really amazing hug. He's genuinely happy to see me, which is a huge boost for me after all the shit that's been happening in the last few weeks.

I'm there, 'What the fock are you doing home? And why didn't you tell us you were coming?'

He goes, 'It's only a flying visit. Arrived last night, going back tomorrow. My sister's getting married today.'

I laugh. I'm there, 'Are we talking Eleanor?'

'Yes, Eleanor,' he goes. 'She and David feel they're finally ready to make the commitment to each other.'

I rode Eleanor while they were on a break. She's a great little mount, but she's as needy as fock and she quotes, like, Paulo Coelho books to express her feelings. Rather David than me is what I think I'm saying.

He suddenly goes, 'I tried to see you last night. I went to Kielys straight from the airport. Christian was there. Oisinn was there. JP was there. No sign of Ross, though.'

I'm like, 'And they told you, I'm presuming – all the shit that's been going on?'

'They did. And I told them it was ridiculous. How long have we all been friends?'

'We played rugby together, Fionn. It's like that suddenly doesn't mean anything to them.'

'You've got to sort it out – the four of you. I said it to them. We're all too old to start falling out now.'

'I'm glad to you hear you say that.'

'I'm not saying I'm on your side. Well, maybe with the Oisinn thing. I really don't know what he's playing at. I mean, how did he *think* you were going to react?'

'Yeah, no, *I* walked in on them. Jesus, he was going at her like a fat dude with a bucket of chicken.'

'But then, you haven't always respected familial boundaries, have you, Ross?'

He has me there. Even though I'm not a hundred percent sure what familial means.

I go, 'I know, Dude. I know all too well.'

'And what you did to Christian and Lauren's son . . .'

'That was nothing.'

'You gave him concussion and told him he was a sissy and said his parents would be ashamed of him if he couldn't play rugby.'

'It sounds definitely bad the way you phrase it.'

'And Shoshanna . . .'

I automatically laugh. I'm there, 'Was *she* in Kielys last night?'

He laughs as well. He can't help himself. He goes, 'She was there alright.'

I'm like, 'Isn't she the most focking ridiculous person you've ever met?'

'I was telling her some of the stories about Uganda and everything was . . .'

'*Sad story! Happy story!*'

He laughs – as in *really* laughs? He's always found me very funny. But then he becomes suddenly serious.

He's like, 'Sort it out, Ross. I know it's a cliché, but life really is too short. You see it in Africa. Between Aids and malaria and war and malnutrition. Death is just so ever-present. You can die from something as simple as diarrhoea. The things that we regard as problems aren't problems at all. Promise me you'll sort it out?'

'We will.'

'Just talk to each other, Ross. All those years, don't throw them away.'

My phone all of a sudden rings. The screen says it's K . . . K . . . K . . . Kennet. That's actually what he's in my phone as.

I go, 'I just need to take this. I'm doing jury service at the moment, I don't know if Sorcha mentioned,' and I step out into the gorden, close the door after me and then answer it.

I'm like, 'Hello?'

Kennet goes, 'S . . . s . . . s . . . stordee?'

'What do you mean, stordee? Why are you ringing me?'

'To foyunt out how it's goin – what way is ta j . . . j . . . joory tinkin?'

'Well, they think you're a fockwit, I've gathered that much. Walking around with your thumbs in your ormpits. What are you focking like?'

'Whor about de ebbidence, but? What way are thee th . . . th . . . th . . . thinkin? What's ta genoddle feedin?'

'The general feeling – just from the one or two conversatios I've overheard – is that you're guilty. Which you are, I presume?'

'Of co-erse I f . . . f . . . fooken am.'

I laugh.

I'm there, 'So what actually *did* happen?'

'Dat fooken dope was asleep in ta th . . . th . . . th . . . thruck,' he goes. 'He was always at it. We were arthur been watchin um for w . . . w . . . weeks. So we serrim up.'

'So Say Nuttin knocked the barrels off the truck?'

'Who?'

'Locky – whatever the fock you call him.'

'No, dat was D . . . D . . . D . . . Dadden and Eddie. Then thee joomped off and hid beyount a wall when yer man w . . . w . . . woke up.'

'What a lovely family my son has gotten mixed up with.'

'So you're sayin you doatunt tink they're b . . . b . . . b . . . boyen me st . . . stowery?'

'Some of it maybe. I've heard one or two say they didn't believe the truck driver's evidence. But then the forensics don't look good for you.'

'Reet, well Ine reloyen on you to infloodence tum. Sow a seat of doubt in one or two of their moyunds – do ye get me?'

'Yeah.'

'Remember, ders a lot royden on it for you – knowmsayin?'

He hangs up. I head back into the kitchen to Fionn, who says he'd better make tracks. The wedding's in, like, two hours' time and Eleanor doesn't even know he's home yet – he's going to just show up at the gaff while she's getting ready and surprise her.

He has a good hort, Fionn.

I'm there, 'It's great to see you, Dude. I'm constantly reading your blog, of course. I love all the updates.'

He laughs. He knows I'm full of shit.

'I wouldn't expect you to read it,' he goes.

I'm like, 'Well, I've looked at one or two of your photos – over Sorcha's shoulder.'

Out of the blue, he suddenly hits me with it. He's like, 'I've met someone,' and I swear to God, he can hordly keep the smile off his face.

We all know *that* feeling.

I'm there, 'Come on, Dude, don't hold out on me here – spill.'

'Her name is Jenny,' he goes. 'She's one of the co-ordinators of the school-building project.'

'Jenny the Project Co-Ordinator. She sounds like a complete ride.'

'She's really nice. I'm very happy. I'm coming home for two weeks in August. I'm hoping to bring her with me.'

'Well, I – for one – can't wait to meet her. Dude, I wish you were staying longer. Our vow renewal is this day next week.'

'Yeah, Sorcha seems very excited about it. I didn't think the Catholic Church recognized vow renewals.'

'Dude, do you think even God could have the last word over my wife?'

He cracks his hole laughing. I walk him to the door and I call Sorcha.

I'm like, 'Fionn's going, Babes?'

She comes downstairs and it's, like, all hugs and goodbyes.

I'm there, 'It's great to see you, Dude. Enjoy the wedding.'

He goes, 'Remember what I said, Ross. Sort it out.'

We're watching black-and-white CCTV footage from the door of the hilariously named Club Tropicana – the nightclub above The Broken Arms in Finglas. The image is scratchy, the people in the shot moving in a sort of, like, rapid freeze frame, which is kind of the way northsiders move anyway.

What I see when I look at it is Kennet, Marek and some other, like, random goon standing at the door of the club, doing what bouncers basically do – letting in the not-too-pissed after a short interrogation, sending away anyone who looks like trouble and checking out the rump end of every bird who goes up the stairs behind them, then exchanging either a shake of the head or a nod of approval.

Kennet has been working the door of the Club Tropicana – or Ta Throp, as he calls it – for seven years, according to Ronan. But on the night this footage was taken, exactly one week after his supposed accident, he claims he was, like, lying on boards, on the flat of his basic back, unable to move because of, like, the pain in his neck and upper *shoulders*?

He's now trying to say that the dude on the door isn't actually him. It's some, like, random Albanian called Todor who showed up at the club one night offering his services as a doorman, worked for a few weeks, then moved on again without leaving a forwarding address or any other clue as to his actual identity, except that he was an absolute ringer for Kennet.

Which is so obviously horseshit. I know that it's Kennet in the footage. That leather jacket he's wearing in it is never off his focking back. You can even see his lips forming the same word over and over again as he cross-examines some dude who's trying to get in with an obvious skinful on him.

He's going, 'Wh . . . wh . . . wh . . . where are you cubbin from toneet?' or some bullshit bouncer question like that.

But there's obviously, like, a doubt in the minds of one or two of the jurors, because they ask to see the footage again. Well, two of them ask to see it again. One of them is Simon, this dude who's around my age and is taking the whole thing incredibly seriously – wears a focking suit and tie to court every day. An accountant would be my guess. The other is a much younger dude – he couldn't be more than twenty – called Aidan, who mentioned to someone else that he's from, like, Clonskeagh and who strikes me – rightly or wrongly – as a bit of a pill head.

They watch the footage again. We all watch the footage again. Simon and Aidan and one or two others, I notice, are squinting their eyes, trying to get, like, a clearer *image*?

Three times we watch it in total and I can see that Kennet is suddenly smiling. He's smiling at Dordeen, roysh, and Dordeen is smiling back, because they realize that there's, like, a doubt over whether it's actually him in the footage that supposedly proves that the injury was faked.

I can suddenly see that here is my opportunity to do something, to, like, water those seeds of doubt and get Ronan out of debt to this scumbag and back in hopefully school.

We're dismissed for lunch. The video was, like, the final piece of evidence in the case and both sides will do their summing up in the afternoon.

I ask Simon if he fancies grabbing a bit of lunch and he says yes. Then I ask Aidan and he just shrugs and follows us in, like, moody silence to the Legal Beagle pub around the corner.

I decide *not* to have a pint? I want to keep my mind clear and anyway it's only, like, one o'clock in the day. I order, like, a toasted special and a coffee and the two boys order whatever.

It's actually Simon who brings up the case when we're sitting down at, like, a low *table*?

He goes, 'So what do you think of the famous Kennet?'

I'm there, 'Yeah, no, I actually think he's innocent,' and there's, like, a few seconds of stunned silence before Simon basically laughs in my face.

He goes, 'You're joking, right?'

And I'm there, 'No, I genuinely don't think the poor focker did it.'

'He did it alright. I think we can be reasonably certain about that. The question is whether the prosecution have proven their case beyond a reasonable doubt.'

'And you don't think they have?'

'I was very disappointed with this morning's evidence. I mean, they show us this poor-quality CCTV footage. Look, it probably is him. But where are the eyewitnesses? There must have been, what, two hundred people admitted to the club that night. Didn't any of them see him? Now, I know *they'd* probably say that it was difficult to get people to identify him because of perhaps fear or more likely a simple lazy-minded antipathy towards the Gardaí. But that's not good enough. If they can't find a single eye-witness who's prepared to say, yes, they saw the accused working on the door of the night-club when he was supposed to be suffering with a debilitating personal injury, I can't see how the case is proven.'

I turn to Aidan, who's chewing his sandwich slowly and just staring into space, and I go, 'What do *you* reckon?'

He shrugs and goes, 'Focking insurance companies. I hate them.'

Simon seems a bit surprised by this.

He goes, 'Well, that's not really a legal argument.'

But Aidan's like, 'They're focking robbing bastards.'

Simon goes, 'I wonder what way everyone else is thinking. I'm sure we'll find out soon enough.'

'So how does it work now?' I go.

'Well, after both sides have summed up, we sit down to discuss the evidence and consider our verdict.'

'Does it have to be unanimous, anonymous? I always get those two words confused.'

He looks at me like he's wondering am I taking the piss. Then he realizes that I'm not. I'm actually *genuinely* stupid?

'Unanimous,' he goes. 'No. The judge will accept a ten-to-two majority verdict.'

'But there's three of us here saying we don't know if the dude one hundred percent definitely did it. So will he get off?'

'No, that'd be a hung jury. There'd be a retrial with a new jury sworn in.'

That would not represent a result in Kennet's eyes. As I finish my sandwich, it's instantly clear to me, the tactical master, what I have to do. I've got to go into that jury room and persuade a few more jurors – I haven't done the exact maths yet – that one of Dublin's leading scumbags is an innocent man.

The morquee is up and it's a pretty impressive sight. I'm thinking it's going to look a hell of a lot more impressive when it's, like, full of people.

Sorcha is in her element, by the way. She's holding her iPad like it's basically a clipboard and giving instructions to the minions from the furniture rental company as to where she wants each of the tables.

I'm like, 'Hey, it's really taking shape.'

'Oh my God,' she goes, 'there's *so* much to do between now and Saturday. How did you get on in court today?'

I'm like, 'Yeah, no, both sides summed up. We stort our deliberations tomorrow. We've been told to bring, like, an overnight bag, just in case we need more than a day to decide.'

She's there, 'It's treason! Oh my God, Ross, of course you're going to need more than one day.'

'I suppose. Where's Honor?'

'She's in her room. She's still not talking.'

'Nothing?'

'Nothing. Just dirty looks across the dinner table.'

She suddenly roars at one of the minions that he hasn't left enough room for the dancefloor and I tell her I'll leave her to it.

I tip back into the house.

I'm in the kitchen, roysh, grabbing a beer from the fridge when all of a sudden the intercom buzzer for the front gate goes. I check the phone with the little TV screen on it and – hilariously – it ends up being the old dear.

Instead of, like, answering it, I decide to tip down to the gate to tell her to fock off in person.

She looks a focking state in the exact same Stella jumpsuit that Sorcha has. She needs to stort wearing shit that's more age-appropriate. She storts screaming at me while I'm still a good twenty metres from the gate.

She storts going, 'You took something from me!' her voice all, I don't know, *shrill*? 'You took something from *my* house that wasn't yours! Now you let me in right now!'

As I reach the gate, I suddenly notice that Oisinn is with her. He's sitting in the driver's seat of her red, open-top Nissan 370Z sports cor, every inch the gigolo. He's driving her around now, presumably so *she* can drink gin all day – the woman who thinks a Martini and a muesli bor is a full Irish breakfast.

When I see *him*, I end up totally forgetting what Fionn said about possibly trying to sort shit out. It just gets to me and I stort singing, 'I'm ronery!' like the dude out of *Team America: World Police*, 'I'm so ronery!' Deliberately directing it at him.

He can't even look at me.

She's still having an eppo, by the way.

'Give me that box of books!' she keeps going. 'You give me that box of books this minute!'

I'm there, 'What box of books would that be? The one that proves that you basically ripped off every idea you've ever had and every decent line you've ever used?'

That softens her cough. She suddenly storts to talk to me a bit more politely. 'What are you going to do with it?' she goes, her voice full of fear.

I'm there, 'I'm going to use it to destroy you, of course.'

'Who are you going to give it to?'

'I haven't decided yet. Maybe the *Stor*. Maybe the *Sunday Indo*. Yeah, no, maybe I'll ring your mate, Niamh Horan.'

I turn my back on her and stort walking back to the gaff. She loses it again, screaming at me – we're talking pleas *and* threats.

She's like, 'Ross, I'm begging you! I'll be finished!' and then, almost in the same breath, she goes, 'I'll call the Gords! I will! It's theft!'

I can't help but smile to myself, loving the power that I suddenly have over her.

It turns out that we're on our own – we're talking me, Simon and Aidan. Everyone else around the table thinks Kennet is pretty much guilty as *chorged*? That's after we kick off with, like, a show of hands. It ends up being nine–three in favour of sending the dude down, which means I'll have to persuade, like, four of the others to basically change their minds.

Of course I've never been scared of a challenge in my life. I dig deep, remembering some of the incredible speeches I made when I was captain of the Senior Cup team in Castlerock.

'Can I just say something here?' I go. 'I believe in this dude's innocence. I listened to his summing up yesterday with literally tears in my eyes – the reason being that I think he *is* a victim, as he said himself. He's a victim of the incompetence of the transport company. He's a victim of the greed of an insurance company that's happy to take premiums but then doesn't want to pay out. He's a victim of a criminal justice system that judges people on the basis of what side of the city they come from and that is wrong. As he said himself, there are a lot of people in this country who should be in prison for what they did during the whole Celtic Tiger thing. Yet they're walking around without a care in the world. And here's this poor focker, a family man, a loving husband, a father of God knows how many kids, who loves his soccer and his GAA sports, and we're being asked to send him to prison for something he didn't do. Well, I won't let it happen. I will not let it happen.'

I give the boardroom table a bit of a thump just for emphasis and shout, 'God damn it!' then I look around at the faces, to find out if I've managed to bring anyone with me.

'Ah, leds,' focking Bernadette has to go. She's managed to talk her way into being the foreman of the jury, by the way. She's one of those people who loves power as much as she loves the sound of her own voice. 'His speech was gess altogithor! Robert Immit, how are ya! But sure, you wouldn't believe a word of it!'

This other dude called Toby – focking *Toby*! – goes, 'I have to agree with Bernadette. His summing up was strong on emotion, but, well, let's be honest here, light on anything that refuted the prosecution case, which, to my mind, they proved beyond a reasonable doubt.'

'The forensics,' some dude with a moustache whose name I don't know goes. 'You heard what that chap said. There *was* no crash. All of the evidence suggests that the car was driven into the tree at a reasonably slow pace and that most of the damage to the front of it was done before the accident and almost certainly intentionally.'

Another dude, whose name may or may not be Ian, goes, 'I agree. This Kennet guy – I mean, we all enjoyed him – but he didn't challenge the forensic testimony in any meaningful way. Why didn't he produce his own expert to throw doubt on the official version?'

'Probably,' Bernadette goes, 'because he wasn't eeble to find one.

Not one who'd be pripeered to risk his own priffisional cridibility by becking up his story.'

This isn't focking going well.

'I'd be more inclined to look into the dude's eyes,' I go, 'and decide whether he's lying or not. And he seems like a pretty straight player to me. I think this could end up being a massive – what do they call it? – miscarriage of justice?'

Bernadette literally laughs, while Irla and Sandra, the two older women who've attached themselves to her like a couple of focking rescue dogs, have a bit of a chuckle to themselves as well.

Simon comes riding to my rescue. 'There's so much about this case that bothers me,' he goes. 'If this was, as they claim, a conspiracy involving several people to defraud an insurance company, why has only one man been charged? Where are the others? If Mr Loughran was the man who knocked the barrels from the truck – as the prosecuting barrister claimed – why isn't he on trial, too? Presumably because they didn't have a shard of evidence against him. In other words, they only have *half* a case. The truck driver, one of the prosecution's star witnesses, lied through his teeth on the witness stand. The CCTV footage was inconclusive and was uncorroborated by eyewitness testimony. They couldn't find a single person to say that Kennet Tuite was working on the door of the Club Tropicana that night. Now, I'm not saying that I think he's innocent. I just think the prosecution case was lazy, sloppy and incomplete. They don't deserve a conviction from us. And if we give them one, then we have to ask ourselves, what are juries even for? Are we just part of a system that processes guilty people?'

It's an amazing speech, the kind I would have made if I had two focking brain cells to rub together. Not everyone is won over, though. The dude who I think is called Ian goes, 'I don't know how you can say the CCTV footage was inconclusive. It's clearly him. I don't need an eyewitness to tell me.'

'Ah, leds,' Bernadette goes, 'sure it's obviously him!'

Irla's like, 'The other thing is, did you see his family? One of the sons is wearing a surgical collar as well. They're obviously all at it. Either that or they're the most unfortunate family in Ireland.'

The dude with the 'tache goes, 'I don't think we should allow that to figure in our judgement, though.'

Bernadette obviously cops that Aidan hasn't thrown his two yoyos in yet.

She's like, 'So why do you think he's *not* guilty?'

And all Aidan goes is, 'Insurance companies are wankers. And they can all fock off.'

It continues like this throughout the day. We go through all of the evidence again, piece by piece. We anlayse it. We debate it. We become tired. We shout. We point fingers. We bang the table. Insults are thrown. We phone out for pizza.

By eight o'clock we have the case talked nearly to death and we still haven't shifted from our original positions. Some old dude knocks on the door and asks if we've reached a verdict. Bernadette orders another show of hands and the count is still, like, nine–three. He goes off, then comes back a few minutes later to say we're going to be put up in a hotel overnight to continue our deliberations in the morning.

I ask him what hotel and he says Jury's in Christchurch, then I ask him if I can stay at the Merrion, where my old man has a rate, but the focker says no.

Half an hour later, I'm lying on a bed in some, like, random room with a miniature jug kettle, no mini-bor and a choice of TV channels that makes me wonder have I gone back in time to 1988.

I ring Sorcha and I tell her I won't be home. She seems cool with it.

'Ronan and Shadden are here with Rihanna-Brogan,' she goes. 'Ronan's going to do the reading, Ross. From the Book of Ecclesiastes?'

I'm like, 'Cool.'

I feel weirdly sad. Not sad but homesick. I wish I was there with them.

'How's Honor?' I go.

Sorcha's like, 'In her room. Still not talking.'

'Hopefully she'll have snapped out of it by Saturday.'

'Hey, I have a present for you.'

'What it is?'

'It's for the day. It's only small.'

My phone beeps. I've another call coming through. I check the screen and it ends up being *him*.

'Sorcha,' I go, 'I've got to take this call. I'll talk to you tomorrow.'

I kill one call and answer the other.

'S . . . s . . . s . . . stordee?' is his opening line.

I'm there, 'What do *you* want?'

'Fooken info, what do you tink? Ters no veerdict?'

'We couldn't reach one.'

'Tat's f . . . f . . . f . . . fooken hopeful. What's ta noombers?'

'Nine guilty and three not.'

'F . . . f . . . fook.'

'Your three are bankers, I wouldn't worry about that. Some accountant dude who thinks the prosecution made a balls of the case, then some druggy from Clonskeagh who has a thing about insurance companies.'

'It'll be a fooken r . . . r . . . r . . . rethroyal den.'

'If it stays at nine–three, apparently, yeah.'

'Well, what ta fook are doin abourrit?'

'What?'

He suddenly loses it. 'A rethroyal's no f . . . f . . . f . . . fooking gooth ta me,' he goes, and he, like, shouts it. 'It's no fooken gooth to me and it's no fooken gooth to you eeder.'

I'm there, 'I realize that.'

'You fooken listen to me. If you doatunt get me ourra tis, I'll do t . . . t . . . t . . . two to tree yee-ur max. But Ine gonna owen your son for ta next toorty. So you b . . . b . . . b . . . bethor steert usin your p . . . p . . . p . . . powers of p . . . p . . . p . . . persuasion – knowmean?'

He hangs up.

And as I lie on my bed, watching some random home improvement programme while eating the complimentary pack of three Custard Creams, I suddenly realize exactly what I have to do.

★

She's pretty surprised to see me standing at her door. She's been at the Custard Creams as well, judging from the crumbs on her face.

I'm there, 'Bernadette – how the hell are you?'

She's like, 'Ross?'

Like I said, definitely surprised, but also secretly *delighted*?

'I, er, just wanted to apologize,' I go. 'It got a little heated in that room today. I may have said one or two things that I now regret.'

She's there, 'You told me to feck off back to Tipperary – except you didn't use the word feck.'

I just nod – big sincere head on me.

'Look,' I go, 'I lost it. I'm admitting that. I was bang out of order. I'm actually here to apologize.'

She's there, 'Do you want to come in?' She opens the door a few inches wider.

'Is that okay?' I go. 'It's not against the rules, is it? You being the foreman and blah, blah, blah.'

She's like, 'Ah, leds, we're allowed to talk to each other!'

I give her a little chuckle – of course, silly me! – then in I go.

'I was just meeking some tea,' she goes.

Country people have a serious horn for tea- and coffee-making facilities in hotel rooms. Of course she has the three biscuits horsed before the kettle is even boiled.

'Yeah, no,' I go, 'a cup of tea would be great.'

She makes two cups, then hands me mine and goes, 'You surprised me todee.'

I'm there, 'Surprised you in what way?'

'Look, dawnt teek this the wrong wee, but I had you down as a bit of an esshole.'

'How do you know I'm *not* an orsehole?'

'I dawnt. Actually, I think you probably eer one.'

'But?'

'I dawnt knaw. The wee you believe in thet fella's innocence. If you were a tawtally selfish besturd, you wouldn't keer one wee or the other if he went to jeel. I dawnt agree with you, but I heff to admire your pession.'

I lean against the wall. She's standing beside me.

'If I sent a man to jail,' I go, 'I'd have to be one hundred percent sure of his actual guilt. And in this case, I'm not. Look, I'm not married. I don't have any kids . . .'

I hate myself for saying it – don't you worry.

I'm there, '. . . but this Kennet dude, remember, is somebody's husband and somebody's father. By sending him to jail, you're, like, depriving a woman of her husband and depriving however many children of their father. I just think I'd need to be very, very sure of my facts to do that.'

While she's still processing this, I go, 'Can I kiss you?'

She's like, 'I big your peerdon?'

She's focking thrilled with herself. She just wants to hear me ask again. I just refuse to on principle. She's not Zooey Deschanel. I just put my cup down, take hers out of her hands and put it down too, then I move in close and I stort kissing her.

She responds straight away. Really gets into it as well. Doesn't know her luck.

She's comfortably one of the five ugliest girls I've ever put my mouth to. I realize that I'm crossing a line here. It's my first time actually being with someone since me and Sorcha got back together. But I manage to convince myself that being with a bird who's so far out of my wife's league means that this isn't *actually* cheating?

And anyway, for once in my life, I'm doing it for totally unselfish reasons.

As I'm sucking away on her big Bratwurst lips and running my hands through her steel-wool hair, I'm thinking that all I really have to do is bring *her* around to my point of view. The two rescue dogs will do whatever the fock she tells them to do. Then it'll be six and six and all I'll need is one more person to swap sides and my son will be free.

I stop kissing her, then I unbutton my shirt. She stares at my abs and pecs like she's reading a Tube map, running her thumb over the lines, amazed and confused at the exact same time. You can tell she's never seen a body like it before.

I help her out of her clothes.

'Aw, leds!' she goes as I unhook her bra. 'Aw, Jesus, leds! Aw, leds!'

She has a fantastic set of bumpers on her. I think I mentioned that she was a big goose.

I'm there, 'I've fancied you since the day this whole jury service thing storted. I tried to fight it. I tried to remain professional. I guess I'm just not strong enough.'

I'm on fire.

'Why am I so attracted to essholes!' she goes, then she pushes me back onto the bed, climbs on board and storts going at me like a baboon licking up Fanta.

She wants me and she wants me in a big-time way. I'd say it's a long time since anyone's troubled Bernadette's foundations.

Now, I'm going to draw a discreet blind on proceedings there, obviously out of respect to the girl. All I will say is that I end up pretty much ploughing her into the mattress and she ends up breaking the Third Commandment over and over again with her eyes spinning like a couple of pinwheels.

When we've had our fill of each other, we both drift off and I end up sleeping the sleep of the dead. That's how wrecked I am.

I wake up at, like, eight o'clock the following morning. Or rather I'm woken – by the sound of, like, my *phone* ringing?

Shit, I think. Because it's Sorcha.

I take it into the bathroom to answer it.

'Ross?' she goes.

I can instantly tell that she's crying. My first thought, of course, is how the fock did she find out. In fact, I'm on the point of going, 'Sorcha, it meant nothing,' when *she* all of a sudden goes, 'Ross, I am *so* sorry to ring you like this. I know you're probably busy deliberating.'

I'm there, 'Babes, what's happened?' suddenly wondering if it's something that Honor has done.

'Ross,' she goes, 'did you know that Ronan is in debt to Shadden's father?'

I'm like, 'What?'

'He lent him thirty thousand euros!'

'Did Ro tell you that?'

'Shadden told me. Last night. She's very upset, Ross. I asked her what kind of APR he was paying. She said he's going to end up paying him, like, one hundred and twenty thousand over the next however many years. Kennet has him basically *enslaved*?'

'I'm going to sort it, Sorcha. Don't you worry.'

'There's something else, Ross – which you're not going to like.'

'What?'

'He hit him.'

For a good ten seconds, it's like the world has suddenly stopped. I'm like, 'Say that again.'

'Kennet hit Ronan,' she goes. 'Do you remember the black eye he had the day of the family photo?'

I feel my jaw clench and my face becomes suddenly hot.

I'm there, 'You're saying *Kennet* did that to him?'

'It was because he missed a payment,' she goes. 'Oh my God, Shadden hates him, Ross. She hates her mother as well. She doesn't want little Rihanna-Brogan growing up around that family.'

I stare at my reflection in the bathroom mirror. And in that second, I realize exactly what has to happen now.

I'm there, 'Sorcha, don't worry. I'm going to fix this,' and I hang up.

I go back into the room and stort throwing my clothes on. Bernadette wakes up and she's like, 'Do you heff to gaw?'

She obviously wants more of the same. I don't even bother answering her. You got lucky one night, I think, you didn't win the focking lottery.

I'm there, 'What time are we all meeting up again?'

She goes, 'Eleven.'

I walk out of there without another word. I go down in the lift, then tip outside and I hail a Jo.

The old man is delighted to see me. He's always delighted to see me.

'Have you been listening to *Morning Ireland*?' are pretty much the first words out of his mouth.

I'm like, 'Er, no.'

'The Greek elections,' he goes. 'The Left did a lot better than anyone expected. There's talk of them exiting the bloody well euro now. And of Spain having to be rescued! Anyway, come in, come in!'

I follow him inside, then down to the kitchen, where Helen is sitting at the table, having her breakfast, still in her dressing gown. She's thrilled to see me as well. Hugs. Air-kisses. The full show.

'Look,' I go, 'I'm sorry to crash in on you like this.'

Helen's there, 'Don't be silly, Ross. It's always so lovely to see you. I'll fix you some breakfast – if you can promise to keep it down, that is!'

I laugh.

I'm like, 'Yeah, no, I won't thanks. I'm only here on, like, a *flying* visit?' and then I check out her ring. 'It cleaned up well, didn't it?'

She goes, 'It did.'

'So have you two set a date yet?'

The old man's there, 'We thought we might wait a year,' and he and Helen smile at each other. 'We don't want to do it without Erika being there. Thought we might give it twelve months. See does she come to her senses in that time.'

Helen says she's going to go and get dressed and she leaves me and the old man on our own.

'So,' he goes, 'is everything okay?'

I'm there, 'I need thirty grand.'

It's incredible. He doesn't even blink. He goes, 'I think there's *exactly* thirty thousand in the safe.'

I follow him up to the study. I watch him dial the combination, open the door, then whip out a humungous knacker roll. He counts the fifties out on his desk, then goes, 'Thirty thousand exactly! What are the chances?'

He shoves it all into a white envelope and all I can do is just, like, shake my head.

I'm there, 'Do you not want to know what it's even for?'

He goes, 'Well, I presume it's important, Kicker. Otherwise you wouldn't have asked.'

'It is important, yeah.'

'Well, there you are, see.'

I've always hammered my old man for being a bad father. But I've never given him enough credit for being a good man. I get this sudden flash of memory from, like, 2002. Or maybe it was 2003. It was during the whole Celtic Tiger thing anyway. There was a cor stopped at the traffic lights on the bridge over the dualler, just outside UCD. The driver had been sitting there for an hour, indicating right, but then never actually moving. Every time the lights turned green there was, like, a chorus of angry horns and as people drove around him they threw their hands in the air and gave him another blast or two and called him every prick under the sun.

Anyway, the *reason* the dude didn't move was because he was dead. He'd had, like, a hort attack or something. I sometimes wonder how many cors passed him in that hour. Two hundred? Three hundred? All good people, I'm sure, but too caught up in having to get wherever they were going to see this cor stalled at a green light as anything other than an inconvenience.

And then Charles O'Carroll-Kelly blunders onto the scene. The only man to get out of his cor. You can picture him, can't you? Approaching the passenger door, going, 'What's all this how-do-you-do? Are you okay, old chap?'

I know he pulled the man out of his seat and tried to give him CPR on the road – with people still beeping, by the way. And I know he went to the funeral, because I went with him. The family asked him to do a reading. And I know that every year he rings the man's widow on the anniversary.

I never read that story in any of the, like, acres of coverage my old man got at the time of his trial. I read that he kept money from the Revenue and that he paid bribes and solicited bribes, too. But there's also an incredible kindness in my old man. He genuinely *gives* a shit about people.

He hands me the envelope and I tell him thanks and I stick it in my inside pocket.

Then as I turn to leave, he goes, 'Your mother came to see me yesterday.'

He doesn't say anything else. He just lets it hang there.

I'm like, 'Yeah? What did that focking hatchet-faced ho-nasty want?'

He just sad-smiles me. 'She says you took something,' he goes, 'from her house.'

I'm there, 'Yeah, no, I did. A box of books that she's spent the last few years ripping off.'

'What do you plan to do with them?'

'I was going to leak them to the press. Serve her focking right.'

He nods.

He's there, 'You know that could destroy her?'

I'm like, 'Yeah, no, that's what I'm hoping for.'

'No, I mean *really* destroy her. Before you do it, Kicker, you should ask yourself if it's what you really want.'

'She's having sex with one of my friends.'

'I know. I've always tried to make allowances for your mother, Ross. Especially in the last few years.'

'Allowances? What are you shitting about?'

'She's mad, Ross.'

'What?'

'Sorry, that wasn't very charitable. Look, you know her family history. Her mother went that way. Her grandmother, too. She's always been a bit, well, you know. But the last couple of years I've noticed that she's become, well, a bit more so than usual. Do you understand what I'm saying?'

'She's bananas. I've always said that.'

'Look, I realize that what your mother is doing at the moment is very embarrassing for you. So I'm not going to tell you what to do. Just make sure you realize the likely effect of the course of action you're considering. It *will* destroy her, Ross. Her sense of herself, her credibility, her standing in the community. I'm not telling you what to do. All I'm saying is, be absolutely certain that she deserves it.'

I nod. Then I tell him I have to go. Someone's freedom is in my hands.

*

It's just after lunchtime when we file back into the courtroom. There's, like, a hush as the twelve of us make our way to our seats. Kennet stares straight at me and raises his eyebrows, basically looking for news.

I smile at him and just nod.

He smiles then – a weight obviously lifted from his shoulders. He's probably thinking about all the shit he's going to do now that his ordeal is over and he can, like, return to normal life again.

After a bit of, I don't know, formality, the judge asks Bernadette to stand. I'm surprised she still can after the workout I put her through last night.

'Have you reached a verdict?' the dude goes.

Bernadette's like, 'We heff.'

He's there, 'Very good. On the charge of conspiracy to defraud, how do you find the defendant?'

She goes, 'Guilty.'

There are, like, gasps from the public gallery.

I watch Eddie's face collapse like a detonated building. From smug to devastated in five seconds flat. He looks around him, wondering has he, like, misheard. Then he looks at me. I stare straight at him, my eyes never leaving his.

'Bastoords!' Dadden shouts. 'Yiz doorty-looken bastoords!'

Four or five others, including Say Nuttin, call us doort-boords and wankoors and tell us we'll *be got*. The judge wallops the gavel a few times and says that anyone raising their voices or using threats or profanities in his courtroom will be held in contempt.

I look at Dordeen, sobbing her hort out, then at Eddie, who has his orm around Dadden, trying to basically calm him *down*?

The judge says he will impose sentence tomorrow, when the atmosphere is a little less fraught.

Then he goes, 'Mr Tuite, I suggest you have an enjoyable evening with your family as the sentence is likely to be custodial.'

Then we're all dismissed.

The next major concern for most of the jury members is how do we get out of the building without being basically killed? Ian and the dude with the 'tache are asking about a side entrance, while one or two others are ringing, I don't know, loved ones and family members and asking them to come and get them.

Bernadette sidles over to me as we're leaving the court. She goes, 'Are you doing innything leesher?'

The focking cheek of the girl. I don't know where she gets her confidence from.

'I'll tell you one thing I won't be doing,' I go. 'And that's you.'

She's obviously a bit taken aback by that – and that's to say the least.

She's there, 'I just thought . . .'

I'm like, 'Yeah, I know what you just thought. Let me tell you something, you have no idea how lucky you got last night – focking seriously!'

'What do you mean by thet?'

''Take a look at me and then take a look at you. That's what I mean by lucky.'

There's that old proverb, isn't there? Hell hath no fury like a blahdy blahdy blah blah.

'Lucky?' she tries to go. 'I wouldn't call it lucky to heff someone shoating "Linstor!" in your ear for heff the night.'

I'm like, 'Hey, we can both stand here throwing nasty comments back and forth. Or we can both walk away. You'll always have your memories.'

She shakes her head and goes, 'You're an esshole.'

And I'm like, 'We knew that.'

I walk out of the courtroom into the hallway and I have a look around. I notice Dadden and Eddie comforting their old dear and Say Nuttin on his mobile, obviously phoning in the result to someone, shaking his head and saying it's a teddible day. I spot Kennet disappearing into the jacks and I put my head down and follow him in.

He's standing at the trough, having a hit and miss. He hears my footsteps and he somehow knows it's me without even having to turn around.

He goes, 'Who chenged der m . . . m . . . m . . . moyunt?'

I'm like, 'Excuse me?'

'Last noyt, ter was tree says I w . . . w . . . w . . . wadn't guilty. Ta woorst it'd be, *you* said, wad a h . . . h . . . h . . . hung joowery. So who chenged der moyunt?'

I'm there, 'I did.'

He doesn't actually react to this. He zips up and walks over to the sink to, like, wash his hands.

'You?' he goes.

He seems pretty surprised – impressed, even – that I had it in me.

I'm there, 'You beat my son up. Your daughter's boyfriend. The father of your granddaughter. You beat him up.'

'He m . . . m . . . missed a week.'

'He missed a week? You're lucky I don't split your head open like a focking cantaloupe.'

He runs his hands under the hot tap, then pulls a couple of paper towels out of, like, the dispenser and storts drying them off.

'Veddy brave,' he goes, 'teddin me it was you who s . . . s . . . s . . . sent me dowin.'

I'm there, 'The hilarious thing is I probably *could* have got you off? Then I heard it was you who gave my son that black eye and I decided, no, I've got to get rid of that focking scumbag from his life once and for all.'

'The secont I gerroura prison, you'll be g . . . g . . . got. You're gonna spent ta next few yee-urs lookin overt your sh . . . sh . . . sh . . . showulter.'

'No, I won't. Because I'm not scared of you. See, I'm a lot of things, Kennet. I'm a liar and a cheat. I'm as thick as shit in the neck of a bottle and I'm a total bastard to women. I'm a total waste of rugby-playing talent. I'm a bad son, a bad husband and quite possibly a bad father. But one thing I'm not and definitely never have been is a coward. Ask Gordon D'Arcy about some of the run-ins we had on the rugby field back in the day.'

'Who ta fook is Gordon D . . . D . . . D . . . Deercy?'

'He's one of the legends of the game. One of the legends of the game who could tell you next week's weather from the throb in his hip where I once tackled him. The dude is like Old Man focking River.'

I reach into my inside pocket and pull out the envelope that my old man gave me. I put it down on the side of the sink.

'There's thirty Ks in there,' I go. 'The money you lent Ronan.'

'Waira minute,' he goes. 'Ters also inthorest oawut on it. Eer deal still stands.'

I'm there, 'That's all you're getting. You could make a complaint to the financial regulator if you want, although it'll probably have to wait until you get out of prison.'

He goes, 'You fooken p . . . p . . . p . . . p . . .'

But I'm out of the men's toilet and out of the man's life before he's managed to even say the word.

I pull them out of the box – *Hungry for Naan, Members Only, Riders, The Games People Play, Lethal Seduction, Jew Make Me Feel So Young* and other classics of our time – and, one by one, I place them on the grill of the borbecue. I saturate them in, like, lighter fuel and then – being the lovely goy that I actually am – I drop a match on top and they go up in an instant *whoof.*

I couldn't do it when it came to it. In the end, though, it had fock-all to do with not wanting to destroy *her.* It was about not wanting to disappoint *him.* My old man. It's taken me thirty-two years to discover it, but it would kill me if he thought less of me.

It's, like, six o'clock on Friday, the night before me and Sorcha renew our vows. Everything is arranged. The morquee is up. The tables are set. The caterers arrived two hours ago and put the entire banquet for tomorrow in our fridge. There's an iPod playlist of our favourite songs and a photographic slideshow of our happiest memories. There's a freshly dry-cleaned tux hanging in my wardrobe and a Jenny Packham gown hanging in Sorcha's, which I'm not allowed to see.

Our guests will be here at noon.

I'm enjoying this moment of quiet time, just getting my head around everything that's happened in the last few months, as I step back to avoid the smoke blowing in my face and I watch the flames – I don't know – *devour* the evidence of what a complete and utter fraud my old dear is.

Bernadette pops into my head. That big lump of Tipperary beef – muzzle to focking hoof – is probably bitching about me to her friends as we speak, unaware of just how lucky she got.

Of course, in normal circumstances, all things being equal, I would never cheat on Sorcha with a girl who looks like that. It was all port of a plan. It had to be done. But I'm not going to say it was a one-off. Because I'm a dirtbag. I'm going to try to be faithful to Sorcha. At least I'm going to try not to be unfaithful. Tomorrow, I'll restate my vows, according to the script I'm handed, but then silently – in my head – I'll say, 'I'm going to do my best. I'm going to do my very, very best.'

Because you can't deny your nature. That's just a fact.

My phone rings, suddenly dragging me from this big intellectual moment I'm having. It ends up being Ronan.

'Rosser,' he goes, 'you bender.'

I laugh. I can't help it.

I'm there, 'Hey, Ro. You sound in good form.'

He doesn't say anything for a good five seconds. Then he goes, 'Shadden's da is arthur being sent down.'

I'm like, 'No!' playing the innocent.

''Tis mornin,' he goes. 'The judge gev him foyuv yee-ur.'

'Five?'

'On account of he's utter convicshiddens.'

'I knew he'd a bit of previous alright.'

'He said me and him are squeer, but.'

'Did he?'

'Said I didn't have to pay him back any of the muddy I boddowed.'

'That was nice of him, wasn't it? So what happens now?'

'What do you mean?'

'Do you want to come here and live with us? The three of you.'

'If it's alreet with Sorcha.'

'It'll be alright with Sorcha. It'll make her year. Do me a favour, though. Don't say anything for now. It'll be my surprise for her tomorrow.'

Speak of the devil, she's suddenly walking down the gorden towards me, followed by her sister. Rosemary. Lemon balm. Marjoram. Whatever the fock. She's moving in with us today. I actually forgot.

She's wearing a pink 'I Love Beverly Hills' T-shirt that's straining at the seams with the job of containing those monster focking milk wagons. I'm going to have my work cut out keeping my hands off her.

'What's with the fire?' Sorcha goes.

I'm there, 'I'm just burning a few . . . things.'

'Oh my God, are they books?'

'Yeah, no, they were just ones I found in my old wardrobe in Foxrock. I mean, when am I ever going to read a book? It's crazy.'

I change the subject.

I'm like, 'Have your old pair gone?'

The sister was dropping them to the airport this afternoon. It's actually the sister who answers.

'Yes,' she goes. 'They were on a two o'clock flight.'

I automatically look at Sorcha. She goes, 'I'm fine with it, Ross. Mum and I had breakfast this morning. *He* was invited and he didn't show. But I'm not going to let him cast a shadow over tomorrow. Not him. Not Honor. Not Dechtire Ní Conchobhair.'

I'm like, 'Dechtire? What's the deal there?'

'She finally sent me the piece of music she composed for us.'

'And?'

Sorcha pulls out her iPhone while smiling to herself. She hits a couple of buttons and the music suddenly storts. Well, I *say* music? It ends up being mostly, like, silence, then every six or maybe seven seconds, there's two cello notes. It's like, *duuuhhh-dum*. Then there's a gap, then another *duuuhhh-dum*. It's actually a bit creepy.

I'm there, 'It sounds like the theme music from *Jaws*.'

Sorcha goes, 'That's probably because it *is* the theme music from *Jaws*?'

'Fock!' I go. 'What a bitch!'

The sister smiles. She looks really, really well – I don't know if I mentioned. She's like, 'Oh my God, you must have really hurt her, Ross!' and she has, like, a huge smile on her face.

'Like I said,' Sorcha goes, 'I'm not going to let it get to me. Tomorrow is going to be the most perfect day of my life.'

Epilogue: *How Horrid!*

I hear Sorcha's screams coming from the kitchen. Loud and – I suppose – *piercing*? She's going, 'No! *Nooo!!!!* No, no, no!!!'

At first I just presume she's got the rugby on and, like me, has just watched Dan Corter snatch victory for the All Blacks with a last-minute drop goal. We deserved more from the game. Drico put on a performance that could only be described as supernatural. It would have to go down as one of his ten best games ever.

It's only when the screaming continues – 'Oh, no! Please, no! Oh my God, *please!*' – that I begin to suspect it's possibly something else that's eating Sorcha. I mean, she sometimes watches rugby, but the girl knows fock-all about it, other than which players she thinks are good-looking.

I put down my tactics book and tip down to the kitchen to investigate. And I have to admit, I'm not ready for the sight that greets me.

The fridge door is open and there's, like, green slime everywhere – on the floor, all up Sorcha's orms, on her face. If she told me that she'd just stabbed an alien to death with a Stellar boning knife, I'd have to believe her, because that's what it looks like. But then I see the upturned tureen on the floor and I suddenly realize that it's English pea soup.

'It's ruined!' she goes. Her face is a real mess. 'Everything is ruined!'

I'm like, 'What are you talking about?'

'The soup,' she goes. 'The crème fraîche. The blackberry and walnut salad with lime ginger vinaigrette. Oh my God, the herb panzanella with tomatoes and husk cherries!'

I'm like, 'What do you mean by ruined, though?'

'Someone switched off the fridge!' she goes. 'It was switched off at the wall.'

I'm there, in my total innocence, 'Who, though? Who would have switched off the fridge?'

She actually roars at me – that's how upset she is. She's like, 'Who do you *think*, Ross?'

After about twenty seconds, I'm there, 'Honor?'

She's like, 'Yes, Honor!'

'Do you really think she'd . . .'

'This is her revenge. For sending her to a national school.'

'Fock.'

The kitchen door opens and in walks Sorcha's sister. She's like, 'What's all the screaming . . .' and then she suddenly stops because she sees what *I* first saw. Alien focking entrails.

She's like, 'Oh! My God! What is that?'

She's wearing a pink silk nightshirt with the top three buttons open, offering us a ridiculously good view of her butter bags.

Sorcha's there, 'It *was* our wedding feast,' and then she follows my line of vision and ends up suddenly losing it with the girl. 'Would you put some *focking* clothes on when you're walking around this house?'

I'm there, 'Okay, let's all just be cool like Huggy Bear for a minute. You're saying you definitely think Honor did this?'

Sorcha's like, 'Of course she did it? Do you remember she said she could be an even *bigger* bitch?'

'*This*, though?'

'Oh my God!' the sister suddenly goes. I'll get her name one day and I'm going to write it down. 'Oh my God, Sorcha, I don't want to worry you . . .'

Sorcha's there, 'What?'

'I just saw her coming out of your bedroom.'

Sorcha just freezes. Honestly, she doesn't move – not even a muscle on her face – for a good ten seconds. Then she goes, 'Oh my God, the dress!'

She runs out of the kitchen, wiping her hands on her dressing gown as she goes. I follow her. She takes the stairs, like, two at a time. By the time I catch up with her, she's sitting on the edge of the bed and, like, cradling her white Jenny Packham gown like it's a sick child.

They do say it's unlucky for the groom to see the dress before the actual ceremony, although that rule no longer applies. Because the thing has been hacked to shit. There's, like, pieces of it all over the bedroom floor. She obviously went at it with, like, a *scissors* or something?

From her room, we can both hear Honor singing, 'Going to the chapel and we're gonna get married.'

Sorcha looks up from what used to be an incredibly expensive gown with tears just streaming down her face and goes, 'Ross, what are we going to do?' and I know straight away that she's not talking about the renewal.

I'm just there, 'I don't know, Sorcha. I really don't.'

'We need to take her to counselling. Family counselling.'

'As in, like, all three of us?'

'I just don't know what else there is to do.'

'We'll do it then. We'll ring someone first thing on Monday morning. Leave it to me. I'll get a name.'

She looks back down at what's left of the dress. I'd say it was beautiful up until about five minutes ago.

'No dress,' she goes, shaking her head. 'No food. No music for when I'm walking up the aisle . . .'

I'm there, 'Babes, do you think maybe someone up there is trying to tell us something?'

She's like, 'What do you mean?'

'What I mean is, do we really need to renew our vows, Sorcha?'

'I thought it was what we *both* wanted?'

'I don't know if it is any more. You'd have to admit, it's been a bit of a disaster. None of my friends are going to be there. Your old pair aren't going to be there. My old dear. Our daughter – I doubt if she's welcome now.'

I pick up the iPad from her bedside locker and stort scrolling down through the guest list. 'I mean, who *are* all these people?' I go. 'I've never even heard of most of them.'

She's there, 'It's just our wedding was – oh my God – *such* a disaster the first time around. I just wanted to, I don't know, have a second go of it and make it, like, perfect this time.'

'I know I'm always quoting him, but Father Fehily used to say that you can't rewrite your past – but you can have a hand in directing your future.'

'That's an amazing quote.'

I kneel down on the floor in front of her and I take her hand.

Look,' I go, 'I know in the past I've made mistakes and possibly taken you for granted. I put a lot of things – a lot of other people – before you and did a lot of shit that I maybe wouldn't be a hundred percent proud of. All the trouble in our marriage was down to me. But there's never been a day, Sorcha, when I stopped loving you. Not a day, not an hour, not a minute. The first night I met you – shit, that was a lifetime's worth of luck right there. Look, I'm probably going to fock up again, Sorcha, because that's just genuinely how I am. Old too soon and wise too late – another Fehily quote. I was stupid enough to lose you once. But I won't be stupid enough to let it happen again. I'm going to give our marriage everything I've got.'

She's in, like, floods of tears. It's a definite moment. She wipes her face with the back of her hand.

'All that planning,' she goes. 'The God's knot. The songs. The caterers. Ecclesiastes. The frozen affogato. And I've just realized that what you just said is all I really wanted to hear. And it doesn't matter to me that no one else was here to hear it.'

'Father Seamus was right, Sorcha. We don't need to renew our vows.'

She takes her phone out of her pocket. 'I'll ring him,' she goes. 'I'll tell him he doesn't need to come.'

I'm there, 'Before you do that, I have something to tell you.'

'What is it?'

'Ronan and Shadden are coming to live with us – *with* Rihanna-Brogan.'

Her face lights up like the Hallowe'en sky over Clondalkin. 'What?' she goes. 'How?'

I'm like, 'Kennet got five years in prison for conspiracy to defraud.'

She covers her open mouth with her hand.

I'm there, 'He had fourteen previous convictions. I knew you'd be pleased. It was going to be my present to you.'

She can't help but smile. 'This house,' she goes, 'it suddenly feels full again, doesn't it?'

I'm there, 'It certainly will when Ronan gets here!'

'*I have* something for *you*, Ross.'

'What is it?'

'It's only something small, okay?'

'Okay.'

'It's actually tiny.'

'Okay, what is it?'

She suddenly takes my hand and she holds it to her belly. A wave of shock washes over me. I'm floored. I can't find words. At least I can't find the right words. 'That day you spewed your ring up,' I go, 'outside the old Killiney Court Hotel . . .'

She just nods.

I'm the one who's bawling now.

'Okay,' I go, wiping my own tears away, 'you and me are having our own celebration today. And no one else is invited.'

'People are going to be arriving in the next couple of hours. Should we maybe ring around?'

'No. I'll put a note on the front gate.'

She laughs. 'Ross,' she goes, 'you can't do that.'

I'm there, 'Can't I? You just watch me.'

I grab the lid from the box that the Jenny Packham gown arrived in. I tear off a square of cordboard, then I pick up a pen and I write, on it 'The renewal is off! We've eloped!!!'

Then, underneath, I write, 'Ronan and Shadden, just press the buzzer.'

I'm like, 'There! What do you think?'

Sorcha kisses me and goes, 'It's perfect.'

I'm there, 'I'll be back in thirty seconds.'

I go outside. The sun is shining. It wouldn't have *been* a bad day for a porty. I walk down the gravel path towards the gate. I'm, like, tying the sign onto the bors when a cor all of a sudden pulls up outside and I recognize it straight away as JP's silver Audi A7.

The doors open and out they climb. JP, Oisinn and Christian. None of them are supposedly talking to me, so it's, like, random that they're even *here*?

But right now I'm the happiest I've possibly ever been, to the point where I don't care about any of that shit any more. Not right now. Not today.

In fact, the first words out of my mouth are, 'Some match, wasn't it? We'll possibly never come that close to beating the All Blacks again.'

Then something in their manner tells me that something is wrong. The fact that the three of them are even here.

It's Oisinn who goes, 'Did you see the news this morning?'

I'm like, 'The news? What the fock kind of question is that?'

And Christian goes, 'Ross, it's Fionn.'

I'm there, 'Fionn? Yeah, no, he's in, whatever it's called, Ruganda.'

He's like, 'Ross, he's been kidnapped.'

Acknowledgements

With grateful thanks, as ever, to my editor Rachel Pierce, my agent Faith O'Grady and the artist Alan Clarke. A big thank you to Michael McLoughlin, Patricia Deevy, Cliona Lewis, Patricia McVeigh, Brian Walker and everyone at Penguin Ireland. And with love to my wife, Mary, and my amazing family.